Arthur &
George

JULIAN BARNES

Arthur &
George

RANDOM HOUSE CANADA

www.randomhouse.ca

Originally published in Great Britain by Jonathan Cape, an imprint of the
Random House Group Limited, London.

Library and Archives Canada Cataloguing in Publication

Barnes, Julian
Arthur & George / Julian Barnes.

ISBN 0-679-31417-2

I. Title.   II. Title: Arthur and George.

PR6052.A6657A78 2005   823'.914   C2005-903673-7

Printed and bound in the United States of America

2   4   6   8   9   7   5   3   1

to P.K.

ONE

Beginnings

Arthur

A child wants to see. It always begins like this, and it began like this then. A child wanted to see.

He was able to walk, and could reach up to a door handle. He did this with nothing that could be called a purpose, merely the instinctive tourism of infancy. A door was there to be pushed; he walked in, stopped, looked. There was nobody to observe him; he turned and walked away, carefully shutting the door behind him.

What he saw there became his first memory. A small boy, a room, a bed, closed curtains leaking afternoon light. By the time he came to describe it publicly, sixty years had passed. How many internal retellings had smoothed and adjusted the plain words he finally used? Doubtless it still seemed as clear as on the day itself. The door, the room, the light, the bed, and what was on the bed: a 'white, waxen thing'.

A small boy and a corpse: such encounters would not have been so rare in the Edinburgh of his time. High mortality rates and cramped circumstances made for early learning. The household was Catholic, and the body that of Arthur's grandmother, one Katherine Pack. Perhaps the door had been deliberately left ajar. There might have been a desire to impress upon the child the horror of death; or, more optimistically, to show him that death was nothing to be feared. Grandmother's soul had clearly flown up to Heaven, leaving behind only the sloughed husk of her body. The boy wants to see? Then let the boy see.

An encounter in a curtained room. A small boy and a corpse. A grandchild who, by the acquisition of memory, had just stopped being a thing, and a grandmother who, by losing those attributes the child was developing, had returned to that state. The small boy stared; and over half a century later the adult man was still staring. Quite what a 'thing' amounted to – or, to put it more exactly, quite what happened when the tremendous change took place, leaving only a 'thing' behind – was to become of central importance to Arthur.

George

George does not have a first memory, and by the time anyone suggests that it might be normal to have one, it is too late. He has no recollection obviously preceding all others – not of being picked up, cuddled, laughed at or chastised. He has an awareness of once having been an only child, and a knowledge that there is now Horace as well, but no primal sense of being disturbingly presented with a brother, no expulsion from paradise. Neither a first sight, nor a first smell: whether of a scented mother or a carbolicy maid-of-all-work.

He is a shy, earnest boy, acute at sensing the expectations of others. At times he feels he is letting his parents down: a dutiful child should remember being cared for from the first. Yet his parents never rebuke him for this inadequacy. And while other children might make good the lack – might forcibly install a mother's doting face or a father's supporting arm in their memories – George does not do so. For a start, he lacks imagination. Whether he has never had one, or whether its growth has been stunted by some parental act, is a question for a branch of psychological science which has not yet been devised. George is fully capable of following the inventions of others – the stories of Noah's Ark, David and Goliath, the Journey of the Magi – but has little such capacity himself.

He does not feel guilty about this, since his parents do not regard it as a fault in him. When they say that a child in the village has 'too much imagination', it is clearly a term of dispraise. Further up the scale are 'tellers of tall stories' and 'fibbers'; by far the worst is the child who is 'a liar through and through' – such are to be avoided at all costs. George himself is never urged to speak the truth: this would imply that he needs encouragement. It is simpler than this: he is expected to tell the truth because at the Vicarage no alternative exists.

'I am the way, the truth and the life': he is to hear this many times on his father's lips. The way, the truth and the life. You go on your way through life telling the truth. George knows that this is not exactly what the Bible means, but as he grows up this is how the words sound to him.

Arthur

For Arthur there was a normal distance between home and church; but each place was filled with presences, with stories and instructions. In the cold stone church where he went once a week to kneel and pray, there was God and Jesus Christ and the Twelve Apostles and the Ten Commandments and the Seven Deadly Sins. Everything was very orderly, always listed and numbered, like the hymns and the prayers and the verses of the Bible.

He understood that what he learned there was the truth; but his imagination preferred the different, parallel version he was taught at home. His mother's stories were also about far distant times, and also designed to teach him the distinction between right and wrong. She would stand at the kitchen range, stirring the porridge, tucking her hair back behind her ears as she did so; and he would wait for the moment when she would tap the stick against the pan, pause, and turn her round, smiling face towards him. Then her grey eyes would hold him, while her voice made a moving curve in the air, swooping up and down, then slowing almost to a halt as she reached the part of the tale he could scarcely endure, the part where exquisite torment or joy awaited not just hero and heroine, but the listener as well.

'And then the knight was held over the pit of writhing snakes, which hissed and spat as their twining lengths ensnared the whitening bones of their previous victims . . .'

'And then the black-hearted villain, with a hideous oath, drew a secret dagger from his boot and advanced towards the defenceless . . .'

'And then the maiden took a pin from her hair and the golden tresses fell from the window, down, down, caressing the castle walls until they almost reached the verdant grass on which he stood . . .'

Arthur was an energetic, headstrong boy who did not easily sit still; but once the Mam raised her porridge stick he was held in a state of silent enchant-ment—as if a villain from one of her stories had slipped a secret herb into his food. Knights and their ladies then moved about the tiny kitchen; challenges were issued, quests miraculously fulfilled; armour clanked, chain mail rustled, and honour was always upheld.

These stories were connected, in a way that he did not at first understand, with an old wooden chest beside his parents' bed, which held the papers of the family's descent. Here were different kinds of stories, which more resembled school homework, about the ducal house of Brittany, and the Irish branch of the Percys of Northumberland, and someone who had led Pack's Brigade at Waterloo, and was the uncle of the white, waxen thing he never forgot. And connected to all this were the private lessons in heraldry his mother gave him. From the kitchen cupboard the Mam would pull out large sheets of cardboard, painted and coloured by one of his uncles in London. She would explain the coats of arms, then instruct him in his turn: 'Blazon me this shield!' And he would have to reply, as with multiplication tables: chevrons, estoiles, mullets, cinquefoils, crescents argent, and their glittering like.

At home he learned extra commandments on top of the ten he knew from church. 'Fearless to the strong; humble to the weak', was one, and 'Chivalry towards women, of high and low degree.' He felt them to be more impor-tant, since they came directly from the Mam; they also demanded practical implementation. Arthur did not look beyond his immediate circumstances. The flat was small, money short, his mother overworked, his father erratic. Early on he made a childhood vow and vows, he knew, were never to be swerved from: 'When you are old, Mammie, you shall have a velvet dress and gold glasses and sit in comfort by the fire.' Arthur could see the beginning of the story – where he was now – and its happy end; only the middle was for the moment lacking.

He searched for clues in his favourite author, Captain Mayne Reid. He looked in *The Rifle Rangers: or Adventures of an Officer in Southern Mexico.* He read *The Young Voyageurs* and *The War Trail* and *The Headless Horseman.* Buffaloes and Red Indians were now mixing in his head with chain-mailed knights and the infantrymen of Pack's Brigade. His favourite Mayne Reid of all was *The Scalp-Hunters: or Romantic Adventures in Southern Mexico.* Arthur did not as yet know how the gold glasses and velvet dress were to be obtained; but he suspected it might involve a hazardous journey to Mexico.

George

His mother takes him once a week to visit Great-Uncle Compson. He lives not far away, behind a low granite kerb which George is not allowed to cross. Every week they renew his jug of flowers. Great Wyrley was Uncle Compson's parish for twenty-six years; now his soul is in Heaven while his body remains in the churchyard. Mother explains this as she takes out the shrivelled stems, throws away the smelly water, and stands up the fresh, smooth flowers. Sometimes George is allowed to help her pour in the clean water. She tells him that excessive mourning is unChristian, but George does not understand this.

After Great-Uncle's departure for Heaven, Father took his place. One year he married Mother, the next he obtained his parish, and the next George was born. This is the story he has been told, and it is clear and true and happy, as everything ought to be. There is Mother, who is constantly present in his life, teaching him his letters, kissing him goodnight; and Father, who is often absent because he is visiting the old and the sick, or writing his sermons, or preaching them. There is the Vicarage, the church, the building where Mother teaches Sunday school, the garden, the cat, the hens, the stretch of grass they cross between the Vicarage and the church, and the churchyard. This is George's world, and he knows it well.

Inside the Vicarage, everything is quiet. There are prayers, books, needlework. You do not shout, you do not run, you do not soil yourself. The fire is sometimes noisy, so are the knives and forks if you do not hold them properly; so is his brother Horace when he arrives. But these are the exceptions in a world which is both peaceful and reliable. The world beyond the Vicarage seems to George filled with unexpected noise and unexpected happenings. When he is four, he is taken for a walk in the lanes and introduced to a cow.

It is not the size of the beast that alarms him, nor the swollen udders wobbling in his eye-line, but the sudden hoarse bellow the thing utters for no good reason. It can only be in a very bad temper. George bursts into tears, while his father punishes the cow by hitting it with a stick. Then the animal turns sideways, raises its tail and soils itself. George is transfixed by this outpouring, by the strange splatty noise as it lands on the grass, by the way things have suddenly slipped out of control. But his mother's hand pulls him away before he can consider it further.

It is not just the cow – or the cow's many friends like the horse, the sheep and the pig – that renders George suspicious of the world beyond the Vicarage wall. Most of what he hears about it makes him anxious. It is full of people who are old, and sick, and poor, all of which are bad things to be, judging from Father's attitude and lowered voice when he returns; and people called pit widows, which George does not understand. There are boys beyond the wall who are fibbers and, worse than that, liars through and through. There is also something called a Colliery nearby, which is where the coal in the grate comes from. He is not sure he likes coal. It is smelly and dusty and noisy when poked, and you are told to keep away from its flames; also, it is brought to the house by large fierce men in leather helmets which carry on down their backs. When the outside world brings the door-knocker down, George usually jumps. All things considered, he would prefer to stay here, inside, with Mother, with his brother Horace and new sister Maud, until it is time for him to go to Heaven and meet Great-Uncle Compson. But he suspects that this will not be allowed.

Arthur

They were always moving: half a dozen times in Arthur's first ten years. The flats seemed to get smaller as the family grew larger. Apart from Arthur, there was his older sister Annette, his younger sisters Lottie and Connie, his little brother Innes, and then, later, his sisters Ida and Julia, known as Dodo. Their father was good at engendering children – there were another two who had not survived – but less good at providing for them. This early realization that his father would never furnish the Mam with the proper comforts of old age made Arthur all the more determined to provide them himself.

His father – Dukes of Brittany aside – came from an artistic family. He had talent and fine religious instincts; but was highly strung, and his constitution was not robust. He had come to Edinburgh from London at the age of nineteen; an assistant surveyor in Scotland's Board of Works, he was precipitated at too early an age into a society which, though kindly, was often rough and hard-drinking. He did not progress at the Board of Works, nor at George Waterman & Sons, the lithographic printers. He was a gentle failure of a man, with a soft face behind a full, soft beard; he perceived duty distantly, and had lost his way in life.

He was never violent or aggressive; he was a drunkard of the sentimental, open-pursed, self-pitying kind. He would be brought home, dribbling into his beard, by cabmen whose insistence on being paid would wake the children; the next morning he would lament at maudlin length his inability to support those he loved so tenderly. One year Arthur was sent away to lodgings rather than witness a new stage of his father's decline; but he saw enough to endorse his crescent understanding of what a man could or should be. In his mother's tales of chivalry and romance there were few parts for drunken illustrators.

Arthur's father painted in watercolour, and always intended to supplement his income by selling his work. But his generous nature constantly intervened; he gave his pictures away to all-comers, or at best accepted a few pence for them. His subjects could be wild and fearsome, and often gave evidence of his natural humour. But what he liked to paint best, and was most remembered for painting, was fairies.

George

George is sent to the village school. He wears a deep starched collar with a loose bow tie to hide the stud, a waistcoat which buttons up to just below the tie, and a jacket with high, almost horizontal lapels. Other boys are not so neat: some wear rough, home-knitted jerseys or ill-fitting jackets passed on from elder brothers. A few have starched collars, but only Harry Charlesworth wears a tie as George does.

His mother has taught him his letters, his father simple sums. For the first week he finds himself seated at the rear of the classroom. On Friday they will be tested and rearranged by intelligence: clever boys will sit at the front, stupid boys at the back; the reward for progress being to find yourself closer to the master, to the seat of instruction, to knowledge, to truth. This is Mr Bostock, who wears a tweed jacket, a woollen waistcoat, and a shirt-collar whose points are pulled in behind his tie by a gold pin. Mr Bostock carries a brown felt hat at all times and places it on the desk during class, as if he does not trust it out of his sight.

When there is a break between lessons the boys go outside into what is called the yard, but which is merely a trampled area of grass looking across open fields towards the distant Colliery. Boys who already know one another instantly start fighting, just for something to do. George has never seen boys fight before. As he watches, Sid Henshaw, one of the rougher boys, comes and stands in front of him. Henshaw makes monkey faces, pulling at the sides of his mouth with his little fingers while using his thumbs to flap his ears forward.

'How d'you do, my name's George.' This is what he has been instructed to say. But Henshaw just carries on making gurgling noises and flapping his ears.

Some of the boys come from farms, and George thinks they smell of cows. Others are miners' sons, and seem to talk differently. George learns the names of his schoolfellows: Sid Henshaw, Arthur Aram, Harry Boam, Horace Knighton, Harry Charlesworth, Wallie Sharp, John Harriman, Albert Yates . . .

His father says that he is going to make friends, but he is not sure how this is done. One morning Wallie Sharp comes up behind him in the yard and whispers,

'You're not a right sort.'

George turns round. 'How d'you do, my name's George,' he repeats.

At the end of the first week Mr Bostock tests them at reading, spelling and sums. He announces the results on Monday morning, and then they move desks. George is good at reading from the book in front of him, but his spelling and sums let him down. He is told to remain at the back of the form. He does no better the next Friday, and the one after that. By now he finds himself surrounded by farm boys and mine boys who don't care where they sit, indeed think it an advantage to be farther away from Mr Bostock so they can misbehave. George feels as if he is being slowly banished from the way, the truth and the life.

Mr Bostock stabs at the blackboard with a piece of chalk. '*This*, George, plus *this*' (stab) 'equals *what?*' (stab stab).

Everything in his head is a blur, and George guesses wildly. 'Twelve,' he he says, or 'Seven and a half.' The boys at the front laugh, and then the farm boys join in when they realize he is wrong.

Mr Bostock sighs and shakes his head and asks Harry Charlesworth, who is always in the front row and has his hand up all the time.

'Eight,' Harry says, or 'Thirteen and a quarter,' and Mr Bostock moves his head in George's direction, to show how stupid he has been.

One afternoon, on his way back to the Vicarage, George soils himself. His mother takes off his clothes, stands him in the bath, scrubs him down, dresses him again and takes him to Father. But George is unable to explain to his father why, though he is nearly seven years old, he has behaved like a baby in napkins.

This happens again, and then again. His parents do not punish him, but their evident disappointment in their first-born – stupid at school, a baby on the way home – is as bad as any punishment. They discuss him over the top of his head.

'The child gets his nerves from you, Charlotte.'

'In any event, it cannot be teething.'

'We can rule out cold, since we are in September.'

'And indigestible items of food, since Horace is not affected.'

'What remains?'

'The only other cause the book suggests is fright.'

'George, are you frightened of something?'

George looks at his father, at the shiny clerical collar, at the broad, unsmiling face above it, the mouth which speaks the frequently incomprehensible truth from the pulpit of St Mark's, and the black eyes which now command the truth from him. What is he to say? He is frightened of Wallie Sharp and Sid Henshaw and some others, but that would be telling on them. In any case, it is not what he fears most. Eventually he says, 'I'm frightened of being stupid.'

'George,' his father replies, 'we know you are not stupid. Your mother and I have taught you your letters and your sums. You are a bright boy. You can do sums at home but not at school. Can you tell us why?'

'No.'

'Does Mr Bostock teach them differently?'

'No, Father.'

'Do you stop trying?'

'No, Father. I can do them in the book but I can't do them on the board.'

'Charlotte, I think we should take him into Birmingham.'

Arthur

Arthur had uncles who watched their brother's decline and pitied his family. Their solution was to send Arthur to be schooled by the Jesuits in England. Aged nine, he was put on the train at Edinburgh and wept all the way to Preston. He would spend the next seven years at Stonyhurst, except for six weeks each summer, when he returned to the Mam and to his occasional father.

These Jesuits had come over from Holland, bringing their curriculum and methods of discipline with them. Education comprised seven classes of knowledge – elements, figures, rudiments, grammar, syntax, poetry and rhetoric – with one year allotted to each. There was the usual public-school routine of Euclid, algebra and the classics, whose truths were endorsed by emphatic beatings. The instrument deployed – a piece of India rubber the size and thickness of a boot sole – had also come over from Holland, and was known as the

Tolley. One blow on the hand, delivered with full Jesuitical intent, was enough to cause the palm to swell and change colour. The normal punishment for larger boys consisted of nine blows on each hand. Afterwards, the sinner could barely turn the doorknob of the study in which he had been beaten.

The Tolley, it was explained to Arthur, had received its name as a Latin pun. *Fero*, I bear. *Fero, ferre, tuli, latum. Tuli*, I have borne, the Tolley is what we have borne, yes?

The humour was as rough as the punishments. Asked how he saw his future, Arthur admitted that he had thought of becoming a civil engineer.

'Well, you may be an engineer,' replied the priest, 'but I don't think you'll ever be a civil one.'

Arthur developed into a large, boisterous youth, who found consolation in the school library and happiness on the cricket field. Once a week the boys were set to write home, which most regarded as a further punishment, but Arthur viewed as a reward. For that hour he would pour out everything to his mother. There may have been God, and Jesus Christ, and the Bible, and the Jesuits, and the Tolley, but the authority he most believed in and submitted to was his small, commanding Mam. She was an expert in all matters, from underclothing to hellfire. 'Wear flannel next to your skin,' she advised him, 'and never believe in eternal punishment.'

She had also, less deliberately, taught him a way to popularity. Early on, he began telling his fellow pupils the stories of chivalry and romance he had first heard from beneath a raised porridge stick. On wet half-holidays, he would stand on a desk while his audience squatted around him. Remembering the Mam's skills, he knew how to drop his voice, how to drag out a story, how to leave off at a perilous, excruciating moment with the promise of more the next day. Being large and hungry, he would accept a pastry as the basic price of a tale. But sometimes, he might stop dead at the thrill of a crisis, and could only be got going again at the cost of an apple.

Thus he discovered the essential connection between narrative and reward.

George

The oculist does not recommend spectacles for young children. It is better to let the boy's eyes adjust naturally over the years. In the meanwhile, he should be moved to the front of the classroom. George leaves the farm boys behind and is placed beside Harry Charlesworth, who is regularly top in tests. School now makes sense to George; he can see where Mr Bostock's chalk is stabbing, and he never again soils himself on the way home.

Sid Henshaw carries on making monkey faces, but George barely notices. Sid Henshaw is just a stupid farm boy who smells of cows and probably cannot even spell the word.

One day, Henshaw rushes at George in the yard, barges him with his shoulder, and as George is recovering himself, pulls off his bow tie and runs away. George hears laughter. Back in the classroom, Mr Bostock asks where his tie has got to.

This presents George with a problem. He knows it is wrong to get a schoolfellow into trouble. But he knows it is worse to tell lies. His father is quite clear about this. Once you start telling lies you are led into the paths of sin and nothing will stop you until the hangman slips a noose around your neck. No one has said as much, but this is what George has understood. So he cannot lie to Mr Bostock. He looks for a way out – which is perhaps bad enough anyway, the start of a lie – and then he simply answers the question.

'Sid Henshaw knocked me and took it.'

Mr Bostock leads Henshaw out by the hair, beats him until he howls, comes back with George's tie, and gives the class a lecture about theft. After school, Wallie Sharp stands in George's path and as he steps round him says, 'You're not a right sort.'

George rules out Wallie Sharp as a possible friend.

He rarely feels the lack of what he does not have. The family takes no part in local society, but George cannot imagine what this might involve, let alone what the reason for their unwillingness, or failure, might be. He himself never goes to other boys' houses, so cannot judge how things are conducted elsewhere. His life is sufficient unto itself. He has no money, but also no need of it, and even less when he learns that its love is the root of all evil. He has no toys, but does not miss them. He lacks the skill and eyesight for games; he has never even jumped a hopscotch grid, while a thrown ball makes him flinch. He is happy to play fraternally with Horace, more gently with Maud, and more gently still with the hens.

He is aware that most boys have friends – there are David and Jonathan in the Bible, and he has watched Harry Boam and Arthur Aram huddling at the edge of the yard and showing one another things from their pockets – but he never finds this happening to himself. Is he meant to do something, or are they meant to do something? In any case, though he wants to please Mr Bostock, he is not especially interested in pleasing the boys who sit behind him.

When Great-Aunt Stoneham comes to tea, as she does on the first Sunday of each month, she scrapes her cup noisily across its saucer and through a wrinkled mouth asks him about his friends.

'Harry Charlesworth,' he always replies. 'He sits next to me.'

The third time he gives her the same reply, she puts her cup noisily back in its saucer, frowns, and asks, 'Anyone else?'

'The rest of them are just smelly farm boys,' he replies.

From the way Great-Aunt Stoneham looks at Father, he knows he has said something wrong. Before supper, he is called into the study. His father stands at his desk, with all the authority of the faith shelved behind him.

'George, how old are you?'

This is how conversations often begin with Father. They both of them already know the answer, but George still has to give it.

'Seven, Father.'

'That is an age by which a certain intelligence and judgement may reasonably be expected. So let me ask you this, George. Do you think that in the eyes of God you are more important than boys who live on farms?'

George can tell that the correct answer is No, but is reluctant to give it immediately. Surely a boy who lives in the Vicarage, whose father is the Vicar and whose great-uncle has been Vicar as well, is more important to God than a boy who never goes to church and is stupid and also cruel like Harry Boam?

'No,' he says.

'And why do you call these boys smelly?'

It is less clear what the correct answer to this might be. George considers the matter. The correct answer, he has been taught, is the truthful one.

'Because they are, Father.'

His father sighs. 'And if they are, George, why are they?'

'Why are they what, Father?'

'Smelly.'

'Because they do not wash.'

'No, George, if they are smelly, it is because they are poor. We are fortunate enough to be able to afford soap, and fresh linen, and to have a bathroom, and not to live in close proximity with beasts. They are the humble of the earth. And tell me this, whom does God love more, the humble of the earth or those who are filled with wrongful pride?'

This is an easier question, even if George doesn't particularly agree with the answer. 'The humble of the earth, Father.'

'Blessed are the meek, George. You know the verse.'

'Yes, Father.'

But something in George resists this conclusion. He does not think Harry Boam and Arthur Aram are meek. Nor can he believe it to be part of God's eternal plan for His creation that Harry Boam and Arthur Aram shall end up inheriting the earth. That would scarcely conform to George's sense of justice. They are just smelly farm boys, after all.

Arthur

Stonyhurst offered to remit Arthur's school fees if he was prepared to train for the priesthood; but the Mam declined the proposal. Arthur was ambitious and well capable of leadership, already marked down as a future Captain of Cricket. But she did not foresee any child of hers as a spiritual guide. Arthur, for his part, knew that he could not possibly supply the promised gold glasses and velvet dress and seat by the fire if he vowed himself to a life of poverty and obedience.

The Jesuits were not bad fellows, in his assessment. They considered human nature to be essentially weak, and their mistrust seemed justified to Arthur: you only had to look at his own father. They also understood that sinfulness began early. Boys were never permitted to be alone together; masters always accompanied them on walks; and every night a shadowy figure would perambulate the dormitories. Constant surveillance might undermine self-respect and self-help; but the immorality and beastliness rife at other schools were kept to a minimum.

Arthur believed, in a general way, that God existed, that boys were tempted by sin, and that the Fathers were right to beat them with the Tolley. When it came to particular articles of faith, he argued in private with his friend Partridge. He had been impressed by Partridge when, standing at second slip, he had taken a blinding catch from one of Arthur's fastest deliveries, pocketed the ball quicker than the eye could see, and turned away, pretending to watch the ball disappear to the boundary. Partridge liked to bamboozle a fellow, and not just on the cricket field.

'Are you aware that the doctrine of the Immaculate Conception became an article of faith as recently as 1854?'

'Somewhat late in the day, I'd have thought, Partridge.'

'Imagine. The Church has been debating the dogma for centuries, and all that time it has never been heresy to deny it. Suddenly it is.'

'Hmm.'

'Now why should Rome decide, so far after the event, to downgrade the participation of Mary's corporeal father in the matter?'

'I say, steady on, man.'

But Partridge was already addressing the doctrine of Papal Infallibility, pronounced only five years previously. Why should all the popes of centuries past be implicitly declared fallible, and all popes present and future the opposite? Why indeed, Arthur echoed. Because, Partridge rejoined, it was more a question of Church politics than theological advance. It was all to do with the presence of influential Jesuits high up in the Vatican.

'You are sent to tempt me,' Arthur would sometimes reply.

'On the contrary. I am here to strengthen your faith. Thinking for ourselves within the Church is the path of true obedience. Whenever the Church feels threatened, it responds by imposing stricter discipline. It works in the short term, but not in the long. It's like the Tolley. You are beaten today, and so you do not offend again tomorrow or the next day. But not offending for the rest of your life because of a memory of the Tolley is a nonsense, is it not?'

'Not if it works.'

'But in a year or two we shall be quit of this place. The Tolley will not exist any more. We need to be equipped to resist sin and crime by rational argument, not the fear of physical pain.'

'I doubt rational argument will work on some boys.'

'Then the Tolley by all means. And the same in the world outside. Of course there must be prison, and hard labour, and the hangman.'

'But what is the Church threatened by? It seems strong to me.'

'By science. By the spread of sceptical teaching. By the loss of the Papal States. By the loss of political influence. By the prospect of the twentieth century.'

'The twentieth century.' Arthur mused on this a moment. 'I cannot think that far. I shall be forty by the time the next century begins.'

'And captain of the England team.'

'I doubt it, Partridge. But not a priest, at any rate.'

Arthur was not exactly conscious of his faith weakening. But thinking for himself within the Church slipped easily into thinking for himself outside it. He found that his reason and conscience did not always accept what was placed in front of them. In his last year at school, Father Murphy came to preach. High in the pulpit, fierce and red-faced, the priest threatened sure and certain damnation for all who remained outside the Church. Whether their exclusion came from wickedness, wilfulness or mere ignorance, the consequences were the same: sure and certain damnation for all eternity. There followed a panoramic description of the torments and desolations of Hell, especially designed to make boys squirm; but Arthur had stopped attending. The Mam had told him what was the case; and he now gazed up at Father Murphy as at a storyteller he no longer believed.

George

Mother teaches Sunday school in the building next door to the Vicarage. Its brickwork has a diamond pattern to it which Mother says reminds her of a

Fair Isle comforter. George does not understand this, though wonders if it has anything to do with Job's comforters. He looks forward to Sunday school all week. The rough boys do not attend: they are running wild in the fields, trapping rabbits, telling lies, and generally going down the primrose path to everlasting damnation. Mother has warned him that in class she will treat him exactly the same as everyone else. George understands why: because she is showing them all – equally – the way to Heaven.

She tells them exciting stories which George can follow easily: like Daniel in the Lions' Den, and the Burning Fiery Furnace. But other stories prove more difficult. Christ taught in Parables, and George finds he does not like Parables. Take the Parable of the Wheat and the Tares. George understands the part about the enemy planting Tares among the Wheat, and how you shouldn't gather up the Tares in case you root out the Wheat at the same time – though he isn't entirely sure about this, because he often sees Mother weeding in the Vicarage garden and what is weeding except gathering up the Tares before they and the Wheat are fully grown? But even ignoring this problem, he can go no further. He knows the story is all about something else – that is why it is a Parable – but what this something else might be his mind will not reach to.

He tells Horace about the Wheat and the Tares, but Horace does not even understand what Tares are. Horace is three years younger than George, and Maud is three years younger than Horace. Maud, being a girl, and also being the youngest child, is not as strong as the two boys, who are told it is their duty to protect her. Quite what this involves is left unspecified; it seems to consist mainly of not doing things – not poking her with sticks, not pulling her hair, and not making noises in her face as Horace likes doing.

But George and Horace prove inadequate at protecting Maud. The doctor's visits begin, and his regular inspections cast the family into a state of anxiety. George feels guilty whenever the doctor calls, and stays out of the way, in case he is identified as the prime cause of his sister's illness. Horace feels no such guilt, and cheerfully asks if he may carry the doctor's bag upstairs.

When Maud is four, it is decided that she is too frail to be left on her own all night, and that neither George nor Horace, nor even the combination of the two, can be trusted with her nocturnal care. From now on she will sleep in their mother's room. At the same time, it is decided that George will sleep with his father, and Horace will have the nursery to himself. George is now ten, and Horace seven; perhaps it is thought that the age of sinfulness is approaching, and the two boys should not be left alone together. No explanation is given, and none is sought. George does not ask whether being put to sleep in his father's room is a punishment or a reward. It is how things are, which is all there is to be said.

George and his father pray together, kneeling side by side on the scrubbed boards. Then George climbs into bed while his father locks the door and turns out the light. As he falls asleep, George sometimes thinks of the floor, and how his soul must be scrubbed just as the boards are scrubbed.

Father is not an easy sleeper, and has a tendency to groan and wheeze. Sometimes, in the early morning, when dawn is beginning to show at the edges of the curtains, Father will catechize him.

'George, where do you live?'

'The Vicarage, Great Wyrley.'

'And where is that?'

'Staffordshire, Father.'

'And where is that?'

'The centre of England.'

'And what is England, George?'

'England is the beating heart of the Empire, Father.'

'Good. And what is the blood that flows through the arteries and veins of the Empire to reach even its farthest shore?'

'The Church of England.'

'Good, George.'

And after a while Father begins to groan and wheeze again. George watches the outline of the curtain harden. He lies there thinking of arteries and veins making red lines on the map of the world, linking Britain to all the places coloured pink: Australia and India and Canada and islands dotted every-where. He thinks of tubes being laid along the bed of the ocean like tele-graph cables. He thinks of blood bubbling through these tubes and emerging in Sydney, Bombay, Cape Town. Bloodlines, that is a word he has heard some-where. With the pulse of blood in his ears, he begins to fall asleep again.

Arthur

Arthur passed his Matriculation with Honours; but being still only sixteen, he was sent for a further year among the Jesuits in Austria. At Feldkirch he discovered a kindlier regime, which allowed beer drinking and heated dormi-tories. There were long walks, on which English pupils were deliberately flanked by German-speaking boys, thus obliging them to speak the language. Arthur appointed himself editor and sole contributor of *The Feldkirchian Gazette*, a hand-written literary and scientific magazine. He also played foot-ball on stilts, and was taught the Bombardon tuba, an instrument which wrapped twice around the chest and made a sound like Judgement Day.

On his return to Edinburgh, he discovered that his father was in a nursing home, officially suffering from epilepsy. There would be no more income, not even occasional coppers from watercolours of fairies. So Annette, the eldest sister, was already in Portugal, working as a governess; Lottie would soon join her, and they would send money home. The Mam's other recourse was to take in lodgers. Arthur felt embarrassed and affronted by this. His mother, of all people, should not be reduced to the status of a landlady.

'But Arthur, if people did not take in lodgers, your father would never have come to live with Grandma Pack, and I should never have met him.'

This struck Arthur as an even stronger argument against lodgers. He knew he was not allowed to criticize his father in any way, so he remained silent. But it was a nonsense to pretend that the Mam could not have made a better match.

'And if that had not happened,' she went on, smiling at him with those grey eyes which he could never disobey, 'Not only would there have been no Arthur, there would have been no Annette, no Lottie, no Connie, no Innes and no Ida.'

This was indisputably true, and also one of those insoluble metaphysical conundrums. He wished Partridge were there to help him debate the question: could you remain yourself, or at least enough of yourself, if you had a different father? If not, it also followed that his sisters would not have remained themselves either, especially Lottie, whom he loved the best, even though Connie was said to be prettier. He could just about imagine himself being different, but his brain would not stretch to changing one iota of Lottie.

Arthur might have better stomached the Mam's response to their reduced social condition if he had not already met her first lodger. Bryan Charles Waller: just six years older than Arthur, but already a qualified doctor. Also a published poet, whose uncle had received the dedication of *Vanity Fair*. Arthur did not object to the fact that the fellow was well-read, even scholarly; nor to the fact that he was a hot-hearted atheist; he objected to the way he was far too easy and charming around the house. The way he said, 'So this is Arthur,' and smilingly held out his hand. The way he implied he was one step ahead of you already. The way he wore his two London suits, and talked in generalities and epigrams. The way he was with Lottie and Connie. The way he was with the Mam.

He was easy and charming with Arthur, too, which went down ill with the large, awkward, stubborn ex-schoolboy just back from Austria. Waller behaved as if he understood Arthur even when Arthur could not seem to understand himself, when he stood there by his own fireside feeling as absurd as if he had a Bombardon tuba wrapped twice around him. He wanted to blow a blast of protest, the more so when Waller affected to peer into his very soul and – which was the most annoying part – to take what he found there seriously and yet also not seriously, smiling away as if all the confusion he detected was unsurprising and unimportant.

Far too easy and charming with life itself, dammit.

George

For as long as George can remember, there has been a maid-of-all-work at the Vicarage, someone in the background scrubbing, dusting, polishing, laying fires, blackening grate and setting the copper to boil. Every year or so there is a change of maid, as one gets married, another goes off to Cannock or Walsall or even Birmingham. George never pays them any attention, and now that he is at Rugeley School, taking the train there and back each day, he notices the maid's existence even less.

He is glad to have escaped the village school with its stupid farm boys and odd-talking miners' sons, whose very names he soon forgets. At Rugeley he is generally with the better sort of boy, while the masters consider it a useful thing to be intelligent. He gets on well enough with his fellows, even if he does not make any close friends. Harry Charlesworth goes to school in Walsall, and nowadays they merely nod at one another if they meet. George's work, his family, and his faith, and all the duties that flow from these adherences, are what count. There will be time for other things later.

One Saturday afternoon, George is called to his father's study. There is a large biblical concordance open on the desk, and some notes for tomorrow's sermon. Father looks as he does in the pulpit. At least George can guess what his first question will be.

'George, how old are you?'

'Twelve, Father.'

'An age at which wisdom and discretion might to a certain degree be expected.'

George does not know if this is a question or not, so he remains silent.

'George, Elizabeth Foster complains that you look at her strangely.'

He is puzzled. Elizabeth Foster is the new maid; she has been there a few months. She wears a maid's uniform, like all the previous maids.

'What does she mean, Father?'

'What do you think she means?'

George ponders this for a while. 'Is it something sinful she means?'

'And if it is, what might it be?'

'My only sin, Father, is that I am hardly aware of her, though I know her to be part of God's creation. I have not spoken to her more than twice, on occasions when she has mislaid objects. I have no reason to look at her.'

'No reason at all, George?'

'No reason at all, Father.'

'Then I shall tell her she is a foolish and malicious girl who will be dismissed if she gives further grounds for complaint.'

George is eager for his Latin verbs, and does not mind what becomes of Elizabeth Foster. Nor does he wonder if it is a sin not to mind what becomes of her.

Arthur

It was decided that Arthur would study medicine at Edinburgh University. He was responsible and hard-working; in time he would surely acquire the stolidity patients liked to trust. Arthur was agreeable to the idea, if suspicious about its origins. The Mam had first proposed medicine in a letter to Feldkirch, a letter sent within a month of Dr Waller's arrival into the household. Mere coincidence? Arthur hoped so; he did not care to imagine his future being discussed between his mother and this interloper. Even if he was, as people constantly reminded him, a qualified doctor and published poet. Even if his uncle was the dedicatee of *Vanity Fair*.

It also seemed a little too damned convenient that Waller was now offering to coach him for a scholarship. Arthur accepted with adolescent ill grace, which drew a private word from the Mam. Nowadays he towered over her, and her hair, which had already lost its fairness, was beginning to whiten where it was drawn back behind her ears; but her grey eyes and her quiet voice, and the moral authority implicit in them, remained as powerful as ever.

Waller proved an excellent tutor. Together, they crammed the classics, aiming for the Grierson bursary: £40 a year for two years would be a great help to the household. When the letter came, and the household was united in acclamation, he felt it was his first real achievement, his first act of paying back his mother for her sacrifices over the years. There were handshakes and kisses all round; Lottie and Connie became absurdly sentimental and wept like the girls they were; and Arthur, in a spirit of magnanimity, resolved to lay aside his suspicions of Waller.

A few days later, Arthur called at the University to claim his prize. He was received by a small, embarrassed official whose precise status was never made clear. It was all entirely regrettable. It was still unclear how it had happened. A clerical error of some kind. The Grierson bursary was open only to arts students. Arthur's entry should never have been accepted. They would take steps in future, and so on.

But there were other prizes and bursaries, Arthur pointed out – a whole list of them. Presumably they would give him one of those instead. Well, yes, that could be the case, in theory; indeed, the next bursary down on the list was available for medicals. Unfortunately, it had already been claimed. As, indeed, had all the others.

'But this is daylight robbery,' Arthur shouted. 'Daylight robbery!'

Certainly it was unfortunate. Perhaps something could be done. And the following week it was. Arthur found himself awarded a solatium of £7, which had accumulated in some overlooked fund, and which the authorities graciously felt could be applied to his purpose.

It was his first experience of rank injustice. When he had been beaten with the Tolley, it was rarely without some reasonable cause. When his father was taken away, it had struck a pain to his son's heart, but he could not protest that his father was blameless; it had been a tragedy though not an injustice. But this – this! He had a case in law against the university, everyone agreed. He would sue them and reclaim the bursary. It took Dr Waller to persuade him of the inadvisability of suing the institution you were relying upon to educate you. There was nothing to be done except swallow pride and bear disappointment like a man. Arthur accepted this appeal to a manliness he had yet to inhabit. But the calming phrases he pretended to find persuasive were mere breath in his ear. Everything within him festered and burned and stank, like a tiny corner of the Hell he no longer believed in.

George

It is unusual for George's father to speak to him after prayers have been said and the light turned out. They are supposed to reflect upon the meaning of the words while yielding themselves to the bosom of God's sleep. In truth, George is more inclined to carry on thinking about the next day's lessons. He does not believe God will count this a sin.

'George,' his father suddenly says. 'Have you noticed anyone loitering near the Vicarage?'

'Today, Father?'

'No, not today. Generally. Recently.'

'No, Father. Why would anyone be loitering?'

'Your mother and I have been receiving anonymous letters.'

'From loiterers?'

'Yes. No. I want you to report anything suspicious to me, George. Somebody pushing something through the door. People standing around.'

'Who are these letters from, Father?'

'They are anonymous, George.' Even in the dark he can sense his father's impatience. 'Anonymous. From the Greek, then the Latin. Without a name.'

'What do they say, Father?'

'They say wicked things. About . . . everyone.'

George knows he is meant to be concerned, but finds it all too exciting. He has been given authority to play the detective, and does so as often as possible without interfering with his school work. He peers from behind the trunks of trees; he obscures himself in the cubbyhole beneath the stairs to watch the front door; he examines the behaviour of those who come to the house; he wonders how he might afford a magnifying glass and, perhaps, a telescope. He discovers nothing.

Nor does he know who starts chalking up sinful words about his parents on Mr Harriman's barn and Mr Aram's outbuildings. As soon as they are washed off, the words mysteriously reappear. George is not told what they say. One afternoon, taking a circuitous route like all the best detectives, he creeps up on Mr Harriman's barn, but all he espies is a wall with some wet patches drying.

'Father,' George whispers after the light has been put out. He assumes this is the permitted time to talk about such matters. 'I have an idea. Mr Bostock.'

'What about Mr Bostock?'

'He has lots of chalk. He always had lots of chalk.'

'That is true, George. But I think we may safely eliminate Mr Bostock.'

A few days later George's mother sprains her wrist and wraps it in muslin. She asks Elizabeth Foster to write the butcher's list for her; but instead of sending the girl with it to Mr Greensill, she takes it to George's father. After comparison with the contents of a locked drawer, Elizabeth Foster is dismissed.

Later, Father has to go and explain things to the magistrates at Cannock. George secretly hopes he might also be asked to give evidence. Father reports that the wretched girl claimed it was all a foolish joke, and has been bound over to keep the peace.

Elizabeth Foster is not seen again in the district and a new maid soon arrives. George feels he could have done better at playing the detective. He also wishes he knew what was chalked on Mr Harriman's barn and Mr Aram's outbuildings.

Arthur

Irish by ancestry, Scottish by birth, instructed in the faith of Rome by Dutch Jesuits, Arthur became English. English history inspired him; English freedoms made him proud; English cricket made him patriotic. And the greatest epoch in English history – with many to choose from – was the fourteenth century: a time when the English archer commanded the field, and when both the French and Scottish kings were held prisoner in London.

But he also never forgot the tales heard while the porridge stick was raised. For Arthur the root of Englishness lay in the long-gone, long-remembered, long-invented world of chivalry. There was no knight more faithful than Sir Kaye, none so brave and amorous as Sir Lancelot, none so virtuous as Sir Galahad. There was no pair of lovers truer than Tristan and Iseult, no wife fairer and more faithless than Guinevere. And of course there was no braver or more noble king than Arthur.

The Christian virtues could be practised by everyone, from the humble to the high-born. But chivalry was the prerogative of the powerful. The knight protected his lady; the strong aided the weak; honour was a living thing for which you should be prepared to die. Sadly, the number of grails and quests available to a newly qualified doctor was fairly limited. In this modern world of Birmingham factories and billycock hats the notion of chivalry often seemed to have declined into one of mere sportsmanship. But Arthur practised the code wherever possible. He was a man of his word; he succoured the poor; he kept his guard against baser emotions; he treated women respectfully; he had long-term plans for the rescue and care of his mother. Given that the fourteenth century had regrettably ended, and that he was not William Douglas, Lord of Liddesdale, the Flower of Chivalry himself, this was the best Arthur could currently manage.

It was the rules of chivalry, and not the textbooks of physiology, which governed his first approaches to the fairer sex. He was handsome enough to attract women, and robustly flirtatious; once, he proudly informed the Mam that he was honourably in love with five women at the same time. It was different from being bosom friends with fellows at school, but at least some of the same rules applied. Thus, if you liked a girl, you gave her a nickname. Elmore Weldon, for instance: a pretty, sturdy thing with whom he flirted furiously for weeks. He called her Elmo, after St Elmo's Fire, that miraculous light seen about the masts and yardarms of ships during a storm. He liked to picture himself as a mariner in peril on the seas of life, while she illuminated the dark skies for him. Indeed, he almost became engaged to Elmo; but then, after a while, he didn't.

He was also much concerned at this time about nocturnal emissions, which had featured little in the *Morte d'Arthur*. Damp morning sheets rather detracted from chivalric dreams; also from a sense of what a man was, or might be, if he put his mind and strength to it. Arthur sought to impose discipline upon his sleeping self by increased physical activity. Already he boxed, and played cricket and football. Now he also took up golf. Where lesser men consulted filth, he read Wisden.

He began to submit stories to the magazines. Once again he was the boy standing on the school desk, deploying his vocal tricks; the cynosure of raised eyes, the cause of mouths dropped open in credulity. He wrote the sort of tales he enjoyed reading – this seemed to him the most sensible approach to the writing game. He set his adventures in distant lands, where buried treasure could often be found, and the local population was high on black-hearted villains and rescuable maidens. Only a certain kind of hero was fitted to take part in the hazardous missions he sketched. For a start, those whose constitutions were enfeebled, those given to self-pity and to alcohol, were manifestly unsuitable. Arthur's father had failed in his chivalric duty to the Mam; now the task had devolved upon his son. He could not rescue her by fourteenth-century methods, so would have to apply those available in a lesser age. He would write stories: he would rescue her by describing the fictional rescue of others. These descriptions would bring him money, and money would do the rest.

George

It is two weeks before Christmas. George is now sixteen, and no longer feels the excitement of the season as he once did. He knows our Saviour's birth to be a solemn truth, annually celebrated, but he has left behind the nervous exaltation that still infects Horace and Maud. Nor does he share the trivial hopes his old schoolfellows at Rugeley used openly to express: for frivolous presents of a kind which have no place at the Vicarage. They also annually set their hearts on snow, and would even demean the faith by praying for it.

George has no interest in skating or sledding or the building of snowmen. He has already embarked on his future career. He has left Rugeley and is studying law at Mason College in Birmingham. If he applies himself, and passes the first examination, he will become an articled clerk. After five years of articles, there will be final examinations, and then he will become a solicitor. He sees himself with a desk, a set of bound law books and a suit with a fob chain slung between his waistcoat pockets like golden rope. He imagines himself being respected. He imagines himself with a hat.

It is almost dark when he gets home late on the afternoon of December 12th. As he reaches the front door of the Vicarage he notices an object lying on the step. He bends, then squats to examine it more closely. It is a large key, cold to the touch and heavy in the hand. George does not know what to make of it. The keys to the Vicarage are much smaller; so is that of the schoolroom. The church key is different again; nor does this seem to be a farm key of any kind. But its weight suggests a serious purpose.

He takes it to his father, who is equally puzzled.

'On the step, you say?' Another question to which Father already knows the answer.

'Yes, Father.'

'And you saw no one put it there?'

'No.'

'And did you meet anyone coming away from the Vicarage on your way from the station?'

'No, Father.'

The key is sent with a note to Hednesford police station, and three days later, when George returns from college, Sergeant Upton is sitting in the kitchen. Father is still out on his parish rounds; Mother is hovering anxiously. It crosses George's mind that there is a reward for finding the key. If this was one of those stories the boys at Rugeley used to love, it would open a strongbox or treasure chest, and the hero would next require a crumpled map with an X marked on it. George has no taste for such adventures, which always strike him as far too unlikely.

Sergeant Upton is a red-faced man with the build of a blacksmith; his dark serge uniform constricts him, and is perhaps the cause of the wheezing noises he makes. He looks George up and down, nodding to himself as he does so.

'So you're the young fellow that found the key?'

George remembers his attempts to play the detective when Elizabeth Foster was writing on walls. Now there is another mystery, but this time with a policeman and a future solicitor involved. It feels appropriate as well as exciting.

'Yes. It was on the doorstep.' The Sergeant doesn't respond to this, but carries on nodding to himself. He seems to need putting at his ease, so George tries to help. 'Is there a reward?'

The Sergeant looks surprised. 'Now why would you be wondering if there's a reward? You of all people?'

George takes this to mean that there isn't one. Perhaps the policeman has only come to congratulate him on returning lost property. 'Have you found out where it's from?'

Upton doesn't reply to this either. Instead, he takes out a notebook and pencil.

'Name?'

'You know my name.'

'Name, I said.'

The Sergeant really could be more civil, George thinks.

'George.'

'Yes. Go on.'

'Ernest.'

'Go on.'

'Thompson.'

'Go on.'

'You know my surname. It's the same as my father's. And my mother's.'

'Go on, I say, you uppish little fellow.'

'Edalji.'

'Ah yes,' says the Sergeant. 'Now I think you'd better spell that out for me.'

Arthur

Arthur's marriage, like his remembered life, began in death.

He qualified as a doctor; worked as a locum-tenens in Sheffield, Shropshire and Birmingham; then took a post as surgeon on the steam-whaler *Hope*. They sailed from Peterhead to the Arctic ice field, off after seal and anything else they could chase and kill. Arthur's duties proved light, and since he was a normal young man, happily given to drinking and, if necessary, fighting, he swiftly won the confidence of the crew; he also fell into the sea so often that they nicknamed him the Great Northern Diver. And like any healthy Briton, he enjoyed a good hunt: his game-bag on the voyage came to fifty-five seals.

He felt little but vigorous male competitiveness when they were out on the endless ice battering seals to death. But one day they took a Greenland whale, and he found it an experience of a different order to any he had known before. To play a salmon might be a royal game, but when your Artic prey weighs more than a suburban villa, it dwarfs all comparisons. From no more than a hand's touch away, Arthur watched the whale's eye – to his surprise, no bigger than a bullock's – slowly dim over in death.

The mystery of the victim: something was now changed in his way of thinking. He continued to shoot ducks from the snowy sky, and felt pride in his marksmanship; yet beyond this lay a feeling he could grasp at but not contain. Every bird you downed bore pebbles in its gizzard from a land the maps ignored.

Next he sailed south, on the *Mayumba* out of Liverpool, bound for the Canaries and the west coast of Africa. Shipboard drinking continued, but fighting took place only over the bridge table and the cribbage board. If he regretted swapping the sea boots and informal dress of a whaler for the gilt buttons and serge suit of a passenger vessel, there was at least the compensation of female company. One night the ladies sportingly made an apple-pie of his bed; the next he took his amiable revenge by hiding a flying fish in one of their nightgowns.

He returned to dry land, common sense and a career. He set up his brass plate in Southsea. He became a Freemason, admitted to the third degree in the Phoenix Lodge No. 257. He captained the Portsmouth Cricket Club and was judged one of the safest Association backs in Hampshire. Dr Pike, fellow member of the Southsea Bowling Club, referred patients to him; the Gresham Life Insurance Company hired him to perform medical examinations.

One day Dr Pike sought Arthur's view on a young patient who had recently moved to Southsea with his widowed mother and elder sister. This second opinion was a mere politeness: it was evident that Jack Hawkins had cerebral meningitis, against which the entire medical profession, let alone Arthur, was powerless. No hotel or boarding house would accept the poor fellow; so Arthur offered to take him into his own house as a resident patient. Hawkins was only a month older than his host. Despite a thousand palliative cups of arrow-root, he swiftly deteriorated, became delirious, and smashed up everything in his room. Within days he was dead.

Arthur looked more carefully at this corpse than he had done at the white, waxen thing of his infancy. He had begun to find, during his medical training, that there was often much promise in the faces of the dead – as if the strain and tension of living had given way to a greater peacefulness. Post-mortal muscular relaxation was the scientific answer; but part of him wondered if this was the full explanation. The human dead also bore in their gizzard pebbles from a land the maps ignored.

As he rode in the one-carriage funeral procession from his own house to the Highland Road cemetery, Arthur's chivalrous feelings were aroused by the black-clad mother and sister, now alone in an unfamiliar town with no male support. Louisa, once her veil was raised, proved a shy, round-faced young woman with blue eyes shading to sea-green. After a decent interval, Arthur was allowed to call at her lodgings.

The young doctor began by explaining how the island – for Southsea was an island, despite appearances – could be represented as a series of Chinese rings: open spaces at its centre, then the middle ring of the town, and then the outer ring of the sea. He told her about the gravelly soil and the quick drainage that resulted from it; about the efficiency of Sir Frederick Bramwell's sanitary arrangements; about the town's salubrious reputation. This last item caused Louisa a sudden distress, which she disguised by an enquiry about Bramwell. She was told a great deal about that distinguished engineer.

The groundwork thus laid, it was time to inspect the place properly. They visited both piers, where military bands seemed to play all day. They watched colours being trooped on the Governor's Green, and mimic engagements on the Common; through binoculars they inspected the nation's battle fleet riding at anchor in the middle distance at Spithead. They walked up the Clarence Esplanade while Arthur explained to her, one by one, all the trophies and memorials of warfare on display. Here a Russian gun, there a Japanese cannon and mortar, everywhere tablets and obelisks to sailors and infantrymen who had died in all quarters of the Empire and in every fashion – yellow fever, shipwreck, the perfidious action of Indian mutineers. She wondered if the doctor had a morbid streak to him; but preferred to decide, for the moment, that his interested curiosity matched his physical tirelessness. He even took her by horse-tram to the Royal Clarence Victualling Yard to watch the manufacturing process of ship's biscuit: from bag of flour to dough, to its conversion by heat into a souvenir which visitors had between their teeth as they left.

Miss Louisa Hawkins had not realized that courtship – if this was what it was – could be so strenuous, or so resemble tourism. Next they turned their eyes southward, to the Isle of Wight. From the Esplanade, Arthur pointed to what he termed the azure hills of the Vectrian Isle, a turn of phrase which struck her as most poetic. They had a distant glimpse of Osborne House, and he explained how an increase in water traffic told when the Queen was in residence. Then they took a steamer across the Solent and round the island; her eye was directed to the Needles, Alum Bay, Carisbrooke Castle, the Landslip, the Undercliff – until she was obliged to call for a deckchair and a rug.

One evening, as they gazed out to sea from the South Parade Pier, he described his exploits in Africa and the Arctic; yet the way tears came into her eyes when he mentioned their purpose on the ice field made him refrain from bragging about his game-bag. She had, he discovered, an innate gentleness which he took to be characteristic of all women, once you got to know them. She was always ready to smile; but could not bear any humour which verged on cruelty, or implied the superiority of the humorist. She had an open, generous nature, a lovely head of curls, and a small income of her own.

In his previous dealings with women, Arthur had played the honourable flirt. Now, as they strolled this concentric resort, as she learned to take his arm, as her name changed in his mouth from Louisa to Touie, as he surreptitiously looked at her hips when she turned away, he knew he wanted more than flirtation. He also thought she would improve him as a man; which was, after all, one of the principles of marriage.

First, however, the young prospect had to be approved by the Mam, who travelled to Hampshire for the inspection. She found Louisa timid, tractable and of decent if not distinguished family. There was no vulgarity or obvious moral weakness likely to embarrass her beloved boy. Nor did there seem any lurking vanity which might at some future time make the girl bridle at Arthur's authority. The mother, Mrs Hawkins, seemed both pleasant and respectful. In giving her approval, the Mam even allowed herself to muse that there might perhaps be something about Louisa – just there, when she held herself in the light like that – which was reminiscent of her own younger self. And what more could a mother want than that, after all?

George

Since starting at Mason College, George has developed the habit of walking the lanes most evenings after his return from Birmingham. This is not for exercise – he had a lifetime of that at Rugeley – but to clear his head before settling down to his books again. As often as not, this fails to work, and he finds himself back in the minutiae of contract law. On this cold January evening, with a half-moon in the sky and the verges still shiny from last night's frost, George is muttering his way through his argument for tomorrow's moot debate – the case is about contaminated flour in a granary – when a figure jumps out at him from behind a tree.

'On your way to Walsall, eh?'

It is Sergeant Upton, red-faced and puffing.

'I beg your pardon?'

'You heard what I said.' Upton is standing close to him, staring in a way George finds alarming. He wonders if the Sergeant is a little loony; in which case, best to humour him.

'You asked if I was on my way to Walsall.'

'So you do have a bloody pair of ears after all.' He is wheezing like – like a horse, or a pig or something.

'I only wondered why you asked, because this is not the way to Walsall. As we both know.'

'As we both know. As we both know.' Upton takes a pace forwards and seizes George by the shoulder. 'What we both know, what we both know, is that you know the way to Walsall, and I know the way to Walsall, and you've been up to your little tricks in Walsall, haven't you?'

The Sergeant is definitely loony now; also hurting him. Is there any advantage in pointing out that he hasn't been to Walsall since this time two years ago, when he was buying Christmas presents for Horace and Maud?

'You been into Walsall, you've took the key to the school, you've brought it home and you've put it on your own front step, didn't you?'

'You're hurting me,' says George.

'Oh no I'm not. I'm not hurting you. This isn't hurting you. You want Sergeant Upton to hurt you, all you have to do is ask.'

George now feels as he did when he used to stare at the distant blackboard with no idea what the correct answer was. He feels as he did when he was about to soil himself. Without knowing quite why, he says, 'I'm going to be a solicitor.'

The Sergeant releases his grip, steps back, and laughs in George's face. Then he spits down towards George's boot.

'Is that what you think? A so-li-ci-tor? What a big word for a little mongrel like you. You think you'll become a so-li-ci-tor if Sergeant Upton says you won't?'

George stops himself saying that it is up to Mason College and the examiners and the Incorporated Law Society to decide whether or not he is to be a solicitor. He thinks he must get home as quickly as possible and tell Father.

'Let me ask you a question.' Upton's tone seems to have softened, so George decides to humour him a moment longer. 'What are those things on your hands?'

George lifts his forearms, spreads his fingers automatically in his gloves. 'These?' he asks. The man must be mentally deficient.

'Yes.'

'Gloves.'

'Well then, being a clever young monkey and intending to be a so-li-ci-tor, you will know that a pair of gloves is known as Going Equipped, won't you?'

Then he spits again and stamps off down the lane. George bursts into tears.

He is ashamed of himself by the time he gets home. He is sixteen, he is

30

not allowed to cry. Horace has not cried since he was eight. Maud cries a lot, but then she is an invalid as well as a girl.

George's father listens to his story and announces that he will write to the Chief Constable of Staffordshire. It is disgraceful that a common policeman should manhandle his son on a public highway and accuse him of theft. The officer should be dismissed from the force.

'I think he is rather loony, Father. He spat at me twice.'

'He spat at you?'

George thinks again. He is still frightened, but knows this is no reason to tell less than the truth.

'I cannot be certain of that, Father. He was about a yard away, and he spat twice very close to my foot. It's possible he was spitting just like rough people do. But when he did it he seemed to be cross with me.'

'Do you think that is sufficient proof of intention?'

George likes this. He is being treated as a future solicitor.

'Perhaps not, Father.'

'I agree with you. Good. I shall not mention the spitting.'

Three days later the Reverend Shapurji Edalji receives a reply from Captain the Honourable George A. Anson, Chief Constable of Staffordshire. It is dated January 23rd 1893, and does not contain the expected apology and promise of action. Instead, Anson writes:

> Will you please ask your son George from whom the key was obtained which was laid on your doorstep on Dec. 12? The key was stolen, but if it can be shown that the whole thing was due to some idle freak or practical joke, I should not be inclined to allow any police proceedings to be taken in regard to it. If, however, the persons concerned in the removal of the key refuse to make any explanation of the subject, I must necessarily treat the matter in all seriousness as a theft. I may say at once that I shall not pretend to believe any protestations of ignorance which your son may make about this key. My information on the subject does not come from the police.

The Vicar knows his son to be a decent and honourable boy. He must overcome the nerves he seems to have inherited from his mother, but is already showing much promise. The time has come to begin treating him as an adult. He shows George the letter and asks for his view.

George reads the letter twice and takes a moment to assemble his thoughts. 'In the lane,' he begins slowly, 'Sergeant Upton accused me of going to

Walsall School and stealing the key. The Chief Constable, on the other hand, accuses me of being in alliance with someone else, or several others. One of them took the key, then I accepted the stolen item and put it on the step. Perhaps they realize I have not been in Walsall for two years. At any event, they have changed their story.'

'Yes. Good. I agree. And what else do you think?'

'I think they must both be loony.'

'George, that's a childish word. And in any case it is our Christian duty to pity and cherish the feeble of mind.'

'I'm sorry, Father. Then all I can think is that they . . . that they must suspect me for some reason I do not understand.'

'And what do you think he means when he writes "My information on the subject does not come from the police"?'

'He must mean that someone has sent him a letter denouncing me. Unless . . . unless he is not telling the truth. He might be pretending to know things he doesn't. Perhaps it is just a bluff.'

Shapurji smiles at his son. 'George, with your eyesight you would never have made a detective. But with your brain you will be a very fine solicitor.'

Arthur

Arthur and Louisa did not get married in Southsea. Nor did they get married in Minsterworth, Gloucestershire, the bride's parish of origin. Nor did they get married in the city of Arthur's birth.

When Arthur quit Edinburgh as a newly qualified doctor, he left behind the Mam, his brother Innes, and his three youngest sisters – Connie, Ida and little Julia. He also left behind the flat's other occupant, Dr Bryan Waller, supposed poet, incontrovertible lodger, and a fellow too damned at ease with the world. Despite all Arthur's gratitude for Waller's tutorial help, something still rankled. He could never quite allay his suspicion that the lodger's assistance had not been disinterested; though where exactly that interest might lie Arthur was unable to detect.

When he left, Arthur had imagined that Waller would soon set up his own Edinburgh practice, would acquire a wife and a little local reputation, and then fade into the status of an occasional memory. Such expectations were not to be fulfilled. Arthur went out into the world to forage on behalf of his unprotected family, only to find that Waller had taken on the task of protection himself, which was none of his damned business. He had become, in a phrase Arthur deliberately avoided using in letters to the Mam, a cuckoo in the nest. Each time Arthur came home, he found himself credulously imagining that the family narrative, suspended since his last visit, would resume where it had left off. But each time he was made aware that the story – his favourite story – had moved on without him. He found himself catching at words, at unexpected glances and allusions, at anecdotes in which he no longer featured. There was a life going on here without him, and that life seemed to be animated by the lodger.

Bryan Waller did not set up as a doctor; nor did his poetry-scribbling turn into a professional habit. He inherited an estate at Ingleton in the West Riding of Yorkshire and settled for the idle life of an English squire. The cuckoo now had twenty-four acres of his own woodland surrounding a grey stone nest called Masongill House. Well then, so much the better. Except that Arthur had scarcely absorbed this good news when a letter arrived from the Mam, informing him that she, Ida and Dodo were also leaving Edinburgh; also for Masongill, where a cottage on the estate was being prepared for them. The Mam did not attempt a justification – the healthy air, an unhealthy child, perhaps – merely stated that this was happening. Indeed, had already happened. Oh yes, here was a justification: the rent was very low.

Arthur felt it as a kidnapping and betrayal combined. He entirely failed to persuade himself that this was a chivalrous action on Waller's part. A true courtly knight would have arranged for some mysterious inheritance to come the way of the Mam and her daughters, while himself departing to a distant land on a long and preferably perilous quest. A true courtly knight would also not have jilted Lottie or Connie, whichever of the two it had been. Arthur had no proof, and perhaps it had been no more than a flirting which induced false expectations, but something had been going on, if certain hints and female silences meant what he guessed.

Arthur's suspicions did not, alas, end there. He was a young man who liked things clear and certain, yet found himself in a place where little was clear and some certainties were unacceptable. That Waller was more than just a lodger was as plain as the nose on your face. He was often referred to as a friend of the family, even one of the family. Not so by Arthur: he did not want an elder brother suddenly thrust upon him, let alone a sibling at whom the Mam smiled in a different way. Waller was six years older than Arthur, and fifteen years younger than the Mam. Arthur would have thrust his hand into fire in defence of his mother's honour; his principles, and his sense of family, and the duty owed to it, had all come from her. And yet, he sometimes found himself wondering, how would things appear in a police court? What evidence might be given, and what assumptions made by a jury? Consider, for instance, this item: his father was an enfeebled dipsomaniac occasionally confined to nursing homes, his mother had borne her final child while Bryan Waller was part of the household, and she had given that daughter four Christian names. The last three of these were Mary, Julia and Josephine; the child's nickname was Dodo. But her first given name was Bryan. Apart from anything else, Arthur did not agree that Bryan was a girl's name.

While Arthur was courting Louisa, his father managed to obtain alcohol in his nursing home, broke a window trying to escape and was transferred to the Montrose Royal Lunatic Asylum. On the 6th of August 1885 Arthur and Touie were married at St Oswald's, Thornton-in-Lonsdale, in the county of Yorkshire. The groom was twenty-six, the bride twenty-eight. Arthur's best man was not a fellow member of the Southsea Bowling Club, of the Portsmouth Literary and Scientific Society, or of Phoenix Lodge No. 257. The Mam had made all the arrangements, and Arthur's best man was Bryan Waller, who seemed to have taken over as future provider of velvet dresses, gold glasses, and comfortable seats by the fire.

George

When George pulls back the curtains, there is an empty milk churn standing in the middle of the lawn. He points it out to his father. They dress and investigate. The churn is missing its lid, and when George peers in he sees a dead blackbird lying at the bottom. They bury the bird quickly behind the compost heap. George agrees that they may tell Mother about the churn, which they put to stand in the lane, but not about its contents.

The next day George receives a postcard of a tomb in Brewood Church showing a man with two wives. The message reads, 'Why not go on with your old game of writing things on walls?'

His father receives a letter in the same unformed hand: 'Every day, every hour, my hatred is growing against George Edalji. And your damned wife. And your horrid little girl. Do you think, you Pharisee, that because you are a parson God will absolve you from your iniquities?' He does not show this letter to George.

Father and son receive a joint communication:

> Ha, ha, hurrah for Upton! Good old Upton!
> Blessed Upton. Good old Upton! Upton is blessed!
> Dear old Upton!

Stand up, stand up for Upton
Ye soldiers of the Cross
Lift high your royal banner
It must not suffer loss.

The Vicar and his wife decide that in future they will open all mail addressed to the Vicarage themselves. At all cost, George's studies must not be interfered with. Therefore he does not see the letter which begins: 'I swear by God that I will do harm to some person. the only thing I care about in this world is revenge, revenge, sweet revenge I long for, then I shall be happy in hell.' Nor does he see the one that says: 'Before the end of the year your kid will be either in the graveyard or disgraced for life.' However, he is shown the one beginning: 'You Pharisee and false prophet you accused Elizabeth Foster and sent her away you and your damned wife.'

The letters increase in frequency. They are written on cheap lined paper torn from a notebook, and posted from Cannock, Walsall, Rugeley, Wolverhampton and even Great Wyrley itself. The Vicar does not know what to do about them. Given the behaviour first of Upton and then of the Chief Constable, there seems little point complaining to the police. As the letters pile up, he tries to tabulate their chief characteristics. These are: a defence of Elizabeth Foster; frantic praise of Sergeant Upton and the police generally; insane hatred of the Edalji family; and religious mania, which may or may not be assumed. The penmanship varies in style, as he imagines it might if you were disguising your hand.

Shapurji prays for enlightenment. He also prays for patience, for his family, and – with a slightly reluctant sense of duty – for the letter writer.

George leaves for Mason College before the first post arrives, but on his return can normally detect if an anonymous letter has been delivered that day. His mother will be falsely cheerful, flitting from one topic of conversation to another, as if silence, like gravity, might pull them all down to ground level, to the mud and filth that rest there. His father, less equipped for social dissimulation, is withdrawn, and sits at the head of the table like a granite statue of himself. The reaction of each parent frays the nerves of the other; George tries to find a middle ground by talking more than his father but less than his mother. Meanwhile, Horace and Maud chatter away unchecked, the sole if temporary beneficiaries of the writing campaign.

After the key and the milk churn, other items appear at the Vicarage. A pewter ladle on a window sill; a garden fork pinning a dead rabbit to the lawn; three eggs broken on the front step. Each morning George and his father search the grounds before Mother and the two younger ones are allowed outside. One day they find twenty pennies and halfpennies laid at intervals across the lawn; the Vicar decides to regard them as a donation to the church. There are also dead birds, mostly strangled; and once excrement has been laid where it will be most visible. Occasionally, in the dawn light, George is aware of something that is less than a presence, a possible observer; it is more like a close absence, the feeling of someone having just left. But nobody is ever caught, or even spotted.

And now the hoaxes begin. After church one Sunday, Mr Beckworth of Hangover Farm shakes the Vicar's hand, then winks and murmurs, 'Starting a new line of business, I see.' When Shapurji looks puzzled, Beckworth passes him a clipping from the *Cannock Chase Courier*. It is an advertisement surrounded by a scalloped box:

Eligible Young Ladies
of Good Manners & Breeding
Available for Matrimony
to Gentlemen of Means & Character
Introductions: apply Rev S Edalji,
Great Wyrley Vicarage.
Fee payable.

The Vicar visits the newspaper offices and is told that three more such advertisements have already been ordered. But no one has set eyes upon their purchaser: the instruction came by letter with a postal order enclosed. The commercial manager is sympathetic, and naturally offers to suspend the remaining insertions. If the culprit tries to protest or reclaim his money, the police will of course be summoned. But no, he does not think the editorial pages will be interested in the story. No offence to the cloth, but a newspaper has its reputation to consider, and telling the world it has been hoaxed might undermine the credibility of its other stories.

When Shapurji returns to the Vicarage, there is a young red-headed curate from Norfolk waiting to see him, and holding his Christian temper with some difficulty. He is impatient to know why his fellow servant in Christ has summoned him all the way to Staffordshire on a matter of spiritual urgency, perhaps requiring exorcism, of which the Vicar's wife appears quite ignorant. Here is your letter, here is your signature. Shapurji explains and apologizes. The curate asks to be reimbursed for his expenses.

Next the maid-of-all-work is called to Wolverhampton in order to inspect the dead body of her non-existent sister, which is supposedly lying in a public house. Quantities of goods – fifty linen napkins, twelve young pear trees, a baron of beef, six crates of champagne, fifteen gallons of black paint – are delivered and have to be sent back. Advertisements appear in newspapers offering the Vicarage for rent at such a low price that there is an abundance of takers. Stabling facilities are offered; so is horse manure. Letters are sent in the Vicar's name to private detectives, engaging their services.

After months of persecution, Shapurji decides to counter-attack. He prepares his own advertisement, outlining recent events, and describing the anonymous letters, their handwriting, style and contents; he specifies the times and places of posting. He asks newspapers to refuse requests in his name, readers to report any suspicions they might have, and the perpetrators to examine their consciences.

A broken soup tureen containing a dead blackbird appears on the kitchen step two afternoons later. The following day a bailiff arrives to distrain goods in favour of an imaginary debt. Later, a dressmaker from Stafford comes to measure Maud for her wedding dress. When Maud is silently brought before him, he asks politely if she is to be the child-bride in some Hindoo ceremony. In the midst of this scene, five oilskin jackets arrive for George.

And then, a week later, three newspapers publish a response to the Vicar's appeal. It is in a black box and headed APOLOGY. It reads:

> **We, the undersigned, both residing in the parish of Great Wyrley, do hereby declare that we are the sole authors and writers of certain offensive and anonymous letters received by various persons during the last twelve months. We regret these utterances, and also utterances against Mr Upton the sergeant of police at Cannock, and against Elizabeth Foster. We have examined our consciences as requested and beg forgiveness of all those involved and also of the authorities, both spiritual and criminal.**
>
> **signed, G.E.T. Edalji and Fredk. Brookes.**

Arthur

Arthur believed in looking – at the glaucous eye of a dying whale, at the contents of a shot bird's gizzard, at the facial relaxation of a corpse who was never to become his brother-in-law. Such looking must be without prejudice: this was a practical necessity for a doctor, and a moral imperative for a human being.

He liked to tell how he had been taught the importance of careful looking at the Edinburgh Infirmary. A surgeon there, Joseph Bell, had taken a shine to this large, enthusiastic youth and made Arthur his out-patient clerk. His job was to muster the patients, take preliminary notes, and then lead them to Mr Bell's room, where the surgeon would be sitting among his dressers. Bell would greet each patient, and from a silent yet intense scrutiny try to deduce as much as possible about their lives and proclivities. He would declare that this man was by trade a French polisher, that one a left-handed cobbler, to the amazement of those present, not least of the patient himself. Arthur remembered the following exchange:

'Well, my man, you've served in the army.'

'Aye, sir.'

'Not long discharged?'

'No, sir.'

'A Highland regiment?'

'Aye, sir.'

'Stationed at Barbados?'

'Aye, sir.'

It was a trick, yet it was a true trick; mysterious at first, simple when explained.

'You see, gentlemen, the man was a respectful man but did not remove his hat. They do not in the army, but he would have learned civilian ways had he been long discharged. He has an air of authority and he is obviously Scottish. As to Barbados, his complaint is elephantiasis, which is West Indian and not British.'

Arthur had been educated, during those most plastic years, in the school of medical materialism. Any residue of formal religion had been expunged; yet he remained metaphysically respectful. He admitted the possibility of a central intelligent cause, while being unable to identify that cause, or understand why its designs should be brought to fulfilment in such roundabout and often terrible ways. As far as the mind and the soul went, Arthur accepted the scientific explanation of the day. The mind was an emanation of the brain, just as bile was an excretion of the liver – something purely physical in character; while the soul, as far as such a term could be admitted, was the total effect of all the hereditary and personal functionings of the mind. But he also recognized that knowledge never stayed still, and that today's certainties might become tomorrow's superstitions. Therefore, the intellectual duty to continue looking never ceased.

At the Portsmouth Literary and Scientific Society, which met every second Tuesday, Arthur encountered the city's more speculative minds. Telepathy being much under discussion, Arthur found himself one afternoon sitting in a curtained and unmirrored room with a local architect, Stanley Ball. They placed themselves back to back and several yards apart; Arthur, with a drawing pad on his knee, sketched a shape and attempted by a powerful concentration of the mind to convey the image to Ball. The architect then drew whatever form his own mind seemed to propose. Then they reversed the procedure, with the architect as shape-despatcher and the doctor as recipient. The results, to their astonishment, showed a matching significantly above the random. They repeated the experiment enough times for a scientific conclusion to be reached: namely that, given a natural sympathy between conductor and receiver, thought-transference could indeed take place.

What might this mean? If thought could be transferred across distance without any evident means of conveyance, then the pure materialism of Arthur's teachers was, at the very least, too rigid. The congruence of drawn shapes he had achieved with Stanley Ball did not allow the return of angels with shining swords. But it nevertheless raised a question, and a stubborn one at that.

Many others were simultaneously pushing at the ironclad walls of a materialist universe. The mesmerist Professor de Meyer, who was famous — according to the Portsmouth newspapers — across the continent of Europe, came to town and induced various healthy young men to do his bidding. Some stood with their mouths agape, incapable of closing them despite laughter from the auditorium; others fell to their knees and were unable to rise without the Professor's permission. Arthur inserted himself into the line of candidates on stage, but Meyer's technique left him unmesmerised and unimpressed. It smacked more of vaudeville than of scientific demonstration.

He and Touie began attending seances. Stanley Ball was often present; also General Drayson the Southsea astronomer. They found the instructions for conducting a circle in *Light*, the weekly psychical paper. Proceedings would begin with a reading of the first chapter of Ezekiel: 'Whithersoever the spirit was to go, they went, thither was their spirit to go.' The prophet's vision — of the whirlwind and the great cloud and the brightness and the fire and the four cherubim each with four faces and each with four wings – prepared those present to be receptive. Then it was the flickering candle, the felty dimness, the concentration of mind, the emptying of self and the communal waiting. Once, a spirit answering to the name of Arthur's great-uncle appeared behind him; on another occasion, a black man with a spear. After a few months, spirit lights became occasionally visible, even to him.

Arthur was uncertain how much evidential weight should be granted to these collaborative circles. He was more convinced by an elderly psychic he met at the house of General Drayson. After various preparations of a rather thespian nature, the old man went into a heavy-breathing trance and began dispensing both advice and spirit communications to his small, hushed audience. Arthur had come fully armed with scepticism – until the misted-over eyes were directed towards him, and a frail, distant voice pronounced the words,

'Do not read Leigh Hunt's book.'

This was more than uncanny. For some days, Arthur had been privately wondering whether or not to read Hunt's *Comic Dramatists of the Restoration*. He had not discussed the matter with anyone; and it was hardly a dilemma with which he would bother Touie. But then to be given such a precise answer to his unvoiced question . . . It could not be a magician's trick; it could only have happened through the ability of one man's mind to gain access in a so far inexplicable way to another man's mind.

Arthur was so persuaded by the experience that he wrote it up for *Light*. Here was further proof that telepathy worked; for the moment, nothing more. This much so far he had seen: what was the minimum, not the maximum, that could be deduced? Though if reliable data continued to accrue, then more than the minimum might have to be considered. What if all his previous certainties became less certain? And what, for that matter, might the maximum turn out to be?

Touie regarded her husband's involvement in telepathy and the spirit world with the same sympathetic and watchful interest that she brought to his enthusiasm for sport. The laws of psychical phenomena seemed to her as arcane as the laws of cricket; but she sensed that with each a certain result was desirable, and amiably presumed that Arthur would inform her when such a result had been obtained. Besides, she was now much absorbed in their daughter, Mary Louise, whose existence had come about through the application of the least arcane and least telepathic laws known to mankind.

George

George's 'apology' in the newspaper affords the Vicar a new line of inquiry. He calls on William Brookes, the village ironmonger, father of Frederick Brookes, George's supposed co-signatory. The ironmonger, a small, rotund man in a green apron, takes Shapurji into a storeroom hung with mops and pails and zinc baths. He removes his apron, pulls out a drawer and hands over the half dozen letters of denunciation his family has received. They are written on the familiar lined paper torn from a notebook; although the penmanship varies more.

The top letter is in a childish, unconfident scrawl. 'Unless you run away from the black I'll murder you and mrs brookes I know your names and I'll tell you wrote.' Others are in a hand which, even if disguised, seems more forceful. 'Your kid and Wynn's kid have been spitting in an old woman's face at Walsall station.' The writer demands that money be sent to Walsall Post Office in recompense. A subsequent letter, pinned to this one, threatens prosecution if the demand is not met.

'I assume you sent no money.'

'Course not.'

'But you showed the letters to the police?'

'Police? Not worth their time or mine. It's just kids, isn't it? And as it says in the Bible, sticks and stones may break my bones, but words will ne'er harm me.'

The Vicar does not correct Mr Brookes's source. He also senses something idle about the man's attitude. 'But you didn't merely put the letters in a drawer?'

'I asked around a bit. I asked Fred what he knew.'

'Who is this Mr Wynn?'

Wynn is apparently a draper who lives up the line at Bloxwich. He has a son who goes to school at Walsall with Brookes's boy. They meet on the train each morning and usually return together. A while ago – the ironmonger does not specify how long – Wynn's son and young Fred were accused of breaking a carriage window. Both swore it was the work of a boy called Speck, and eventually the railway officials decided not to press charges. This happened a few weeks before the first letter arrived. Perhaps there was some connection. Perhaps not.

The Vicar now understands Brookes's lack of zeal in the matter. No, the ironmonger does not know who Speck is. No, Mr Wynn hasn't received any letters himself. No, Wynn's boy and Brookes's boy are not friends with George. This last is hardly a surprise.

Shapurji describes the exchange to George before supper, and pronounces himself encouraged.

'Why are you encouraged, Father?'

'The more people involved, the more likely the scoundrel is to be discovered. The more people he persecutes, the more probable it is he will make a mistake. Do you know of this boy called Speck?'

'Speck? No.' George shakes his head.

'And I am also encouraged in one respect by the persecution of the Brookes family. This proves it is not merely race prejudice.'

'Is that a good thing, Father? To be hated for more than one reason?'

Shapurji smiles to himself. These flashes of intelligence, coming from a docile boy who is often too much turned in on himself, always delight him.

'I will say it again, you will make a fine solicitor, George.' But even as he pronounces the words, he is reminded of a line from one of the letters he has not shown his son. 'Before the end of the year your kid will be either in the graveyard or disgraced for life.'

'George,' he says. 'There is a date I wish you to remember. The 6th of July 1892. Just two years ago. On that day Mr Dadabhoy Naoroji was elected to Parliament for the Finsbury Central district of London.'

'Yes, Father.'

'Mr Naoroji was for many years Professor of Gujerati at University College London. I was briefly in correspondence with him, and am proud to say that he had words of praise for my *Grammar of the Gujerati Language.*'

'Yes, Father.' George has seen the Professor's letter brought out on more than one occasion.

'His election was an honourable conclusion to a most dishonourable time. The Prime Minister, Lord Salisbury, said that black men should not and would not be elected to Parliament. He was rebuked for it by the Queen herself. And then the voters of Finsbury Central, only four years later, decided that they agreed with Queen Victoria and not with Lord Salisbury.'

'But I am not a Parsee, Father.' In George's head the words come back: the centre of England, the beating heart of the British Empire, the flowing bloodline that is the Church of England. He is English, he is a student of the laws of England, and one day, God willing, he will marry according to the rites and ceremonies of the Church of England. This is what his parents have taught him from the beginning.

'George, this is true enough. You are an Englishman. But others may not always entirely agree. And where we are living –'

'The centre of England,' George responds, as if in bedroom catechism.

'The centre of England, yes, where we find ourselves, and where I have ministered for nearly twenty years, the centre of England – despite all God's creatures being equally blessed – is still a little primitive, George. And you will furthermore find primitive people where you least expect them. They exist in ranks of society where better might be anticipated. But if Mr Naoroji can become a university professor and a Member of Parliament, then you, George, can and will become a solicitor and a respected member of society. And if unfair things happen, if even wicked things happen, then you should remember the date of the 6th of July 1892.'

George thinks about this for a while, and then repeats, quietly yet firmly, 'But I am not a Parsee, Father. That is what you and Mother have taught me.'

'Remember the date, George, remember the date.'

Arthur

Arthur began to write more professionally. As he put on literary muscle, his stories grew into novels, the best of them naturally being set in the heroic fourteenth century. Each page of work would be read aloud to Touie after supper, and the completed text sent to the Mam for editorial comment. Arthur also took on a secretary and amanuensis: Alfred Wood, a master from Portsmouth School, a discreet efficient fellow with the honest look of a pharmacist; an all-round sportsman too, with a very decent cricket arm on him.

But medicine remained Arthur's current livelihood. And if he was to advance in his profession, he knew it had become time to specialize. He had always prided himself, through every aspect of his life, in looking carefully; so it did not require a spirit voice, or a table leaping into the air, to spell out his chosen calling – ophthalmologist. He was not a man to prevaricate or palter, and knew at once where best it was to train.

'Vienna?' repeated Touie wonderingly, for she had never left England. It was now November; winter was coming on; little Mary was beginning to walk, as long as you held her sash. 'When do we leave?'

'Immediately,' replied Arthur.

And Touie – bless her – merely rose from her needlework and murmured, 'Then I must be quick.'

They sold up, left Mary with Mrs Hawkins, and took off to Vienna for six months. Arthur signed up for a course of eye lectures at the Krankenhaus; but quickly discovered that the German learned while walking along flanked by two Austrian schoolboys whose phraseology was often less than choice did not fully prepare a fellow for rapid instruction littered with technical terms. Still, the Austrian winter provided fine skating, and the city excellent cakes; Arthur even knocked off a short novel, *The Doings of Raffles Haw*, which paid all their Viennese expenses. After a couple of months, however, he admitted that he would have been better off studying in London. Touie responded to the change of plan with her usual equanimity and despatch. They returned via Paris, where Arthur managed to put in a few days' study with Landolt.

Thus able to claim he had been trained in two countries, he took rooms in Devonshire Place, was elected a member of the Ophthalmological Society, and waited for patients. He also hoped for work passed on by the big men in the profession, who were often too busy to calculate refractions for themselves. Some regarded it as mere donkey-labour; but Arthur considered himself competent in this field, and counted on overflow work drifting his way.

Devonshire Place consisted of a waiting room and a consulting room. Yet after a few weeks he began to joke that both were waiting rooms, and that he, Arthur, was the one doing the waiting. Idleness being repugnant, he sat at his desk and wrote. He was now well-apprenticed in the literary game, and turned his mind to one of its current bedevilments: magazine fiction. Arthur loved a problem, and the problem went like this. Magazines published two kinds of stories: either lengthy serializations which ensnared the reader week by week and month by month; or single, free-standing tales. The trouble with the tales was that they often didn't give you enough to bite on. The trouble with the serializations was that if you happened to miss a single issue, you lost the plot. Applying his practical brain to the problem, Arthur envisaged combining the virtues of the two forms: a series of stories, each complete in itself, yet filled with running characters to reignite the reader's sympathy or disapproval.

He needed therefore the kind of protagonist who could be relied upon to have regular and diverse adventures. Clearly, most professions need not apply. As he turned the matter over in Devonshire Place, he began to wonder if he hadn't already invented the appropriate candidate. A couple of his less successful novels had featured a consulting detective closely modelled on Joseph Bell of the Edinburgh Infirmary: intense observation followed by rigorous deduction was the key to criminal as well as to medical diagnosis. Arthur had initially called his detective Sheridan Hope. But the name felt unsatisfactory, and in the writing Sheridan Hope had changed first into Sherringford Holmes and then – inevitably as it seemed thereafter – into Sherlock Holmes.

George

The letters and hoaxes continue; Shapurji's plea to the malefactor to examine his conscience seems to have acted as further provocation. Newspapers announce that the Vicarage is now a boarding house offering rock-bottom terms; that it has become a slaughterhouse; that it will despatch free samples of ladies' corsetry on request. George has apparently set up as an oculist; he also offers free legal advice and is qualified to arrange tickets and accommodation for travellers to India and the Far East. Enough coal is delivered to stoke a battleship; encyclopaedias arrive, along with live geese.

It is impossible to continue for ever in the same state of nerves; and after a while the household almost turns its persecution into a routine. The Vicarage grounds are patrolled at first light; goods are refused at the gate or returned; explanations are given to disappointed customers for esoteric services. Charlotte even becomes adept at appeasing clergymen summoned from distant counties by urgent pleas for assistance.

George has left Mason College and is now articled to a firm of Birmingham solicitors. Each morning, as he takes the train, he feels guilty for abandoning his family; yet the evenings bring no relief, merely another form of anxiety. His father has also chosen to respond to the crisis in what seems to George a peculiar fashion: by giving him short lectures on how the Parsees have always been much favoured by the British. George thus learns that the very first Indian traveller to Britain was a Parsee; that the first Indian to study Christian theology at a British university was a Parsee; so was the first Indian student at Oxford, and later the first woman student; so was the first Indian man presented at Court, and, later, the first Indian woman. The first Indian to enter the Indian Civil Service was a Parsee. Shapurji tells George about surgeons and lawyers trained in Britain; about Parsee charity during the Irish famine and later towards suffering millworkers in Lancashire. He even tells George about the first Indian cricket team to tour England – Parsees every one of them. But George is quite without interest in cricket, and finds his father's stratagem more desperate than helpful. When the family is required to toast the election of a second Parsee Member of Parliament, Muncherji Bhownagree in the constituency of North-East Bethnal Green, George finds a shameful sarcasm rising within him. Why not write to the new MP and suggest he help prevent the arrival of coal, encyclopaedias and live geese?

Shapurji is more concerned about the letters than the deliveries. Increasingly, they seem to be the work of a religious maniac. They are signed by God, Beelzebub, the Devil; the writer claims to be eternally lost in Hell, or earnestly desiring that destination. When this mania begins to show violent intent, the Vicar fears for his family. 'I swear by God that I will murder George Edalji soon.' 'May the Lord strike me dead if mayhem and blood-shed do not ensue.' 'I will descend into Hell showering curses upon you all and will meet you there in God's time.' 'You are nearing the end of your time on this Earth and I am God's chosen instrument for the task.'

After more than two years of persecution, Shapurji decides to approach the Chief Constable again. He writes an account of events, encloses samples of the correspondence, points out respectfully that a clear intention to murder is now being expressed, and asks for the police to protect an innocent family thus threatened. Captain Anson's reply ignores the request. Instead he writes:

I do not say that I know the name of the offender, though I have my particular suspicions. I prefer to keep these suspicions to myself until I am able to prove them, and I trust to be able to obtain a dose of penal servitude for the offender; as although great care has apparently been exercised to avoid, as far as possible, anything which would constitute any serious offence in law, the person who writes the letters has over-reached himself in two or three instances, in such manner as to render him liable to the most serious punishment. I have no doubt that the offender will be detected.

Shapurji hands his son the letter and asks his opinion. 'On the one hand,' says George, 'the Chief Constable maintains that the hoaxer is skilfully using his knowledge of the law to avoid committing any actual offence. On the other hand, he seems to think that clear offences liable to result in penal servi-tude have already been committed. In which case the hoaxer is not such a clever fellow after all.' He pauses and looks at his father. 'He means me, of course. He believes I took the key and he now believes that I wrote the letters. He knows I am studying law – the reference is clear. I think, to be honest, Father, the Chief Constable might be more of a threat to me than the hoaxer.'

Shapurji is not so sure. One threatens penal servitude and the other threatens death. He finds it hard to keep bitterness against the Chief Constable out of his thoughts. He still has not shown George the vilest of the letters. Could Anson really believe that George wrote them? If so, he would like to be told in what way it is an offence to write an anonymous letter to yourself threat-ening to murder yourself. He worries night and day about his first-born son. He sleeps badly, and often finds himself out of bed, urgently and unneces-sarily checking that the door is locked.

In December of 1895 an advertisement appears in a Blackpool newspaper offering the entire contents of the Vicarage for sale by public auction. There will be no reserve price on any item as the Vicar and his wife are eager to dispose of everything prior to their imminent departure for Bombay.

Blackpool is at least a hundred miles as the crow flies. Shapurji has a vision of the persecution spreading throughout the whole country. Blackpool might be only the beginning: next it will be Edinburgh, Newcastle, London. Follower by Paris, Moscow, Timbuctoo – why not?

And then, as suddenly as it began, it stops. No more letters, no unwanted goods, no hoax advertisements, no intemperate brothers in Christ on the doorstep. For a day, then a week, then a month, then two months. It stops. It has stopped.

TWO

Beginning with an Ending

George

The month the persecutions stop marks the twentieth anniversary of Shapurji Edalji's appointment to Great Wyrley; it is followed by the twentieth – no, the twenty-first – Christmas celebrated at the Vicarage. Maud receives a tapestry bookmark, Horace his own copy of Father's *Lectures on St Paul's Epistle to the Galatians*, George a sepia print of Mr Holman Hunt's *The Light of the World* with the suggestion that he might hang it on the wall of his office. George thanks his parents, but can well imagine what the senior partners would think: that an articled clerk of only two years' standing, who is trusted to do little more than write out documents in fair copy, is hardly entitled to make decisions about furnishing; further, that clients come to a solicitor for a specific kind of guidance, and might well find Mr Hunt's advertisement for a different kind distracting.

As the first months of the new year pass, the curtains are parted each morning with the increased certainty that there will be nothing but God's shining dew upon the lawn; and the postman's arrival no longer causes alarm. The Vicar begins to repeat that they have been tested with fire, and their faith in the Lord has helped them endure this trial. Maud, fragile and pious, has been kept in as much ignorance as possible; Horace, now a sturdy and straightforward sixteen-year-old, knows more, and will privately confess to George that in his view the old method of an eye for an eye is an unimprovable system of justice, and that if he ever catches anyone tossing dead blackbirds over the hedge, he will wring their necks in person.

George does not, as his parents believe have his own office at Sangster, Vickery & Speight. He has a stool and a high-top desk in an uncarpeted corner where the access of the sun's rays depends upon the goodwill of a distant skylight. He does not yet possess a fob watch, let alone his own set of law books. But he has a proper hat, a three-and-sixpenny bowler from Fenton's in Grange Street. And though his bed remains a mere three yards from Father's, he feels the beginnings of independent life stirring within him. He has even made the acquaintance of two articled clerks from neighbouring practices. Greenway and Stentson, who are slightly older, took him one lunchtime to a public house where he briefly pretended to enjoy the horrible sour beer he paid for.

During his year at Mason College, George paid little attention to the great city he found himself in. He felt it only as a barricade of noise and bustle lying between the station and his books; in truth, it frightened him. But now he begins to feel more at ease with the place, and more curious about it. If he is not crushed by its vigour and energy, perhaps he will one day become part of it himself.

He begins to read up on the city. At first he finds it rather stodgy stuff, about cutlers and smiths and metal manufacture; next come the Civil War and the Plague, the steam engine and the Lunar Society, the Church and King Riots, the Chartist upheavals. But then, little more than a decade ago, Birmingham begins to shake itself into modern municipal life, and suddenly George feels he is reading about real things, relevant things. He is tormented to realize that he could have been present at one of Birmingham's greatest moments: the day in 1887 when Her Majesty laid the foundation stone of the Victoria Law Courts. And thereafter, the city has arrived in a great rush of new buildings and institutions: the General Hospital, the Chamber of Arbitration, the meat market. Money is currently being raised to establish a university; there is a plan to build a new Temperance Hall, and serious talk that Birmingham might soon become a bishopric, no longer under the see of Worcester.

On that day of Queen Victoria's visit, 500,000 people came to greet her, and despite the vast crowd there were neither disturbances nor casualties. George is impressed, yet also not surprised. The general opinion is that cities are violent, overcrowded places, while the countryside is calm and peaceable. His own experience is to the contrary: the country is turbulent and primitive, while the city is where life becomes orderly and modern. Of course Birmingham is not without crime and vice and discord – else there would be less of a living for solicitors – but it seems to George that human conduct is more rational here, and more obedient to the law: more civil.

George finds something both serious and comforting in his daily transit into the city. There is a journey, there is a destination: this is how he has been taught to understand life. At home, the destination is the Kingdom of Heaven; at the office, the destination is justice, that is to say, a successful outcome for your client; but both journeys are full of forking paths and booby traps laid by the opponent. The railway suggests how it ought to be, how it could be: a smooth ride to a terminus on evenly spaced rails and according to an agreed timetable, with passengers divided among first-, second- and third-class carriages.

Perhaps this is why George feels quietly enraged when anyone seeks to harm the railway. There are youths – men, perhaps – who take knives and razors to the leather window straps; who senselessly attack the picture frames above the seats; who loiter on footbridges and try to drop bricks into the locomotive's chimney. This is all incomprehensible to George. It may seem a harmless game to place a penny on the rail and see it flattened to twice its diameter by a passing express; but George regards it as a slippery slope which leads to train wrecking.

Such actions are naturally covered by the criminal law. George finds himself increasingly preoccupied by the civil connection between passengers and the railway company. A passenger buys a ticket, and at that moment, with consideration given and received, a contract springs into being. But ask that passenger what kind of contract he or she has entered into, what obligations are laid upon the parties, what claim for compensation might be pursued against the railway company in case of lateness, breakdown or accident, and answer would come there none. This may not be the passenger's fault: the ticket alludes to a contract, but its detailed terms are only displayed at certain main-line stations and at the offices of the railway company – and what busy traveller has the time to make a diversion and examine them? Even so, George marvels at how the British, who gave railways to the world, treat them as a mere means of convenient transport, rather than as an intense nexus of multiple rights and responsibilities.

He decides to appoint Horace and Maud as the Man and Woman on the Clapham Omnibus – or, in the present instance, the Man and Woman on the Walsall, Cannock & Rugeley Train. He is allowed to use the schoolroom as his law court. He sits his brother and sister at desks and presents them with a case he has recently come across in the foreign law reports.

'Once upon a time,' he begins, walking up and down in a way that seems necessary to the story, 'there was a very fat Frenchman called Payelle, who weighed twenty-five stones.'

Horace starts giggling. George frowns at his brother and grips his lapels like a barrister. 'No laughter in court,' he insists. He proceeds. 'Monsieur Payelle bought a third-class ticket on a French train.'

'Where was he going?' asks Maud.

'It doesn't matter where he was going.'

'Why was he so fat?' demands Horace. This *ad hoc* jury seems to believe it may ask questions whenever it likes.

'I don't know. He must have been even greedier than you. In fact, he was so greedy that when the train pulled in, he found he couldn't get through the door of a third-class carriage.' Horace starts tittering at the idea. 'So next he tried a second-class carriage, but he was too fat to get into that as well. So then he tried a first-class carriage –'

'And he was too fat to get into that too!' Horace shouts, as if it were the conclusion to a joke.

'No, members of the jury, he found that this door was indeed wide enough. So he took a seat, and the train set off for – for wherever it was going. After a while the ticket collector came along, examined his ticket, and asked for the difference between the third-class fare and the first-class fare. Monsieur Payelle refused to pay. The railway company sued Payelle. Now, do you see the problem?'

'The problem is he was too fat,' says Horace, and starts giggling again.

'He didn't have enough money to pay,' says Maud. 'Poor man.'

'No, neither of those is the problem. He had money enough to pay, but he refused to. Let me explain. Counsel for Payelle argued that he had fulfilled his legal requirements by buying a ticket, and it was the company's fault if all the train doors were too narrow for him except the first-class ones. The company argued that if he was too fat to get into one kind of compartment, then he should take a ticket for the sort of compartment he could get into. What do you think?'

Horace is quite firm. 'If he went into a first-class compartment, then he has to pay for going into it. It stands to reason. He shouldn't have eaten so much cake. It's not the railway's fault if he's too fat.'

Maud tends to side with the underdog, and decides that a fat Frenchman comes into this category. 'It's not his fault he's fat,' she begins. 'It might be a disease. Or he may have lost his mother and got so sad he ate too much. Or – any reason. It wasn't as if he was making someone get out of their seat and go into a third-class compartment instead.'

'The court was not told the reasons for his size.'

'Then the law is an ass,' says Horace, who has recently learned the phrase.

'Had he ever done it before?' asks Maud.

'Now that's an excellent point,' says George, nodding like a judge. 'It goes to the question of intent. Either he knew from previous experience that he was too fat to enter a third-class compartment and bought a ticket despite this knowledge, or he bought a ticket in the honest belief that he could indeed fit through the door.'

'Well, which is it?' asks Horace, impatiently.

'I don't know. It doesn't say in the report.'

'So what's the answer?'

'Well, the answer here is a divided jury – one for each party. You'll have to argue it out between you.'

'I'm not going to argue with Maud,' says Horace. 'She's a girl. What's the real answer?'

'Oh, the Correctional Court at Lille found for the railway company. Payelle had to reimburse them.'

'I won!' shouts Horace. 'Maud got it wrong.'

'No one got it wrong,' George replies. 'The case could have gone either way. That's why things go to court in the first place.'

'I still won,' says Horace.

George is pleased. He has engaged the interest of his junior jury, and on succeeding Saturday afternoons he presents them with new cases and problems. Do passengers in a full compartment have the right to hold the door closed against those on the platform seeking to enter? Is there any legal difference between finding someone's pocketbook on the seat, and finding a loose coin under the cushion? What should happen if you take the last train home and it fails to stop at your station, thereby obliging you to walk five miles back in the rain?

When he finds his jurors' attention waning, George diverts them with interesting facts and odd cases. He tells them, for instance, about dogs in Belgium. In England the regulations state that dogs have to be muzzled and put in the van; whereas in Belgium a dog may have the status of a passenger so long as it has a ticket. He cites the case of a hunting man who took his retriever on a train and sued when it was ejected from the seat beside him in favour of a human being. The court – to Horace's delight and to Maud's dissatisfaction – found for the plaintiff, a ruling which meant that from now on if five men and their five dogs were to occupy a ten-seated compartment in Belgium, and all ten were the bearers of tickets, that compartment would legally be classified as full.

Horace and Maud are surprised by George. In the schoolroom there is a new authority about him; but also, a kind of lightness, as if he is on the verge of telling a joke, something he has never done to their knowledge. George, in return, finds his jury useful to him. Horace arrives quickly at blunt positions – usually in favour of the railway company – from which he will not be budged. Maud takes longer to make up her mind, asks the more pertinent questions, and sympathizes with every inconvenience that might befall a passenger. Though his siblings hardly amount to a cross section of the travelling public, they are typical, George thinks, in their almost complete ignorance of their rights.

Arthur

He had brought detectivism up to date. He had rid it of the slow-thinking representatives of the old school, those ordinary mortals who gained applause for deciphering palpable clues laid right across their path. In their place he had put a cool, calculating figure who could see the clue to a murder in a ball of worsted, and certain conviction in a saucer of milk.

Holmes provided Arthur with sudden fame and – something the England captaincy would never have done – money. He bought a decent-sized house in South Norwood, whose deep walled garden had room for a tennis ground. He put his grandfather's bust in the entrance hall and lodged his Arctic trophies on top of a bookcase. He found an office for Wood, who seemed to have attached himself as permanent staff. Lottie had returned from working as a governess in Portugal and Connie, despite being the decorative one, was proving an invaluable hand at the typewriter. He had acquired a machine in Southsea but never managed to manipulate it with success himself. He was more dextrous with the tandem bicycle he pedalled with Touie. When she became pregnant again, he exchanged it for a tricycle, driven by masculine power alone. On fine afternoons he would project them on thirty-mile missions across the Surrey hills.

He became accustomed to success, to being recognized and inspected; also to the various pleasures and embarrassments of the newspaper interview.

'It says you are a happy, genial, homely man.' Touie was smiling back at the magazine. 'Tall, broad-shouldered and with a hand that grips you heartily, and, in its sincerity of welcome, hurts.'

'Who is that?'

The Strand Magazine.'

'Ah. Mr How, as I recall. Not one of nature's sportsmen, I suspected at the time. The paw of a poodle. What does he say of you, my dear?'

'He says . . . Oh, I cannot read it.'

'I insist. You know how I love to see you blush.'

'He says . . . I am "a most charming woman".' And, on cue, she blushed, and hurriedly changed the subject. 'Mr How says, that "Dr Doyle invariably conceives the end of his story first, and writes up to it." You never told me that, Arthur.'

'Did I not? Perhaps because it is as plain as a packstaff. How can you make sense of the beginning unless you know the ending? It's entirely logical when you reflect upon it. What else does our friend have to say for himself?'

'That your ideas come to you at all manner of times – when out walking, cricketing, tricycling, or playing tennis. Is that the case, Arthur? Does that account for your occasional absent-mindedness on the court?'

'I might have been putting on dog a little.'

'And look – here is little Mary standing on this very chair.'

Arthur leaned over. 'Engraved from one of my photographs – there, you see. I made sure they put my name underneath.'

Arthur had become a face in literary circles. He counted Jerome and Barrie as friends; had met Meredith and Wells. He had dined with Oscar Wilde, finding him thoroughly civil and agreeable, not least because the fellow had read and admired his *Micah Clarke*. Arthur now reckoned he would run Holmes for not more than two years – three at most, before killing him off. Then he would concentrate on historical novels, which he had always known were the best of him.

He was proud of what he had done so far. He wondered if he would have been prouder had he fulfilled Partridge's prophecy and captained England at cricket. It was quite clear this would never happen. He was a decent right-hand bat, and could bowl slows with a flight that puzzled some. He might make a good all-round MCC man, but his final ambition was now more modest – to have his name inscribed in the pages of Wisden.

Touie bore him a son, Alleyne Kingsley. He had always dreamed of filling a house up with his family. But poor Annette had died out in Portugal; while the Mam was as stubborn as ever, preferring to stick in her cottage on that fellow's estate. Still, he had sisters, children, wife; and his brother Innes was not far away at Woolwich, preparing for an army life. Arthur was the bread-winner, and a head of the family who enjoyed dispensing largesse and blank cheques. Once a year he did it formally, dressing as Father Christmas.

He knew the proper order should have been: wife, children, sisters. How long had they been married – seven, eight years? Touie was all anyone could possibly want in a wife. She was indeed a most charming woman, as *The Strand Magazine* had noted. She was calm and had grown competent; she had given him a son and daughter. She believed in his writing down to the last adjective, and supported all his ventures. He fancied Norway; they went to Norway. He fancied dinner parties; she organized them to his taste. He had married her for better for worse, for richer for poorer. So far there had been no worse, and no poorer.

And yet. It was different now, if he was honest with himself. When they had met, he had been young, awkward and unknown; she had loved him, and never complained. Now he was still young, but successful and famous; he could keep a table of Savile Club wits interested by the hour. He had found his feet, and – partly thanks to marriage – his brain. His success was the deserved result of hard work, but those themselves unfamiliar with success imagined it the end of the story. Arthur was not yet ready for the end of his own story. If life was a chivalric quest, then he had rescued the fair Touie, he had conquered the city, and been rewarded with gold. But there were years to go before he was prepared to accept a role as wise elder to the tribe. What did a knight errant do when he came home to a wife and two children in South Norwood?

Well, perhaps it was not such a difficult question. He protected them, behaved honourably, and taught his children the proper code of living. He might depart on further quests, though obviously not quests which involved the saving of other maidens. There would be plenty of challenges in his writing, in society, travel, politics. Who knew in what direction his sudden energies would take him? He would always give Touie whatever attention and comfort she could need; he would never cause her a moment's unhappiness.

And yet.

George

Greenway and Stentson tend to hang about together, but this does not bother George. At lunchtime he has no desire for the tavern, preferring to sit under a tree in St Philip's Place and eat the sandwiches his mother has prepared. He likes it when they ask him to explain some aspect of conveyancing, but is often puzzled by the way they go off into secretive spurts about horses and betting offices, girls and dance-halls. They are also currently obsessed with Bechuana Land, whose chiefs are on an official visit to Birmingham.

Besides, when he does hang about with them, they like to question a fellow and tease him.

'George, where do you come from?'

'Great Wyrley.'

'No, where do you *really* come from?'

George ponders this. 'The Vicarage,' he replies, and the dogs laugh.

'Have you got a girl, George?'

'I beg your pardon?'

'Some legal definition you don't understand in the question?'

'Well, I just think a chap should mind his own business.'

'Hoity-toity, George.'

It is a subject to which Greenway and Stentson are tenaciously and hilariously attached.

'Is she a stunner, George?'

'Does she look like Marie Lloyd?'

When George does not reply, they put their heads together, tip their hats at an angle, and serenade him. 'The-boy-I-love-sits-up-in-the-ga-ll-ery.'

'Go on, George, tell us her name.'

'Go on, George, tell us her name.'

After a few weeks of this, George can take no more. If that's what they want, that's what they can have. 'Her name's Dora Charlesworth,' he says suddenly.

'Dora Charlesworth,' they repeat. 'Dora Charlesworth. Dora Charlesworth?' They make it sound increasingly improbable.

'She's Harry Charlesworth's sister. He's my friend.'

He thinks this will shut them up, but it only seems to encourage them.

'What's the colour of her hair?'

'Have you kissed her, George?'

'Where does she come from?'

'No, where does she really come from?'

'Are you making her a Valentine?'

They never seem to tire of the subject.

'I say, George, there's one question we have to ask you about Dora. Is she a darkie?'

'She's English, just like me.'

'Just like you, George? *Just* like you?'

'When can we meet her?'

'I bet she's a Bechuana girl.'

'Shall we send a private detective to investigate? What about that fellow some of the divorce firms use? Goes into hotel rooms and catches the husband with the maid? Wouldn't want to get caught like that, George, would you?'

George decides that what he has done, or has allowed to happen, isn't really lying; it is just letting them believe what they want to believe, which is different. Happily, they live on the other side of Birmingham, so each time George's train pulls out from New Street, he is leaving that particular story behind.

On the morning of February 13th, Greenway and Stentson are in skittish mood, though George never discovers why. They have just posted a Valentine addressed to Miss Dora Charlesworth, Great Wyrley, Staffordshire. This sets off considerable puzzlement in the postman, and even more in Harry Charlesworth, who has always longed for a sister.

George sits on the train, his newspaper unfolded across his knee. His brief-case is on the higher, and wider, of the two string racks above his head; his bowler on the lower, narrower one, which is reserved for hats, umbrellas, sticks and small parcels. He thinks about the journey everyone has to make in life. Father's, for instance, began in distant Bombay, at the far end of one of the bubbling bloodlines of Empire. There he was brought up, and was converted to Christianity. There he wrote a grammar of the Gujerati language which funded his passage to England. He studied at St Augustine's College, Canterbury, was ordained a priest by Bishop Macarness, and then served as a curate in Liverpool before finding his parish at Wyrley. That is a great journey by any reckoning; and his own, George thinks, will doubtless not be so extensive. Perhaps it will more closely resemble Mother's: from Scotland, where she was born, to Shropshire, where her father was Vicar of Ketley for thirty-nine years, and then to nearby Staffordshire, where her husband, if

God spares him, may prove equally long-serving. Will Birmingham turn out to be George's final destination, or just a staging post? He cannot as yet tell.

George is beginning to think of himself less as a villager with a season ticket and more as a prospective citizen of Birmingham. As a sign of this new status, he decides to grow a moustache. It takes far longer than he imagines, allowing Greenway and Stentson to ask repeatedly if he would like them to club together and buy him a bottle of hair tonic. When the growth finally covers the full breadth of his upper lip, they begin calling him a Manchoo.

When they tire of this joke, they find another.

'I say, Stentson, do you know who George reminds me of?'

'Give a chap a clue.'

'Well, where did he go to school?'

'George, where did you go to school?'

'You know very well, Stentson.'

'Tell me all the same, George.'

George lifts his head from the Land Transfer Act 1897 and its consequences for wills of realty. 'Rugeley.'

'Think about it, Stentson.'

'Rugeley. Now I'm getting there. Hang on – could it be William Palmer –'

'The Rugeley Poisoner! Exactly.'

'Where did he go to school, George?'

'You know very well, you fellows.'

'Did they give everyone poisoning lessons there? Or just the clever boys?'

Palmer had killed his wife and brother after insuring them heavily; then a bookmaker to whom he was in debt. There may have been other victims, but the police contented themselves with exhuming only the next-of-kin. The evidence was enough to ensure the Poisoner a public execution in Stafford before a crowd of fifty thousand.

'Did he have a moustache like George's?'

'Just like George's.'

'You don't know anything about him, Greenway.'

'I know he went to your school. Was he on the Honours Board? Famous alumnus and all that?'

George pretends to put his thumbs in his ears.

'Actually, the thing about the Poisoner, Stentson, is that he was devilish clever. The prosecution was completely unable to establish what kind of poison he'd used.'

'Devilish clever. Do you think he was an Oriental gentleman, this Palmer?'

'Might have been from Bechuana Land. You can't always tell from someone's name, can you, George?'

'And did you hear that afterwards Rugeley sent a deputation to Lord Palmerston in Downing Street? They wanted to change the name of their town because of the disgrace the Poisoner had brought upon it. The PM thought about their request for a moment and replied, "What name do you propose – Palmerstown?"'

There is a silence. 'I don't follow you.'

'No, not Palmerston. Pal-mers-town.'

'Ah! Now that's very amusing, Greenway.'

'Even our Manchoo friend is laughing. Underneath his moustache.'

For once, George has had enough. 'Roll up your sleeve, Greenway.'

Greenway smirks. 'What for? Are you going to give me a Chinese burn?'

'Roll up your sleeve.'

George then does the same, and holds his forearm next to that of Greenway, who is just back from a fortnight sunning himself at Aberystwyth. Their skins are the same colour. Greenway is unabashed, and waits for George to comment; but George feels he has made his point, and starts putting the link back through his cuff.

'What was that about?' Stentson asks.

'I think George is trying to prove I'm a poisoner too.'

Arthur

They had taken Connie on a European tour. She was a robust girl, the only woman on the Norway crossing who wasn't prostrate with seasickness. Such imperviousness made other female sufferers irritated. Perhaps her sturdy beauty irritated them too: Jerome said that Connie could have posed for Brünnhilde. During that tour Arthur discovered that his sister, with her light dancing step, and her chestnut hair worn down her back like the cable of a man-o'-war, attracted the most unsuitable men: lotharios, card-sharps, oleaginous divorcees. Arthur had almost been obliged to raise his stick to some of them.

Back home, she seemed at last to have fixed her eye on a presentable fellow: Ernest William Hornung, twenty-six years old, tall, dapper, asthmatic, a decent wicketkeeper and occasional spin bowler; well-mannered, if liable to talk a streak if in the least encouraged. Arthur recognized that he would find it difficult to approve of anyone who attached themselves to either Lottie or Connie; but in any case, it was his duty as head of the family to cross-examine his sister.

'Hornung. What is he, this Hornung? Half Mongol, half Slav, by the sound of him. Could you not find someone wholly British?'

'He was born in Middlesbrough, Arthur. His father is a solicitor. He went to Uppingham.'

'There's something odd about him. I can sniff it.'

'He lived in Australia for three years. Because of his asthma. Perhaps what you can sniff are the gum trees.'

Arthur suppressed a laugh. Connie was the sister who most stood up to him; he loved Lottie more, but Connie was the one who liked to pull him up and surprise him. Thank God she had not married Waller. And the same went, *a fortiori*, for Lottie.

'And what does he do, this fellow from Middlesbrough?'

'He is a writer. Like you, Arthur.'

Never heard of him.'

He has written a dozen novels.'

'A dozen! But he's just a young pup.' An industrious pup, at least.

'I can lend you one if you wish to judge him that way. I have *Under Two Skies* and *The Boss of Taroomba*. Many of them are set in Australia, and I find them very accomplished.'

'Do you just, Connie?'

'But he realizes that it is difficult to make a living from writing novels, and so he works also as a journalist.'

'Well, it is a name that sticks,' Arthur grunted. He gave Connie permission to introduce the fellow into the household. For the moment he would give him the benefit of the doubt by not reading any of his books.

Spring was early that year, and the tennis ground was marked out by the end of April. From his study Arthur would hear the distant pop of racquet on ball, and the familiar irritating cry made by a female missing an easy shot. Later, he would wander out and there would be Connie in flowing skirts and Willie Hornung in straw hat and peg-topped white flannels. He noted the way Hornung did not give her any easy points, but at the same time held back from a full weight of shot. He approved: that was how a man ought to play a girl.

Touie sat to one side in a deckchair, warmed less by the frail sun of early summer than by the heat of young love. Their laughing chatter across the net and their shyness with one another afterwards seemed to delight her, and Arthur therefore decided to be won over. In truth, he rather liked the role of grudging paterfamilias. And Hornung was proving himself a witty fellow at times. Perhaps too witty, but that could be ascribed to youth. What was that first jest of his? Yes, Arthur had been reading the sporting pages, and remarked upon a story in which a runner was credited with completing the hundred yards in a mere ten seconds.

'What do you make of that, Mr Hornung?'

And Hornung had replied, quick as a flash, 'It must be a sprinter's error.'

That August, Arthur was invited to lecture in Switzerland; Touie was still a little weak from the birth of Kingsley, but naturally accompanied him. They visited the Reichenbach Falls, splendid yet terrifying, and a worthy tomb for Holmes. The fellow was rapidly turning into an old man of the sea, clinging round his neck. Now, with the help of an arch-villain, he would shrug his burden off.

At the end of September, Arthur was walking Connie up the aisle, she pulling back on his arm for striking too military a pace. As he handed her over symbolically at the altar, he knew he should be proud and happy for her. But amid all the orange blossom and backslapping and jokes about bowling maidens over, he felt his dream of an ever-increasing family around him taking a knock.

Ten days later, he learned that his father had died in a Dumfries lunatic asylum. Epilepsy was given as the cause. Arthur had not visited him in years, and did not attend the funeral; none of the family did. Charles Doyle had let down the Mam and condemned his children to genteel poverty. He had been weak and unmanly, incapable of winning his fight against liquor. Fight? He had barely raised his gloves at the demon. Excuses were occasionally made for him, but Arthur did not find the claim of an artistic temperament persuasive. That was just self-indulgence and self-exculpation. It was perfectly possible to be an artist, yet also to be robust and responsible.

Touie developed a persistent autumn cough, and complained of pains in her side. Arthur judged the symptoms insignificant, but eventually called in Dalton, the local practitioner. It was strange to find himself transformed from doctor to mere patient's husband; strange to wait downstairs while somewhere above his head his fate was being decided. The bedroom door was closed for a long time, and Dalton emerged with a face as dismal as it was familiar: Arthur had worn it himself all too many times.

'Her lungs are gravely affected. There is every sign of rapid consumption. Given her condition and family history . . .' Dr Dalton did not need to continue, except to add, 'You will want a second opinion.'

Not just a second, but the best. Douglas Powell, consulting physician at the Brompton Hospital for Consumption and Diseases of the Chest, came down to South Norwood the following Saturday. A pale, ascetic man, clean-shaved and correct, Powell regretfully confirmed the diagnosis.

'You are, I believe, a medical man, Mr Doyle?'

'I rebuke myself for my inattention.'

'The pulmonary system was not your speciality?'

'The eye.'

'Then you should not rebuke yourself.'

'No, the more so. I had eyes, and did not see. I did not spot the accursed microbe. I did not pay her enough attention. I was too busy with my own . . . success.'

'But you were an eye doctor.'

'Three years ago I went to Berlin to report on Koch's findings – supposed findings – about this very disease. I wrote about it for Stead, in the *Review of Reviews*.'

'I see.'

'And yet I did not recognize a case of galloping consumption in my own wife. Worse, I let her join me in activities which will have made it worse. We tricycled in every weather, we travelled to cold climates, she followed me in outdoor sports . . .'

'On the other hand,' said Powell, and the words briefly lifted Arthur's spirits, 'in my view there are promising signs of fibroid growth around the seat of the disease. And the other lung has enlarged somewhat to compensate. But that is the best I can say.'

'I do not accept it!' Arthur whispered the words because he could not bellow them at the top of his voice.

Powell took no offence. He was accustomed to pronouncing the gentlest, courtliest sentence of death, and familiar with the ways it took those affected. 'Of course. If you would like the name –'

'No. I accept what you have told me. But I do not accept what you have not told me. You would give her a matter of months.'

'You know as well as I do, Mr Doyle, how impossible it is to predict –'

'I know as well as you do, Dr Powell, the words we use to give hope to our patients and those near to them. I also know the words we hear within ourselves as we seek to raise their spirits. About three months.'

'Yes, in my view.'

'Then again, I say, I do not accept it. When I see the Devil, I fight him. Wherever we need to go, whatever I need to spend, he shall not have her.'

'I wish you every good fortune,' replied Powell, 'And remain at your service. There are, however, two things I am obliged to say. They may be unnecessary, but I am duty-bound. I trust you will not take offence.'

Arthur stiffened his back, a soldier ready for orders.

'You have, I believe, children?'

'Two, a boy and a girl. Aged one and four.'

'There is, you must understand, no possibility –'

'I understand.'

'I am not talking to her ability to conceive –'

'Mr Powell, I am not a fool. And neither am I a brute.'

'These things have to be made crystal clear, you must understand. The second matter is perhaps less obvious. It is the effect – the likely effect – on the patient. On Mrs Doyle.'

'Yes?'

'In our experience, consumption is different from other wasting diseases. On the whole, the patient suffers very little pain. Often the disease will proceed with less inconvenience than a toothache or an indigestion. But what sets it apart is the effect upon the mental processes. The patient is often very optimistic.'

'You mean light-headed? Delirious?'

'No, I mean optimistic. Tranquil and cheerful, I would say.'

'On account of the drugs you prescribe?'

'Not at all. It is in the nature of the disease. Regardless of how aware the patient is of the seriousness of her case.'

'Well, that is a great relief to me.'

'Yes, it may be so at first, Mr Doyle.'

'What do you mean by that?'

'I mean that when a patient does not suffer and does not complain and remains cheerful in the face of grave illness, then the suffering and the complaining has to be done by someone.'

'You do not know me, sir.'

'That is true. But I wish you the necessary courage nonetheless.'

For better, for worse; for richer, for poorer. He had forgotten: in sickness and in health.

The lunatic asylum sent Arthur his father's sketchbooks. Charles Doyle's last years had been miserable, as he lay unvisited at his grim final address; but he did not die mad. That much was clear: he had continued to paint water-colours and to draw; also to keep a diary. It now struck Arthur that his father had been a considerable artist, undervalued by his peers, worthy indeed of a posthumous exhibition in Edinburgh – perhaps even in London. Arthur could not help reflecting on the contrast in their fates: while the son was enjoying the embrace of fame and society, his abandoned father knew only the occasional embrace of the straitjacket. Arthur felt no guilt – just the beginnings of filial compassion. And there was one sentence in his father's diary which would drag at any son's heart. 'I believe,' he had written, 'I am branded as mad solely from the Scotch Misconception of Jokes.'

In December of that year, Holmes fell to his death in the arms of Moriarty; both of them propelled downwards by an impatient authorial hand. The London newspapers had contained no obituaries of Charles Doyle, but were full of protest and dismay at the death of a non-existent consulting detective whose popularity had begun to embarrass and even disgust his creator. It seemed to Arthur that the world was running mad: his father was fresh in the ground, and his wife condemned, but young City men were apparently tying crepe bands to their hats in mourning for Mr Sherlock Holmes.

Another event took place during this morbid year's end. A month after his father's death, Arthur applied to join the Society for Psychical Research.

George

In the Solicitors' Final Examinations George receives Second Class Honours, and is awarded a Bronze Medal by the Birmingham Law Society. He opens an office at 54 Newhall Street with the initial promise of some overflow work from Sangster, Vickery & Speight. He is twenty-three, and the world is changing for him.

Despite being a child of the Vicarage, despite a lifetime of filial attention to the pulpit of St Mark's, George has often felt that he does not understand the Bible. Not all of it, all of the time; indeed, not enough of it, enough of the time. There has always been some leap to be made, from fact to faith, from knowledge to understanding, of which he has proved incapable. This makes him feel a sham. The tenets of the Church of England have increasingly become a distant given. He does not sense them as close truths, or see them working from day to day, from moment to moment. Naturally, he does not tell his parents this.

At school, additional stories and explanations of life were put before him. This is what science says; this is what history says; this is what literature says ... George became adept at answering examination questions on these subjects, even if they had no real vivacity in his mind. But now he has discovered the law, and the world is beginning finally to make sense. Hitherto invisible connections – between people, between things, between ideas and principles – are gradually revealing themselves.

For instance, he is on the train between Bloxwich and Birchills, looking out of the window at a hedgerow. He sees not what his fellow passengers would see – a few intertwined bushes blown by the wind, home to some nesting birds – but instead a formal boundary between owners of land, a delineation settled by contract or long usage, something active, something liable to promote either amity or dispute. At the Vicarage, he looks at the maid scrubbing the kitchen table, and instead of a coarse and clumsy girl likely to misplace his books, he sees a contract of employment and a duty of care, a complicated and delicate tying together, backed by centuries of case law, all of it unfamiliar to the parties concerned.

He feels confident and happy with the law. There is a great deal of textual exegesis, of explaining how words can and do mean different things; and there are almost as many books of commentary on the law as there are on the Bible. But at the end there is not that further leap to be made. At the end, you have an agreement, a decision to be obeyed, an understanding of what something means. There is a journey from confusion to clarity. A drunken mariner writes his last will and testament on an ostrich egg; the mariner drowns, the egg survives, whereupon the law brings coherence and fairness to his sea-washed words.

Other young men divide their lives between work and pleasure; indeed, spend the former dreaming of the latter. George finds that the law provides him with both. He has no need or desire to take part in sports, to go boating, to attend the theatre; he has no interest in alcohol or gourmandising, or in horses racing one another; he has little desire to travel. He has his practice, and then, for pleasure, he has railway law. It is astonishing that the tens of thousands who travel daily by train have no useful pocket explicator to help them determine their rights vis-à-vis the railway company. He has written to Messrs Effingham Wilson, publishers of the 'Wilson's Legal Handy Books' series, and on the basis of a sample chapter they have accepted his proposal.

George has been brought up to believe in hard work, honesty, thrift, charity and love of family; also to believe that virtue is its own reward. Further, as the eldest child, he is expected to set an example to Horace and Maud. George increasingly realizes that, while his parents love their three children equally, it is on him that expectation weighs the heaviest. Maud is always likely to be a source of concern. Horace, while in all respects a thoroughly decent fellow, has never been cut out for a scholar. He has left home and, with help from a cousin of Mother's, managed to enter the Civil Service at the lowest clerical level.

Still, there are moments when George catches himself envying Horace, who now lives in diggings in Manchester, and occasionally sends a cheery postcard from a seaside resort. There are also moments when he wishes that Dora Charlesworth really did exist. But he knows no girls. None comes to the house; Maud has no female friends he might practise acquaintance on. Greenway and Stentson liked to boast experience in such matters, but George was often dubious of their claims, and is glad to have left those two behind. When he sits on his bench in St Philip's Place eating his sandwiches, he glances admiringly at young women who pass; sometimes he will remember a face, and have yearnings for it at night, while his father growls and snuffles a few feet away. George is familiar with the sins of the flesh, as listed in

Galatians, chapter five – they begin with Adultery, Fornication, Uncleanness and Lasciviousness. But he does not believe his own quiet hankerings qualify under either of the last two heads.

One day he will be married. He will acquire not just a fob watch but a junior partner, and perhaps an articled clerk, and after that a wife, young children, and a house to whose purchase he has brought all his conveyancing skills. He already imagines himself discussing, over luncheon, the Sale of Goods Act 1893 with the senior partners of other Birmingham practices. They listen respectfully to his summary of how the Act is being interpreted, and cry 'Good old George!' when he reaches for the bill. He is not sure exactly how you get to there from here: whether you acquire a wife and then a house, or a house and then a wife. But he imagines it all happening, by some as yet unrevealed process. Both acquisitions will depend upon his leaving Wyrley, of course. He does not ask his father about this. Nor does he ask him why he still locks the bedroom door at night.

When Horace left home, George hoped he might move into the empty room. The small desk fitted up for him in Father's study when he first went to Mason College was no longer adequate. He imagined Horace's room with his bed in it, his desk in it; he imagined privacy. But when he put his request to Mother, she gently explained that Maud was now judged strong enough to sleep by herself, and George wouldn't want to deprive her of that chance, would he? It was now too late, he realized, to put in evidence Father's snoring, which had got worse and sometimes kept him awake. So he continues to work and sleep within touching distance of his father. However, he is awarded a small table next to his desk, on which to place extra books.

He still retains the habit, which has now grown into a necessity, of walking the lanes for an hour or so after he gets back from the office. It is one detail of his life in which he will not be ruled. He keeps a pair of old boots by the back door, and rain or shine, hail or snow, George takes his walk. He ignores the landscape, which does not interest him; nor do the bulky, bellowing animals it contains. As for the humans, he will occasionally think he recognizes someone from the village school in Mr Bostock's day, but he is never quite sure. No doubt the farm boys have now grown into farm-hands, and the miners' sons are down the pit themselves. Some days George gives a kind of half-greeting, a sideways raising of the head, to everyone he meets; at other times he greets no one, even if he remembers having acknowledged them the day before.

His walk is delayed one evening by the sight of a small parcel on the kitchen table. From its size and weight, and the London postmark, he knows immediately what it contains. He wants to delay the moment for as long as possible. He unknots the string and carefully rolls it round his fingers. He removes the waxed brown paper and smooths it out for reuse. Maud is by now thoroughly excited, and even Mother shows a little impatience. He opens the book to its title page:

RAILWAY LAW

FOR

THE " MAN IN THE TRAIN "

CHIEFLY INTENDED AS A GUIDE FOR THE TRAVELLING PUBLIC ON ALL POINTS LIKELY TO ARISE IN CONNECTION WITH THE RAILWAYS

BY

GEORGE E. T. EDALJI

SOLICITOR

Second Class Honours, Solicitors' Final Examination, November, 1898 ;
Birmingham Law Society's Bronze Medallist, 1898

LONDON

EFFINGHAM WILSON

ROYAL EXCHANGE

1901

[*Entered at Stationers' Hall*]

He turns to the Contents. Bye-Laws and Their Validity. Season Tickets. Unpunctuality of Trains, etc. Luggage. The Carriage of Cycles. Accidents. Some Miscellaneous Points. He shows Maud the cases they considered in the schoolroom with Horace. Here is the one about fat Monsieur Payelle; and here the one about Belgians and their dogs.

This is, he realizes, the proudest day of his life; and over supper it is clear that his parents allow a certain amount of pride to be justifiable and Christian. He has studied and passed his examinations. He has set up his own office, and now shown himself an authority upon an aspect of the law which is of practical help to many people. He is on his way: that journey in life is now truly beginning.

He goes to Horniman & Co to get some flyers printed. He discusses layout and typeface and print run with Mr Horniman himself, as one professional to another. A week later he is the owner of four hundred advertisements for his book. He leaves three hundred in his office, not wishing to appear vain-glorious, and takes a hundred home. The order form invites interested purchasers to send a Postal Order for 2/3 – the 3d to cover postage – to 54 Newhall Street Birmingham. He gives handfuls of the flyer to his parents, with instructions that they press them upon likely looking Men and Women 'In the Train'. Next morning he gives three to the stationmaster at Great Wyrley & Churchbridge, and distributes others to respectable fellow passengers.

Arthur

They put the furniture into store and left the children with Mrs Hawkins. From the fog and damp of London to the clean, dry chill of Davos, where Touie was installed at the Kurhaus Hotel under a pile of blankets. As Dr Powell had predicted, the disease brought with it a strange optimism; and this, combined with Touie's placid nature, made her not just stoical but actively cheerful. It was perfectly clear that she had been transformed within a few weeks from wife and companion to invalid and dependant; but she did not fret at her condition, let alone rage as Arthur would have done. He did the raging for both of them, in silence, by himself. He also concealed his blacker feelings. Each uncomplaining cough sent a pain, not through her, but through him; she brought up a little blood, he brought up gouts of guilt.

Whatever his fault, whatever his negligence, it was done, and there was only one course of action: a violent attack on the accursed microbe which was intending to consume her vitals. And when his presence was not required, only one course of distraction: violent exercise. He had brought his Norwegian skis to Davos, and took instruction in their use from two brothers called Branger. When their pupil's skill began to match his brute determination, they took him on the ascent of the Jacobshorn; at the summit he turned, and saw far below him the flags of the town being lowered in acclamation. Later that winter the Brangers led him over the 9,000-foot Furka Pass. They set off at four in the morning and arrived in Arosa by noon, Arthur thus becoming the first Englishman to cross an Alpine pass on skis. At their hotel in Arosa, Tobias Branger registered the three of them. Next to Arthur's name, in the space for Profession, he wrote: *Sportesmann.*

With Alpine air, the best doctors, and money, with Lottie's nursing help and Arthur's tenacity in wrestling down the Devil, Touie's condition stabilized, then began to improve. By the late spring, she was judged strong enough to come back to England, allowing Arthur to depart for an American publication tour. The following winter they returned to Davos. That initial sentence of three months had been overturned; every doctor agreed that the patient's health was somewhat more secure. The next winter they spent in the desert outside Cairo at the Mena House Hotel, a low white building with the Pyramids looming behind. Arthur was irritated by the brittle air; but soothed by billiards, tennis and golf. He foresaw a life of annual winter exiles, each a little longer than the previous one, until . . . No, he must not let himself think beyond the spring, beyond the summer. At least he could still manage to write during this jerky existence of hotels and steamers and trains. And when he couldn't write he went out into the desert and whacked a golf ball as far as it would fly. The whole course was in effect nothing but one vast sand-hole; wherever you landed, you were in it. This, it seemed, was what his life had become.

Back in England, however, he ran into Grant Allen: like Arthur a novelist, and like Touie a consumptive. Allen assured him that the disease could be resisted without recourse to exile, and offered himself as living proof. The solution lay in his postal address: Hindhead, Surrey. A village on the Portsmouth road, almost halfway, as it happened, between Southsea and London. More to the point, a spot with its own private climate. It was high up, sheltered from the winds, dry, full of fir trees and sandy soil. They called it the Little Switzerland of Surrey.

Arthur was immediately convinced. He thrived on action, on having an urgent plan to implement; he loathed waiting, and feared the passivity of exile. Hindhead was the answer. Land must be bought, a house designed. He found four acres, wooded and secluded, where the ground dropped away into a small valley. Gibbet Hill and the Devil's Punchbowl were close at hand,

Hankley Golf Course five miles away. Ideas came to him in a rush. There must be a billiards room, and a tennis ground, and stables; quarters for Lottie, and perhaps Mrs Hawkins, and of course Woodie, who had now signed up for the duration. The house must be impressive yet welcoming: a famous writer's house, but also a family house and an invalid's house. It must be full of light, and Touie's room must have the best view. Every door must have a push-pull knob, as Arthur had once tried to calculate the amount of time lost to the human race in turning the conventional kind. It would be quite feasible for the house to have its own electricity plant; and given that he had now attained a certain eminence, it would not be inappropriate to have his family arms in stained glass.

Arthur sketched a ground plan and handed the work over to an architect. Not just any architect, but Stanley Ball, his old telepathic friend from Southsea. Those early experiments now struck him as appropriate training. He would be taking Touie to Davos again, and would communicate with Ball by letter and, if necessary, telegram. But who knew what architectural shapes might not flit sympathetically between their brains, while their bodies were hundreds of miles apart?

His stained-glass window would rise to the full height of a double-storey hallway. At the top the rose of England and the thistle of Scotland would flank the entwined initials ACD. Below there would be three rows of heraldic shields. First rank: Purcell of Foulkes Rath, Pack of Kilkenny, Mahon of Cheverney. Second rank: Percy of Northumberland, Butler of Ormonde, Colclough of Tintern. And at eye level: Conan of Brittany (Per fess Argent and Gules a lion rampant counterchanged), Hawkins of Devonshire (for Touie) and then the Doyle arms: three stags' heads and the red hand of Ulster. The true Doyle motto was *Fortitudine Vincit*; but here, beneath the shield, he placed a variant – *Patientia Vincit*. This is what the house would proclaim, to all the world and to the accursed microbe: with patience he conquers.

Stanley Ball and his builders saw little but impatience. Arthur, having set up headquarters at a nearby hotel, would constantly drive over and badger them. But at last the house took recognizable shape: a long, barn-like structure, red-bricked, tile-hung, heavy-gabled, lying across the neck of the valley. Arthur stood on his newly laid terrace and cast an inspecting eye on the broad lawn, recently rolled and seeded. Beyond it the ground fell away in an ever narrowing V to where the woods took over. There was something wild and magical about the view: from the first moment Arthur had found it evocative of some German folk tale. He thought he would plant rhododendrons.

On the day the hall window was hoisted into place, he took Touie with him to witness the unveiling. She stood before it, her eye passing over the colours and the names, then coming to rest on the house's motto.

'The Mam will be pleased,' he observed. Only the slight pause before her smile made him realize something might be awry.

'You are right,' he said immediately, though she had still not uttered a word. How could he have been such a dunderhead? To put up a tribute to your own illustrious ancestry and forget your very mother's family? For a moment he thought of ordering the workmen to take the whole damn window down. Later, after guilty reflection, he commissioned a second, more modest window for the turning of the stair. Its central panel would hold the over-looked arms and name: Foley of Worcestershire.

He decided to call the house Undershaw, after the hanging grove of trees beneath which it lay. The name would give this modern construction a fine old Anglo-Saxon resonance. Here life might continue as before, if cautiously and within limits.

Life. How easily everyone, including himself, said the word. Life must go on, everyone routinely agreed. And yet how few asked what it was, and why it was, and if it was the only life or the mere amphitheatre to something quite different. Arthur was frequently baffled by the complacency with which people went on with . . . with what they insouciantly called their lives, as if both the word and the thing made perfect sense to them.

His old Southsea friend General Drayson had become convinced of the spiritualist argument after his dead brother spoke to him at a seance. Thereafter, the astronomer maintained that the continuance of life after death was not just a supposition but a provable fact. Arthur had politely demurred at the time; even so, his list of Books To Be Read that year included seventy-four on the subject of Spiritualism. He had despatched them all, noting down sentences and maxims which impressed him. Like this from Hellenbach: 'There is a scepticism which surpasses in imbecility the obtuseness of a clodhopper.'

Until Touie's illness announced itself, he had everything the world assumed necessary to make a man contented. And yet he could never quite shake off the feeling that all he had achieved was just a trivial and specious beginning; that he was made for something else. But what might that something else be? He returned to a study of the world's religions, but could no more get into any of them than he could into a boy's suit. He joined the Rationalist Association, and found their work necessary, but essentially destructive and therefore sterile. The demolition of antique faiths had been fundamental to human advancement; but now that those old buildings had been levelled, where was man to find shelter in this blasted landscape? How could anyone glibly decide that the history of what the species had for millennia agreed to call the soul was now at an end? Human beings would continue to develop, and therefore whatever was inside them must also develop. Even a clodhopping sceptic could surely see that.

Outside Cairo, while Touie was breathing deep the desert air, Arthur had read histories of Egyptian civilization and visited the tombs of the pharaohs. He concluded that while the ancient Egyptians had indubitably raised the arts and sciences to a new level, their reasoning power was in many ways contemptible. Especially in their attitude to death. The notion that the dead body, an old, outworn greatcoat which once briefly wrapped the soul, should be preserved at any cost was not just risible; it was the last word in materialism. As for those baskets of provisions placed in the tomb to feed the soul upon its journey: how could a people of such sophistication be so emasculated in their minds? Faith endorsed by materialism: a double curse. And the same curse blighted every subsequent nation and civilization that came under the rule of a priesthood.

Back in Southsea, he had not found General Drayson's arguments sufficient. But now psychic phenomena were being vouched for by scientists of high distinction and manifest probity, like William Crookes, Oliver Lodge and Alfred Russel Wallace. Such names meant that the men who best understood the natural world – the great physicists and biologists – had also become our guides to the supernatural world.

Take Wallace. The co-discoverer of the modern theory of evolution, the man who stood at Darwin's side when they jointly announced the idea of natural selection to the Linnaean Society. The fearful and the unimaginative had concluded that Wallace and Darwin had delivered us into a godless and mechanistic universe, had left us alone upon the darkling plain. But consider what Wallace himself believed. This greatest of modern men maintained that natural selection accounted only for the development of the human body, and that the process of evolution must at some point have been supplemented by a supernatural intervention, when the spirit's flame was inserted into the rough developing animal. Who dared claim now that science was the enemy of the soul?

George & Arthur

It was a cold, clear February night, with half a moon and a heavenful of stars. In the distance the head gear of Wyrley Colliery stood out faintly against the sky. Close by was the farm belonging to Joseph Holmes: house, barn, outbuildings, with not a light showing in any of them. Humans were sleeping and the birds had not yet woken.

But the horse was awake as the man came through a gap in the hedge on the far side of the field. He was carrying a feed-bag over his arm. As soon as he became aware that the horse had noticed his presence, he stopped and began to talk very quietly. The words themselves were a gabble of nonsense; it was the tone, calming and intimate, that mattered. After a few minutes, the man slowly began to advance. When he had made a few paces, the horse shook its head, and its mane was a brief blur. At this, the man stopped again.

He continued his gabble of nonsense, however, and continued looking straight towards the horse. Beneath his feet the ground was solid after nights of frost, and his boots left no print on the soil. He advanced slowly, a few yards at a time, stopping at the least sign of restiveness from the horse. At all times he made his presence evident, holding himself as tall as possible. The feed-bag over his arm was an unimportant detail. What mattered were the quiet persistence of the voice, the certainty of the approach, the direct-ness of the gaze, the gentleness of the mastery.

It took him twenty minutes to cross the field in this way. Now he stood only a few yards distant, head on to the horse. Still he made no sudden move, but continued as before, murmuring, gazing, standing straight, waiting. Eventually, what he had been expecting took place: the horse, reluctantly at first, but then unequivocally, lowered its head.

The man, even now, made no sudden reach. He let a minute or two pass, then crossed the final yards and hung the feed-bag gently round the horse's neck. The animal kept its head lowered as the man proceeded to stroke it, murmuring all the while. He stroked its mane, its flank, its back; sometimes he just rested his hand against the warm skin, making sure that contact between the two of them was never broken.

Still stroking and murmuring, the man slipped the feed-bag from the horse's neck and slung it over his shoulder. Still stroking and murmuring, the man then felt inside his coat. Still stroking and murmuring, one arm across the horse's back, he reached underneath to its belly.

The horse barely gave a start; the man at last ceased his gabble of nonsense, and in the new silence he made his way, at a deliberate pace, back towards the gap in the hedge.

George

Each morning George takes the first train of the day into Birmingham. He knows the timetable by heart, and loves it. Wyrley & Churchbridge 7.39. Bloxwich 7.48. Birchills 7.53. Walsall 7.58. Birmingham New Street 8.35. He no longer feels the need to hide behind his newspaper; indeed, from time to time he suspects that some of his fellow passengers are aware that he is the author of *Railway Law for the 'Man in the Train'* (237 copies sold). He greets ticket collectors and stationmasters and they return his salute. He has a respectable moustache, a briefcase, a modest fob chain, and his bowler has been augmented by a straw hat for summer use. He also has an umbrella. He is rather proud of this last possession, often taking it with him in defiance of the barometer.

On the train he reads the newspaper and tries to develop views on what is happening in the world. Last month there was an important speech at the new Birmingham Town Hall by Mr Chamberlain about the colonies and pref-erential tariffs. George's position – though as yet no one has asked for his opinion on the matter – is one of cautious endorsement. Next month Lord Roberts of Kandahar is due to receive the freedom of the city, an honour with which no reasonable man could possibly quarrel.

His paper tells him other news, more local, more trivial: another animal has been mutilated in the Wyrley area. George wonders briefly which part of the criminal law covers this sort of activity: would it be destruction of property under the Theft Act, or might there be some relevant statute covering one or other particular species of animal involved? He is glad he works in Birmingham, and it will only be a matter of time before he lives there too. He knows he must make the decision; he must stand up to Father's frowns and Mother's tears and Maud's silent yet more insidious dismay. Each morning, as fields dotted with livestock give way to well-ordered suburbs, George feels a perceptible lift in his spirits. Father told him years ago that farm boys and farm-hands were the humble whom God loved and who would inherit the earth. Well, only some of them, he thinks, and not according to any rules of probate that he is familiar with.

There are often schoolboys on the train, at least until Walsall, where they alight for the Grammar School. Their presence and their uniforms occasionally remind George of the dreadful time he was accused of stealing the school's key. But that was all years ago, and most of the boys are quite respectful. There is a group who are sometimes in his carriage, and by overhearing he learns their names: Page, Harrison, Greatorex, Stanley, Ferriday, Quibell. He is even on nodding terms with them, after three or four years.

Most of his days at 54 Newhall Street are spent in conveyancing – work he has seen described by one superior legal expert as 'void of imagination and the free play of thought'. This disparagement does not bother George in the slightest; to him such work is precise, responsible and necessary. He has also drawn up a few wills, and recently begun to obtain clients as a result of his *Railway Law*. Cases involving lost luggage, or unreasonably delayed trains; and one in which a lady slipped and sprained her wrist on Snow Hill station after a railway employee carelessly spilt oil near a locomotive. He has also handled several running-down cases. It appears that the chances of a citizen of Birmingham being struck by a bicycle, horse, motor car, tram or even train are considerably higher than he would ever have anticipated. Perhaps George Edalji, solicitor-at-law, will become known as the man to call in when the human body is surprised by a reckless means of transportation.

George's train home from New Street leaves at 5.25. On the return journey, there are rarely schoolboys. Instead, there is sometimes a larger and more loutish element whom George views with distaste. Remarks are occasionally passed in his direction which are quite unnecessary: about bleach, and his mother forgetting the carbolic, and enquiries about whether he has been down the mine that day. Mostly he ignores such words, though if a young rough chooses to make himself especially offensive, George might be obliged to remind him who he is dealing with. He is not physically brave, but at such times he feels surprisingly calm. He knows the laws of England, and knows he can count on their support.

Birmingham New Street 5.25. Walsall 5.55. This train does not stop at Birchills, for reasons George has never been able to ascertain. Then it is Bloxwich 6.02, Wyrley & Churchbridge 6.09. At 6.10 he nods to Mr Merriman the stationmaster – a moment that often reminds him of His Honour Judge Bacon's 1899 ruling in the Bloomsbury County Court on the illegal retention of expired season tickets – and positions his umbrella over his left wrist for the walk back to the Vicarage.

Campbell

Since his appointment to the Staffordshire Constabulary two years previously, Inspector Campbell had met Captain Anson on several occasions, but never before been summoned to Green Hall. The Chief Constable's house lay on the outskirts of town, among the water meadows on the farther side of the River Sow, and was reputed to be the largest residence between Stafford and Shugborough. As he walked up the gravel drive off the Lichfield Road and the size of the Hall gradually revealed itself, Campbell found himself wondering how big Shugborough must be. That was in the possession of Captain Anson's elder brother. The Chief Constable, being merely a second son, was obliged to content himself with this modest white-painted mansion:

three storeys high, seven or eight windows wide, with a daunting entrance porch supported by four pillars. Over to the right there was a terrace and a sunken rose garden, with beyond it a summer house and a tennis ground.

Campbell took all this in without breaking stride. When the parlourmaid admitted him, he tried to suspend his natural professional habits: working out the likely probity and income of the occupants, and committing to memory items worth stealing – in some cases, items perhaps already stolen. Deliberately incurious, he was nonetheless aware of polished mahogany, white panelled walls, an extravagant hall stand, and to his right a staircase with curious twisted balusters.

He was shown into a room directly to the left of the front door. Anson's study, by the look of it: two high leather chairs on either side of the fire-place, and above it the looming head of a dead elk, or moose. Something antlered anyway; Campbell did not hunt, nor did he aspire to. He was a Birmingham man who had reluctantly applied for transfer when his wife grew sick of the city and longed for the slowness and space of her childhood. Fifteen miles or so, but to Campbell it felt like exile in another land. The local gentry ignored you; the farmers kept to themselves; the miners and iron-workers were a rough lot even by slum standards. Any vague notions that the countryside was romantic were swiftly extinguished. And people out here seemed to dislike the police even more than they did in the city. He'd lost count of the times he'd been made to feel superfluous. A crime might have been committed and even reported, but its victims had a way of letting you know that they preferred their own notion of justice to any purveyed by an inspector whose three-piece suit and bowler hat still smelt of Brummagem.

Anson bustled in, shook hands and seated his visitor. He was a small, compact man in his middle forties, with a double-breasted suit and the neatest moustache Campbell had ever seen: its sides seemed to be mere extensions of his nose, and the whole fitted the triangulation of his upper lip as if bought from a catalogue after precise measurement. His tie was held in place with a gold pin in the shape of the Stafford knot. This proclaimed what everyone already knew: that Captain the Honourable George Augustus Anson, Chief Constable since 1888, Deputy Lieutenant of the county since 1900, was a Staffordshire man through and through. Campbell, being one of the newer breed of professional policemen, did not see why the head of the Constabulary should be the only amateur in the force; but then much in the functioning of society appeared to him arbitrary, based more on antique prejudice than modern sense. Still, Anson was respected by those who worked under him; he was known as a man who backed his officers.

'Campbell, you will have guessed why I asked you to come.'

'I assume the mutilations, sir.'

'Indeed. How many have we now had?'

Campbell had rehearsed this part, but even so reached for his notebook.

'February second, valuable horse belonging to Mr Joseph Holmes. April second, cob belonging to Mr Thomas ripped in exactly the same fashion. May fourth, a cow of Mrs Bungay's similarly treated. Two weeks later, May eighteenth, a horse of Mr Badger's terribly mutilated, and also five sheep on the same night. And then last week, June sixth, two cows belonging to Mr Lockyer.'

'All at night?'

'All at night.'

'Any discernible pattern to events?'

'All the attacks happened within a three-mile radius of Wyrley. And . . . I don't know if it's a pattern, but they all occurred in the first week of the month. Except for those of May eighteenth, which didn't.' Campbell was aware of Anson's eye on him, and hurried on. 'The method of ripping is, however, largely consistent from attack to attack.'

'Consistently disgusting, no doubt.'

Campbell looked at the Chief Constable, unsure if he did, or didn't, want the details. He took silence for regretful assent.

'They were ripped under the belly. Crosswise, and generally in a single cut. The cows . . . the cows also had their udders mutilated. And there was damage inflicted upon . . . upon their sexual parts, sir.'

'It beggars belief, Campbell, doesn't it? Such senseless cruelty to defence-less beasts?'

Campbell pretended to himself that they were not sitting beneath the glassy eye and severed head of the elk or moose. 'Yes, sir.'

'So we are looking for some maniac with a knife.'

'Probably not a knife, sir. I spoke to the veterinary surgeon who attended the later mutilations – Mr Holmes' horse was treated as an isolated incident at the time – and he was puzzled as to the instrument used. It must have been very sharp, but on the other hand it cut into the skin and the first layer of muscle and no further.'

'So why not a knife?'

'Because a knife – a butcher's knife, say – would have gone deeper. At some point, anyway. A knife would have opened up the guts. None of the animals was actually killed in the attacks. Not at the time. They either bled to death or were in such a state when found that they had to be put down.'

'So if not a knife?'

'Something that cuts easily but shallowly. Like a razor. But with more strength than a razor. It could be a tool from the leather trade. Or a farm instrument of some kind. I would assume the man was accustomed to handling animals.'

'Man or men. A vile individual, or a gang of vile individuals. And a vile crime. Have you come across it before?'

'Not in Birmingham, sir.'

'No, indeed.' Anson gave a wan smile and fell briefly silent. Campbell allowed himself to think about the police horses in the Stafford stables: how alert and responsive they were, how warm and smelly and almost furry in their hairiness; how they twitched their ears and put their heads down at you; how they blew through their noses in a way that reminded him of a boiling kettle. What species of human could wish such an animal harm?

'Superintendant Barrett remembers a case some years ago of a wretch who fell into debt and killed his own horse for the insurance. But a murderous spree like this . . . it seems so foreign. In Ireland, of course, the midnight houghing of the landlord's cattle is practically part of the social calendar. But then, little would ever surprise me of a Fenian.'

'Yes, sir.'

'It must be brought to a swift end. These outrages are blackening the reputation of the entire county.'

'Yes, the newspapers –'

'I do not give a fig about the newspapers, Campbell. I care about the honour of Staffordshire. I do not want it deemed the haunt of savages.'

'No, sir.' But the Inspector thought the Chief Constable must be aware of certain recent editorials, none of them complimentary, and some of them personal.

'I would suggest you look into the history of crime in Great Wyrley and its environs in the last years. There have been some . . . peculiar goings-on. And I suggest you work with those who know the area best. There's a very sound Sergeant, can't remember his name. Large, red-faced fellow . . .'

'Upton, sir?'

'Upton, that's it. He's a man who keeps his ear close to the ground.'

'Very well, sir.'

'And I am also drafting in twenty special constables. They can report to Sergeant Parsons.'

'Twenty!'

'Twenty, and damn the expense. It'll come out of my own pocket if necessary. I want a constable under every hedge and behind every bush until this man is caught.'

Campbell was not concerned about the expense. He wondered how you disguised the presence of twenty special constables in an area where the least rumour travelled quicker than the telegraph. Twenty specials, most of them unfamiliar with the territory, against a local man who might just choose to stay at home and laugh at them. And in any case, how many animals could twenty constables protect? Forty, sixty, eighty? And how many animals were there in the district? Hundreds, probably thousands.

'Any further questions?'

'No, sir. Except . . . if I may ask a non-professional question?'

'Go ahead.'

'The porch outside. With the pillars. Do they have a name? The style, I mean?'

Anson looked as if this was the most extraordinary question a serving officer had ever asked. 'Pillars? I wouldn't have the slightest idea. It's the sort of thing my wife would know.'

In the next days, Campbell reviewed the history of crime in Great Wyrley and its immediate purlieus. He found it much as he would have expected. A certain amount of theft, mostly of livestock; various cases of assault; some vagrancy and public drunkenness; one attempted suicide; a girl sentenced for writing abuse on farm buildings; five cases of arson; threatening letters and unsolicited goods received at Wyrley Vicarage; one indecent assault and two indecent behaviours. There had been no previous attacks on animals in the last ten years, as far as he could discover.

Nor could Sergeant Upton, who had policed the district for twice that time, recall any. But the question did remind him of a farmer, now passed on to a better world – unless, sir, it turned out to be a worse one – who was suspected of loving his goose too much, if you catch my meaning. Campbell cut off this parish-pump tittle-tattle; he had quickly marked Upton as someone left over from the time when Constabularies were happy to recruit almost anyone except the obviously halt, lame and half-witted. You might consult Upton about local rumours and grudges, but would hardly trust his hand upon a Bible.

'So, you worked it out then, sir?' the Sergeant wheezed at him.

'Is there something specific you have to tell me, Upton?'

'I wouldn't say that. But takes one to know one. Set one to catch one. I'm sure you'll get there in the end, Inspector. What with you being an Inspector from Birmingham. Oh yes, you'll get there in the end.'

Upton struck him as a mixture of sly ingratiation and vague obstructiveness. Some of the farm-hands were exactly the same. Campbell felt more at ease with Birmingham thieves, who at least lied to you directly.

On the morning of June 27th, the Inspector was called to the Quinton Colliery, where two of the company's valuable horses had been ripped during the night. One had bled to death, and the other, a mare which had suffered additional mutilation, was in the process of being destroyed. The veterinary surgeon confirmed that the same instrument – or, at least, one with precisely the same effects – had been used as before.

Two days later, Sergeant Parsons brought Campbell a letter addressed to 'The Sergeant, Police Station, Hednesford, Staffordshire.' It had been posted from Walsall, and was signed by one William Greatorex.

> I have got a dare-devil face and can run well, and when they formed that gang at Wyrley they got me to join. I knew all about horses and beasts and how to catch them best. They said they would do me if I funked it, so I did, and caught them both lying down at ten minutes to three, and they roused up; and then I caught each under the belly, but they didn't spurt much blood, and one ran away, but the other fell. Now I'll tell you who are in the gang, but you can't prove it without me. There is one named Shipton from Wyrley, and a porter they call Lee, and he's had to stay away, and there's Edalji the lawyer. Now I haven't told you who is at the back of them all, and I shan't unless you promise to do nothing at me. It is not true we always do it when the moon is young, and the one Edalji killed on April 11 was full moon. I've never been locked up yet, and I don't think any of the others have, except the Captain, so I guess they'll get off light.

Campbell reread the letter. *I caught each under the belly, but they didn't spurt much blood, and one ran away, but the other fell.* This all sounded knowledgeable; but any number of people could have examined the dead animals. After the last two cases, the police had to mount guard and turn away sightseers until the surgeon had done his work. Still, *ten minutes to three* . . . there was a strange precision about it.

'Do we know this Greatorex?'

'I take him to be the son of Mr Greatorex of Littleworth Farm.'

'Any dealings? Any reason for him to write to Sergeant Robinson at Hednesford?'

'None at all.'

'And what do you make of this moon business?'

Sergeant Parsons was a stocky, black-haired fellow with a tendency to move his lips while thinking. 'That's what some people have been saying. The new moon, pagan rites and such like. I wouldn't know. But I do know there was no animal killed on April 11th. Not within a week of that date, if I'm not mistaken.'

'You're not.' Parsons was much more to the Inspector's taste than someone like Upton. He was the next generation on, and better trained; not quick, but thoughtful.

William Greatorex proved to be a fourteen-year-old schoolboy whose hand-writing in no way matched the letter. He had never heard of Lee or Shipton, but admitted knowing Edalji, who was sometimes on the same train in the mornings. He had never been to the police station at Hednesford, and did not know the name of the Sergeant who kept it.

Parsons and five special constables searched Littleworth Farm and its outbuildings, but found nothing preternaturally sharp, or spotted with blood, or recently wiped clean. As they left, Campbell asked the Sergeant what he knew about George Edalji.

'Well, sir, he's Indian, isn't he? Half Indian, that is. Little fellow. A bit odd-looking. Lawyer, lives at home, goes up to Birmingham every day. Doesn't exactly involve himself in village life, if you understand me.'

'So not known to go round in a gang?'

'Far from it.'

'Any friends?'

'Not known for it. They're a close family. Something wrong with the sister, I think. Invalid, simple-minded, something. And they say he walks the lanes every evening. Not that he's got a dog or anything. There was a campaign against the family a few years back.'

'I saw it in the day-book. Any reason for that?'

'Who can tell? There was some . . . ill feeling when the Vicar was first given the living. People saying they didn't want a black man in the pulpit telling them what sinners they were, that sort of thing. But this was donkey's years ago. I'm chapel myself. We're more welcoming, in my opinion.'

'This fellow – the son – does he look like a horse-ripper to you?'

Parsons chewed his lips before replying. 'Inspector, let me put it this way. After you've served around here as long as I have, you'll find that no one looks like anything. Or, for that matter, not like anything. Do you follow?'

George

The postman shows George the official marking on the envelope: POSTAGE DEFICIENT. The letter has come from Walsall; his name and office address are written in a clear and decent hand, so George decides to liberate the item.

It costs him twopence, twice the overlooked postage. He is pleased when he recognizes the contents: an order form for *Railway Law*. But there is no cheque or postal order accompanying it. The sender has asked for 300 copies, and filled in his name as Beelzebub.

Three days later, the letters begin again. The same sort of letters; libellous, blasphemous, lunatic. They come to his office, which he feels as an insolent intrusion: this is where he is safe, and respected, where life is orderly. Instinctively he throws the first one away; then puts the rest in a bottom drawer to keep as evidence. George is no longer the anxious adolescent of the earlier persecutions; he is a person of substance now, a solicitor of four years' standing. He is well capable of ignoring such things if he chooses, or of dealing with them appropriately. And the Birmingham police are doubtless more efficient and modern than the Staffordshire Constabulary.

One evening, just after 6.10, George has returned his season ticket to his pocket and is placing his umbrella over his forearm when he becomes aware of a figure falling into step beside him.

'Keeping well, are we, young sir?'

It is Upton, fatter and more red-faced than all those years ago, and probably more stupid too. George does not break stride.

'Good evening,' he replies briskly.

'Enjoying life, are we? Sleeping well?'

At one time George might have felt alarmed, or stopped to await Upton's point. But he is no longer like that.

'Not sleepwalking, anyway, I hope.' George consciously increases his pace, so that the Sergeant is now obliged to puff and pant to keep up. 'Only, you see, we've flooded the district with specials. Flooded it. So even for a so-li-ci-tor to sleepwalk, oh yes, that would be a bad idea.' Without pausing in his step, George casts a scornful glance in the direction of the empty, blustering fool. 'Oh yes, a so-li-ci-tor. I hope you're finding it useful, young sir. Forewarned is forearmed as they say, unless it be the other way round.'

George does not tell his parents about the incident. There is a more immediate concern: the afternoon post has brought a letter from Cannock in familiar handwriting. It is addressed to George and signed 'A Lover of Justice':

> I do not know you, but have sometimes seen you on the
> railway, and do not expect I would like you much if I did
> know you, as I do not like natives. But I think everyone ought
> to have fair treatment, and that is why I write to you, because
> I do not think you have anything to do with the horrid crimes
> that everyone talks about. The people all said it must be you,

because they do not think you are a right sort, and you would
like to do them. So the police got watching you, but they
could not see anything, and now they are watching someone
else . . . If another horse is murdered they will say it is you,
so go away for your holiday, and be away when the next case
happens. The police say it will come at the end of the month
like the last one. Go away before that.

George is quite calm. 'Libel,' he says. 'Indeed, prima facie I would judge
it a criminal libel.'

'It's starting again,' says his mother, and he can tell she is on the edge of
tears. 'It's all starting again. They'll never go away until they have us out.'

'Charlotte,' says Shapurji firmly, 'There is no question of that. We shall
never leave the Vicarage until we go to rest with Uncle Compson. If it is the
Lord's will that we suffer on our journey there, it is not for us to question
the Lord.'

Nowadays, there are moments when George finds himself close to ques-
tioning the Lord. For instance: why should his mother, who is virtue incar-
nate and who succours the poor and sickly of the parish, have to suffer in
this way? And if, as his father maintains, the Lord is responsible for everything, then the Lord is responsible for the Staffordshire Constabulary and its
notorious incompetence. But George cannot say this; increasingly, there are
things he cannot even hint.

He is also beginning to realize that he understands the world a little better
than his parents. He may be only twenty-seven, but the working life of a
Birmingham solicitor offers insights into human nature which may be unavail-
able to a country Vicar. So when his father suggests complaining once more to
the Chief Constable, George disagrees. Anson was against them on the previous
occasion; the man to address is the Inspector charged with the investigation.

'I shall write to him,' says Shapurji.

'No, Father, I think that is my task. And I shall go to see him by myself.
If we both went, he might feel it as a delegation.'

The Vicar is taken aback, but pleased. He likes these assertions of manliness in his son, and lets him have his way.

George writes to request an interview – preferably not at the Vicarage but
at a police station of the Inspector's choice. This strikes Campbell as a little
strange. He nominates Hednesford, and asks Sergeant Parsons to attend.

'Thank you for seeing me, Inspector. I am grateful for your time. I have
three items on my agenda. But first, I would like you to accept this.'

Campbell is a ginger-haired, camel-headed, long-backed man of about forty, who seems even taller sitting down than standing up. He reaches across the table and examines his present: a copy of *Railway Law for the 'Man in the Train'*. He flicks slowly through a few pages.

'The two hundred and thirty eighth copy,' says George. It comes out sounding vainer than he means.

'Very kind of you, sir, but I'm afraid police regulations forbid the accepting of gifts from the general public.' Campbell slides the book back across the desk.

'Oh it's hardly a bribe, Inspector,' says George lightly. 'Can you not regard it as . . . an addition to the library?'

'The library. Do we have a library, Sergeant?'

'Well, we could always start one, sir.'

'Then in that case, Mr Edalji, count me grateful.'

George half-wonders if they are making fun of him.

'It is pronounced *Ay*dlji. Not Ee-dal-ji.'

'Aydlji.' The Inspector makes a rough stab, and pulls a face. 'If you don't mind, I'll settle for calling you Sir.'

George clears his throat. 'The first item on the agenda is this.' He produces the letter from 'A Lover of Justice'. 'There have been five others addressed to my place of business.'

Campbell reads it, passes it to the Sergeant, takes it back, reads it again. He wonders if this is a letter of denunciation or support. Or the former disguised as the latter. If it is a denunciation, why would anyone bring it to the police? If it is support, then why bring it unless you have already been accused? Campbell finds George's motive almost as interesting as the letter itself.

'Any idea who it's from?'

'It's unsigned.'

'I can see that, sir. May I ask if you intend to take the fellow's advice? *Go away for your holiday?*'

'Really, Inspector, that seems to be getting hold of the wrong end of the stick. Do you not regard this letter as a criminal libel?'

'I don't know sir, to be honest. It's lawyers like yourself that decide what's the law and what isn't. From a police point of view, I would say someone was having a lark at your expense.'

'A lark? Do you not think that if this letter were broadcast, with the allegation he pretends to be denying, that I would not be in danger from local farm-hands and miners?'

'I don't know, sir. All I can say is, I can't remember an anonymous letter giving rise to an assault in this district since I've been here. Can you, Parsons?'

The Sergeant shakes his head. 'Now what do you make of this phrase, towards the middle . . . *they do not think you are a right sort*?'

'What do you make of it yourself?'

'Well, you see, it's not anything that's ever been said to me.'

'Very well, Inspector, what I "make" of it is that it is almost certainly a reference to the fact that my father is of Parsee origin.'

'Yes, I suppose it could refer to that.' Campbell bends his ginger head over the letter again, as if scrutinizing it for further meaning. He is trying to make his mind up about this man and his grievance; whether he is a straightforward complainant, or something more complicated.

'Could? Could? What else might it mean?'

'Well, it might mean that you don't fit in.'

'You mean, I do not play in the Great Wyrley cricket team?'

'Do you not, sir?'

George can feel his exasperation rising. 'Nor for that matter do I patronize public houses.'

'Do you not, sir?'

'Nor for that matter do I smoke tobacco.'

'Do you not sir? Well, we'll have to wait and ask the letter writer what he meant by it. If and when we catch him. You said there was something else?'

The second item on George's agenda is to register a complaint against Sergeant Upton, both for his manner and his insinuations. Except that, when repeated back by the Inspector, they somehow cease to be insinuations. Campbell turns them into the plodding remarks of a not very bright member of the Constabulary to a rather pompous and over-sensitive complainant.

George is now in some disarray. He came expecting gratitude for the book, shock at the letter, interest in his predicament. The Inspector has been correct, yet slow; his studied politeness strikes George as a kind of rudeness. Well, he must press on to his third item nevertheless.

'I have a suggestion. For your enquiry.' George pauses, as he planned to, in order to command their full attention. 'Bloodhounds.'

'I beg your pardon?'

'Bloodhounds. They have, as I am sure you are aware, an excellent sense of smell. Were you to acquire a pair of trained bloodhounds, they would surely lead you from the scene of the next mutilation directly to the criminal. They can follow a scent with uncanny precision, and in this district there are no large streams or rivers into which the criminal might wade to confuse them.'

The Staffordshire Constabulary appears unused to practical suggestions from members of the public.

'Bloodhounds,' Campbell repeats. 'Indeed, a pair of them. It sounds like something out of a shilling shocker. "Mr Holmes, they were the footprints of a gigantic hound!"' Then Parsons starts chuckling, and Campbell does not order him to be silent.

It has all gone horribly wrong, especially this last part, which George has thought up on his own account, and not even discussed with Father. He is downcast. As he leaves the station, the two policemen stand on the step watching him go. He hears the Sergeant observe, in a voice that carries, 'Maybe we could keep the bloodhounds in the library.'

The words seem to accompany him all the way back to the Vicarage, where he gives his parents an abbreviated account of the meeting. He decides that if the police decline his suggestions, he will help them even so. He places an advertisement in the *Lichfield Mercury* and other newspapers describing the renewed campaign of letters, and offering a reward of £25 to be paid in the event of criminal conviction. He remembers that his father's advertisement all those years ago merely had an inflammatory effect; but he hopes that this time the offer of money will produce results. He states that he is a solicitor-at-law.

Campbell

Five days later, the Inspector was summoned back to Green Hall. This time he found himself less shy of looking around. He noticed a long-case clock displaying the cycles of the moon, a mezzotint of a biblical scene, a fading Turkey rug, and a fireplace crammed with logs in anticipation of autumn. In the study he was less alarmed by the glassy-eyed moose, and registered leather-bound volumes of *The Field* and *Punch*. The sideboard held a large stuffed fish in a glass case, and a three-decanter tantalus.

Captain Anson waved Campbell to a chair and remained standing himself: a trick of small men in the presence of taller ones, as the Inspector well knew. But he had no time to reflect on the stratagems of authority. The mood this time was not genial.

'Our man has now started taunting us. These Greatorex letters. How many have we had so far?'

'Five, sir.'

'And this came for Mr Rowley at Bridgetown station last evening.' Anson put on his spectacles and began to read:

> Sir, A party whose initials you'll guess will be bringing a new
> hook home by the train from Walsall on Wednesday night,

and he will have it in his special pocket under his coat, and if
you or your pals can get his coat pulled aside a bit you'll get
sight of it, as it's an inch and a half longer than the one he
threw out of sight when he heard someone a sloping it after
him this morning. He will come by that after five or six, or if
he don't come home tomorrow he is sure on Thursday, and
you have made a mistake not keeping all the plain clothes men
at hand. You sent them away too soon. Why, just think, he
did it close where two of them were hiding only a few days
gone by. But sir, he has got eagle eyes, and his ears is as sharp
as a razor, and he is as fleet of foot as a fox, and as noiseless,
and he crawls up on all fours to the poor beasts, and fondles
them a bit, and then he pulls his hook smart across 'em, and
out their entrails fly, before they guess they are hurt. You
want 100 detectives, to run him in red-handed, because he is
so fly, and knows every nook and corner. You know who it is,
and I can prove it; but until £100 reward is offered for a
conviction, I shan't split no more.

Anson looked at Campbell, inviting comment. 'None of my men saw
anything thrown away, sir. And nothing resembling a hook has been found.
He may or may not mutilate animals like that, but the entrails do not fly out,
as we know. Do you want me to watch the Walsall trains?'

'I hardly think that after this letter some fellow is going to turn up in a
long overcoat in the middle of summer, inviting to be searched.'

'No, sir. Do you think the £100 requested is a deliberate response to the
lawyer's offer of a reward?'

'Possibly. That was a gross piece of impertinence.' Anson paused, and
picked another sheet of paper from his desk. 'But the other letter – to Sergeant
Robinson at Hednesford – is worse. Well, judge for yourself.' Anson handed
it over.

There will be merry times at Wyrley in November, when they
start on little girls, for they will do twenty wenches like the
horses before next March. Don't think you are likely to catch
them cutting the beasts; they are too quiet, and lie low for
hours, till your men have gone . . . Mr Edalji, him they said
was locked up, is going to Brum on Sunday night to see the
Captain, near Northfield, about how it's to be carried on with
so many detectives about, and I believe they are going to do

some cows in the daytime instead of at night . . . I think they
are going to kill beasts nearer here soon, and I know Cross
Keys Farm and West Cannock Farm are the first two on the
list . . . You bloated blackguard, I will shoot you with your
father's gun through your thick head if you come in my way
or go sneaking to any of my pals.

'That's bad, sir. That's very bad. This'd better not get out. There'll be
panic in every village. Twenty wenches . . . People are worried enough for
their livestock as it is.'

'You have children, Campbell?'

'A boy. And a little girl.'

'Yes. The only good thing in this letter is the threat to shoot Sergeant
Robinson.'

'That's a good thing, sir?'

'Oh, maybe not for Sergeant Robinson himself. But it means our man has
overstepped himself. Threatening to murder a police officer. Put that on the
indictment and we'll be able to get penal servitude for life.'

If we can find the letter writer, thought Campbell. 'Northfield, Hednesford,
Walsall – he's trying to send us in all directions.'

'No doubt. Inspector, let me summarize, if you have no objection, and you
tell me if you disagree with my thinking.'

'Yes, sir.'

'Now, you are a capable officer – no, don't disagree already.' Anson gave
the slightest smile he had in his repertoire. 'You are a very capable officer.
But this investigation is now three and a half months old, including three
weeks with twenty specials under your command. No one has been charged,
no one arrested, no one even seriously taken aside and looked over. And the
mutilations have continued. Agreed?'

'Agreed, sir.'

'Local cooperation, which I am aware you compare unfavourably with
what you experienced in the great city of Birmingham, has been better than
usual. There is, for once, a wider interest than normal in aiding the
Constabulary. But the best suspicions we have obtained so far have come in
anonymous denunciations. This mysterious "Captain", for example, who
lives so inconveniently on the other side of Birmingham. Should we be tempted
by him? I think not. What possible interest might some Captain miles away
have in mutilating animals belonging to people he has never met? Though it
would be poor detective work not to take a visit to Northfield.'

'Agreed.'

'So we are looking for local people, as we have always assumed. Or a local person. I favour the notion of more than one. Three or four, perhaps. It makes more sense. I would imagine one letter writer, one postboy to travel to different towns, one person skilled at handling animals, and one planner to guide them all. A gang, in other words. Whose members have no love for the police. Indeed, take pleasure in trying to mislead us. Who like to boast.

'They name names to confuse us. Of course. But even so, one name comes up again and again. Edalji. Edalji who is going to meet the Captain. Edalji who they said was locked up. Edalji the lawyer is in the gang. I have always had my suspicions, but so far have felt it proper to keep them to myself. I told you to look up the files. There was a campaign of letter-writing before, mainly against the father. Pranks, hoaxes, petty theft. We nearly got him at the time. Eventually I gave the Vicar a pretty heavy warning that we knew who was behind it, and not long afterwards it stopped. QED, you might say, though regrettably not enough to convict. Still, if he didn't own up, at least I put a stop to it. For – what? – seven, eight years.

'Now it's started again, and in the same place. And Edalji's name keeps coming up. That first Greatorex letter mentions three names, but the only one of them the lad himself knows is Edalji. Therefore, Edalji knows Greatorex. And he did the same the first time round – included himself in the denunciations. Only this time he's older, and not satisfied with catching blackbirds and wringing their necks. This time he's after bigger things, literally. Cows, horses. And not being much of a physical specimen himself, he recruits others to help him do the work. And now he's raising the stakes, and threatens us with twenty wenches. Twenty wenches, Campbell.'

'Indeed, sir. You will allow me to put one or two questions?'

'I will.'

'For a start, why should he denounce himself?'

'To put us off the scent. He deliberately includes his own name in lists of people we know can have nothing to do with the matter.'

'So he also offers a reward for his own capture?'

'That way he knows there will be no one to claim it but himself.' Anson gave a dry chuckle, but the joke seemed lost on Campbell. 'And of course, it's a further provocation to the police. Look how the Constabulary blunders about, while a poor honest citizen has to offer his own tin to clear up crime. Come to think of it, that advertisement might be construed as a libel on the force . . .'

'But – excuse me, sir – why should a Birmingham solicitor assemble a gang of local roughs in order to mutilate animals?'

'You've met him, Campbell. How did he strike you?'

The Inspector reviewed his impressions. 'Intelligent. Nervous. Rather eager to please at first. Then a little quick to take offence. He offered us some advice and we didn't seem keen on it. Suggested we try using bloodhounds.'

'Bloodhounds? You're sure he didn't say native trackers?'

'No, sir, bloodhounds. The odd thing was, listening to his voice – it was an educated voice, a lawyer's voice – I found myself thinking at one point, if you shut your eyes, you'd think him an Englishman.'

'Whereas if you left them open, you wouldn't exactly mistake him for a member of the Brigade of Guards?'

'You could put it that way, sir.'

'Yes. It sounds as if – eyes open or eyes shut – your impression was of someone who feels himself superior. How might I put it? Someone who thinks he belongs to a higher caste?'

'Possibly. But why should such a person wish to rip horses? Rather than prove he's clever and superior by, say, embezzling large sums of money?'

'Who's to say he isn't up to that as well? Frankly, Campbell, the why interests me much less than the how and the when and the what.'

'Yes, sir. But if you're asking me to arrest this fellow, it might help to have a clue as to his motive.'

Anson disliked this sort of question, which in his view was nowadays asked far too frequently in police work. There was a passion for delving into the mind of the criminal. What you did was catch a fellow, arrest him, charge him, and get him sent away for a few years, the more the merrier. It was of little interest to probe the mental functionings of a malefactor as he discharged his pistol or smashed in your window. The Chief Constable was about to say as much when Campbell prompted him.

'We can, after all, rule out profit as a motive. It is not as if he were destroying his own property with a view to making some claim against the insurance.'

'A man who sets fire to his neighbour's rick does not do so for profit. He does it out of malice. He does it for the pleasure of seeing flames in the sky and fear on people's faces. In Edalji's case there might be some deep hatred of animals. You will doubtless enquire into that. Or if there is some pattern in the timing of the attacks, if most of them happen at the start of the month, there might be some sacrificial principle involved. Perhaps the mysterious instrument we are seeking is a ritual knife of Indian origin. A kukri or something. Edalji's father is a Parsee, I understand. Do they not worship fire?'

Campbell acknowledged that professional methods had so far turned up nothing; but was unwilling to see them replaced by such loose speculation. And if Parsees worshipped fire, then would you not expect the man to be committing arson?

'By the way, I am not asking you to arrest the lawyer.'

'No, sir?'

'No. What I am asking – ordering – you to do is concentrate your resources on him. Watch the Vicarage discreetly in the day, have him followed to the station, assign a man to Birmingham – in case he is lunching with the mysterious Captain – and then cover the house entirely after dark. Have it so that he cannot step out of the back door and spit without hitting a special constable. He will do something, I know he will do something.'

George

George attempts to continue his life as normal: this is, after all, his right as a freeborn Englishman. But it is difficult when you feel yourself spied upon; when dark figures trespass the Vicarage grounds at night; when things have to be kept from Maud and even, at times, from Mother. Prayers are uttered as forcefully as ever by Father, and repeated as anxiously by the womenfolk. George feels himself ever less confident of the Lord's protection. The one moment in the day he considers himself safe is when his father locks the bedroom door.

At times he wants to pull back the curtains, throw open the window, and hurl sarcastic words at the watchers he knows are out there. What a ludicrous squandering of public money, he thinks. To his surprise, he finds that he is becoming the owner of a temper. To his further surprise, it makes him feel rather grown up. One evening, he is tramping the lanes as usual and there is a special constable trailing a distance behind him. George does a sudden about-face and accosts his pursuer, a foxy-faced man in a tweed suit who looks as if he would be more at home in a low public house.

'Can I help you with your route?' George asks, barely holding on to politeness.

'I can look after myself, thank you.'

'You're not from hereabouts?'

'Walsall, since you ask.'

'This is not the way to Walsall. Why are you walking the lanes of Great Wyrley at this time of day?'

'I might very well ask you the same question.'

This is one insolent fellow, thinks George. 'You are following me on the instructions of Inspector Campbell. It's perfectly obvious. Do you take me for an idiot? The only point of interest is whether Campbell ordered you to make yourself visible at all times, in which case your behaviour may amount to obstruction of the public thoroughfare, or whether he instructed you to remain concealed, in which case you are an entirely incompetent special constable.'

The fellow just gives a grin. 'That's between him and me, wouldn't you say?'

'I would say this, my good man,' – and the anger is now as strong as sin – 'you and your sort are a considerable waste of the public budget. You have been clambering over the village for weeks and have nothing, absolutely nothing, to show for it.'

The constable simply grins once more. 'Softly, softly,' he says.

That suppertime, the Vicar suggests that George take Maud to Aberystwyth for a day's outing. His tone is that of a command, but George flatly refuses: he has too much work, and no desire for a holiday. He does not budge until Maud joins in the plea, then accedes reluctantly. On the Tuesday, they are away from dawn until late at night. The sun shines; the train journey – all 124 miles by the GWR – is pleasant and without mishap; brother and sister feel an unwonted sense of freedom. They walk the seafront, inspect the façade of University College, and stroll to the end of the pier (admission, 2d). It is a beautiful August day with a gentle wind, and they are absolutely agreed that they do not want to take a pleasure boat around the bay; nor will they join the crouching pebble-pickers on the beach. Instead, they take the tramway from the north end of the promenade up to Cliff Gardens on Constitution Hill. As the tram ascends, and afterwards descends, they have a fine retrospect of the town and of Cardigan Bay. Everyone they talk to in the resort is civil, including the uniformed policeman who advises the Belle Vue Hotel for lunch, or the Waterloo if they are strictly temperance. Over roast chicken and apple pie they discuss safe topics, like Horace and Great-Aunt Stoneham, and the people at other tables. After lunch they climb to the Castle, which George describes good-humouredly as an offence under the Sale of Goods Act, consisting as it does of only a few ruined towers and fragments. A passer-by points out, over there, just to the left of Constitution Hill, the peak of Snowdon. Maud is delighted, but George cannot make it out at all. One day, she promises, she will buy him a pair of binoculars. On the train home she asks if the Aberystwyth tramway would be governed by the same laws as the railway; then pleads with George to set her another conundrum, as he used to do in the schoolroom. He does his best, because he loves his sister, who for once is looking almost joyful; but his heart is not in it.

The next day, a postcard is delivered to Newhall Street. It is a vile effusion accusing him of having guilty relations with a woman in Cannock: 'Sir. Do you think it seemly for one in your position to be having connection with ----- -----'s sister every night seeing she is going to marry Frank Smith the

Socialist.' Needless to say, he has heard of neither party. He looks at the post-mark: Wolverhampton 12.30 p.m. Aug 4, 1903. This disgusting libel was being thought up just as he and Maud were sitting down to lunch at the Belle Vue Hotel.

The postcard throws him into envious thoughts of Horace, now a happy-go-lucky penpusher with the Income Tax in Manchester. Horace seems to glide through life unscathed; he goes from day to day, his ambition amounting to no more than a slow climb of the ladder, his contentment deriving from female companionship, about which he drops unsubtle hints. Most of all, Horace has escaped Great Wyrley. George as never before feels it a curse to be the first-born, and to have expectations placed upon him; also a curse to have been given more intelligence and less self-confidence than his brother. Horace has every reason to doubt himself, but doesn't; George, despite his academic success and professional qualifications, is blighted by shyness. When he is behind a desk, explaining the law, he can be clear and even assertive. But he has no ability to talk lightly or superficially; he does not know how to put people at their ease; he is aware that some consider him odd-looking.

On Monday 17th August 1903, George takes the 7.39 to New Street, as normal; he returns by the 5.25, as normal, reaching the Vicarage shortly before half past six. He works for a while, then puts on a coat and walks to see the bootmaker, Mr John Hands. He returns to the Vicarage just before 9.30, eats supper, and retires to the room where he sleeps with his father. The Vicarage doors are locked and bolted, the bedroom door is locked, and George sleeps as interruptedly as he has done in recent weeks. The next morning he is awake at 6, the bedroom door is unlocked at 6.40, and he catches the 7.39 to New Street.

He does not realize that these are the last normal twenty-four hours of his life.

Campbell

It rained heavily on the night of the 17th, with the wind coming in squalls. But by dawn it had cleared, and as the miners set off for the early shift at Great Wyrley Colliery there was a freshness in the air that comes after summer rain. A pit lad named Henry Garrett was passing a field on his way to work when he noticed one of the Colliery's ponies in a state of distress. Drawing nearer, he saw that it was barely able to stand, and dropping blood fast.

The lad's cries brought a group of miners squelching across the field to examine the lengthy cut across the pony's abdomen, and the churned mud beneath it spotted with red. Within the hour Campbell had arrived with half a dozen specials, and Mr Lewis the veterinary surgeon had been sent for. Campbell asked who had been responsible for patrolling this sector. PC Cooper replied that he had passed the field at about eleven o'clock, and the animal had appeared to be all right. But the night was dark, and he had not got close to the pony.

It was the eighth case in six months, and the sixteenth animal to be mutilated. Campbell thought a little about the pony, and the affection even the roughest miners often displayed towards such beasts; he thought a little about Captain Anson and his concern for the honour of Staffordshire; but what was most in his head as he looked at the oozing slash and watched the pony stagger was the letter the Chief Constable had shown him. *There will be merry times at Wyrley in November*, he recalled. And then: *for they will do twenty wenches like the horses before next March*. And two other words: *little girls*.

Campbell was a capable officer, as Anson had said; he was dutiful and level-headed. He did not have preconceptions about a criminal type; nor was he given to over-hasty theorizing or self-indulgent intuition. Even so: the field in which the outrage had occurred lay directly between the Colliery and Wyrley. If you drew a straight line from the field to the village, the first house you would come to was the Vicarage. Common logic, as well as the Chief Constable, argued for a visit.

'Anyone here watching the Vicarage last night?'

Constable Judd identified himself, and talked rather too much about the devilish weather and the rain getting in his eyes, which may have meant that he had spent half the night sheltering under a tree. Campbell did not imagine policemen to be free of human failings. But in any case, Judd had seen no one come and no one go; the lights had been turned out at half past ten, as they invariably were. Still, it had been a wild old night of it, Inspector . . .

Campbell looked at the time: 7.15. He sent Markew, who knew the solicitor, to detain him at the station. He told Cooper and Judd to wait for the surgeon and keep away gawpers, then led Parsons and the remaining specials by the most direct route to the Vicarage. There were a couple of hedges to squeeze through, and the railway to cross by a subterranean passage, but they managed it without difficulty in under fifteen minutes. Well before eight o'clock Campbell had posted a constable at each corner of the house while he and Parsons made the knocker thunder. It was not just the twenty wenches; there was also the threat to shoot Robinson in the head with somebody's gun.

The maid showed the two policemen into the kitchen, where the Vicar's wife and daughter were finishing breakfast. To Parsons' eye the mother looked scared and the half-caste daughter sickly.

'I should like to speak to your son George.'

The Vicar's wife was thin and slightly built; most of her hair had gone white. She spoke quietly, with a pronounced Scottish accent. 'He has already left for his office. He takes the seven thirty-nine. He is a solicitor in Birmingham.'

'I am aware of that, Madam. Then I must ask you to show me his clothing. All his clothing, without exception.'

'Maud, go and fetch your father.'

Parsons asked with a mere turn of the head whether he should follow the girl, but Campbell indicated not. A minute or so later the Vicar appeared: a short, powerful, light-skinned fellow with none of the oddities of his son. White-haired, but good-looking in a Hindoo sort of a way, Campbell thought.

The Inspector repeated his request.

'I must ask you what the subject of your inquiry is, and whether you have a search warrant.'

'A pit pony has been found . . .' Campbell hesitated briefly, given the presence of women, '. . . in a field nearby . . . someone has injured it.'

'And you suspect my son George of the deed.'

The mother put an arm around her daughter.

'Let us say that it would be very helpful to exclude him from the investigation if possible.' That old lie, Campbell thought, almost ashamed of bringing it out again.

'But you do not have a search warrant?'

'Not with me at the moment, sir.'

'Very well. Charlotte, show him George's clothes.'

'Thank you. And you will not object, I take it, if I ask my constables to search the house and the immediate grounds.'

'Not if it helps exclude my son from your investigation.'

So far, so good, thought Campbell. In the slums of Birmingham, he'd have had the father going for him with a poker, the mother bawling, and the daughter trying to scratch his eyes out. Though in some ways that was easier, being almost an admission of guilt.

Campbell told his men to look out for any knives or razors, agricultural or horticultural implements that might have been used in the attack, then went upstairs with Parsons. The lawyer's clothing was laid out on a bed, including, as had been requested, shirts and underlinen. It appeared clean, and dry to the touch.

'This is all his clothing?'

The mother paused before answering. 'Yes,' she said. And then, after a few seconds, 'Apart from what he has on.'

Well of course, thought Parsons, I didn't believe he went to work naked. What a queer statement. 'I need to see his knife,' he said casually.

'His knife?' She looked at him wonderingly. 'You mean, the knife he eats with?'

'No, his knife. Every young man has a knife.'

'My son is a solicitor,' said the Vicar rather sharply. 'He works in an office. He does not sit around whittling sticks.'

'I do not know how many times I have been told that your son is a solicitor. I am well aware of that. As I am of the fact that every young man has a knife.'

After some whispering, the daughter went away and returned with a short, stubby item which she handed over defiantly. 'This is his botany spud,' she said.

Campbell saw at a glance that the item could not possibly have inflicted the sort of damage he had recently witnessed. Nevertheless, he pretended to considerable interest, taking the spud over to the window and turning it in the light.

'We've found these, sir.' A constable was holding out a case containing four razors. One of them seemed to be wet. Another had red stains on the back.

'Those are my razors,' said the Vicar quickly.

'One of them is wet.'

'No doubt because I shaved myself with it barely an hour ago.'

'And your son – what does he shave with?'

There was a pause. 'One of these.'

'Ah. So they are not, strictly speaking, your razors, sir?'

'On the contrary. This has always been my set of razors. I have owned them for twenty years or more, and when it became time for my son to shave, I allowed him to use one.'

'Which he still does?'

'Yes.'

'You do not trust him with razors of his own?'

'He does not need razors of his own.'

'Now why should he not be allowed razors of his own?' Campbell aired it as a half-question, waiting to see if anyone chose to pick it up. No, he thought not. There was something slightly queer about the family, not that he could put his finger on it. They weren't being uncooperative; but at the same time he felt them less than straightforward.

'He was out last night, your son.'

'Yes.'

'How long for?'

'I'm not really sure. An hour, perhaps more. Charlotte?'

Again, the wife seemed to take an unconscionable time considering a simple question. 'One and a half, one and three-quarters,' she finally whispered.

Time enough and plenty to get to the field and back, as Campbell had just proved. 'And when would this be?'

'Between about eight and nine thirty,' answered the Vicar, even though Parsons' question had been addressed to his wife. 'He went to the boot-maker.'

'No, I meant after that.'

'After that, no.'

'But I asked if he went out in the night and you said that he did.'

'No, Inspector, you asked if he went out last night, not in the night.'

Campbell nodded. He was no fool, this clergyman. 'Well, I should like to see his boots.'

'His boots?'

'Yes, the boots he went out in. And show me which trousers he was wearing.'

These were dry, but now that Campbell looked at them again, he saw black mud around the bottoms. The boots, when produced, were also encrusted with mud, and were still damp.

'I found this too, sir,' said the sergeant who brought the boots. 'Feels damp to me.' He handed over a blue serge coat.

'Where did you find this?' The Inspector passed his hand over the coat. 'Yes, it's damp.'

'Hanging by the back door just above the boots.'

'Let me feel that,' said the Vicar. He ran a hand down a sleeve and said, 'It's dry.'

'It's damp,' repeated Campbell, thinking, And what's more, I'm a policeman. 'So who does this belong to?'

'To George.'

'To George? I asked you to show me all his clothing. Without exception.'

'We did' – the mother this time. 'All this is what I think of as his clothing. That's just an old house-coat he never wears.'

'Never?'

'Never.'

'Does anyone else wear it?'

'No.'

'How very mysterious. A coat that nobody wears yet which hangs usefully by the back door. Let me start again. This is your son's coat. When did he last wear it?'

The parents looked at one another. Eventually the mother said, 'I have no idea. It is too shabby for him to go out in, and he has no cause to wear it in the house. Perhaps he wore it for gardening.'

'Now let me see,' said Campbell, holding the coat to the window. 'Yes, there's a hair here. And . . . another. And . . . yes, another. Parsons?'

The Sergeant took a look and nodded.

'Let me see, Inspector.' The Vicar was allowed to inspect the coat. 'That's not a hair. I don't see any hairs.'

Now mother and daughter joined in, tugging at the blue serge, like in a bazaar. He waved them away and laid the coat on a table. 'There,' he said, pointing at the most obvious hair.

'That's a roving,' said the daughter. 'It's not a hair, it's a roving.'

'What's a roving?'

'A thread, a loose thread. Anyone can see that, anyone who's ever sewn anything.'

Campbell had never sewn in his life, but he could recognize panic in a young woman's voice.

'And look at these stains, Sergeant.' On the right sleeve there were two separate patches, one whitish, one darkish. Neither he nor Parsons spoke, but they were each thinking the same. Whitish, the pony's saliva; darkish, the pony's blood.

'I told you, it's just his old house-coat. He would never go out in it. Certainly not to the bootmaker's.'

'Then why is it damp?'

'It's not damp.'

The daughter came up with another explanation useful to her brother. 'Perhaps it just feels damp to you because it was hanging by the back door.'

Unimpressed, Campbell gathered up the coat, the boots, the trousers and other clothing identified as having been worn the previous evening; he also took the razors. The family was instructed not to make contact with George until given police permission. He stationed one man outside the Vicarage, and ordered the others to quarter the grounds. Then he returned with Parsons to the field, where Mr Lewis had completed his examination and sought leave to destroy the pony. The surgeon's report would be with Campbell the following day. The Inspector asked him to cut a piece of skin from the dead animal. PC Cooper was to take this, along with the clothes, to Dr Butter in Cannock.

At Wyrley station Markew reported that the lawyer had curtly refused his request to wait. Campbell and Parsons therefore took the first available train – the 9.53 – into Birmingham.

'Strange family,' said the Inspector, as they were crossing the canal between Bloxwich and Walsall.

'Very strange.' The Sergeant chewed his lip for a while. 'If you don't mind my saying, sir, they seemed honest enough in themselves.'

'I know what you mean. It's something the criminal classes would do well to study.'

'What's that, sir?'

'Lying no more than you need to.'

'That'll be the day.' Parsons chuckled. 'Still, you have to feel sorry for them, in a way. Happening to that sort of family. A black sheep, if you'll pardon the expression.'

'I certainly will.'

Shortly after 11 o'clock the two policemen presented themselves at 54 Newhall Street. It was a small, two-room office, with a woman secretary guarding the solicitor's door. George Edalji sat passively behind his desk, looking ill.

Campbell, alert for any sudden movement from the man, said, 'We don't want to search you here, but you must let me have your pistol.'

Edalji looked at him blankly. 'I have no pistol.'

'What's that, then?' The Inspector gestured at a long, shiny object on the desk before him.

The solicitor sounded intensely weary as he spoke. 'That, Inspector, is the key to the door of a railway carriage.'

'Just joking,' Campbell replied. But he was thinking: keys. The key to Walsall School all those years ago, and now here's another one. There's something very queer about this fellow.

'I use it as a paperweight,' the lawyer explained. 'As you might have cause to recall, I am an authority on railway law.'

Campbell nodded. Then he cautioned the man and arrested him. In a cab on the way to the Newton Street lock-up, Edalji said to the officers, 'I am not surprised at this. I have been expecting it for some time.'

Campbell glanced at Parsons, who made a contemporaneous note of these words.

George

At Newton Street they took away his money, his watch and a small pocket knife. They also attempted to take his handkerchief, in case he sought to strangle himself. George protested that it was quite inadequate to such a purpose, and was allowed to keep it.

They put him in a light, clean cell for an hour, then took him by the 12.40 from New Street to Cannock. 1.08 depart Walsall, George thought. Birchills 1.12. Bloxwich 1.16. Wyrley & Churchbridge 1.24. Cannock 1.29. The two policemen said they would not restrain him on the journey, for which George was grateful. Even so, when the train pulled in to Wyrley, he lowered his head and raised a hand to his cheek in case Mr Merriman or the porter spotted the Sergeant's uniform and spread the news.

At Cannock he was driven in a trap to the police station. There his height was measured and his particulars taken. His clothing was examined for bloodstains. An officer asked him to remove his cuffs and then inspected his wristbands. He said, 'Did you wear this shirt in the field last night? You must have changed it. There's no blood on it.'

George did not answer. He saw no point in doing so. If he replied No to the question, the officer would come back with, 'So you admit being in the field last night. What shirt *did* you wear?' George felt that he had been entirely cooperative so far; he would henceforth give sufficient answers to questions that were necessary and not leading.

They put him in a tiny cell with little light and less air, and which smelt of a public convenience. It lacked even water for washing purposes. They had taken his watch but he imagined it to be about half past two. A fortnight ago, he thought, just a fortnight ago, Maud and I had finished our roast chicken and apple pie at the Belle Vue, and were walking along Marine Terrace towards the Castle Grounds, where I made a light remark about the Sale of Goods Act and a passer-by attempted to point out Snowdon. Now he sat on a low bed in a police cell, taking the shortest breaths he could, and waiting for the next thing to happen. After a couple of hours he was brought to the interview room where Campbell and Parsons awaited him.

'So, Mr Edalji, you know what we're here for.'

'I know what you're here for. And it's *Ay*dlji, not Ee-dal-ji.'

Campbell ignored this. He thought: I'll call you what I like from now on, Mr Solicitor. 'And you understand your legal rights?'

'I think I do, Inspector. I understand the rules of police procedure. I understand the laws of evidence, and the right of the accused to remain silent. I understand the redress available in cases of wrongful arrest and false imprisonment. I understand, for that matter, the laws of defamation. And I also know how soon you must charge me, and how soon after that you must bring me before the magistrates.'

Campbell had been expecting some show of defiance; although not of the normal kind, which often required a sergeant and several constables to subdue.

'Well, that makes it easier for us too. You'll doubtless inform us if we step out of line. So, you know why you're here.'

'I am here because you have arrested me.'

'Mr Edalji, there's no point in being clever with me. I've dealt with far harder cases than you. Now, tell me why you're here.'

'Inspector, I do not intend to answer the sort of general remarks you doubtless employ when seeking to gull common criminals. Nor do I intend to respond if you set off on what our judiciary would dismiss as a fishing expedition. I shall answer, as truthfully as I can, any specific and relevant questions you choose to ask.'

'That's very good of you. Then tell me about the Captain.'

'What Captain?'

'You tell me.'

'I don't know anyone called the Captain. Unless you mean Captain Anson.'

'Don't try impertinence with me, George. We know you visit the Captain at Northfield.'

'I have never been to Northfield in my life, as far as I am aware. On what dates am I supposed to have visited Northfield?'

'Tell me about the Great Wyrley gang.'

'The Great Wyrley gang? Now *you* are talking like a shilling shocker, Inspector. I have never heard anyone speak of such a gang.'

'When did you meet Shipton?'

'I know no one called Shipton.'

'When did you meet Lee the porter?'

'The porter? A station porter, do you mean?'

'Let's call him a station porter, if that's what you're telling me.'

'I know no porters called Lee. Though for all I know I may have greeted porters not knowing their names, and one of them might have been called Lee. The porter at Wyrley & Churchbridge is called Janes.'

'When did you meet William Greatorex?'

'I know no one . . . Greatorex? That boy on the train? The one who goes to Walsall Grammar School? What's he got to do with this?'

'You tell me.'

Silence.

'So are Shipton and Lee members of the Great Wyrley gang?'

'Inspector, my answer to that is fully implied in my previous answers. Please do not insult my intelligence.'

'Your intelligence is important to you, isn't it, Mr Edalji?'

Silence.

'It's important to you to be more intelligent than other people, isn't it?'

Silence.

'And to demonstrate that greater intelligence.'

Silence.

'Are you the Captain?'

Silence.

'Tell me exactly what your movements were yesterday.'

'Yesterday. I went to work as usual. I was at my office at Newhall Street all day, except for when I ate my sandwiches in St Philip's Place. I returned as usual, about 6.30. I transacted some business –'

'What business?'

'Some legal business I had brought from the office. The conveyancing of a small property.'

'And then?'

'Then I left the house and walked to see Mr Hands the bootmaker.'

'Why?'

'Because he is making me a pair of boots.'

'Is Hands in on this too?'

Silence.

'And?'

'And I talked to him while he made a fitting. Then I walked around for a while. Then I returned shortly before nine thirty for my supper.'

'Where did you walk?'

'Around. Around the lanes. I walk every day. I never really pay attention.'

'So you walked over towards the Colliery?'

'No, I don't think so.'

'Come on, George, you can do better than this. You said you walked in every direction but you didn't remember which. One of the directions from Wyrley is towards the Colliery. Why wouldn't you walk in that direction?'

'If you will give me a moment.' George pressed his fingers to his forehead. 'I remember now. I walked along the road to Churchbridge. Then I turned right towards Watling Street Road, then to Walk Mill, then along the road as far as Green's farm.'

Campbell thought this very impressive for someone who didn't remember where he walked. 'And who did you meet at Green's farm?'

'No one. I didn't go in. I don't know those people.'

'And who did you meet on your walk?'

'Mr Hands.'

'No. You met Mr Hands before your walk.'

'I'm not sure. Did you not have one of your special constables following me? You need only consult the man to get a full account of my movements.'

'Oh, I will, I will. And not just him either. So then you had your supper. And then you went out again.'

'No. After supper I went to bed.'

'And then got up later and went out?'

'No, I have told you when I went out.'

'What were you wearing?'

'What was I wearing? Boots, trousers, jacket, overcoat.'

'What sort of coat?'

'Blue serge.'

'The one that hangs by the kitchen door where you leave your boots?'

George frowned. 'No, that's an old house-coat. I wore one I keep on the hall stand.'

'Then why was your coat by the back door damp?'

'I have no idea. I haven't touched that coat for weeks, if not months.'

'You wore it last night. We can prove it.'

'Then this is clearly a matter for the court.'

'The clothes you were wearing last night had animal hairs on them.'

'That's not possible.'

'Are you calling your mother a liar?'

Silence.

'We asked your mother to show us the clothes you were wearing last night. She did so. Some of them had animal hairs on them. How do you explain that?'

'Well, I do live in the country, Inspector. For my sins.'

'For your sins? But you don't milk cows and shoe horses, do you?'

'That is self-evident. Perhaps I leaned on a gate into a field which had cows in it.'

'It rained last night and your boots were wet this morning.'

Silence.

'That is a question, Mr Edalji.'

'No, Inspector, that is a tendentious statement. You have examined my boots. If they were wet, it does not surprise me. The lanes are wet at this time of year.'

'But the fields are wetter, and it rained last night.'

Silence.

'So you are denying that you left the Vicarage between the hours of 9.30 p.m. and daybreak?'

'Later than daybreak. I leave the house at 7.20.'

'But you cannot possibly prove that.'

'On the contrary. My father and I sleep in the same room. Each night he locks the door.'

The Inspector stopped in his tracks. He looked across at Parsons, who was still writing the last words down. He'd heard some jerry-built alibis in his time, but really . . . 'I'm sorry, but could you repeat what you just said.'

'My father and I sleep in the same room. Each night he locks the door.'

'How long has this . . . arrangement been going on?'

'Since I was ten.'

'And you are now?'

'Twenty-seven.'

'I see.' Campbell doesn't see at all. 'And your father – when he locks the door – you know where he puts the key?'

'He doesn't put it anywhere. He leaves it in the lock.'

'So it is perfectly easy for you to leave the room?'

'I have no need to leave the room.'

'Call of nature?'

'There is a pot beneath my bed. But I never use it.'

'Never?'

'Never.'

'Very well. The key is always in the lock. So you would not have to go hunting for it?'

'My father is a very light sleeper, and is currently suffering from lumbago. He wakes very easily. The key makes a very loud squeak when it turns.'

It was all Campbell could do not to laugh in the man's face. Who did he take them for?

'That all seems remarkably convenient, if you don't mind my saying, sir. Have you never thought of oiling the lock?'

Silence.

'How many razors do you own?'

'How many razors? I don't own a razor.'

'But you do shave, I presume?'

'I shave with one of my father's.'

'Why are you not trusted with your own razor?'

Silence.

'How old are you, Mr Edalji?'

'I have already answered that question three times today. I suggest you consult your notes.'

'A twenty-seven-year-old man who is not allowed a razor and is locked in his bedroom every night by his father who is a light sleeper. You realize what an exceptionally rare individual you are?'

Silence.

'Exceptionally rare, I'd say. And . . . tell me about animals.'

'That's not a question, that's a fishing expedition.' George realized the incongruity of his reply, and couldn't help smiling.

'My apologies.' The Inspector was becoming increasingly riled. He'd gone easy on the man so far. Well, it wouldn't take much to turn a conceited lawyer into a snivelling schoolboy. 'Here is a question, then. What do you think about animals? Do you like them?'

'What do I think about animals? Do I like them? No, generally, I do not like them.'

'I might have guessed that.'

'No, Inspector, let me explain.' George had sensed a hardening in Campbell's attitude, and thought it good tactics to relax his rules of engagement. 'When I was four, I was taken to see a cow. It soiled itself. That is almost my first memory.'

'Of a cow soiling itself?'

'Yes. I think from that day I have distrusted animals.'

'Distrusted?'

'Yes. What they might do. They are unreliable.'

'I see. And that is your first memory, you say?'

'Yes.'

'And since then you have distrusted animals. All animals.'

'Well, not the cat we have at home. Or Aunt Stoneham's dog. I am very fond of them.'

'I see. But large animals. Like cows.'

'Yes.'

'Horses?'

'Horses are unreliable, yes.'

'Sheep?'

'Sheep are just stupid.'

'Blackbirds?' asks Sergeant Parsons. It is the first word he has spoken.

'Blackbirds are not animals.'

'Monkeys?'

'There are no monkeys in Staffordshire.'

'Quite sure of that, are we?'

George feels his anger rising. He deliberately waits before replying. 'Inspector, may I say that your Sergeant's tactics are quite misconceived.'

'Oh, I don't think that was tactics, Mr Edalji. Sergeant Parsons is a good friend of Sergeant Robinson at Hednesford. Someone has threatened to shoot Sergeant Robinson in the head.'

Silence.

'Someone has also threatened to slice up twenty wenches in the village where you live.'

Silence.

'Well, he doesn't seem shocked by either of those statements, Sergeant. They can't have come as much of a surprise, then.'

Silence. George thought: it was a mistake to give him anything. Anything that isn't a straight answer to a straight question is giving him something. So don't.

The Inspector consulted a notebook in front of him. 'When we arrested you, you said, "I am not surprised at this. I have been expecting it for some time." What did you mean by that?'

'I meant what I said.'

'Well, let me tell you what I understood by what you said, and what the Sergeant understood by what you said, and what the man on the Clapham omnibus would understand by it. That at last you have been caught, and that you are rather relieved to be caught.'

Silence.

'So why do you think you are here?'

Silence.

'Perhaps you think it's because your father is a Hindoo.'

'My father is actually a Parsee.'

'Your boots have mud on them.'

Silence.

'Your razor has blood on it.'

Silence.

'Your coat has horse hairs on it.'

Silence.

'You were not surprised to be arrested.'

Silence.

'I don't think any of that has anything to do with whether your father is a Hindoo or a Parsee or a Hottentot.'

Silence.

'Well, he seems to have run out of words, Sergeant. He must be saving them for the Cannock magistrates.'

George was taken back to his cell where a plate of cold mess awaited him. He ignored it. Every twenty minutes, he heard the scrape of the spy hole; every hour – or so he guessed – the door was unlocked and a constable inspected him.

On his second visit, the policeman, evidently speaking to a script, said, 'Well, Mr Edalji, I'm sorry to see you here, but how did you manage to slip by all our chaps? What time did you put the horse through it?'

George had never met the constable before, so the expression of sympathy made little impact, and did not draw any reply.

An hour later, the policeman said, 'My advice, sir, frankly, is to give the show away. Because if you don't, someone else is bound to.'

On the fourth visit, George asked if these constant checks would continue through the night.

'Orders is orders.'

'And your orders are to keep me awake?'

'Oh no, sir. Our orders is to keep you alive. It's my neck if you do any harm to yourself.' George realized that no protest of his could stop the hourly interruptions. The constable continued, 'Of course, it would be easier for all concerned, yourself included, if you were to commit yourself.'

'Commit myself? Where to?'

The constable shuffled slightly. 'To a place of safety.'

'Oh, I see,' said George, his temper suddenly returning. 'You want me to say I am loony.' He used the word deliberately, in the full memory of his father's disapproval.

'It's often easier on the family all round. Think about it, sir. Think about how it will affect your parents. I understand they're a bit elderly.'

The cell door closed. George lay on his bed too exhausted and angry to sleep. His mind raced to the Vicarage, to the knock on the door and the house full of policemen. His father, his mother, Maud. His office at Newhall Street, now locked and deserted, his secretary sent home until further notice. His brother Horace opening a newspaper the next morning. His fellow solicitors in Birmingham telephoning one another with the news.

But beneath the exhaustion, the anger and the fear, George discovered another emotion: relief. It had come at last to this: then so much the better. There had been little he could do against the hoaxers and persecutors and writers of anonymous filth; and not much more when the police were blundering away – except offer them sensible advice they had contemptuously refused. But those tormenters and these blunderers had delivered him to a place of safety: to his second home, the laws of England. He knew where he was now. Though his work rarely took him to a courtroom, he knew it as part of his natural territory. He had sat in on cases enough times to have seen members of the public, dry-mouthed with panic, scarcely able to give evidence when faced with the solemn splendour of the law. He had seen policemen, at first all brass buttons and self-assurance, be reduced to lying fools by a half-decent defence counsel. And he had observed – no, not just observed, sensed, almost been able to touch – those unseen, unbreakable strands which linked everyone whose business was the law. Judges, magistrates, barristers, solicitors, clerks, ushers: this was their kingdom, where they spoke to one another in a *lingua franca* others could often barely comprehend.

Of course it would not get as far as judges and barristers. The police had no evidence against him, and he had the clearest proof of an alibi it was possible to have. A clergyman of the Church of England would swear on the Holy Bible that his son had been fast asleep in a locked bedroom at the time when the crime was being committed. Whereupon the magistrates would take one look at each other and not even bother to retire. Inspector Campbell would be on the receiving end of a sharp rebuke and that would be that. Naturally, he needed to engage the right solicitor, and he thought Mr Litchfield Meek the man for the job. Case dismissed, costs awarded, released without a stain on his character, police heavily criticized.

No, he was getting light-headed. He was also jumping much too far ahead, like some naive member of the public. He must never stop thinking like a solicitor. He must anticipate what the police might allege, what his solicitor would need to know, what the court would admit. He must remember, with absolute certainty, where he was, what he did and said, and who said what to him, throughout the whole period of alleged criminal activity.

He went through the last two days systematically, preparing himself to prove beyond reasonable doubt the simplest and least controversial event. He listed the witnesses he might need: his secretary, Mr Hands the bootmaker, Mr Merriman the stationmaster. Anyone who saw him do anything. Like Markew. If Merriman was unable to corroborate the fact that he had taken the 7.39 to Birmingham, then he knew whom to call. George had been standing on the platform when Joseph Markew accosted him and suggested he took a later train as Inspector Campbell wished to speak to him. Markew was a former police constable who currently kept an inn; it was entirely possible that he had been signed up as a special, but he did not say as much. George had asked what Campbell wanted, but Markew said he did not know. George had been deciding what to do, and also wondering what his fellow passengers were making of the exchange, when Markew had adopted a hectoring tone and said something like – no, not like, for the exact words now came back to George. Markew had said, 'Oh, come on, Mr Edalji, can't you give yourself a holiday for a single day?' And George had thought, actually, my good man, I took a holiday a fortnight ago this very day, I went to Aberystwyth with my sister, but if it is to be a question of holidays then I shall take my own advice, or that of my father, above that of the Staffordshire Constabulary, whose behaviour in recent weeks has hardly been marked by the greatest civility. So he had explained that urgent business awaited him at Newhall Street, and when the 7.39 drew in, left Markew on the platform.

George went through other exchanges, even the most trivial, with the same scrupulousness. Eventually, he slept; or rather, he became less aware of the peephole's scrape and the constable's intrusions. In the morning, he was brought a bucket of water, a lump of mottled soap, and a bit of rag to serve as a towel. He was allowed to see his father, who had brought him breakfast from the Vicarage. He was also allowed to write two brief letters, explaining to clients why there would have to be some delay in their immediate business.

An hour or so later, two constables arrived to take him to the magistrates' court. While waiting to set off, they ignored him and talked over the top of his head about a case that evidently interested them much more than his. It concerned the mysterious disappearance of a lady surgeon in London.

'Five foot ten and all.'

'Not too hard to spot, then.'

'You'd think, wouldn't you?'

They walked him the hundred and fifty yards from the police station, through crowds whose mood appeared to be mainly one of curiosity. There was an old woman shouting incoherent abuse at one point, but she was taken away. At the court Mr Litchfield Meek was waiting for him: a solicitor of the old school, lean and white-haired, known equally for his courtesy and his obduracy. Unlike George, he did not expect a summary dismissal of the case.

The magistrates appeared: Mr J. Williamson, Mr J.T. Hatton and Colonel R.S. Williamson. George Ernest Thompson Edalji was charged with unlawfully and maliciously wounding a horse, the property of the Great Wyrley Colliery Company, on August 17th. A plea of not guilty was entered, and Inspector Campbell was called to present the police evidence. He described being summoned to a field near the Colliery at about 7 a.m. and finding a distressed pony which subsequently had to be shot. He went from the field to the prisoner's house, where he found a jacket with bloodstains on the cuffs, whitish saliva stains on the sleeves, and hairs on the sleeves and breast. There was a waistcoat with a saliva patch. The pocket of the jacket contained a handkerchief marked SE with a brownish stain in one corner, which might have been blood. He then went with Sergeant Parsons to the prisoner's place of business in Birmingham, arrested him, and brought him to Cannock for interrogation. The prisoner denied that the clothing described to him had been what he was wearing the previous night; but on being told that his mother had confirmed this to be the case, had admitted the fact. Then he was asked about the hairs on his clothing. At first he denied there were any, but then suggested he might have picked them up by leaning on a gate.

George looked across at Mr Meek: this was hardly the tenor of his conversation with the Inspector yesterday afternoon. But Mr Meek was not interested in catching his client's eye. Instead he got to his feet and asked Campbell a few questions, all of which seemed to George innocuous, if not positively friendly.

Then Mr Meek called the Reverend Shapurji Edalji, described as 'a clerk in holy orders'. George watched his father outline, in a precise way but with rather long pauses, the sleeping arrangements at the Vicarage; how he always locked the bedroom door; how the key was hard to turn, and squeaked; how he was a very light sleeper, who in recent months had been plagued with lumbago, and would certainly have woken had the key been turned; how in any case he had not slept beyond five in the morning.

Superintendent Barrett, a plump man with a short white beard, his cap held against the swell of his belly, told the court that the Chief Constable had instructed him to object to bail. After a brief consultation, the magistrates remanded the prisoner to appear before them again the following Monday, when arguments for bail would be heard. In the meantime he would be transferred to Stafford Gaol. And that was that. Mr Meek promised to visit George the next day, probably in the afternoon. George asked him to bring a Birmingham paper. He would need to know what his colleagues were being told. He preferred the *Gazette*, but the *Post* would suffice.

At Stafford Gaol they asked what religion he belonged to, and also whether he could read and write. Then he was told to strip naked and instructed to place himself in a humiliating posture. He was taken to see the Governor, Captain Synge, who told him he would be housed in the hospital wing until a cell became available. Then his privileges as a prisoner on remand were explained: he would be allowed to wear his own clothes, to take exercise, to write letters, to receive newspapers and magazines. He would be allowed private conversations with his solicitor, which would be observed by a warder from behind a glass door. All other meetings would be supervised.

George had been arrested in his light summer suit, his only headgear a straw hat. He requested permission to send for a change of clothing. This, he was told, was against the regulations. It was a privilege for a prisoner on remand to retain his own clothes; but this should not be understood as conveying the right to build up a private wardrobe in his cell.

THE GREAT WYRLEY SENSATION, George read the next afternoon. VICAR'S SON IN COURT. 'The sensation which the arrest caused throughout the Cannock Chase district was evidenced by the large crowds which yesterday frequented the roads leading to the Great Wyrley Vicarage, where the accused man resided, and the Police Court and Police Station, Cannock.' George was dismayed at the idea of the Vicarage being besieged. 'The police were allowed to search without warrant. So far as can be ascertained at present the result of the search is a quantity of bloodstained apparel, a number of razors, and a pair of boots, the latter found in a field close to the scene of the last mutilation.'

'Found in a field,' he repeated to Mr Meek. 'Found in a field? Has someone been putting my boots in a field? Quantity of blood-stained apparel? *Quantity?*'

Meek seemed astonishingly calm about all this. No, he did not intend to ask the police about the supposed discovery of a pair of boots in a field. No, he did not propose asking the Birmingham *Daily Gazette* to publish a retraction concerning the amount of bloodstained clothing.

'If I may make a suggestion, Mr Edalji.'

'Of course.'

'I have, as you may imagine, had many clients in positions similar to yours, and they mostly insist upon reading the newspaper accounts of their case. It sometimes makes them a trifle over-heated. When this occurs, I always advise them to read the next column along. It often seems to help.'

'The next column along?' George shifted his gaze two inches to the left. MISSING LADY DOCTOR was the heading. And beneath it: NO CLUE TO MISS HICKMAN.

'Read it aloud,' said Mr Meek.

'"No clue as to the disappearance of Miss Sophie Frances Hickman, a lady surgeon at the Royal Free Hospital, has yet emerged . . ."'

Meek made George read the whole column to him. He listened attentively, sighing and shaking his head, even sucking in his breath from time to time.

'But Mr Meek,' said George at the end, 'how am I to tell if any of this is true either, given what they say about me?'

'That is rather my point.'

'Even so . . .' George's eyes were reverting magnetically to his own column. 'Even so. "The accused man, as his name implies, is of Eastern origin." They make me sound like a Chinaman.'

'I promise you, Mr Edalji, if ever they say you are a Chinaman, I'll have a quiet word with the editor.'

The following Monday, George was taken from Stafford back to Cannock. This time the crowd on the way to court seemed more turbulent. Men ran alongside the cab, jumping up and peering in; some thumped on the doors and waved sticks in the air. George grew alarmed; but the escorting constables acted as if it were all quite normal.

This time Captain Anson was in court; George became aware of a neat, authoritative figure staring fiercely at him. The magistrates announced that they would require three separate sureties, given the gravity of the charge. George's father doubted he could find so many. The magistrates therefore adjourned to Penkridge that day week.

At Penkridge the magistrates specified their bail terms further. The sureties required were as follows: £200 from George, £100 each from his father and mother, and a further £100 from a third party. But this was four sureties, not the three they had announced at Cannock. George felt it was all a charade. Not waiting for Mr Meek, he stood up himself.

'I do not desire bail,' he told the magistrates. 'I have had several offers, but I prefer not to have bail.'

Committal proceedings were then set for the following Thursday, September 3rd, at Cannock. On the Tuesday Mr Meek came to see him with bad news.

'They are adding a second charge, that of threatening to murder Sergeant Robinson at Hednesford by shooting him.'

'Have they found a gun next to my boots in the field?' asked George incredulously. 'Shooting him? Shooting Sergeant Robinson? I've never touched a gun in my life, and I've never to my knowledge laid eyes on Sergeant Robinson. Mr Meek, have they taken leave of their senses? What on earth can it possibly mean?'

'What it means,' replied Mr Meek, as if his client's outburst had been a simple, measured question, 'What it means is that the magistrates are certain to commit. However weak the evidence, it's most unlikely they could now discharge.'

Later, George sat on his bed in the hospital wing. Disbelief still burned in him like an ailment. How could they do this to him? How could they think that? How could they begin to believe that? George was so new to feeling anger that he did not know against whom to direct it – Campbell, Parsons, Anson, the police solicitor, the magistrates? Well, the magistrates would do for a start. Meek said they were certain to commit – as if they had no mental capacity, as if they were glove puppets or automata. But then, what were magistrates anyway? They scarcely qualified as members of the legal profession. Most were just self-important amateurs dressed in a little brief authority.

He felt thrilled by his contemptuous words, and then immediate shame at his own excitement. This was why wrath was a sin: it led to untruth. The magistrates at Cannock were doubtless no better and no worse than magistrates anywhere else; nor could he remember them uttering a word from which he could fairly dissent. And the more he thought of them, the more his professional self began taking over again. Incredulity weakened to mere vivid disappointment, and then to a resigned practicality. It was clearly much better that his case went to a higher court. Barristers and graver surroundings were required to deliver the proper justice and the proper rebuke. Cannock magistrates' court was quite the wrong setting. For a start, it was scarcely bigger than the schoolroom at the Vicarage. There was not even a proper dock: prisoners were obliged to sit on a chair in the middle of the court.

This was where he was placed on the morning of September 3rd; he felt himself observed from all quarters, uncertain whether his position made him look more like the classroom scholar or its dunce. Inspector Campbell gave evidence at length, but departed little from what he had previously said. The first new police testimony came from Constable Cooper, who described how in the hours after the discovery of the injured animal he had taken possession of one of the prisoner's boots, which had a peculiarly worn-down heel. This he had compared with footprints in the field where the pony was found, and also with marks close to a wooden footbridge near the Vicarage. He had pressed Mr Edalji's boot-heel down into the wet earth and found, when he withdrew the boot, that the prints matched.

Sergeant Parsons then agreed that he was in charge of the band of twenty special constables deployed to pursue the gang of mutilators. He told how a search of Edalji's bedroom had disclosed a case of four razors. One of them had wet, brown stains on it, and one or two hairs adhering to the blade. The sergeant had pointed this out to Edalji's father, who had commenced wiping the blade with his thumb.

'That's not true!' shouted the Vicar, rising to his feet.

'You must not interrupt,' said Inspector Campbell, before the magistrates could respond.

Sergeant Parsons continued with his evidence, and described the moment when the prisoner was put into the Newton Street lock-up in Birmingham. Edalji had turned to him and said, 'This is a bit of Mr Loxton's work, I suppose. I'll make him sit up before I am done.'

The next morning, the Birmingham *Daily Gazette* wrote of George:

> **He is 28 years of age but looks younger. He was dressed
> in a shrunken black and white check suit, and there was**

little of the typical solicitor in his swarthy face, with its full, dark eyes, prominent mouth, and small round chin. His appearance is essentially Oriental in its stolidity, no sign of emotion escaping him beyond a faint smile as the extraordinary story of the prosecution unfolded. His aged Hindoo father and his white-haired English mother were in court, and followed the proceedings with pathetic interest.

'I am twenty-eight but look younger,' he remarked to Mr Meek. 'Perhaps that is because I am twenty-seven. My mother is not English, she is Scottish. My father is not a Hindoo.'

'I warned you against reading the newspapers.'

'But he is not a Hindoo.'

'It's near enough for the *Gazette*.'

'But Mr Meek, what if I said you were a Welshman?'

'I would not hold you inaccurate, as my mother had Welsh blood.'

'Or an Irishman?'

Mr Meek smiled back at him, unoffended, perhaps even looking a little Irish.

'Or a Frenchman?'

'Now there, sir, you go too far. There you provoke me.'

'And I am stolid,' George continued, looking down at the *Gazette* again. 'Isn't that a good thing to be? Isn't stolid what a typical solicitor is meant to be? And yet I am not a typical solicitor. I am a typical Oriental, whatever that means. Whatever I am, I am typical, isn't that it? If I were excitable, I would still be a typical Oriental, wouldn't I?'

'Stolid is good, Mr Edalji. And at least they didn't call you inscrutable. Or wily.'

'What would that signify?'

'Oh, full of devilish low cunning. We like to avoid devilish. Also diabolical. The defence will settle for stolid.'

George smiled at his solicitor. 'I do apologize, Mr Meek. And I thank you for your good sense. I am likely to need more of it, I fear.'

On the second day of the proceedings, William Greatorex, a fourteen-year-old scholar of Walsall Grammar School, gave evidence. Numerous letters written over his signature were read out in court. He denied both authorship and knowledge of them, and could even show that he had been in the Isle of Man when two of them had been posted. He said that it was his custom to take the train every morning from Hednesford to Walsall, where he was at school. Other boys who generally travelled with him were Westwood Stanley, son of the well-known miners' agent; Quibell, son of the Vicar of Hednesford; Page, Harrison and Ferriday. The names of all these boys were mentioned in the letters which had just been read out.

Greatorex stated that he had known Mr Edalji by sight for three or four years. 'He has often travelled to Walsall in the same compartment as us boys. Quite a dozen times, I should think.' He was asked when was the last time the prisoner had travelled with him. 'The morning after two of Mr Blewitt's horses were killed. It was June 30, I think. We could see the horses lying in the field as we went by in the train.' The witness was asked if Mr Edalji had said anything to him that morning. 'Yes, he asked me if the horses that had been killed belonged to Blewitt. Then he looked out of the window.' The witness was asked if there had been any previous conversation with the prisoner about the maimings. 'No, no, never,' he replied.

Thomas Henry Gurrin agreed that he was a handwriting expert of many years' standing. He gave his report on the letters that had been read out in court. In the disguised writing he found a number of peculiarities very strongly marked. Exactly the same peculiarities were found in the letters of Mr Edalji, which had been handed to him for comparison.

Dr Butter, the police surgeon, who had examined the stains on Edalji's clothing, stated that he had performed tests which revealed traces of mammalian blood. On the coat and waistcoat he found twenty-nine short, brown hairs. These he compared with hairs on the skin of a Colliery pony maimed the evening before Mr Edalji was arrested. Under the microscope they were found to be similar.

Mr Gripton, who was keeping company with a young lady near Coppice Lane, Great Wyrley, on the night in question, gave evidence that he saw Mr Edalji, and passed him at about nine o'clock. Mr Gripton was not quite certain of the spot.

'Well,' asked the police solicitor, 'Give us the name of the nearest public house to the place you saw him.'

'The old police station,' replied Mr Gripton cheerily.

The police sternly stopped the laughter which greeted this remark.

Miss Biddle, who wished to make it clear that she was engaged to Mr Gripton, had also seen Mr Edalji; so had a number of other witnesses.

Details of the mutilation were given: the wound to the Colliery Company's pony was described as being of fifteen inches in length.

The prisoner's father, the Hindoo Vicar of Great Wyrley, also gave evidence.

The prisoner stated: 'I am perfectly innocent of the charge, and reserve my defence.'

On Friday 4th September, George Edalji was committed for trial at the Stafford Court of Quarter Sessions on two counts. Next morning, he read in the Birmingham *Daily Gazette*:

> **Edalji looked fresh and cheerful, and, sitting in his chair in the middle of the court, he conversed briskly with his solicitor with a keen discrimination of evidence, proceeding from thorough legal training. Mostly, however, he sat with arms folded and legs crossed, watching the witnesses with stolid interest, one boot raised and exhibiting plainly to the spectator the curious wearing down of one heel, which is one of the strongest links in the chain of circumstantial evidence against him.**

George was glad still to be regarded as stolid, and wondered if he could effect a change of footwear before the Court of Quarter Sessions.

He also noted another newspaper's description of William Greatorex as 'a healthy young English boy, with a frank, sunburnt face, and a pleasing manner'.

Mr Litchfield Meek was confident of an eventual acquittal.

Miss Sophie Frances Hickman, the lady surgeon, was still missing.

George

George spent the six weeks between the committal proceedings and the Quarter Sessions in the hospital wing of Stafford Gaol. He was not discontented; he thought it the correct decision to refuse bail. He could hardly have carried on his business with such charges hanging over him; and while he missed his family, he judged it best for all of them that he stayed in safe custody. That report of crowds besieging the Vicarage had alarmed him; and he remembered fists pounding on the cab doors as he was driven to court in Cannock. He would not be able to count himself safe if such hotheads sought him out among the lanes of Great Wyrley.

But there was another reason why he preferred to be in prison. Everyone knew where he was; every moment of the day he was spied upon and accounted for. So if a further outrage occurred, the whole pattern of events would be shown to have nothing to do with him. And were the first charge against him found untenable, then the second one – the ludicrous proposition that he had threatened to murder a man he had never met – would also have to be withdrawn. It was strange to find himself, a solicitor-at-law, actually hoping for another animal to be maimed; but a further crime seemed to him the speediest way to freedom.

Still, even if the case came to trial, there could be no doubt over the outcome. He had regained both his composure and his optimism; he did not have to play-act either with Mr Meek or with his parents. He could already imagine the headlines. **GREAT WYRLEY MAN CLEARED. SHAMEFUL PROSECUTION OF LOCAL SOLICITOR. POLICE WITNESSES DECLARED INCOMPETENT.** Perhaps even **CHIEF CONSTABLE RESIGNS.**

Mr Meek had more or less convinced him that it mattered little how the newspapers depicted him. It seemed to matter even less on September 21st, when a horse at the farm belonging to Mr Green was found ripped and disembowelled. George greeted the news with a kind of cautious exultation. He could hear keys turning in locks, could smell the early morning air, and his mother's powder when he embraced her.

'Now this proves I am innocent, Mr Meek.'

'Not exactly, Mr Edalji. I don't think we can go quite that far.'

'But here I am in prison . . .'

'Which only goes to prove, in the court's view, that you are and must be entirely innocent of mutilating Mr Green's horse.'

'No, it proves there was a pattern to events, before and after the Colliery pony, which has now been shown to have absolutely nothing to do with me.'

'*I* know that, Mr Edalji.' The solicitor rested his chin on his fist.

'But?'

'But I always find it useful in these moments to imagine what the prosecution might say in the circumstances.'

'And what might they possibly say?'

'Well, on the night of August 17th, as I remember, when the defendant was walking from the bootmaker, he went as far as Mr Green's farm.'

'Yes, I did.'

'Mr Green is the defendant's neighbour.'

'That is true.'

'So what could be of greater benefit to the defendant in his present circumstances than for a horse to be mutilated even closer to the Vicarage than in any other previous incident?'

Litchfield Meek watched George work this out.

'You mean that after getting myself arrested by writing anonymous letters denouncing myself for crimes I did not commit, I then incite someone else to commit another crime in order to exculpate me?'

'That's about the long and the short of it, Mr Edalji.'

'It's utterly ridiculous. And I don't even know Green.'

'I'm just telling you how the prosecution might choose to see it. If they had the mind.'

'Which they doubtless will. But the police must at least hunt the criminal, mustn't they? The newspapers hint quite openly that this throws doubt on the prosecution case. If they found the man, and he confessed to the string of crimes, then that would be my freedom?'

'If that were to happen, Mr Edalji, then yes, I would agree.'

'I see.'

'And there's another development. Does the name Darby mean anything to you? Captain Darby?'

'Darby. Darby. I don't think so. Inspector Campbell asked me about someone called the Captain. Perhaps this is him. Why?'

'More letters have been sent. To all and sundry it appears. One even to the Home Secretary. All signed "Darby, Captain of the Wyrley Gang". Saying how the maimings are going to continue.' Mr Meek saw the look in George's eye. 'But no, Mr Edalji, this only means that the prosecution must accept you almost certainly didn't write them.'

'You seem determined to discourage me this morning, Mr Meek.'

'That is not my intention. But you must accept we are going to trial. And with that in mind we have secured the services of Mr Vachell.'

'Oh, that's excellent news.'

'He will not, I think, let us down. And Mr Gaudy will be at his side.'

'And for the prosecution?'

'Mr Disturnal, I'm afraid. And Mr Harrison.'

'Is Disturnal bad for us?'

'To be honest with you, I would have preferred another.'

'Mr Meek, now it is my turn to put heart into you. A barrister, however competent, cannot make bricks without straw.'

Litchfield Meek gave George a worldly smile. 'In my years in the courts, Mr Edalji, I've seen bricks made from all sorts of materials. Some you didn't even know existed. Lack of straw will be no hardship to Mr Disturnal.'

Despite this approaching threat, George spent the remaining weeks at Stafford Gaol in a tranquil state of mind. He was treated respectfully and there was an order to his days. He received newspapers and mail; he prepared for the trial with Mr Meek; he awaited developments in the Green case; and he was allowed books. His father had brought him a Bible, his mother a one-volume Shakespeare and a one-volume Tennyson. He read the latter two; then, out of idleness, some shilling shockers which a warder passed on to him. The fellow also lent him a tattered cheap edition of *The Hound of the Baskervilles*. George judged it excellent.

He opened the newspaper each morning with less apprehension, given that his own name had temporarily vanished from its pages. Instead, he learned with interest that there were new cabinet appointments in London; that Dr Elgar's latest oratorio had been performed at the Birmingham musical festival; that Buffalo Bill was on a tour of England.

A week before the trial, George met Mr Vachell, a cheerful and corpulent barrister with twenty years' service on the Midland Circuit.

'How do you judge my case, Mr Vachell?'

'I judge it well, Mr Edalji, very well. That is to say, I consider the prosecution scandalous and largely devoid of merit. Of course I shall not say so. I shall merely concentrate on what seem to me to be the strong points of your case.'

'And what, to you, do they seem to be?'

'I would put it like this, Mr Edalji.' The barrister gave him a smile which was almost a grin. 'There is no evidence that you committed this crime. There is no motive for you committing this crime. And there was no opportunity for you to commit this crime. I shall wrap it up a little for the judge and jury. But that will be the essence of my case.'

'It is perhaps a pity,' put in Mr Meek, 'that we are in Court B.' His tone punctured George's temporary elation.

'Why is that a pity?'

'Court A is run by Lord Hatherton. Who at least has legal training.'

'You mean I am to be judged by someone who doesn't know the law?'

Mr Vachell intervened. 'Don't alarm him, Mr Meek. I've been before both courts in my time. Who do we get in Court B?'

'Sir Reginald Hardy.'

Mr Vachell's expression did not flicker. 'Perfectly all right. In some ways I consider it an advantage not to be governed by some stickler who aspires to the High Court. You can get away with a little more. Not pulled up so often for meretricious demonstrations of procedural knowledge. On the whole, an advantage to the defence, I'd say.'

George sensed that Mr Meek did not agree; but he was impressed by Mr Vachell, whether the barrister was being altogether sincere or not.

'Gentlemen, I do have one request.' Mr Meek and Mr Vachell briefly caught one another's eye. 'It is about my name. It is *Ay*dlji. *Ay*dlji. Mr Meek pronounces it more or less correctly, but I should have mentioned the matter earlier to you, Mr Vachell. The police, it seems to me, have always gone out of their way to ignore any correction I have offered them. Might I suggest that Mr Vachell makes an announcement at the beginning of the case as to how to pronounce my name. To tell that court that it is not Ee-*dal*-jee but *Ay*dlji.'

The barrister gave the solicitor an instructing nod, and Mr Meek replied.

'George, how can I best put this? Of course it's your name, and of course Mr Vachell and I shall endeavour to pronounce it correctly. When we are here with you. But in court . . . in court . . . I think the argument would be: when in Rome. We would get off on the wrong foot with Sir Reginald Hardy if we made such an announcement. We are unlikely to succeed in giving pronunciation lessons to the police. And as for Mr Disturnal, I suspect he would greatly enjoy the confusion.'

George looked at the two men. 'I am not sure I follow you.'

'What I'm saying, George, is that we should acknowledge the court's right to decide a prisoner's name. It's not written down anywhere, but that's more or less the fact of the matter. What you call mispronouncing, I would call . . . making you more English.'

George took a breath. 'And less Oriental?'

'Less Oriental, yes, George.'

'Then I would ask you both kindly to mispronounce my name on all occasions, so that I may get used to it.'

The trial was set to begin on October 20th. On the 19th, four young boys playing near the Sidmouth plantation in Richmond Park came upon a body in an advanced state of decomposition. It proved to be that of Miss Sophie Frances Hickman, the lady doctor from the Royal Free Hospital. Like George, she had been in her late twenties. And, he reflected, she was only one column away.

On the morning of October 20th, 1903, George was brought from Stafford Gaol to Shire Hall. He was taken to the basement and shown the holding cell where prisoners were usually placed. As a privilege, he would be allowed to occupy a large, low-ceilinged room with a deal table and a fireplace; here, under the eye of Constable Dubbs, he would be able to confer with Mr Meek. He sat at the table for twenty minutes while Dubbs, a muscular officer with a chinstrap beard and a gloomy air, firmly avoided his eye. Then, at a signal, George was led through dim, winding passages and past inadequate gas lamps to a door giving on to the foot of a narrow staircase. Dubbs gave him a gentle shove, and he climbed up towards light and noise. As he emerged into the view of Court B, noise became silence. George stood self-consciously in the dock, an actor propelled unwillingly on stage through a trapdoor.

Then, before the Assistant Chairman Sir Reginald Hardy, two flanking magistrates, Captain Anson, the properly sworn members of an English jury, representatives of the Press, representatives of the public, and three members of his family, the indictment was read. George Ernest Thompson Edalji was charged with wounding a horse, the property of the Great Wyrley Colliery Company, on the 17th or 18th September; also with sending a letter, on or about 11th July, to Sergeant Robinson at Cannock, threatening to kill him.

Mr Disturnal was a tall, sleek figure, with a swift manner to him. After a brief opening speech, he called Inspector Campbell, and the whole story began again: the discovery of the mutilated pony, the search of the Vicarage, the bloodstained clothing, the hairs on the coat, the anonymous letters, the prisoner's arrest and subsequent statements. It was just a story, George knew, something made up from scraps and coincidences and hypotheses; he knew too that he was innocent; but something about the repetition of the story by an authority in wig and gown made it take on extra plausibility.

George thought Campbell's evidence was finished, when Mr Disturnal produced his first surprise.

'Inspector Campbell, before we conclude, there is a matter of great public anxiety, about which you are, I think, able to enlighten us. On September 21st, I understand, a horse was found maimed at the farm of a Mr Green.'

'That is correct, sir.'

'Mr Green's farm is very close to the Vicarage of Great Wyrley?'

'It is.'

'And the police have conducted an investigation into this outrage?'

'Indeed. As a matter of urgency and priority.'

'And has this investigation been successful?'

'Yes it has, sir.'

Mr Disturnal hardly needed the elaborate pause he now threw in; the whole courtroom was waiting like an open-mouthed child.

'And will you tell the court the result of your investigation?'

'John Harry Green, who is the son of the farmer on whose land the outrage took place, and who is a Yeomanry trooper of the age of nineteen, has admitted committing the action against his own horse. He has signed a confession to this effect.'

'He admitted full and sole responsibility?'

'He did.'

'And you questioned him about any possible connection between this outrage and previous ones in the district?'

'Yes, we did. Extensively, sir.'

'And what did he state?'

'That this was an isolated occurrence.'

'And did your investigations confirm that the outrage at Green's farm had absolutely nothing to do with any other outrage in the vicinity?'

'They did.'

'No connection at all?'

'No connection at all, sir.'

'And is John Harry Green in court today?'

'Yes, he is, sir.'

George, like everyone else in the crowded court, started looking around for a nineteen-year-old trooper who admitted mutilating his own horse without apparently supplying the police with any good reason for having done so. But at that moment, Sir Reginald Hardy decided that it was time for his luncheon.

Mr Meek's first duties were with Mr Vachell; only then did he come to the room where George was held during adjournments. His demeanour was lugubrious.

'Mr Meek, you did warn us about Disturnal. We knew to expect something. And at least we shall be able to have a go at Green this afternoon.'

The solicitor shook his head grimly. 'Not a chance of it.'

'Why not?'

'Because he's their witness. If they don't put him up, we can't cross-examine him. And we can't take the risk of calling him blind as we don't know what he might say. It could be devastating. Yet they produce him in court so it looks as if they're being open with everyone. It's clever. It's typical Disturnal. I should have thought of it, but I didn't know anything about this confession. It's bad.'

George felt it only his duty to cheer his solicitor up. 'I can see it's frustrating, Mr Meek, but is there any real harm? Green said – and the police said – it had nothing to do with any other outrage.'

'That's just the point. It's not what they say – it's how it looks. Why should a man disembowel a horse – his own horse – for no apparent reason? Answer: to help out a friend and neighbour charged with a similar offence.'

'But he's not my friend. I doubt I would even recognize him.'

'Yes, I know. And when we take the considered risk of putting you in the box, you will tell Mr Vachell that. But it's bound to look as if you're denying an allegation that hasn't in fact been made. It's clever. Mr Vachell will assail the Inspector this afternoon, but I don't think we should be optimistic.'

'Mr Meek, I could not help noticing that in Campbell's evidence he said that the clothing of mine he found – the coat I hadn't worn for weeks – was wet. He said wet twice. At Cannock he merely called it damp.'

Meek gave a soft smile. 'It's a pleasure to work with you, Mr Edalji. It's the sort of thing we notice but tend not to mention to the client in case it dispirits him. The police will be making a few more adjustments of the kind, I don't doubt.'

That afternoon Mr Vachell got little of value from the Inspector, who knew his way round a witness box. During their first encounter at Hednesford police station, Campbell had struck George as rather slow-minded and vaguely impertinent. At Newhall Street and at Cannock, he had been more alert and openly hostile, if not always coherent of thought. Now his manner was measured and sombre, while his height and his uniform seemed to impart logic as well as authority. George reflected that if his story was subtly changing around him, then so too were some of the characters.

Mr Vachell had more success with PC Cooper, who described, as he had done at the magistrates' court, his matching of George's boot-heel to the prints in the mud.

'Constable Cooper,' Mr Vachell began, 'may I enquire who gave you the instruction to proceed as you did?'

'I'm not quite sure, sir. I think it was the Inspector, but it might have been Sergeant Parsons.'

'And where precisely were you told to look?'

'Anywhere on the route the culprit might have taken between the field and the Vicarage.'

'Assuming the culprit came from the Vicarage? And was returning there?'

'Yes, sir.'

'Anywhere?'

'Anywhere, sir.' Cooper looked no more than about twenty to George's eye: a red-eared, awkward boy trying to imitate the confidence of his superiors.

'And did you assume the culprit, as you refer to him, took the most direct route?'

'Yes, I suppose I did, sir. It's what they usually do when leaving the scene of the crime.'

'I see, Constable. So you did not look anywhere other than on a direct route?'

'No, sir.'

'And how long did your search last?'

'An hour or more, I would estimate.'

'And at what time did it take place?'

'I suppose I started looking at nine thirty, more or less.'

'And the pony was discovered at six thirty, approximately?'

'Yes, sir.'

'Three hours previously. In the course of which time anyone could have walked across that route. Miners on the way to the Colliery, sightseers brought by news of the outrage. Policemen, indeed.'

'That's possible, sir.'

'And who accompanied you, Constable?'

'I was on my own.'

'I see. And you found a few heelmarks which in your opinion matched the boot you held in your hand.'

'Yes, sir.'

'And then you went back and reported your discovery?'

'Yes, sir.'

'And then what happened?'

'What do you mean, sir?'

George was pleased to observe a slight change in Cooper's tone; as if he knew he were being led somewhere but could not yet make out the destination.

'I mean, Constable, what happened after you reported what you had found?'

'I was put to searching the grounds of the Vicarage, sir.'

'I see. But at some point, Constable, you went back and showed someone of higher rank the marks you had discovered.'

'Yes, sir.'

'And when would that be?'

'In the middle of the afternoon.'

'In the middle of the afternoon. By which you mean, three o'clock, four o'clock?'

'Around then, sir.'

'I see.' Mr Vachell frowned and gave himself rather theatrically to reflection, in George's view. 'Six hours later, in other words.'

'Yes, sir.'

'During which time the area was guarded and cordoned off to prevent further trampling?'

'Not exactly.'

'Not exactly. Does that mean yes or no, Officer?'

'No, sir.'

'Now, I understand that it is often normal procedure in such cases to take a plaster of Paris cast of the heelmarks in question. Can you tell me whether this was done?'

'No, sir, it wasn't.'

'I understand that another technique would be to photograph such marks. Was that done?'

'No, sir.'

'I understand that another technique is to dig up the relevant piece of turf and bring it for forensic analysis. Was that done?'

'No, sir. The ground was too soft.'

'How long have you been a police constable, Mr Cooper?'

'Fifteen months.'

'Fifteen months. Thank you very much.'

George felt like cheering. He looked across at Mr Vachell, as he had done before, but failed to catch his eye. Perhaps this was court etiquette; or perhaps Mr Vachell was just thinking about the next witness.

The rest of the afternoon seemed to go well. A number of the anonymous letters were read out, and it was clear to George that nobody in his right mind could possibly imagine he might have written them. The one he had given Campbell, for instance, from the 'Lover of Justice': 'George Edalji – I do not know you, but have sometimes seen you on the railway, and do not expect I would like you much if I did know you, as I do not like natives.' How on earth could he have written that? It was followed by an even more grotesque attribution of authorship. A letter was read out describing the behaviour of the so-called 'Wyrley Gang', which might have come from the cheapest novel: 'They all take a fearful oath of secrecy, and repeat it after the Captain, and each says, "May I be struck dead if I ever split."' George thought he could rely on the jury to work out that this was not how solicitors expressed themselves.

Mr Hodson, the general dealer, gave evidence that he had seen George on his way to Mr Hands of Bridgetown, and that the solicitor was wearing his old house-coat. But then Mr Hands himself, who had been with George for half an hour or so, asserted that his client had not been wearing the said coat. Two other witnesses reported seeing him, but were unable to remember his garments.

'I feel they're shifting their ground,' said Mr Meek after the court had risen for the day. 'I sense they're up to something.'

'What kind of something?' asked George.

'At Cannock their case was that you went to the field during your walk before dinner. That was why they called so many witnesses who had seen you out and about. That canoodling couple, do you remember? They haven't been put up this time, and they're not the only ones. The other thing is that at the committal the only date mentioned was the 17th. Now the indictment reads the 17th *or* the 18th. So they're hedging their bets. I sense they're moving to the night-time option. They might have something we don't know about.'

'Mr Meek, it doesn't matter which they go for, or why they go for it. If they want the evening, they haven't a single witness who saw me anywhere near the field. And if they want the night, they have my father's evidence to contend with.'

Mr Meek ignored his client and continued thinking aloud. 'Of course, they don't have to go for one or the other. They can merely suggest possibilities to the jury. But they put more stress on the bootmarks this time. And the bootmarks only come into play if they go for the second option, because of the rain in the night. And if your house-coat has moved from damp to wet, that also confirms my supposition.'

'So much the better,' said George. 'There was nothing left of Constable Cooper after Mr Vachell had finished with him this afternoon. And if Mr Disturnal wants to continue with that line, he will have to claim that a clergyman of the Church of England is not telling the truth.'

'Mr Edalji, if I may . . . You must not see it all as so clear-cut.'

'But it is clear-cut.'

'Would you say that your father is robust? From a mental point of view, I mean?'

'He's the robustest man I know. Why do you ask?'

'I suspect he will need to be.'

'You will be surprised how robust Hindoos can turn out to be.'

'And your mother? And your sister?'

The morning of the second day began with the testimony of Joseph Markew, innkeeper and former police constable. He described being sent by Inspector Campbell to Great Wyrley & Churchbridge railway station, and how the prisoner had declined his request to take a later train.

'Did he tell you,' asked Mr Disturnal, 'what business was so important that it required him to ignore the urgent request of a police inspector?'

'No, sir.'

'Did you repeat your request?'

'I did, sir. I suggested that he might take a day's holiday for once. But he refused to change his mind.'

'I see. And Mr Markew, did something happen at this point?'

'Yes, sir. A man on the platform came up and said he'd heard another horse had been ripped that night.'

'And when the man said this, where were you looking?'

'I was looking the prisoner full in the face.'

'And would you describe his reaction to the court.'

'Yes, sir. He smiled.'

'He smiled. He smiled at the news that another horse had been ripped. Are you sure of that, Mr Markew?'

'Oh yes, sir. Perfectly sure. He smiled.'

George thought: but that isn't true. I know it isn't true. Mr Vachell must prove it isn't true.

Mr Vachell knew better than to attack the statement directly. He concentrated instead on the identity of the man who had allegedly come up to Markew and George. Where had he come from, what kind of man was he, where did he go to? (And, by implication, why was he not in court?) Mr Vachell managed to express, by hints and pauses and finally by direct statement, considerable astonishment that a publican and former policeman, with the widest acquaintance across the district, should be unable to identify the useful yet mysterious stranger who might be able to corroborate his fanciful and tendentious claim. But this was as far as the defence could get with Markew.

Mr Disturnal then had Sergeant Parsons repeat the prisoner's remarks about expecting his arrest, and his alleged statement at the Birmingham lock-up about making Mr Loxton sit up before he had done. No one attempted to explain who the said Loxton might be. Another member of the Wyrley gang? A policeman George was also threatening to shoot? The name was left hanging, for the jury to make of it what they might. A Constable Meredith, whose face and name George did not recall, cited something harmless George had said to him about bail, but managed to make it sound incriminating. Then William Greatorex, the healthy young English boy with the pleasing manner, repeated his story of George looking out of the carriage window and showing unaccountable interest in Mr Blewitt's dead horses.

Mr Lewis, the veterinary surgeon, described the condition of the Colliery pony, the manner in which it was dropping blood, the length and nature of the wound, and the regrettable necessity to shoot the animal. He was asked by Mr Disturnal what conclusions he might be able to draw as to the time the mutilation had taken place. Mr Lewis declared that in his professional opinion the injury had been inflicted within six hours of his examining the pony. In other words, not earlier than two thirty in the morning of the 18th.

This felt to George like the first good news of the day. The argument about which clothes he had been wearing on his visit to the bootmaker's was now quite irrelevant. The prosecution had just closed off one of its own avenues. They had boxed themselves in.

But if so, it did not show in Mr Disturnal's demeanour. His whole attitude implied that some initial ambiguity in the case had now been cleared up thanks to diligent work by police and prosecution. We no longer allege that at some point in a twelve-hour period . . . we are now able to allege that it was very close to two thirty in the morning when . . . And somehow Mr Disturnal made this growing precision imply an equally increasing confidence that the prisoner in the dock was there for the reasons stated in the indictment.

The last part of the day was given up to Thomas Henry Gurrin, who agreed to the description of himself as an orthographical expert with nineteen years' experience in the identification of feigned and anonymous handwriting. He confirmed that he had frequently been engaged by the Home Office, and that his most recent professional appearance had been as a witness in the Meat Farm murder trial. George did not know what he expected an orthographical expert to look like; perhaps dry and scholarly, with a voice like a scratchy pen. Mr Gurrin, with his ruddy face and muttonchop whiskers, could have been the brother of Mr Greensill, the butcher in Wyrley.

Regardless of physiognomy, Mr Gurrin then took over the court. Specimens of George's handwriting were produced in enlarged photographic form. Specimens of the anonymous letters were also produced in enlarged photographic form. Original documents were described and passed across to members of the jury, who took what seemed to George an interminable time examining them, constantly breaking off to stare lengthily at the prisoner. Certain characteristic loops and hooks and crossings were indicated by Mr Gurrin with a wooden pointer; and somehow description moved to inference, then to theoretical probability and then to absolute certainty. It was, finally, Mr Gurrin's considered professional and expert opinion that the prisoner was as responsible for the anonymous letters as he was for those manifestly in his own hand over his own signature.

'All of these letters?' asked Mr Disturnal, waving his hand around the court, which seemed to have been turned into a scriptorium.

'No, sir, not all.'

'There are some which in your opinion were not written by the prisoner?'

'Yes, sir.'

'How many of them?'

'One, sir.'

Mr Gurrin indicated the single letter whose authorship he did not ascribe to George. An exception, George realized, which had the effect of endorsing Gurrin's assertions about all the others. It was a piece of slyness disguised as caution.

Mr Vachell then spent some time on the difference between personal opinion and scientific proof, between thinking something and knowing it; but Mr Gurrin showed himself an adamantine witness. He had been in this position many times before. Mr Vachell was not the first defence counsel to suggest that his procedures were no more rigorous than those of a crystal-gazer, a thought-reader or a spiritualist medium.

Afterwards, Mr Meek assured George that the second day was often the worst for the defence; but that the third, when they presented their own evidence, would be the best. George hoped so; he was struggling with the sense that, slowly yet irrevocably, his story was being taken away from him. He feared that by the time the defence case was put, it would be too late. People – and in particular, the jury – would respond by thinking, But no, we've already been told what happened. Why should we change our minds now?

The next morning, he obediently practised Mr Meek's patent method of putting his own case into perspective. **MURDER AT MIDNIGHT. CANAL-SIDE TRAGEDY IN BIRMINGHAM. TWO BARGEMEN ARRESTED.** For once, the ploy failed to have its usual effect. He moved across the page to **TIPTON LOVE TRAGEDY**, about some poor devil who for the love of a bad woman ended up throwing himself into the canal. But the stories failed to engage him, and his eye kept being drawn back to the headlines. He found himself resenting the fact that a squalid canalside murder was a **TRAGEDY**, and a miserable suicide was also a **TRAGEDY**. Whereas his own case had remained, from the beginning, an **OUTRAGE**.

And then, almost to his relief, he found **LADY DOCTOR'S DEATH**. He felt it almost a social duty to keep up with Miss Hickman, whose decomposing body was still withholding its secrets. She had been his companion in misfortune since the committal proceedings began. Yesterday, according to the *Post*, a medical knife or lancet had been discovered near the Sidmouth plantation in Richmond Park. The newspaper surmised that it had fallen out of the woman's clothing while her body was being moved. George wondered how credible this was. You found the corpse of a missing lady surgeon, and as you moved it, things dropped from the pockets and you did not even notice? George was not sure he would believe this if he were on the coroner's jury.

The *Post* further suggested that the knife or lancet had been the property of the deceased, and that it might have been used to sever an artery, thus causing her to bleed to death. In other words, a suicide, and another **TRAGEDY**. Well, thought George, that was one possible explanation. Although if Wyrley Vicarage were in Surrey rather than Staffordshire, the police would construct a more convincing theory: that the Vicar's son had broken out of a locked room, acquired a lancet he had never seen before in his life, followed the poor woman until she reached the plantation, and then, lacking any conceivable motive, slaughtered her.

This slug of bitterness revived him. And picturing his own fantastical appearance in the Hickman case also reminded him of the assurance Mr Vachell had given him at their first conference. My defence, Mr Edalji? Merely that there is no evidence that you committed the crime, no motive for you to have done so, and no opportunity. Of course I shall wrap it up for the judge and jury, but that will be the essence of my case.

First, however, there was Dr Butter's evidence to deal with. Dr Butter was not like Mr Gurrin, who appeared to George a charlatan posing as a professional. The police surgeon was a grey-haired gentleman, calm and cautious, who came from a world of test tubes and microscopes, who dealt only in specifics. He explained to Mr Disturnal his procedures when examining the razors, the jacket, the waistcoat, the boots, the trousers, the house-coat. He described the various stains found on various garments, and identified which could be classified as mammalian blood. He had counted the hairs picked from the sleeve and left breast of the jacket: there were twenty-nine of them in total, all short and red-coloured. He had compared them with the hairs on a piece of skin cut from the dead Colliery pony. These were also short and red-coloured. He had examined them under the microscope and pronounced them to be 'similar in length, colour and structure'.

Mr Vachell's technique with Dr Butter was to grant both his competence and his knowledge full respect, and then attempt to turn them to the defence's advantage. He drew attention to the whitish stains on the jacket which the police had concluded were the saliva and foam from the wounded animal. Was there any confirmation of this from Dr Butter's scientific analysis?

'No.'

'What, in your view, did the stains consist of?'

'Starch.'

'And how might such residues come to be on clothing, in your experience?'

'Most probably, I would say, they were residues of bread and milk from breakfast.'

At which point George heard a noise whose existence he had almost forgotten: laughter. There was laughter in court at the idea of bread and milk. It seemed to him the sound of sanity. He looked across at the jury as the public hilarity continued. One or two of them were smiling, but most had retained sober countenances. George judged all this a heartening sign.

Mr Vachell now moved on to the bloodstains on the sleeve of the defendant's jacket.

'You say these stains are of mammalian blood?'

'Yes.'

'There is no possible doubt about that, Dr Butter?'

'None at all.'

'I see. Now, Dr Butter, a horse is a mammal?'

'Indeed.'

'So is a pig, a sheep, a dog, a cow?'

'Certainly.'

'Indeed, everything in the animal kingdom that is not a bird, a fish or a reptile may be classified as a mammal?'

'Yes.'

'You and I are mammals, and so are members of the jury?'

'Certainly.'

'So Dr Butter, when you say that the blood is mammalian, you are merely saying that it could belong to any of the above-mentioned species?'

'That is true.'

'You do not for a moment claim that you are showing, or would be capable of showing, that the small spots of blood on the defendant's jacket came from a horse or pony?'

'It would not be possible to make such a claim, no.'

'And is it possible to tell from examination the age of bloodstains? Could you say, for instance, that this stain was produced today, this one yesterday, this one a week ago, this one several months ago?'

'Well, if it is still wet —'

'Were any of the bloodstains on George Edalji's jacket wet when you examined them?'

'No.'

'They were dry?'

'Yes.'

'So on your own evidence, they could have been there for days, weeks, even months?'

'That is the case.'

'And is it possible to tell from a bloodstain whether it has been produced by blood from a living animal or a dead one?'

'No.'

'Or indeed from a joint of meat?'

'That neither.'

'So Dr Butter, you cannot, by examining bloodstains, distinguish between those caused by a man mutilating a horse and those which might have landed on his clothes several months previously when, say, he was carving the Sunday roast — or indeed, consuming it?'

'I would have to agree.'

'And can you remind the court how many bloodstains you found on the cuff of Mr Edalji's jacket?'

'Two.'

'And I believe you said that each was the size of a threepenny bit?'

'I did.'

'Dr Butter, if you were to rip a horse so violently that it was bleeding to death and had to be shot, do you imagine that you could do so while leaving scarcely more blood on your clothes than might be found if you were a careless eater?'

'I would not wish to speculate –'

'And I certainly shall not press you to do so, Dr Butter. I certainly shall not press you.'

Buoyant from this exchange, Mr Vachell opened the case for the defence with a short statement, then called George Ernest Thompson Edalji.

'He stepped briskly round from the dock and faced the crowded court with perfect composure.' This was what George read the next day in the Birmingham *Daily Post*, and it was a sentence which would always make him feel proud. No matter what lies had been told, no matter the whispering campaign, the slurs on his ancestry, the deliberate distortions of the police and of other witnesses, he would, and did, face his accusers with perfect composure.

Mr Vachell began by taking his client through his precise movements on the evening of the 17th. Both of them knew this was strictly unnecessary, given the effect of Mr Lewis's evidence on the known timing of events. But Mr Vachell wanted to accustom the jury to the sound of George's voice and the trustworthiness of his evidence. It was barely six years since defendants had been allowed to give evidence, and putting your client into the box was still regarded as a dangerous novelty.

So the visit to Mr Hands the bootmaker was recounted again, and that evening's route traced for the jury – though in response to an earlier hint from Mr Vachell, George did not mention going as far as the Green farm. Then he described the family dinner, the sleeping arrangements, the locked bedroom door, his rising, breakfast and departure for the station.

'Now, at the station, do you recall speaking to Mr Joseph Markew?'

'Yes, indeed. I was standing on the platform waiting for my usual train – the 7.39 – when he accosted me.'

'Do you recall what he said?'

'Yes, he said that he had a message from Inspector Campbell. I was to miss my train and wait at the station until such time as he could speak to me. But it was more Markew's tone of voice that I recall.'

'How would you describe that tone of voice?'

'Well, it was very rude. As if he was giving me an order, or passing one on with as little civility as possible. I asked what the Inspector wished to see me about, and Markew said he did not know and would not tell me anyway.'

'Did he identify himself as a special constable?'

'No.'

'So you saw no reason not to go to work?'

'Indeed, I had pressing business at my office, and I told him so. Then his manner changed. He became ingratiating and suggested that I might for once in my life take a day's holiday.'

'And how did you react to that?'

'I thought he did not have the slightest idea what being a solicitor consisted of, and what the responsibilities of the profession are. It is not like being a publican and taking the day off and getting someone else to draw the beer.'

'Indeed not. And at this point did a man come up to you with the news that another horse had been ripped in the district?'

'What man?'

'I refer to Mr Markew's evidence, in which he said that a man came up to the two of you and reported that a horse had been ripped.'

'That is quite untrue. No man came up to us.'

'And then you took your train?'

'There was no reason supplied why I should not.'

'So there is no question of your smiling at the news that an animal had been mutilated?'

'No question at all. No man came up to us. And I would hardly smile at such a matter. The only time I might have smiled was when Markew suggested I take a holiday. He is well known in the village as a layabout, so the suggestion fitted easily in his mouth.'

'I see. Now, moving on to a little later in the morning, when Inspector Campbell and Sergeant Parsons came to your office and arrested you. On the way to the lock-up, they allege that you said, "I am not surprised at this. I have been expecting it for some time." Did you say those words?'

'Yes, I did.'

'Will you explain what you meant by them?'

'Certainly. There had been a campaign of rumour against me for some time. I had received anonymous letters, which I had shown to the police. It was quite evident that they were following my movements and watching the Vicarage. Comments made to me by a policeman indicated that they had an animus against me. And there had even been a rumour a week or two earlier that I had been arrested. The police seemed determined to prove something against me. So, no, I was not surprised.'

Mr Vachell next put to him the supposed remark about the mysterious Mr Loxton; George denied both making the statement, and ever having known anyone called Loxton.

'Let us turn to another statement you are alleged to have made. At the Cannock magistrates' court, you were offered bail, which you refused. Will you tell the court why?'

'Certainly. The terms were extremely onerous, not just on myself but on my family. Besides, I was in the prison hospital at the time, and being comfortably treated. I was content to remain there until my trial.'

'I see. Police Constable Meredith has given evidence that while you were in custody, you said to him, "I won't have bail, and when the next horse is ripped it will not be by me." Did you say those words?'

'Yes.'

'And what did you mean by them?'

'Merely what I said. There had been attacks on animals for weeks and months before my arrest, and because they had nothing to do with me, I expected them to continue. And if they did, that would prove the matter.'

'You see, Mr Edalji, it has been suggested, and will doubtless be suggested again, that there was a sinister reason why you refused bail. The supposition is that the Great Wyrley Gang, whose existence is constantly alluded to but entirely unproven, was to come to your rescue by deliberately mutilating another animal to demonstrate your innocence.'

'All I can say in reply is that if I had been clever enough to think up such a cunning plan, then I would also have been clever enough not to confess it in advance to a police constable.'

'Indeed, Mr Edalji, indeed.'

Mr Disturnal, as George had expected, was sarcastic and disrespectful in cross-examination. He asked George to explain many things he had already explained, solely in order to exhibit a theatrical disbelief. His strategy was designed to show that the prisoner was extremely cunning and devious, yet constantly incriminating himself. George knew that he must leave Mr Vachell to point this out. He must not allow himself to be provoked; he must take his time in answering; he must be stolid.

Of course Mr Disturnal did not fail to bring up the fact that George had walked as far as Mr Green's farm on the evening of the 17th, and allowed himself to wonder why this might have slipped George's mind while giving evidence. The prosecuting counsel also showed himself ruthless when it came, as it inevitably did, to the matter of the hairs on George's clothing.

'Mr Edalji, you said in sworn evidence that the hairs on your clothing were acquired by leaning against a gate into a field where cows were paddocked.'

'I said that is possibly how they got there.'

'Yet Dr Butter picked twenty-nine hairs from your clothing, which he then examined under a microscope and found to be identical in length, colour and structure to the hairs of the coat cut from the dead pony.'

'He did not say identical. He said similar.'

'Did he?' Mr Disturnal was briefly disconcerted, and pretended to consult his papers. 'Indeed. "Similar in length, colour and structure." How do you explain this similarity, Mr Edalji?'

'I am unable to. I am not an expert in animal hairs. I am only able to suggest how such hairs might have appeared on my clothing.'

'Length, colour and structure, Mr Edalji. Are you seriously asking the court to believe that the hairs on your coat came from a cow in a paddock, when they had the length, colour and structure belonging to the pony ripped scarcely a mile from your house on the night of the 17th?'

George had no reply to make.

Mr Vachell called Mr Lewis back to the witness box. The police veterinary surgeon repeated his statement that the pony could not, in his view, have been injured before 2.30 a.m. He was then asked what kind of instrument might have inflicted the damage. A curved weapon with concave sides. Did Mr Lewis think the wound could have been made with a domestic razor? No, Mr Lewis did not think the wound could have been made with a razor.

Mr Vachell then called Shapurji Edalji, clerk in holy orders, who repeated his evidence about sleeping arrangements, the door, the key, his lumbago and his time of awakening. George thought his father, for the first time, was beginning to look like an old man. His voice seemed less compelling, his certainties less obviously irrefutable.

George became anxious as Mr Disturnal rose to cross-examine the Vicar of Great Wyrley. The prosecution counsel exuded courtesy, assuring the witness he would not detain him long. This, however, turned out to be a grossly false promise. Mr Disturnal took every tiny detail of George's alibi and held it up before the jury, as if trying to assess for the first time its exact weight and value.

'You lock the bedroom door at night?'

George's father looked surprised to be asked again a question he had already answered. He paused for longer than seemed natural. Then he said, 'I do.'

'And unlock it in the morning?'

Again, an unnatural pause. 'I do.'

'And where do you put the key?'

'The key remains in the lock.'

'You do not hide it?'

The Vicar looked at Mr Disturnal as if at some impertinent schoolboy. 'Why on earth should I hide it?'

'You never hide it? You have never hidden it?'

George's father looked quite puzzled. 'I do not understand why you are asking me that question.'

'I am merely trying to establish if the key is always in the lock.'

'But that is what I said.'

'Always in full view? Never hidden?'

'But that is what I said.'

When George's father had given evidence at Cannock, the questions had been straightforward, and the witness box might as well have been a pulpit, with the Vicar bearing witness to God's very existence. Now, under Mr Disturnal's interrogation, he – and the world with him – was beginning to appear more fallible.

'You have said that the key squeaks as it turns in the lock.'

'Yes.'

'Is this a recent development?'

'Is what a recent development?'

'The key squeaking in the lock.' The prosecuting counsel's attitude was one of helping an old man over a stile. 'Has it always done this?'

'For as long as I can remember.'

Mr Disturnal smiled at the Vicar. George did not like the look of that smile. 'And – in all this time – as long as you can remember – no one has ever thought to oil the lock?'

'No.'

'May I ask you, sir, and this may seem a minor question to you, but I should like your answer nonetheless – why has no one ever oiled the lock?'

'I suppose it has never seemed important.'

'It is not from lack of oil?'

The Vicar unwisely allowed his irritation to show. 'You had better ask my wife about our supplies of oil.'

'I may do so, sir. And, this squeak, how would you describe it?'

'What do you mean? It is a squeak.'

'Is it a loud squeak or a soft squeak? Might it be compared, for instance, to the squeak of a mouse or the creak of a barn door?'

Shapurji Edalji looked as if he had stumbled into a den of triviality. 'I suppose I would characterize it as a loud squeak.'

'All the more surprising, perhaps, that the lock was not oiled. But be that as it may. The key squeaks loudly, once in the evening, once in the morning. And on other occasions?'

'I fail to follow you.'

'I mean, sir, when you or your son leave the bedroom at night.'

'But neither of us ever does.'

'Neither of you ever does. I understand this . . . sleeping arrangement has been in existence now for sixteen or seventeen years. You are saying that in all this time neither one of you has ever left the bedroom during the night?'

'No.'

'You are quite sure of this?'

Again, there was a long pause, as if the Vicar were running through the years in his head, night by night. 'As sure as I can be.'

'You have a memory of each night?'

'I do not see the point of that question.'

'Sir, I do not ask you to see its point. I merely request that you answer it. Do you have a memory of each night?'

The Vicar looked around the court, as if expecting someone to rescue him from this imbecilic catechism. 'No more than anybody else.'

'Exactly. You have given evidence that you are a light sleeper.'

'Yes, very light. I wake easily.'

'And, sir, you have testified that if the key was turned in the lock, it would wake you up?'

'Yes.'

'Do you not see the contradiction in that statement?'

'No, I do not.' George could see his father becoming flustered. He was not used to having his word challenged, however courteously. He was looking old, and irritable, and less than master of the situation.

'Then let me explain. No one has left the room in seventeen years. So – according to you – no one has ever turned the key while you were asleep. So how can you possibly assert that if the key were turned, it would wake you up?'

'This is angels dancing on pinheads. I mean, obviously, that the slightest noise wakes me.' But he sounded more petulant than authoritative.

'You have never been woken by the sound of the key turning?'

'No.'

'So you cannot swear that you would be woken by that sound?'

'I can only repeat what I have just said. The slightest noise wakes me.'

'But if you have never been woken by the sound of the key turning, is it not entirely possible that the key has been turned and you have not woken?'

'As I say, it has never happened.'

George watched his father as a dutiful, anxious son, but also as a professional solicitor and apprehensive prisoner. His father was not doing well. Mr Disturnal was easing him first one way, then the other.

'Mr Edalji, you stated in your evidence that you woke at five and did not go back to sleep until you and your son rose at six thirty?'

'Are you doubting my word?'

Mr Disturnal did not exhibit pleasure at this response; but George knew that he would be feeling it.

'No, I am merely asking for confirmation of what you have already said.'

'Then I confirm it.'

'You did not, perhaps, fall asleep again between five and six thirty and wake later?'

'I have said not.'

'Do you ever dream that you wake up?'

'I do not follow you.'

'Do you have dreams when you sleep?'

'Yes. Sometimes.'

'And do you sometimes dream that you wake up?'

'I do not know. I cannot remember.'

'But you accept that people do sometimes dream that they wake up?'

'I had never thought about it. It does not seem important to me what other people dream.'

'But you will accept my word that other people do have such dreams?'

The Vicar now looked like some hermit in the desert being led into temptations whose nature he was quite unable to comprehend. 'If you say so.' George was equally baffled by Mr Disturnal's procedure; but soon the prosecutor's intention became clearer.

'So you are as certain as you are reasonably able to be that you were awake between five and six thirty?'

'Yes.'

'And so you are equally certain that you were asleep between the hours of eleven and five?'

'Yes.'

'You do not remember waking in that period?'

George's father looked as if his word were being doubted again.

'No.'

Mr Disturnal nodded. 'So you were asleep at one thirty, for instance. At –' he seemed to pluck the time from the air '– at two thirty, for instance. At three thirty, for instance. Yes, thank you. Now, moving to another matter . . .'

And so it went, on and on, with George's father turning, before the court's eyes, into a dotard as uncertain as he doubtless was honourable; a man whose peculiar attempts at domestic security could easily have been outwitted by his clever son who, shortly before, had been so confident in the witness box. Or perhaps something even worse: a father who, suspecting his son might possibly have had some involvement in the outrages, was anxiously but incompetently adjusting his evidence as he proceeded.

Next came George's mother, the more nervous for just having witnessed her husband's unprecedented fallibility. After Mr Vachell had taken her through her evidence, Mr Disturnal, with a kind of idle civility, took her through it all again. He seemed only mildly interested in her replies; he was no longer the pitiless prosecutor, but rather the new neighbour dropping in for a polite tea.

'You have always been proud of your son, Mrs Edalji?'

'Oh yes, very proud.'

'And he has always been a clever boy, and a clever young man?'

'Oh, yes, very clever.'

Mr Disturnal made an oleaginous pretence of deep concern for the distress Mrs Edalji must feel at finding herself and her son in their current circumstances.

This was not a question, but George's mother automatically took it as such, and began to praise her son. 'He was always a studious boy. He gained many prizes at school. He studied at Mason College in Birmingham, and was a Law Society medallist. His book on railway law was very well received by many newspapers and law journals. It is published, you know, as one of the Wilson's Legal Handy Books.'

Mr Disturnal encouraged this effusion of maternal pride. He asked if there was anything else she would like to say.

'I would.' Mrs Edalji looked across at her son in the dock. 'He has always been kind and dutiful to us, and from a child he was always kind to any dumb creature. It would have been impossible for him to maim or injure anything, even if we had not known he was not out of the house.'

You would almost have thought Mr Disturnal was himself a son of hers from the way he thanked her; a son, that is, who was deeply indulgent towards the blind good-heartedness and naivety of his old white-headed mother.

Maud was called next, to give her account of the state of George's clothing. Her voice was steady, and her evidence lucid; even so, George felt petrified as Mr Disturnal rose, nodding to himself.

'Your evidence, Miss Edalji, is exactly the same, down to the smallest detail, as that of your parents.'

Maud looked evenly back at him, waiting to see if this was a question, or the precursor to some deadly assault. Whereupon Mr Disturnal, with a sigh, sat down again.

Later, at the deal table in the basement of Shire Hall, George felt exhausted and dispirited. 'Mr Meek, I fear my parents were not good witnesses.'

'I would not say that, Mr Edalji. It is rather the case that the best people are not necessarily the best witnesses. The more scrupulous they are, the more honest, the more they dwell on each word of the question and doubt themselves out of modesty, then the more they can be played with by counsel like Mr Disturnal. This is not the first time it has happened, I can assure you. How can I put it? It's a question of belief. What we believe, why we believe it. From a purely legal point of view, the best witnesses are those whom the jury believes most.'

'In fact, they were bad witnesses.' All through the trial it had been not George's hope but his certainty that his father's evidence would bring him instant vindication. The prosecuting counsel's attack would break against the rock of his father's integrity, and Mr Disturnal would come away like a miscreant parishioner rebuked for idle slander. But the attack had never come, or rather not in the form that George had anticipated; and his father had failed him, had failed to reveal himself as an Olympian deity whose sworn word was irrebuttable. Instead, he had shown himself pedantic, prickly and at times confused. George had wanted to explain to the court that if as a boy he had committed the slightest misdemeanour, his father would have marched him to the police station and demanded exemplary punishment: the higher the duty, the greater the sin. But instead the opposite impression had emerged: that his parents were indulgent fools who could easily be duped. 'They were bad witnesses,' he repeated dismally.

'They spoke the truth,' replied Mr Meek. 'And we should not have expected them to do otherwise, or in a fashion that was not their own. We should trust the jury to be able to see that. Mr Vachell is confident for tomorrow; so must we be.'

And by the next morning, as George was taken from Stafford Gaol to Shire Hall for the last time, as he prepared to hear his story laid out in its final and ever-diverging form, he felt in good heart again. It was Friday 23rd October. By tomorrow he would be back at the Vicarage. On Sunday he would worship again beneath the upturned keel of St Mark's. And on Monday the 7.39 would take him back to Newhall Street, to his desk, his work, his books. He would celebrate his freedom by beginning a subscription to *Halsbury's Laws of England*.

As he emerged from the narrow staircase into the dock, the courtroom seemed even more crowded than on previous days. The excitement was both palpable and, to George, alarming: it did not feel like the grave anticipation of justice, more like a vulgar theatrical expectation. Mr Vachell looked across and smiled at him, the first time he had made such a gesture openly. George did not know whether to return the greeting in the same fashion, but settled for a slight inclination of the head. He looked across at the jury, twelve good Staffordshire men and true, who from the start had struck him as being of decent and sober mien. He noted the presence of Captain Anson and Inspector Campbell, his twin accusers. Though not his real accusers – they were perhaps out on Cannock Chase, gloating at what they had done, and even now sharpening what in Mr Lewis's view was a curved weapon with concave sides.

At Sir Reginald Hardy's invitation, Mr Vachell began his final address. He asked members of the jury to put aside the sensational aspects of the case – the newspaper headlines, the public hysteria, the rumours and allegations – and concentrate their minds on the simple facts. There was not the slightest evidence to show that George Edalji had left the Vicarage – a building closely watched by the Staffordshire Constabulary for days previously – on the night of the 17th to 18th of August. There was not the slightest evidence to connect him to the crime with which he was charged: the minuscule bloodstains found could have come from any source, and were quite incompatible with the violent damage wreaked upon the Colliery pony; as for the hairs supposedly found upon his clothing, there was a complete discrepancy of evidence, and, even had hairs existed, there were alternative explanations for their presence. Then there were the anonymous letters denouncing George Edalji, which the prosecution maintained had been written by the defendant himself, a ludicrous suggestion quite out of keeping with both logic and the criminal mind; as for Mr Gurrin's testimony, it was no more than a matter of opinion, from which the jury was entitled, and indeed expected, to dissociate itself.

Mr Vachell then dealt with the various innuendos made against his client. His refusal to accept bail had been made out of reasonable, not to say admirable, sentiments: the filial desire to lighten the burden on his frail and elderly parents. Then there was the murky business of John Harry Green to consider. The prosecution had sought to tarnish George Edalji by association; yet not the slightest link had been established between the defendant and Mr Green, whose absence from the witness box spoke volumes. In this, as in other regards, the prosecution case amounted to no more than a thing of shreds and patches, of hints and innuendos and insinuations, none of which connected to one another. 'What have we left,' counsel for the defence asked in peroration, 'what have we left after four days here in this courtroom, except the crumbling, crumpled and shattered theories of the police?'

George was pleased as Mr Vachell regained his seat. It had been clear, well-argued, with no false emotional appeals of the kind some advocates went in for; and it had been most professional – that is to say, George had noted the places where Mr Vachell took more liberties of phrasing and inference than might have been allowed in Court A under Lord Hatherton.

Mr Disturnal was in no hurry; he stood and waited, as if for the effect of Mr Vachell's closing words to dissipate. Then he began to take those shreds and patches alluded to by his adversary, and patiently sewed them back together again, making a cloak to hang round George's shoulders. He asked the jury to consider first the behaviour of the prisoner, and reflect upon whether or not it was that of an innocent man. The refusal to wait for Inspector Campbell and the smile at the railway station; the lack of surprise at his arrest; the question about Blewitt's dead horses; the threat to the mysterious Loxton; the refusal of bail and the confident prediction that the Great Wyrley gang would strike again and effect his liberation. Was this the behaviour of an innocent man, Mr Disturnal asked as he reconnected each of these links for the jury's mind.

The bloodstains; the handwriting; and then the clothing yet again. The prisoner's clothes were wet, his house-coat and boots in particular. The police had stated this, and sworn this. Every policeman who had examined his house-coat had testified that it was wet. If so, and if the police were not completely mistaken – and how could or should they be? – then there was only one possible explanation. George Edalji had, as the prosecution maintained, stealthily crept out of the Vicarage into the stormy night of the 17th to the 18th of August.

But even so, despite the overwhelming evidence of the prisoner's deep involvement in the crime, whether alone or with others, there was, Mr Disturnal admitted, one question that needed to be answered. What had been his motive? It was a question the jury had every right to raise. And Mr Disturnal was there to help with the reply.

'If you are to ask yourselves, as others in the courtroom have done over these past days, But what is the prisoner's motive? Why should an outwardly respectable young man commit such a heinous act? Various explanation might offer themselves to the mind of the reasonable observer. Might the prisoner have been acting out of specific spite and malice? It is possible, though perhaps unlikely, given that far too many victims have been involved in the Great Wyrley Outrages and the campaign of anonymous libel that accompanied it. Could he have acted out of insanity? You might judge so, when faced with the unspeakable barbarity of his actions. And yet this too falls short of an explanation, for the crime was too well planned, and too cleverly executed, for it to have been carried out by someone who was insane. No: we must, I would suggest, look for the motivation in a brain that was not diseased, but rather formed differently from that of ordinary men and women. The motive was not financial gain, or revenge against an individual, but rather a desire for notoriety, a desire for anonymous self-importance, a desire to cheat the police at every turn, a desire to laugh in the face of society, a desire to prove oneself superior. Like you, members of the jury, I have at different moments of the trial, convinced as I am and as you will be of the prisoner's guilt, I have found myself asking, but why, but why? And this is what I would say to that question. It really does seem to point to a person who did these outrages from some diabolical cunning in the corner of his brain.'

George, who had been listening with his head slightly bowed, so as to concentrate on Mr Disturnal's words, realized that the address had come to a close. He looked up, and found the prosecutor staring dramatically across at him as if, only now, he was finally seeing the prisoner in the full light of truth. The jury, thus authorized by Mr Disturnal, was also openly scrutinizing him; as was Sir Reginald Hardy; as was the whole courtroom, with the exception of his family. Perhaps PC Dubbs and the other constable standing behind him in the dock were even now examining the jacket of his suit for bloodstains.

The Chairman began his summing-up at a quarter to one, referring to the Outrages as 'a blot on the name of the county'. George listened, but was constantly aware that he was being assessed by twelve good men and true for manifestations of diabolical cunning. There was nothing he could do about it, except try to look as stolid as possible. That was how he must appear in the last few minutes before his fate was decided. Be stolid, he told himself, be stolid.

At two o'clock, Sir Reginald sent the jury away and George was taken down to the basement. PC Dubbs stood guard, as he had done for the previous four days, with the slightly embarrassed air of one who knew George was hardly the escaping type. He had treated his prisoner with respect, and never once manhandled him. Given that there was now no chance of his words being misinterpreted, George engaged him in conversation.

'Constable, in your experience, is it a good thing or a bad thing if the jury takes a long time making up its mind?'

Dubbs thought about this for a while. 'In my experience, sir, I'd say it could be either a good thing or a bad thing. One or the other. It depends really.'

'I see,' said George. He did not usually say 'I see', and recognized he must have caught the mannerism from the barristers. 'And in your experience, what if the jury makes its mind up speedily?'

'Ah, now that, sir, that could be either a good thing or a bad thing. It depends on circumstances really.'

George allowed himself a smile, and Dubbs or anyone else could make of it what they would. It seemed to him that if the jury returned quickly, that must – given the gravity of the case and the need for all twelve to agree – be good for him. And a slow return would not be bad either, because the longer they considered the matter, the more its essentials would rise to the surface and the furious distractions of Mr Disturnal would be seen for what they were.

Constable Dubbs seemed as surprised as George when the call came after only forty minutes. They made their last journey together along the dim passages and up the stairs into the dock. At a quarter to three the clerk of the court put to the foreman words long familiar to George.

'Gentlemen of the jury, have you reached a verdict on which you are all agreed?'

'Yes, sir.'

'Do you find the prisoner, George Ernest Thompson Edalji, guilty or not guilty on the charge of maiming a horse, the property of the Great Wyrley Colliery Company?'

'Guilty, sir.'

No, that's wrong, George thought. He looked at the foreman, a white-haired, schoolmasterly fellow with a light Staffordshire accent. You just said the wrong words. Unsay them. You meant to say, Not guilty. That is the correct answer to the question. All this rushed through George's mind, until he realized that the foreman was still on his feet and about to speak. Yes, of course, he was going to correct his mistake.

'The jury, on reaching its verdict, has a recommendation to mercy.'

'On what grounds?' asked Sir Reginald Hardy, peering across at the foreman.

'His position.'

'His personal position?'

'Yes.'

The Chairman and the two other justices retired to consider sentence. George could scarcely look at his family. His mother was pressing a handkerchief to her face; his father staring dully ahead. Maud, whom he had expected to be wailing, surprised him. She had turned her whole body in his direction and was gazing up towards him, gravely, lovingly. He felt that if he could retain that look in his memory, then the worst things might possibly be bearable.

But before he could think further, George was being addressed by the Chairman, who had taken barely a few minutes to make his decision.

'George Edalji, the verdict of the jury is a right one. They have recommended you to mercy in consideration of the position you hold. We have to determine what punishment to award. We have to take into consideration your personal position, and what any punishment means to you. On the other hand, we have to consider the state of the county of Stafford, and of the Great Wyrley district, and the disgrace inflicted on the neighbourhood by this condition of things. Your sentence is one of penal servitude for seven years.'

A kind of under-murmur went through the court, a throaty yet inexpressive noise. George thought: no, seven years, I cannot survive seven years, even Maud's look cannot sustain me that long. Mr Vachell must explain, he must say something in protest.

Instead, it was Mr Disturnal who rose. Now that a conviction had been achieved, it was time for magnanimity. The charge of sending a threatening letter to Sergeant Robinson would not be proceeded with.

'Take him down' – and Constable Dubbs's hand was on his arm, and before he had time for one last exchange of glances with his family, one last look around the light of the courtroom where he had so confidently expected justice to be delivered, he was thrust down through the trapdoor, down into the flickering gaslight of the crepuscular basement. Dubbs explained politely that, given the verdict, he was now required to put the prisoner in the holding cell while awaiting transport to the gaol. George sat there inertly, his mind still in the courtroom, slowly going over the events of the last four days: evidence supplied, answers given in cross-examination, legal tactics. He had no complaints about his solicitor's diligence or his barrister's effectiveness. As for the prosecution: Mr Disturnal had put his case cleverly and antagonistically, but this had been expected; and yes, Mr Meek had been correct about the fellow's skill at making bricks despite the unavailability of straw.

And then his capacity for calm professional analysis ran out. He felt immensely tired and yet also over-excited. His sequential thoughts lost their steady pace; they lurched, they plunged ahead, they followed emotional gravity. It was suddenly borne in upon him that until minutes ago only a few people – mostly policemen, and perhaps some foolishly ignorant members of the public, the sort who would beat on the doors of a passing cab – had actually assumed him guilty. But now – and shame broke over him at the realization – now almost everyone would think him so. Those who read the newspapers, his fellow solicitors in Birmingham, passengers on the morning train to whom he had distributed flyers for *Railway Law*. Next he started picturing specific individuals who would think him guilty: like Mr Merriman the stationmaster, and Mr Bostock the schoolteacher, and Mr Greensill the butcher who from now on would always remind him of Gurrin the handwriting expert, the man who judged him capable of writing blasphemy and filth. And not just Gurrin – Mr Merriman and Mr Bostock and Mr Greensill would believe that as well as slitting the bellies of animals George was also the author of blasphemy and filth. So would the maid at the Vicarage, and the churchwarden, and so would Harry Charlesworth, whose friendship he had invented. Even Harry's sister Dora – had she existed – would have been revolted by him.

He imagined all these people looking at him – and now they were joined by Mr Hands the bootmaker. Mr Hands would think that George, after having himself expertly fitted for a new pair of boots, had gone calmly home, eaten his supper, deceitfully retired to bed, then crept out, struck across the fields and mutilated a pony. And when George imagined all these witnesses and accusers he felt such a wash of sorrow for himself, and for what had been done to his life, that he wanted to be allowed to stay in this subterranean dimness for ever. But before he could even hold himself at this level of misery, he was swept away again, because of course all these Wyrley folk would not be looking at him in this accusatory way – at least, not for many years. No, they would be looking at his parents: at Father in the pulpit, at Mother as she made her parish rounds; they would be looking at Maud when she entered a shop, at Horace when he came home from Manchester – if he ever came home again, given his brother's downfall. Everyone would look, and point, and say: their son, their brother did the Wyrley outrages. And he had inflicted this public and continuing humiliation upon his family, who were everything to him. They knew him innocent, but this only doubled his sense of guilt towards them.

They knew him innocent? And then despair bore him down further. They knew him innocent, but how could they stop turning over in their heads what they had seen and heard over the last four days? What if their belief in him began to falter? When they said they knew him innocent, what did that really mean? To know him innocent, they must either have sat up all night and observed him sleep, or else been on watch in the Colliery field when some lunatic farm-hand arrived with an evil instrument in his pocket. Only thus could they truly know. So what they did was believe, truly believe. And what if, over time, some words of Mr Disturnal, some assertion of Dr Butter, or some private long-held doubt about George, began to undermine their faith in him?

And this would be another thing he would have done to them. He would have sent them on a dismal journey of self-questioning. Today: we know George and we know him innocent. But perhaps in three months: we think we know George and we believe him innocent. And then in a year: we realize we did not know George, yet we still think him innocent. Who could blame anyone for this declension?

It was not just he who had been sentenced; his family had been too. If he was guilty, then some would conclude that his parents must have perjured themselves. So when the Vicar preached the difference between right and wrong, would his congregation think him either a hypocrite or a dupe? When his mother visited the downtrodden, might they not tell her she would be better off saving her sympathy for her criminal son in his distant gaol? This was another thing he had done: he had sentenced his own parents. Was there no end to these tormented imaginings, to this pitiless moral vortex? He waited for a further descent, a washing-away, a drowning; but then he thought again of Maud. He sat on his hard stool behind iron bars, while somewhere in that gloom Constable Dubbs whistled tunelessly to himself, and he thought of Maud. She was his source of hope, she would keep him from falling. He believed in Maud; he knew she would not falter, because he had seen the look she gave him in court. It was a look that did not need interpretation, that could not be corroded by time or malice; it was a look of love and trust and certainty.

When the crowds outside the courtroom had dispersed, George was taken back to Stafford Gaol. Here he encountered another realignment of his world. Having been in prison since his arrest, George had naturally come to regard himself as a prisoner. But in fact he had been lodged in the best hospital cell; he received newspapers every morning, food from his family, and was allowed to write business letters. Unreflectingly, he had assumed his circumstances to be temporary, attendant, briefly purgatorial.

Now he was truly a prisoner, and to prove it they took his clothes away. In itself this was ironic, since for weeks he had regretted and resented his inappropriate summer suit and otiose straw hat. Had the suit made him look less serious in court, and thus harmed his cause? He could not tell. In any case, suit and hat were taken away, and exchanged for the heavy weight and felty roughness of prison attire. The jacket overhung his shoulders, the trousers bagged at knee and ankle; he did not care. They also gave him a waistcoat, a forage cap, and a pair of wife-kickers.

'You'll find it a bit of a shock,' said the warder, bundling up the summer suit. 'But most get used to it. Even people like yourself, if you don't take offence.'

George nodded. He observed, gratefully, that the officer had spoken to him in just the same tone, and with just as much civility, as he had done over the previous eight weeks. This came as a surprise. He had somehow expected to be spat upon and reviled on his return to the gaol, an innocent man now publicly labelled guilty. But perhaps the terrifying change was only in his own mind. The officers' manner remained the same for a simple and dispiriting reason: from the start they had presumed him guilty, and the jury's decision had merely confirmed that presumption.

The next morning, as a favour, he was brought a newspaper, so that he might see, one final time, his life turned into headlines, his story no longer divergent but now consolidated into legal fact, his character no longer of his own authorship but delineated by others.

SEVEN YEARS PENAL SERVITUDE.

WYRLEY CATTLE-KILLER SENTENCED.

PRISONER UNMOVED

Dully, yet automatically, George looked over the rest of the page. The story of Miss Hickman the lady doctor appeared also to have reached its end, subsiding into silence and mystery. George noted that Buffalo Bill, after a London season and a provincial tour lasting 294 days, had concluded his programme at Burton-on-Trent before returning to the United States. And as important to the *Gazette* as the sentencing of the Wyrley 'cattle-killer' was the story right next to it:

YORKSHIRE RAILWAY SMASH

Two trains wrecked in a tunnel

One killed, 23 injured

BIRMINGHAM MAN'S THRILLING EXPERIENCE

He was held at Stafford for another twelve days, during which time his parents were allowed daily visits. He found this more painful than if he had been hustled into a van and driven to the most distant part of the kingdom. In this long farewelling each of them behaved as if George's current predicament was some bureaucratic error soon to be remedied by an appeal to the appropriate official. The Vicar had received many letters of support and was already talking enthusiastically of a public campaign To George this zeal seemed to border on hysteria, and its origins to lie in guilt. George did not feel his situation to be temporary, and his father's plans did not bring him any comfort. They seemed more an expression of religious belief than anything else.

After twelve days George was transferred to Lewes. Here he received a new uniform of coarse biscuit-coloured linen. There were two broad vertical stripes up the front and back, and thick, clumsily printed arrows. They gave him ill-fitting knickerbockers, black stockings and boots. A prison officer explained that he was a star man, and therefore would begin his sentence with three months' separate – it might be longer, it wouldn't be shorter. Separate meant solitary confinement. That was what all star men began with. George misunderstood at first: he thought he was being called a star man because his case had attracted notoriety; perhaps the perpetrators of especially heinous crimes were deliberately kept apart from other prisoners, who might vent their anger on a horse-mutilator. But no: a star man was simply the term for a first offender. If you come back, he was told, you will be classed as an intermediary; and if your returns are frequent, as an ordinary or a professional. George said he had no intention of coming back.

He was taken before the Governor, an old military man who surprised him by staring at the name before him and asking politely how it was to be pronounced.

'*Ay*dlji, sir.'

'Ay-dl-ji,' repeated the Governor. 'Not that you'll be much except a number here.'

'No, sir.'

'Church of England, it says.'

'Yes. My father is a Vicar.'

'Indeed. Your mother . . .' The Governor did not seem to know how to ask the question.

'My mother is Scottish.'

'Ah.'

'My father is a Parsee by birth.'

'Now I'm with you. I was in Bombay in the Eighties. Fine city. You know it well, Ay-dl-ji?'

'I'm afraid I've never left England, sir. Though I have been to Wales.'

'Wales,' said the Governor musingly. 'You're one up on me then. Solicitor, it says.'

'Yes, sir.'

'We've rather a slump in solicitors at the moment.'

'I beg your pardon?'

'Solicitors – we've a slump in 'em at the moment. Normally we have one or two. One year we had more than half a dozen, I recall. But we got rid of our last solicitor a few months ago. Not that you'd have been able to talk to him much. You'll find the rules here are strict, and fully enforced, Mr Aydl-ji.'

'Yes, sir.'

'Still, we've got a couple of stockbrokers with us, and a banker as well. I tell people, if you want to see a true cross-section of society, you should visit Lewes Prison.' He was accustomed to saying this, and paused for the usual effect. 'Not that we have any members of the aristocracy, I hasten to add. Or,' – with a glance at George's file – 'any Church of England ministers at present. Though we have had the occasional one. Indecency, that sort of thing.'

'Yes, sir.'

'Now I'm not going to ask exactly what you did, or why you did it, or whether you did it, or whether any petition you might forward to the Home Secretary stands more chance than a mouse with a mongoose, because in my experience all that's a waste of time. You're in prison. Serve your sentence, obey the rules, and you won't get into any further trouble.'

'As a lawyer, I am used to rules.'

George meant this neutrally, but the Governor looked up as if it might have been a piece of insolence. Eventually, he settled for saying, 'Quite.'

There were indeed a large number of rules. George found the prison officers to be decent fellows, yet bound hand and foot by red tape. There was no talking to other prisoners. There was no crossing of legs or folding of arms in chapel. There was a bath once a fortnight, and a search of the prisoner's self and belongings whenever the necessity arose.

On the second day, a warder came into George's cell and asked if he had a bed-rug.

George thought this an unnecessary question. It was perfectly plain that he had a multi-coloured and reasonably heavy bed-rug, which the officer could not miss.

'Yes, I do, thank you very much.'

'What do you mean, thank you very much?' asked the warder with more than a touch of belligerance.

George remembered his police interrogations. Perhaps his tone had been too forward. 'I mean, I do,' he said.

'Then it must be destroyed.'

Now he was completely lost. This was a rule which had not been explained to him. He was careful with his reply, and especially with its tone.

'I do apologize, but I have not been here long. Why should you wish to destroy my bed-rug, which is both a comfort and, I imagine, in the harsher months, a necessity?'

The warder looked at him and slowly began to laugh. He laughed so much that a colleague ducked into the cell to see if he was all right.

'Not bed-rug, number 247, bed-bug.'

George half-smiled in return, uncertain if prisoners were allowed to do so under prison regulations. Perhaps only if granted permission. At any rate, the story passed into prison lore, and followed him down the succeeding months. That Hindoo lived such a sheltered life he didn't even know what a bed-bug was.

He discovered other discomforts instead. There were no proper conveniences, and a lack of privacy when it was most required. Soap was of a very poor quality. There was also an idiotic regulation that all shaving and barbering had to be done in the open air, which resulted in many prisoners – George included – catching colds.

He quickly became accustomed to the altered rhythm of his life. 5.45 rise. 6.15 doors unlocked, slops collected, bedclothes hung up to air. 6.30 tools served round, then work. 7.30 breakfast. 8.15 fold up bedding. 8.35 chapel. 9.05 return. 9.20 go to exercise. 10.30 return. Governor's rounds and other bureaucracy. 12 dinner. 1.30 dinner tins collected, then work. 5.30 supper, then tools collected and put outside for the next day. 8 bed.

Life was harsher and colder and more lonely than he had ever known it; but he was helped by this rigid structure to the day. He had always lived to a strict timetable; also with a heavy workload, whether as schoolboy or solicitor. There had been very few holidays in his life – that outing to Aberystwyth with Maud was a rare exception – and fewer luxuries, except those of the mind and spirit.

'The things star men miss the most,' said the Chaplain, on the first of his weekly visits, 'is the beer. Well, not just the star men. Intermediaries and ordinaries too.'

'Fortunately, I do not drink.'

'And the second thing is the cigarettes.'

'Again, I am lucky in that regard.'

'And the third is the newspapers.'

George nodded. 'That has been a severe deprivation already, I admit. I have been in the habit of reading three papers a day.'

'If there was anything I could do to help . . .' said the Chaplain. 'But the rules . . .'

'It is perhaps better to do entirely without something than hope from time to time that you might receive it.'

'I wish others had your attitude. I've seen men go crazy for a cigarette or a drink. And some of them miss their girls terribly. Some of them miss their clothes, some of them miss things they never even knew they were fond of, like the smell outside the back door on a summer's night. Everyone misses something.'

'I am not being complacent,' replied George. 'I am just able to think practically in the matter of newspapers. In other respects I am like everyone else, I am sure.'

'And what do you miss most?'

'Oh,' replied George, 'I miss my life.'

The Chaplain seemed to imagine that George, as the son of a clergyman, would draw his principal comfort and consolation from the practise of his religion. George did not disabuse him, and he attended chapel more willingly than most; but he knelt and sang and prayed in the same spirit as he put out his slops and folded his bedding and worked, as something to help get him through the day. Most of the prisoners went to work in the sheds, where they made mats and baskets; a star man doing three months' separate had to work in his own cell. George was given a board and bundles of heavy yarn. He was shown how to plait the yarn, using the board as a pattern. He produced, slowly and with great effort, oblongs of thick plaited material to a determined size. When he had finished six, they were taken away. Then he started another batch, and another.

After a couple of weeks, he asked a prison officer what the purpose of these shapes might be.

'Oh, you should know, 247, you should know.'

George tried to think where he might have come across such material before. When it was clear he was at a loss, the warder picked up two of the completed oblongs, and pressed them together. Then he held them beneath George's chin. When this gained no response, he put them beneath his own chin and started opening and closing his mouth in a wet and noisy fashion.

George was baffled by this charade. 'I am afraid not.'

'Oh, come on. You can get it.' The warder made noisier and noisier chomping sounds.

'I cannot guess.'

'Horses' nose-bags, 247, horses' nose-bags. Must be congenial, seeing as you're a man familiar with about horses.'

George felt a sudden numbness. So he knew; they all knew; they talked and joked about it. 'Am I the only person making these?'

The warder grinned. 'Don't count yourself so special, 247. You're doing the plaiting, you and half a dozen others. Some do the sewing together. Some make the ropes for tying round the horse's head. Some put them all together. And some pack them up for sending off.'

No, he wasn't special. That was his consolation. He was just a prisoner among prisoners, working as they worked, someone whose crime was no more alarming than that of many others, someone who could choose to be well-behaved or badly behaved, but had no choice about his fundamental status. Even being a solicitor here was not unusual, as the Governor had pointed out. He decided to be as normal as it was possible to be, given the circumstances.

When told that he would serve six months' separate rather than just three, George did not complain, or even ask the reason. The truth was, he thought that what newspapers and books referred to as 'the horrors of solitary confinement' were grossly exaggerated. He would rather have too little company than too much of the wrong sort. He was still permitted to exchange words with the warders, the Chaplain, and the Governor on his rounds, even if he did have to wait for them to speak first. He could use his voice in chapel, singing the hymns and joining in the responses. And during exercise, permission was usually given to talk; though finding common ground with the fellow walking beside you was not always straightforward.

There was, furthermore, a capital library at Lewes, and the librarian called twice a week to take away books he had finished with and replenish his shelf. He was allowed to borrow one work of an educational nature and one 'library' book per week. By 'library' book he was to understand anything from a popular novel to a volume of the classics. George set himself to read all the great works of English literature, and the histories of significant nations. He was naturally permitted a Bible in his cell; though he found increasingly that after four hours struggling with board and yarn each afternoon, it was not the cadences of Holy Writ that he yearned for, but the next chapter of Sir Walter Scott. At times, shut in his cell, reading a novel, safe from the rest of the world, his brightly coloured bed-rug catching the corner of his eye, George felt a sense of order that was almost edging towards contentment.

He learned from his father's letters that there had been a public outcry at his verdict. Mr Voules had taken up his case in *Truth*, and a petition was being raised by Mr R.D. Yelverton, late Chief Justice of the Bahamas, now of Pump Court in the Temple. Signatures were being gathered, and already many solicitors in Birmingham, Dudley and Wolverhampton had given their support. George was touched to discover that the signatories included Greenway and Stentson; they had always been decent dogs, those two. Witnesses were being interviewed, and testimonials to George's character gathered from schoolmasters, professional colleagues, and members of his family. Mr Yelverton had even been in receipt of a letter from Sir George Lewis, the greatest criminal lawyer of the day, expressing his considered opinion that George's conviction was fatally flawed.

It was clear that some official representations had been made on his behalf, because George was allowed to receive more communications regarding his case than would normally have been allowed. He read some of the testimonials. There was a purple carbon copy of a letter from his mother's brother, Uncle Stoneham of The Cottage, Much Wenlock. 'Whenever I have seen or heard of my nephew (until these abominable things were spoken of) I always found him nice and heard of his being nice and clever also.' There was something about the underlining that went straight to George's heart. Not the praise of him, which he found embarrassing, but the underlining. Here it was again. 'I first met Mr Edalji when he had been in orders for five years and had very good testimonials from other clergymen. Our friends at that time too felt as we did that Parsees are a very old and cultivated race, and have many good qualities.' And then again, in a post-scriptum. 'My Father and Mother gave their full consent to the marriage and they were deeply attached to my sister.'

As a son and a prisoner, George could not help being moved to tears by these words; as a lawyer, he doubted how much effect they would have on whichever Home Office functionary might eventually be appointed to review his case. He felt, at the same time, both keenly optimistic and entirely resigned. Part of him wanted to stay in his cell, plaiting nose-bags and reading the works of Sir Walter Scott, catching colds when his hair was cut in the freezing courtyard, and hearing the old joke about bed-bugs again. He wanted this because he knew it was likely to be his fate, and the best way to be resigned to your fate was to want it. The other part of him, which wanted to be free tomorrow, which wanted to embrace his mother and sister, which wanted public acknowledgement of the great injustice done him – this was the part he could not give full rein to, since it could end by causing him the most pain.

So he tried to remain stolid when he learned that ten thousand signatures had now been gathered, headed by those of the President of the Incorporated Law Society, of Sir George Lewis, and Sir George Birchwood, K.C.I.E., the high medical authority. Hundreds of solicitors had signed, not just from the Birmingham area; also King's Counsel, Members of Parliament – including those from Staffordshire – and citizens of every political hue. Sworn statements had been gathered from witnesses who had seen workmen and sightseers trampling the ground where subsequently PC Cooper had discovered his bootmarks. Mr Yelverton had also obtained a favourable statement from Mr Edward Sewell, a veterinary surgeon consulted by the prosecution and then not called in evidence. The petition, the statutory declarations and the testimonials together formed 'the Memorials', which were to be addressed to the Home Office.

In February, two things happened. On the 13th of the month, the *Cannock Advertiser* reported that another animal had been mutilated in exactly the same fashion as in previous outrages. A fortnight later, Mr Yelverton submitted the Memorials to the Home Secretary, Mr Akers-Douglas. George allowed himself the full indulgence of hope. In March two more things happened: the petition was rejected, and George was informed that on completion of his six months' separate, he would be moved to Portland.

He was not told the reason for the transfer, and did not ask. He assumed it was a way of saying: now you will get on and serve your sentence. Since part of him had always expected to do so, part of him – though not a large part – could be philosophical at the news. He told himself that he had exchanged the world of laws for the world of rules, and they were not perhaps so different. Prison was a simpler environment, since rules allowed no latitude for interpretation; but it was likely that the change was less disconcerting to him than to those whose previous existence had always been outside the law.

The cells at Portland did not impress him. They were made of corrugated iron, and to his eye resembled dog-kennels. Ventilation was also poor, and achieved by cutting a hole in the bottom of the door. There were no bells for prisoners, and if you wished to speak to a warder you placed your cap beneath the door. This was also the system by which the roll-call was made. Upon the cry of 'Caps under!' you placed your cap into the ventilation hole. There were four such roll-calls every day, but since counting caps proved less accurate than counting bodies, the laborious process often had to be repeated.

He acquired a new number, D462. The letter indicated his year of conviction. The system had started with the century: 1900 was year A; George had therefore been convicted in year D, 1903. A badge bearing this number, and the prisoner's term of sentence, was worn on the jacket, and also on the cap. Names were used more frequently here than at Lewes, but still you tended to know a man by his badge. So George was D462–7.

There was the usual interview with the Governor. This one, though perfectly civil, was from his first words less encouraging in manner than his colleague at Lewes. 'You should know it is pointless trying to escape. No one has ever escaped from Portland Bill. You will merely lose remission and discover the delights of solitary confinement.'

'I think I am probably the last person in the entire gaol who might try to escape.'

'I have heard that before,' said the Governor. 'Indeed, I have heard everything before.' He looked down at George's file. 'Religion. It says Church of England.'

'Yes, my father –'

'You can't change.'

George did not understand this remark. 'I have no desire to change my religion.'

'Good. Well, you can't anyway. Don't think you can get round the Chaplain. It's a waste of time. Serve your term and obey the warders.'

'That has always been my intention.'

'Then you're either wiser or more foolish than most.' With this enigmatic remark, the Governor waved for George to be taken away.

His cell was smaller and meaner than at Lewes, though he was assured by a warder who had served in the Army that it was better than a barracks. Whether this was true, or intended as unverifiable consolation, George had no means of knowing. For the first time in his prison career, his fingerprints were taken. He feared the moment when the doctor assessed his capacity for work. Everyone knew that those sent to Portland were given a pickaxe and ordered to break rocks in a quarry; leg-irons doubtless came into the reckoning as well. But his anxieties turned out to be misconceived: only a small percentage of the prisoners worked in the quarries, and star men were never sent there. Further, George's eyesight meant that he was judged fit only for light work. The doctor also deemed it unsafe for him to go up and down stairs; so he was located to No. 1 Ward on the ground floor.

He worked in his cell. He picked coir for stuffing beds, and hair for stuffing pillows. The coir had to be first combed out on a board, and then picked as fine as thread: only thus, he was told, would it be suitable to make the softest of beds. No proof of this claim was afforded; George never saw the next stage of the process, and his own mattress was definitely not filled with finely picked coir.

Halfway through his first week at Portland, the Chaplain visited him. His jovial manner implied that they were meeting in the vestry at Great Wyrley rather than a dog-kennel with a ventilation hole cut from the bottom of the door.

'Settling in?' he asked cheerily.

'The Governor seems to imagine my only thoughts are of escape.'

'Yes, yes, he says that to everyone. I think he rather enjoys the occasional escape, just between the two of us. The black flag raised, the cannon booming, the barracks turning out. And he always wins the game – he likes that too. No one ever gets off the Bill. If the soldiers don't get them, the citizenry does. There's a five-pound bounty for turning in an escaper, so there's no incentive to look the other way. Then it's a spell of chokey and a loss of remission. Just not worth it.'

'And the other thing the Governor told me was that I am not allowed to change my religion.'

'True enough.'

'But why should I want to?'

'Ah, you're a star man, of course. Don't know the ins and outs yet. You see, Portland has only Protestants and Catholics. About six to one, the ratio. But no Jews at all. If you were a Jew, you'd be sent to Parkhurst.'

'But I'm not a Jew,' said George, rather doggedly.

'No. Indeed not. But if you were an old lag – an ordinary – and you decided that Parkhurst was an easier billet than Portland, you might be released from Portland this year as an ardent member of the Church of England, but by the time the police caught you next time, you might have decided you were a Jew. Then you'd get sent to Parkhurst. But they made it a rule that you can't change your faith in the middle of a sentence. Otherwise prisoners would be coxing-and-boxing every six months, just for something to do.'

'The rabbi at Parkhurst must get some surprises.'

The Chaplain chuckled. 'Strange how a life of crime can turn a man into a Jew.'

George discovered that it was not just Jews who were sent to Parkhurst; invalids and those known to be a little bit off the top were also despatched there. You might not change religion at Portland, but if you broke down physically or mentally, you could be transferred. It was said that some prisoners deliberately put pickaxes through their feet, or pretended to be a little bit off the top – howling like dogs and tearing out their hair in clumps – in an attempt to gain a move. Most of them ended up in chokey instead, a few days' bread and water their only reward.

'Portland is in a most healthy situation,' George wrote to his parents. 'The air is very strong and bracing, and there is not much sickness.' He might as well have been writing a postcard from Aberystwyth. But it was true too, and he must find what comfort he could for them.

He soon grew used to his cramped accommodation and decided that Portland was a better place than Lewes. There was less red tape, and no idiotic regulation about being shaved and barbered in the open air. Also, the rules governing conversation between prisoners were more relaxed. The food was better too. He was able to inform his parents that there was a different dinner every day, and two kinds of soup. The bread was wholemeal – 'Better than baker's bread', he wrote, not as an attempt to evade censorship or ingratiate himself, but as a true expression of opinion. There were also green vegetables and lettuce. The cocoa was excellent, though the tea was poor stuff. Still, if you did not want tea, you might have porridge or gruel, and it surprised George that many insisted on having inferior tea rather than something more nutritious.

He was able to tell his parents that he had plenty of warm underclothing; also jerseys, leggings and gloves. The library was even better than at Lewes, and the terms of borrowing more generous: he could take out two 'library' books, plus four of an educational nature, every week. All the leading magazines were available in volume form, though both books and journals had been purged of undesirable matter by the prison authorities. George borrowed a history of recent British art, only to discover that all the illustrations of work by Sir Lawrence Alma-Tadema had been neatly removed by the official razor. At the front of the volume was the warning written in every book borrowed from the library: 'No turning down of pages.' Underneath it a prison wag had written, 'And no tearing out of pages.'

Hygiene was no better, though no worse, than at Lewes. If you wanted a toothbrush you had to apply to the Governor, who seemed to answer Yes or No according to some private, whimsical system.

One morning, in need of metal polish, George asked a warder if there was any chance of obtaining some Bath-brick.

'Bath-brick, D462!' replied the officer, his eyebrows leaping towards his cap. 'Bath-brick! You'll ruin the firm – you'll be asking for Bath-buns next.'

And that was the end of that.

George picked coir and hair each day; he took exercise as instructed, though with no great zeal; he borrowed his full allowance of books from the library. At Lewes he had become accustomed to eating with only a tin knife and a wooden spoon, and to the fact that the knife was often insufficient against prison beef and mutton. He no longer missed using a fork, any more than he missed newspapers. Indeed, he saw the absence of a daily paper as an advantage: lacking this daily prod from the outside world, he adapted more easily to the passage of time. Such events as occurred in his life now occurred within the prison walls. One morning, an inmate – C183, serving eight years for robbery – managed to climb on to the roof, whence he declared to the world that he was the Son of God. The Chaplain offered to go up a ladder and discuss the theological implications, but the Governor decided it was just another attempt to gain a transfer to Parkhurst. Eventually they starved him down and packed him off to chokey. C183 admitted in the end that he was the son of a potman and not of a carpenter.

After George had been in Portland a few months, there was an escape attempt. Two men – C202 and B178 – managed to hide a crowbar in their cell; they broke through the ceiling, gained the yard with the aid of a rope, and scaled a wall. The next time 'Caps under!' was called, there was hubbub: they were two caps short. There was another cap-count, followed by a count of bodies. The black flag was raised, the cannon fired, and the prisoners locked in for the interim. George did not mind this, even if he failed to share the general excitement, or join in the bet-laying over the outcome.

The two men had a couple of hours' start, but in the judgement of the ordinaries they would be lying low until nightfall, and only then attempt to get off the Bill. But when the dogs were loosed into the prison grounds, B178 was swiftly discovered, sheltering in a workshed and cursing an ankle broken when jumping from a roof. C202 took longer to find. Sentries were posted on all the heights of Chesil Beach; boats were launched in case the escapee had decided to swim for it; soldiers sealed the Weymouth Road. Quarries were scrutinized, and searches conducted of outlying properties. But the soldiers and prison guards did not find C202; he was brought in roped and bound by an innkeeper who had come upon him in his cellar and subdued him with the help of a drayman. The publican insisted on handing him over to the receiving officer at the gaol, and obtaining a promissory note in the sum of £5 for the capture.

The hubbub among the prisoners turned to disappointment, and the searching of cells became more frequent for a while. This was one aspect of life George found more disruptive than at Lewes; not least because the searches were in his case entirely pointless. First would come the order to 'unbutton'; then the officers would 'rub down' the prisoner to make sure nothing was concealed in his clothing. They would feel him all over, and examine his pocket, and even unfold his handkerchief. This was embarrassing for the prisoner, and George thought it must be hateful to the officers, since the clothes of many inmates were dirty and greasy from their work. Some officers were very careful in their searches, while others would not notice if a prisoner had a hammer and chisel concealed about his person.

Then there was 'turn over', which seemed to consist of the systematic wrecking of a cell, the sweeping of books from surfaces, the unmaking of the bed, and the scouring of potential places of concealment which George would never have guessed at. Worst by far, however, was the 'dry bath' search. You were taken to the bathhouse and made to stand on the wooden slats. You removed every stitch of clothing except your shirt. The officers minutely inspected each item. Then you were obliged to undergo humiliations – raising your legs, bending over, opening your mouth, putting out your tongue. Dry searches were sometimes ordered systematically, sometimes on a random basis. George estimated that he suffered this indignity at least as often as other prisoners. Perhaps, when he had expressed his disinclination to escape, they had taken it for a bluff.

And so the months went by, and then the first year, and then much of the second. Every six months his parents made the long journey from Staffordshire, and were allowed to spend an hour with him under the eyes of a guard. These visits were excruciating to George: not because he did not love his parents, but because he hated to see their suffering. His father seemed shrunken nowadays, and his mother could not bring herself to look around at the place where her son was incarcerated. George found it hard to strike the proper tone with them: if he was cheerful, they would think he was putting it on; if gloomy, he would make them gloomier themselves. Instead, he found himself adopting a neutral manner, helpful but inexpressive, like that of a booking office clerk.

Maud was initially judged too sensitive for such visits; but one year she arrived in the place of her mother. She had little chance to say anything, but whenever George glanced across at her, he encountered that steady, intense gaze he remembered from the courtroom at Stafford. It was as if she was trying to give him strength, to convey something from her mind to his mind without the medium of word or gesture. Later, he found himself wondering if he – they – had been wrong about Maud and her supposed frailty.

The Vicar did not notice. He was too busy telling George how, in the light of the change of government – a matter of which George was scarcely aware – the indefatigable Mr Yelverton was renewing his campaign. A fresh series of articles was planned by Mr Voules in *Truth*; while the Vicar intended issuing a pamphlet of his own about the case. George made a show of being heartened, but privately judged his father's enthusiasm to be foolish. More signatures might be acquired, but the essence of his case would not have changed, so why should officialdom's response change? He, as a lawyer, could see that.

He also knew that the Home Office was flooded with petitions from every gaol in the country. Four thousand Memorials were sent in annually; and a further thousand arrived from other sources on behalf of prisoners. But the Home Office was neither equipped nor empowered to retry a case; it could neither interview witnesses, nor hear counsel. All it could do was examine paperwork and advise the Crown accordingly. This meant that a free pardon was a statistical rarity. It might perhaps be different if there were some court of appeal, able to take a more active part in overturning injustice. But as things stood, the Vicar's belief that a frequent reiteration of innocence, backed up by the power of prayer, would bring about his son's release struck George as naive.

It grieved him to admit the fact, but George found his father's visits unhelpful. They disturbed the orderliness and calm of his life, and without orderliness and calm he did not think he could survive his sentence. Some prisoners counted off each day until their future release; George could only get through prison life by treating it as the only life he had or could ever have. His parents upset this illusion, as did his father's hopeful trust in Mr Yelverton. Perhaps if Maud were allowed to visit him by herself, she would fill him with strength, whereas his parents filled him with anxiety and shame. But he knew this would never be permitted.

The searches continued, the rub-downs and the dry baths. He read more history than he knew existed, had despatched all the classic authors and was now proceeding through the lesser ones. He had also read his way through entire runs of the *Cornhill Magazine* and the *Strand*. He was beginning to worry about exhausting the library's resources.

One morning he was taken to the Chaplain's office, photographed in both full face and profile, then instructed to grow a beard. He was told that in three months' time he would be photographed again. George could work out for himself the purpose of this record: it would be there for the police if he gave them future reason to search for him.

He did not like growing a beard. He had worn a moustache since Nature permitted, but had been ordered to shave it off at Lewes. Now he did not enjoy the daily prickle that spread across his cheeks and under his chin; he missed the feel of the razor. Nor did he like the look of himself with a beard: it gave him a criminal mien. There were remarks from the warders about him having a new hiding place. He carried on picking coir and reading Oliver Goldsmith. There were four years of his sentence left.

And then things suddenly became confusing. He was taken to be photographed, both full face and in profile. Then he was sent to be shaved. The barber told him he was lucky not to be in Strangeways, where they would charge him eighteen pence for the service. When he returned to his cell, he was ordered to collect his few belongings together and be ready for a transfer. He was driven to the station and put on a train with an escort. He could scarcely bring himself to look at the countryside, whose existence seemed to mock him, as did every horse and cow within it. He understood how men went mad from missing ordinary things.

When the train reached London, he was put in a cab and driven to Pentonville. There he was told that he was being prepared for discharge. He spent a day locked up by himself – the most miserable day, in retrospect, of his entire three years in gaol. He knew he should be happy; instead, he was as bewildered by his release as he had been by his arrest. Two detectives came and served him with papers; he was ordered to report to Scotland Yard, there to receive further instructions.

At ten thirty on the morning of October 19th, 1906, George Edalji left Pentonville in a cab with a Jew who was also being released. He did not enquire whether the fellow was a real Jew, or just a prison Jew. The cab dropped his fellow passenger at the Jewish Prisoners' Aid Society, and took him on to the Church Army's Aid Society. Prisoners who had joined such societies qualified for a double gratuity upon release. George was handed £2 9s.10d. Officers of the Society then took him to Scotland Yard, where the terms of his release on licence were explained. He was to supply the address where he would be staying; he was to report once a month to Scotland Yard; and he was to inform them in advance of any plans to leave London.

A newspaper had sent a photographer to Pentonville to obtain a snapshot of George Edalji leaving the prison. By mistake the man photographed a prisoner released half an hour before George; and so the newspaper printed a picture of the wrong man.

From Scotland Yard he was driven to meet his parents.

He was free.

Arthur

And then he meets Jean.

He is a few months short of his thirty-eighth birthday. He is painted that year by Sidney Paget, sitting straight-backed in an upholstered tub chair, frock coat half open, fob chains on show; in his left hand a notebook, in his right a silver propelling pencil. His hair is now receding above the temples, but this loss is made irrelevant by the compensating glory of the moustache: it colonizes his face above and beyond the upper lip and extends in waxed toothpicks out beyond the line of the earlobes. It gives Arthur the commanding air of a military prosecutor; one whose authority is endorsed by the quartered coat of arms in the top corner of the portrait.

Arthur is the first to admit that his knowledge of women is that of a gentleman rather than a cad. There were certain boisterous flirtations in his early life – even an episode which had to do with flying fish. There was Elmore Weldon who, if it was not an ungentlemanly observation, did weigh eleven stone. There is Touie who, over the years, became a companionable sister to him and then, suddenly, an invalid sister. There are, of course, his real sisters. There are the statistics of prostitution which he reads at his club. There are stories told over port which he sometimes declines to hear, stories involving, for instance, private rooms in discreet restaurants. There are the gynaecological cases he has seen, the confinements he has attended, and the cases of disease among Portsmouth sailors and other men of low morals. His understanding of the sexual act is diverse, though related more to its unfortunate consequences than to its joyful preliminaries and processes.

His mother is the only woman to whose governance he is prepared to submit. With other members of the sex he has been, variously, large brother, substitute father, dominant husband, prescribing doctor, generous writer of blank cheques and Father Christmas. He is solidly content with the separation and distinction of the sexes as developed by society in its wisdom through the centuries. He is resolutely against the notion of votes for women: when a man comes home from work, he does not want a politician sitting opposite him at the fireside. Knowing women less, he is able to idealize them more. This is as he thinks it should be.

Jean therefore comes as a shock to him. It is now a long time since he looked at a young woman as young men habitually do. Women – young women – it seems to him, are meant to be unformed; they are malleable, pliant, waiting to be shaped by the impress of the man they marry. They hide themselves; they watch and wait, they indulge in decorous social display (which should always fall short of coquetry) until such time as the man makes apparent his interest, and then his greater interest, and then his especial interest, by which time they are walking alone together, and the families have met, and finally he asks for her hand and sometimes, perhaps, in a last act of concealment, she makes him wait upon her answer. This is how it has all evolved, and social evolution has its laws and its necessities just as biological evolution does. It would not be thus if there were not a very good reason for its being thus.

When he is introduced to Jean – at an afternoon tea party in the house of a prominent London Scotsman, the sort of event he normally avoids – he notices at once that she is a striking young woman. He knows from long experience what to expect: the striking young woman will asks him when he is going to write another Sherlock Holmes story, and did he really die at the Reichenbach Falls, and perhaps it would be better if the consulting detective were to marry, and how did he think up such an idea in the first place? And sometimes he answers with the weariness of a man wearing five overcoats, and sometimes he manages a faint smile and replies, 'Your question, young lady, reminds me why I had the good sense to drop him over the Falls in the first place.'

But Jean does none of this. She does not give an agreeable start at his name, or shyly confess herself a devoted reader. She asks him if he has seen the exhibition of photographs of Dr Nansen's voyage to the far North.

'Not yet. Although I was present at the Albert Hall last month when he lectured to the Royal Geographical Society and received a medal from the Prince of Wales.'

'So was I,' she replies. This is unexpected.

He tells her how, after reading Nansen's account a few years previously of crossing Norway on skis, he acquired a pair of them; how from Davos he skiied the high slopes with the Branger brothers, and how Tobias Branger wrote '*Sportesmann*' in the hotel registration book. Then he begins a story, which he often tells as an adjunct to this one, about losing his skis at the top of a snow-face and being obliged to come down without them, and how the strain on the seat of his tweed knickerbockers . . . and this really is one of his best stories, though perhaps in the present circumstances he will amend the conclusion about being happiest for the rest of the day when standing with his trouster-seat to a wall . . . but she seems to have stopped paying attention. Taken aback, he pauses.

'I should like to learn to ski,' she says.

This is also unexpected.

'I have excellent balance. I have ridden since I was three.'

Arthur is somewhat piqued at not being allowed to finish his story about tearing his knickerbockers, which includes mimicry of his tailor's assurances about the durability of Harris tweed. So he tells her firmly that it is most unlikely that women — by which he means society women, as opposed to female Swiss peasants — will ever learn to ski, given the physical strength required and the dangers attendant on the activity.

'Oh, I am quite strong,' she replies. 'And I imagine I have better balance than you, given your size. It must be an advantage to have a lower centre of gravity. And being much less heavy, I should not do so much damage were I to fall.'

Had she said 'less heavy' he might have taken offence at such pertness. Because she says 'much less heavy' he bursts out laughing, and promises, one day, to teach her to ski.

'I shall hold you to it,' she replies.

It was all a rather extraordinary encounter, he reflects to himself in the subsequent days. The way she declined to acknowledge his fame as a writer, set the subject of the conversation, interrupted one of his most popular stories, exhibited an ambition some might call unladylike, and laughed — well, as good as laughed — at his size. And yet she managed to do it all lightly, seriously, enchantingly. Arthur congratulates himself on not having taken offence, even if none was intended. He feels something he has not felt for years: the self-satisfaction of the successful flirt. And then he forgets her.

Six weeks later he walks into a musical afternoon and she is singing one of Beethoven's Scottish songs while an earnest little fellow in white tie accompanies her. He finds her voice superb, the pianist mannered and vain. Arthur draws back so that she will not see him observing her. After her recital they meet in the presence of others, and she behaves with the sort of politeness which makes it difficult to judge whether she remembers him or not.

They separate; a few minutes later, with some ghastly cellist groaning away in the background, they meet again, this time alone. She says at once, 'I see I shall have to wait at least nine months.'

'For what?'

'For my skiing lesson. There is no possibility of snow now.'

He does not find this forward, or flirtatious, though he knows he should.

'Are you planning it for Hyde Park?' he asks. 'Or St James's? Or perhaps the slopes of Hampstead Heath?'

'Why not? Wherever you wish. Scotland. Or Norway. Or Switzerland.'

They seem to have passed, without his noticing, through some French windows, across a terrace, and are now standing under that very sun which has long banished all hope of snow. He has never resented a fine day more.,

He looks down into her hazel-green eyes. 'Are you flirting with me, young lady?'

She looks straight back at him. 'I am talking to you about skiing.' But those, it feels, are only her nominal words.

'Because if you are, be careful I do not fall in love with you.'

He barely knows what he has said. He half means it entirely and half cannot imagine what has got into him.

'Oh, you are already. In love with me. And I with you. There is no doubt about it. No doubt at all.'

And so it is said. And no more words are needed, or uttered, for a while. All that matters is how he is to see her again, and where, and when, and it must be arranged before someone interrupts them. But he has never been a lothario or seducer, and never known how to say those things which are necessary to arrive at the stage beyond the one where he currently stands – not really knowing either what that further stage might be, since where he is at the moment appears, in its own way, to be final. All he can feel rising up in his head are difficulties, prohibitions, reasons why they will never meet again, except perhaps decades later, in passing, when they are old and grey and will be able to joke about that ever-remembered moment on someone's sunny lawn. It is impossible for them to meet in a public place, because of her reputation and his fame; impossible for them to meet in a private place because of her reputation and . . . and all the things that make up his life. He stands there, a man approaching forty, a man secure in his life and famous in the world, and he has become a schoolboy again. He feels as if he has learned the most beautiful love-speech in Shakespeare and now that he needs to recite it his mouth is dry and his memory empty. He also feels as if he has ripped the seat of his tweed knickerbockers and must instantly find a wall against which to set his back.

Yet almost without his being aware of her questions and his answers, it is somehow arranged. And it is not an assignation, or the start of an intrigue, it is merely the next time they will see one another, and in the five days he is obliged to wait he cannot work, and he can barely think, and even if he plays two rounds of golf in one day he finds, in the seconds between addressing the ball and bringing the club-face down against it, that her face has come into his head, and his game that day is all hooks and slices and the endangering of wildlife. When he propels the ball from one sandhole directly into another, he suddenly recalls golfing at the Mena House Hotel, and feeling then that he was in a perpetual bunker. Now he cannot tell whether this is still true, indeed truer than ever, with the sand even deeper and his ball buried invisibly, or whether he is somehow on the green forever.

It is not an assignation, though he finds himself getting out of the cab on the corner of the street. It is not an assignation, though there is a woman of indeterminate age and class who opens the door and disappears. It is not an assignation though they are at last alone together sitting on a sofa covered in satin brocatelle. It is not an assignation because he tells himself it is not.

He takes her hand and looks at her. Her glance is neither shy nor bold; it is frank and constant. She does not smile. He knows that one or other of them must speak, but seems to have lost his daily familiarity with words. But it does not matter. And then she half-smiles and says, 'I could not wait for the snow.'

'I shall give you snowdrops on every anniversary of the day we met.'

'March the fifteenth,' she says.

'I know. I know because it is engraved upon my heart. If they cut me open they will be able to read that date.'

There is another silence. He sits there, perched on the sofa's edge, longing to concentrate on her words, her face, the date and the thought of snowdrops; but they are all driven out by the awareness that he has the most tremendous cockstand of his entire life. It is not the decorous swelling of a pure-hearted chevalier, it is a thumping and unavoidable presence, something

166

rowdy, something in off the street, something living up to that word cock-stand which he has never himself uttered but which is pressingly in his head. His only other thought is a relief that his trousers are loosely cut. He shifts a little to ease the constriction, and in doing so inadvertently moves a few inches closer to her. She is an angel, he thinks, her look so pure, her complexion so fair, but she has taken his movement as a sign that he intends to kiss her, and so is trustingly offering her face to his, and as a gentleman he cannot slight her, and as a man he cannot help himself from kissing her. Being no lothario or seducer but a burly, honourable man in early middle age leaning awkwardly across a sofa, he tries to think of nothing but love and chivalry as her lips reach towards his moustache and inexpertly seek the mouth beneath it; still holding, but now beginning to crush the hand he has held since the moment he arrived, he becomes aware of a vast and violent leakage taking place inside his trousers. And the groan he gives is almost certainly miscon-strued by Miss Jean Leckie, as is the way he suddenly throws himself back from her as if struck by an assegai between the shoulder blades.

An image comes into Arthur's head, an image from decades earlier. Night-time at Stonyhurst, with a Jesuit quietly patrolling the dormitories to prevent beast-liness among the boys. It worked. And what he needs now, and for all the time he can foresee, is his own patrolling Jesuit. What happened in that room must never happen again. As a doctor, he might find such a moment of weakness explicable; as an English gentleman, he finds it shameful and perturbing. He does not know whom he has betrayed the most: Jean, Touie or himself. All three to some degree, certainly. And it must never happen again.

It is the suddenness which has undone him; also, the gap between dream and reality. In chivalric romance, the knight loves an impossible object – the wife of his lord, for instance – and performs courageous actions in her name; his valour is matched by his purity. But Jean is less than an impossible object, and Arthur is no obscure gallant or unattached knight. Rather, he is a married man whose chasteness has been imposed upon him for the last three years by physician's orders. He is fifteen – no, sixteen – stone, fit and energetic; and yesterday he discharged into his underlinen.

But now that the dilemma has manifested itself in full clarity and awful-ness, Arthur is able to address it. His brain begins to work on the practical-ities of love as once it worked on the practicalities of illness. He defines the problem – the problem! the aching, wracking joy and torment! – thus. It is impossible for him not to love Jean; and for her not to love him. It is impos-sible for him to divorce Touie, the mother of his children, whom he still regards with affection and respect; besides, only a cad would abandon an invalid. Finally, it is impossible to turn the affair into an intrigue by making Jean his mistress. Each of the three parties has his or her honour, even if Touie does not know hers is being considered *in absentia*. For that is an essential condition: Touie must not know.

The next time he and Jean meet, he takes charge. He must do so: he is the man, he is older; she is a young woman, possibly impetuous, whose reputation must not be tarnished. At first she appears anxious, as if he is going to dismiss her; but when it becomes clear that he is merely organizing the terms of their relationship, she relaxes, and at times appears almost not to be listening. She becomes anxious again when he is stressing how careful they must be.

'But we are allowed to kiss one another?' she asks, as if verifying the terms of a contract she has signed while happily blindfolded.

Her tone makes his heart melt and his brain blur. As confirmation of the contract they kiss. She likes to peck at him rather, with eyes open, in bird-like attacks; he prefers the long adhesion of the lips, with eyes closed. He cannot believe he is kissing someone again, let alone her. He tries to stop himself thinking in what ways it is different from kissing Touie. After a while, however, the perturbance starts up again, and he pulls back.

They are to meet; they are to be alone together for limited periods; they are allowed to kiss; they are not to become carried away. Their situation is intensely dangerous. But again she appears to be only half-listening.

'It is time I left home,' she says. 'I can share a flat with other women. Then you may come and see me freely.'

She is so different from Touie: direct, frank, open-minded. She has treated him from the start as an equal. And she is an equal in terms of their love, of course. But he has the responsibility for them, and for her. He must see that her straightforwardness does not lead her into dishonour.

There are times, in the following weeks, when he even begins to wonder if she was not expecting him to make her his mistress. The eagerness of her kisses, the disappointment at his drawing back; the way she presses herself against him, the sense he sometimes has that she knows precisely what is going through him. And yet he cannot think this. She is not that sort of woman; her lack of false modesty is a sign that she trusts him entirely, and would trust him even if he were not the man of principle that he is.

But it is not enough to solve the practical difficulties of their relationship; he also needs moral approval. Arthur takes the Leeds train from St Pancras in a state of trepidation. The Mam remains his final arbiter. She reads every word he writes before it is published; and she has done the equivalent for his emotional life. Only the Mam can confirm that the course of action he proposes is correct.

At Leeds he takes the Carnforth train, changing at Clapham for Ingleton. She is waiting at the station in her wickerwork pony-and-dog cart; she wears a red coat and the white cotton cap she has taken to affecting in recent years. The two ambling miles in the cart seem interminable to Arthur. The Mam defers constantly to her pony, which is called Mooi, and has its eccentricities, such as a refusal to go past steam engines. This means that roadworks have to be avoided, and each whim of equine inattention flattered. At last, they are inside Masongill Cottage. Arthur immediately tells the Mam everything. Everything, at least, that counts. Everything necessary for her to give him advice on this high and heaven-sent love of his. Everything about the sudden wonder and sudden impossibility of his life. Everything about his feelings, his sense of honour and his sense of guilt. Everything about Jean, her sweetly direct nature, her incisive intelligence, her virtue. Everything. Almost everything.

He backtracks; he starts again; he goes into different detail. He stresses Jean's ancestry, her Scottishness, a lineage designed to seduce any amateur genealogist. Her descent from Malise de Leggy in the thirteenth century, and by another line from Rob Roy himself. Her present condition, living with wealthy parents in Blackheath. The Leckie family, respectable and religious, who made their money in tea. Her age, twenty-one. Her fine mezzo voice, trained in Dresden and soon to be perfected in Florence. Her supreme ability as a horsewoman, which he has yet to witness. Her quickness of sympathy, her sincerity and strength of character. And then her personal appearance, which sends Arthur into rapturous mode. Her slender frame, small hands and feet, dark gold hair, hazel-green eyes, gently elongated face, delicate white complexion.

'You paint a photograph, Arthur.'

'I wish I had one. I asked her, but she says she takes a poor picture. She is reluctant to smile for the camera, because she is self-conscious about her teeth. She told me quite straightforwardly. She considers them oversized. Of course they are nothing of the sort. She is such an angel.'

The Mam, listening to her son's account, does not fail to observe the strange parallel that life has thrown up. For years she was married to a man whom society politely chose to regard as an invalid, whether he was being brought home by cadging cabmen or locked away under the disguise of an epileptic. In his absence and incapacity, she had found comfort in the presence of Bryan Waller. Back then, her sulky, aggressive son had dared to criticize; at times, by silence, almost to impugn her honour. And now her favourite, her most adored child, has in turn discovered that the complications of life do not end at the altar; some might say that this is where they begin.

The Mam listens; she understands; and she condones. What Arthur has done is correct, and consistent with honour. And she would like to know Miss Leckie.

They meet; and the Mam approves, as she approved of Touie back in Southsea days. This is not an unthinking endorsement of an indulged son. In the Mam's view, Touie, pliant and agreeable, was exactly the right wife for an ambitious yet confused young doctor needing acceptance in the kind of society that would provide him with patients. But were Arthur to marry now, he would need someone like Jean, someone with capabilities of her own, and with a clear, forthright nature which at times reminds the Mam a little of herself. Privately, she notes that this is the first intimate woman friend to whom her son has not given a nickname.

A Gower-Bell loudspeaking telephone, shaped like a candlestick, stands on the hall table at Undershaw. It has its own number – Hindhead 237 – and, thanks to Arthur's name and reputation, it does not, as many others do, share a party line with a neighbouring house. Even so, Arthur never uses it to telephone Jean. He cannot imagine working out when Undershaw will be empty of servants, the children at school, Touie resting and Wood off on his walk, and then standing in the hall with lowered voice and his back to the stairs: standing beneath the stained-glass names and shields of his ancestors. He cannot picture himself doing that; it would be proof of intrigue, not so much to anyone who might see him in that posture, but to himself. The telephone is the chosen instrument of the adulterer.

So he communicates by letter, by note, by telegram; he communicates by word and by gift. After a few months Jean is moved to explain that the flat she occupies has only a certain amount of space, and though she shares it with trusted friends, the ring of the delivery boy has become embarrassing. Women who receive large numbers of presents from gentlemen – or, more compromisingly, from one particular gentleman – are assumed to be mistresses; at the very least, potential mistresses. When she points this out, Arthur rebukes himself for a fool.

'Besides,' says Jean. 'I do not need assurances. I am certain of your love.'

On the first anniversary of their meeting, he gives her a single snowdrop. She tells him that this brings her more pleasure than any amount of jewellery or dresses or potted plants or expensive chocolates, or whatever it is that men give to women. She has few material needs, and these are easily met by her allowance. Indeed, the fact of not receiving presents is a way of marking that their relationship is different from the humdrum arrangements of others in the world.

But there is the question of the ring. Arthur wants her to wear something, however discreet, on her finger – it does not matter which – to send him a secret message whenever they are in one another's company. Jean does not favour this idea. Men give rings to three categories of women: wife, mistress, fiancée. She is none of these, and will wear no such ring. She will never be a mistress; Arthur already has a wife; nor is she, can she be, a fiancée. To be a fiancée is to say: I am waiting for his wife to die. There were such understandings between couples, she knew, but that is not to be theirs. Their love is different. It has no past, and no future that can be thought about; it has only the present. Arthur says that in his mind she is his mystical wife. Jean agrees, but says that mystical wives do not wear physical rings.

Naturally, it is the Mam who solves the matter. She invites Jean to Ingleton, suggesting that Arthur come himself the following day. On the evening of Jean's arrival, the Mam has a sudden idea. She takes from the little finger of her left hand a small ring and slips it onto the same finger of Jean's hand. It is a pale cabochon sapphire which once belonged to the Mam's great-aunt.

Jean looks at it, twirls her hand, and promptly removes it. 'I cannot accept jewellery that belongs in your family.'

'My great-aunt gave it to me because she thought it went with my colouring. It did then; but no longer. It goes better with yours. And I think of you as part of the family. I have done so from the first day I met you.'

Jean cannot refuse the Mam; few can. When Arthur arrives, he is theatrically slow to notice the ring; finally, it is pointed out to him. Even then he disguises the pleasure he feels, commenting that it is not very large, and giving the women a chance to laugh at him. Now Jean wears not Arthur's ring but a Doyle ring, and that is just as good; perhaps better. He imagines seeing it against the cloth of a cluttered dining table and the keys of a piano, against the arm of a theatre stall and the reins of a horse. He thinks of it as a symbol of what binds her to him. His mystical wife.

Two white lies are allowed to a gentleman: in order to shield a woman, and to get into a fight when the fight is a rightful one. The white lies Arthur tells Touie are far more numerous than he ever imagined. At the beginning he assumed that somehow, in the bustle of his days and weeks, his ventures and enthusiasms, his sports and travels, the need to tell her lies would not arise. Jean would disappear into the interstices of his calendar. But since she cannot disappear from his heart, she equally cannot disappear from his mind and his conscience. So he finds that every meeting, every plan, every note and every letter sent, every thought of her, is hedged around with lies of one sort or another. Mostly they are lies of omission, though sometimes, necessarily, lies of commission; lies anyway, all of them. And Touie is so utterly trusting; she accepts, she has always accepted, Arthur's sudden changes of plan, his impulses, his decisions to stay or to go. Arthur knows she is without suspicion, and this scrapes at his nerves the more. He cannot imagine how adulterers can live with their consciences; how morally primitive they must be simply to sustain the necessary lying.

But beyond practical difficulty, ethical impasse and sexual frustration, there is something darker, something harder to face directly. The key moments in Arthur's life have always been shadowed by death, and this is another one. The sudden, wondrous love that has arrived can only be consummated and acknowledged to the world if Touie dies. She will die; he knows that, and so does Jean; consumption always claims its victims. But Arthur's determination to fight the Devil has resulted in a ceasefire. Touie's condition is stable; she no longer even needs the cleansing air of Davos. She lives contentedly at Hindhead, grateful for what she has, and exuding the gentle optimism of the consumptive. He cannot wish for her death; equally, he cannot wish for Jean's impossible position to continue without end. If he believed in one of the established religions, he would doubtless put everything in the hands of God; but he cannot do this. Touie must continue to receive the best medical attention and the strongest domestic support in order that Jean's suffering may continue as long as possible. If he takes any action, he is a brute. If he tells Touie, he is a brute. If he breaks off with Jean, he is a brute. If he makes her his mistress, he is a brute. If he does nothing, he is merely a passive, hypocritical brute vainly holding on to as much honour as he can.

Slowly, however, and discreetly, the relationship is acknowledged. Jean is introduced to Lottie. Arthur is introduced to Jean's parents, who give him a a pearl and diamond pin-stud for Christmas. Jean is even introduced to Touie's mother, Mrs Hawkins, who accepts the relationship. Connie and Hornung are also apprised, though nowadays they are much taken up with marriage, their son Oscar Arthur, and life in Kensington West. Arthur gives assurances to everyone that Touie will be shielded at all cost from knowledge, pain and dishonour.

There are high-minded declarations, and there is daily reality. Despite family approval, Arthur and Jean are each liable to bouts of low spirits; Jean also becomes prone to migraines. Each feels guilt at having dragged the other into an impossible situation. Honour, like virtue, may be its own reward; but sometimes it does not feel enough. At least, the despair it provokes can be as sharp as any of the exaltation. Arthur prescribes for himself the collected works of Renan. Hard reading, with plenty of golf and cricket, will steady a man, keep him right in body and mind.

But these recourses can only do so much. You can thrash the other side's bowlers to all quarters, then pitch short into their batsmen's ribs; you can take a driver and punish a golf ball into the farthest distance. You cannot keep the thoughts at bay for ever; always the same thoughts, and the same repellent paradoxes. An active man doomed to inactivity; lovers forbidden to love; death which you fear and are ashamed to beckon.

Arthur's cricket season has been going well; scores made and wickets taken are relayed to the Mam with filial pride. She in return continues to give him the benefit of her opinions: about the Dreyfus Case, about the sacerdotal bullies and bigots in the Vatican, about the odious attitude towards France of that dismal paper the *Daily Mail*. One day, Arthur is playing at Lord's for the MCC. He invites Jean to watch him, and knows, when he comes out to bat, just where in 'A' Enclosure she will be sitting. It is one of those days when the bowlers have no secrets from him; his bat is impregnable, and scarcely registers the impact as he smacks and wheedles the ball around the field. Once or twice he lifts it straight into the crowd, and even has time to make sure beforehand that there is no danger of it dropping near her like a shell. He is jousting in the name of his lady; he should have asked for a favour to wear in his cap.

Between innings, he comes to seek her out. He needs no words of praise – he sees the pride in her eyes. She needs to walk a little after sitting on a slatted bench so long. They take a turn around the ground, behind the stands; beer wafts on the hot air. Amid an idling, anonymous throng they feel more alone together than under the friendliest chaperoning eye at a dinner table. They talk as if they had just met. Arthur says how he wishes he could have worn her favour in his cap. She slips her arm through his and they walk silently on, deep in happiness.

'Hello, there's Willie and Connie.'

It is indeed; coming towards them, also arm in arm. They must have left little Oscar with his nurse back in Kensington. Arthur now feels even prouder of his performance with the bat. Then he becomes aware of something. Willie and Connie are not slowing their pace, and Connie has started looking away, as if the back of the pavilion had become something of irreducible interest. Willie at least does not appear to be denying their existence; but as the couples pass, he raises an eyebrow at his brother-in-law, at Jean, and at their linked arms.

Arthur's bowling after the change of innings is faster and wilder than usual. He takes only a single wicket, thanks to an over-greedy swipe at one of his long-hops. When he is sent to field in the deep, he keeps turning to look for Jean, but she must have moved. He cannot spot Willie and Connie either.

His throwing-in causes more alarm to the wicketkeeper than usual, and has him scuttling in all directions.

Afterwards, it is clear that Jean has left. He is now in a state of pure rage. He wants to take a cab straight to Jean's flat, lead her out on to the pavement, put her arm through his, and walk her past Buckingham Palace, Westminster Abbey and the Houses of Parliament. And with him still in his cricket clothes. And shouting, 'I am Arthur Conan Doyle and I am proud to love this woman, Jean Leckie.' He visualizes the scene. When he stops doing so, he thinks he is running mad.

Rage and madness subside, leaving him with a steady, inflexible anger. He takes a shower-bath and changes, all the while swearing internally at Willie Hornung. How dare that asthmatic short-sighted part-time spin bowler raise his bloody eyebrow. At *him*. At *Jean*. Hornung, the journalist, the writer of no-account stories about the Australian outback. Totally unheard of until he purloined – with permission – the idea of Holmes and Watson; turned them upside down and made them into a pair of criminals. Arthur let him do it. Even provided the name of his so-called hero, Raffles, as in *The Doings of Raffles Haw*. Allowed the damned book to be dedicated to him. 'To A.C.D., this form of flattery.'

Gave him more than his best idea, gave him his wife. Literally: walked her up the aisle and handed her over to him. Made them an allowance to get started on. All right, made Connie an allowance, but Willie Hornung didn't say it was a stain on his honour as a man to accept such help, didn't say he'd go out and work harder to keep his young wife, oh no, none of that. And he thinks that gives him the right to raise a priggish eyebrow.

Arthur takes a cab straight from Lord's to Kensington West. Number Nine, Pitt Street. His anger begins to subside as they cross the Harrow Road. In his head he can hear Jean telling him it was all her fault, she was the one who put her arm through his. He knows exactly the tone of self-reproach she will use, and how it will probably drive her into a wretched migraine. All that matters, he tells himself, is to minimize her suffering. His every instinct and his very manliness demand that he break down Hornung's door, drag him on to the pavement, and beat him about the brains with a cricket bat. Yet by the time the cab draws up he knows how he must behave.

He is quite calm as Willie Hornung admits him. 'I have come to see Constance,' he says. Hornung is at least sensible enough not to go in for any damn-fool bluster, or insist on being present himself. Arthur goes upstairs to Connie's sitting room. He explains to her, in straightforward terms, as he has never done – never needed to do – before. About what Touie's illness entails. About his sudden love, his utter love, for Jean. About how that love will remain platonic. Yet how a large side of his life, so long unoccupied, has now been filled. About the strain and depression they both suffer from intermittently. About how Connie only saw them together, obviously in love, because they let their guard down; and how it is a torment never to be able to show their love in front of others. How every smile, every laugh has to be measured and rationed, every companion tested. How Arthur does not think he can survive if his family, who are as dear to him as the world itself, does not understand his plight and support him.

He is playing at Lord's again tomorrow, and he asks, no, he entreats Connie to come, and this time meet Jean properly. It is the only way. What happened today must be set aside, put behind them at once, else it will fester. She will come tomorrow, and have lunch with Jean and know her better. Won't she?

Connie agrees. Willie, as he lets him out, says, 'Arthur, I'm prepared to back your dealings with any woman at sight and without question.' In the cab, Arthur feels as if something terrible has just been averted. He is quite weary, and a little light-headed. He knows he can count on Connie, as he can on all his family. And he is a little ashamed of what he caught himself thinking about Willie Hornung. This damn temper of his is not getting any better. He puts it down to being half Irish. The Scottish half of him has the devil of a job keeping the upper hand.

No, Willie is a fine fellow, who will back him without question. Willie has a good, sharp brain, and is a very decent wicketkeeper. He may dislike golf, but at least gives the best reason Arthur has yet heard for such a prejudice: 'I consider it unsportsmanlike to hit a sitting ball.' That was good. And the one about the sprinter's error. And the one Arthur has spread most widely, which is Willie's assessment of his brother-in-law's consulting detective: 'Though he might be more humble, there is no police like Holmes.' No police like Holmes! Arthur throws himself back against the seat at the memory of the line.

The next morning, as he is preparing to leave for Lord's, a telegram is delivered. Constance Hornung must excuse herself from their lunch engagement today because she has a toothache and is obliged to go to the dentist.

He sends a note to Jean, his apologies to Lord's – 'urgent family business' for once is no euphemism – and takes a cab to Pitt Street. They will be expecting him. They know he is not the man for intrigue or diplomatic silence. You look a fellow in the eye, you speak the truth, and you take the consequences: such is the Doyle creed. Women are allowed different rules, of course – or rather, women seem to have developed different rules for themselves regardless; but even so, he does not think much of emergency dental treatment as an excuse. Its very transparency gets Arthur's dander up. Perhaps she knows this; perhaps it is designed as the plainest rebuke, like that turned-away head of hers. Connie, to her credit, does not palter any more than he does.

He knows he must keep his temper. What matters is first of all Jean, and then the unity of the family. He wonders if Connie has changed Hornung's mind, or Hornung Connie's. 'I'm prepared to back your dealings with any woman at sight and without question.' Nothing equivocal there. But neither had there been about Connie's apparent understanding of his situation. In advance, he searches for reasons. Perhaps Connie has become a respectable married woman rather more quickly than he would have thought possible; perhaps she has always been jealous that Lottie is his favourite sister. As for Hornung: doubtless he is envious of his brother-in-law's fame; or maybe the success of *Raffles* has gone to his head. Something has sparked this sudden display of independence and rebellion. Well, Arthur will soon find out.

'Connie is upstairs, resting,' says Hornung as he opens the door. Plain enough. So it will be man to man, which is how Arthur prefers it.

Little Willie Hornung is the same height as Arthur, a fact he occasionally forgets. And Hornung in his own house is different from the Hornung of Arthur's furious re-creation; also different from the flattering, eager-to-please Willie who darted across the tennis court at West Norwood and brought *bons mots* to the table by way of ingratiation. In the front sitting room he indicates a leather armchair, waits for Arthur to be seated, and than remains standing himself. As he speaks, he begins to prance around the room. Nerves, doubtless, but it has the effect of a prosecuting counsel showing off to a non-existent jury.

'Arthur, this is not going to be easy. Connie has told me what you said to her last night, and we have discussed the matter.'

'And you have changed your minds. Or you have changed her mind. Or she yours. Yesterday you said you would back me without question.'

'I know what I said. And it is not a matter of my changing Connie's mind, or her changing mine. We have discussed it, and we are agreed.'

'I congratulate you.'

'Arthur, let me put it this way. Yesterday we spoke to you with our hearts. You know how Connie loves you, how she always has. You know my enormous admiration for you, how proud I am to say that Arthur Conan Doyle is my brother-in-law. That's why we went to Lord's yesterday, to watch you with pride, to support you.'

'Which you have decided no longer to do.'

'But today we are thinking, and speaking, with our heads.'

'And what do your two heads tell you?' Arthur reins his anger back to mere sarcasm. It is the best he can do. He sits four-square in his chair and watches Willie dance and shuffle in front of him, as he dances and shuffles his argument.

'Our heads – our two heads – tell us what our eyes see and our consciences dictate. Your behaviour is . . . compromising.'

'To whom?'

'To your family. To your wife. To your . . . lady-friend. To yourself.'

'You do not wish to include the Marylebone Cricket Club as well? And the readers of my books? And the staff of Gamages emporium?'

'Arthur, if you cannot see it, others must point it out to you.'

'Which you seem to be relishing. I thought I had merely acquired a brother-in-law. I did not realize the family had acquired a conscience. I was not aware we needed one. You should get yourself a priest's robe.'

'I do not need a priest's robe to tell me that if you stroll around Lord's with a grin on your face and a woman who is not your wife on your arm, you compromise that wife and your behaviour reflects upon your family.'

'Touie will always be shielded from pain and dishonour. That is my first principle. It will remain so.'

'Who else saw you yesterday apart from us? And what might they conclude?'

'And what did you conclude, you and Constance?'

'That you were extremely reckless. That you did the reputation of the woman on your arm no good. That you compromised your wife. And your family.'

'You are a sudden expert on my family for such a johnny-come-lately.'

'Perhaps because I see more clearly.'

'Perhaps because you have less loyalty. Hornung, I do not pretend the situation is not difficult, damned difficult. There's no denying it. At times it is intolerable. I do not need to rehearse what I said to Connie yesterday. I am doing the best I can, we both are, Jean and I. Our . . . alliance has been accepted, has been approved by the Mam, by Jean's parents, by Touie's mother, by my brother and sisters. Until yesterday, by you. When have I ever failed in loyalty to any member of my family? And when before have I appealed to them?'

'And if your wife heard of yesterday's behaviour?'

'She will not. She cannot.'

'Arthur. There is always gossip. There is always the tattle of maids and servants. People write anonymous letters. Journalists drop hints in newspapers.'

'Then I shall sue. Or, more likely, I shall knock the fellow down.'

'Which would be a further act of recklessness. Besides, you cannot knock down an anonymous letter.'

'Hornung, this conversation is fruitless. Evidently you grant yourself a higher sense of honour than you do me. If a vacancy occurs as head of the family, I shall consider your application.'

'*Quis custodiet*, Arthur? Who tells the head of the family he is at fault?'

'Hornung, for the last time. I shall state the matter plainly. I am a man of honour. My name, and the family's name, mean everything to me. Jean Leckie is a woman of the utmost honour, and the utmost virtue. The relationship is platonic. It always will be. I shall remain Touie's husband, and treat her with honour, until the coffin lid closes over one or the other of us.'

Arthur is used to making definitive statements which conclude discussions. He thinks he has made another, but Hornung is still shuffling about like a batsman at the crease.

'It seems to me,' he replies, 'that you attach too much importance to whether these relations are platonic or not. I can't see that it makes much difference. What is the difference?'

Arthur stands up. 'What is the difference?' he bellows. He does not care if his sister is resting, if little Oscar Arthur is taking a nap, if the servant has her ear to the door. 'It's all the difference in the world! It's the difference between innocence and guilt, that's what it is.'

'I disagree, Arthur. There is what you think and what the world thinks. There is what you believe and what the world believes. There is what you know and what the world knows. Honour is not just a matter of internal good feeling, but also of external behaviour.'

'I will not be lectured on the subject of honour,' Arthur roars. 'I will not. I will not. And especially not by a man who writes a thief for a hero.'

He takes his hat from the peg and crushes it down to his ears. Well, that is that, he decides, that is that. The world is either for you or against you. And it makes things clearer, at least, to see how a prissy prosecuting counsel goes about his business.

Despite this disapproval – or perhaps to prove it misconceived – Arthur begins, very cautiously, to introduce Jean into the social life of Undershaw. He has made the acquaintance in London of a charming family called the Leckies, who have a country place in Crowborough; Malcolm Leckie, the son, is a splendid fellow with a sister called – what is it now? And so Jean's name appears in the Undershaw visitors' book, always beside that of her brother or one of her parents. Arthur cannot claim to be entirely at his ease when uttering sentences such as, 'Malcolm Leckie said he might motor over with his sister', but they are sentences that have to be uttered if he is not to go mad. And on these occasions – a large lunch party, a tennis afternoon – he is never entirely sure his behaviour is natural. Has he been over-attentive to Touie, and did she notice? Was he too stiffly correct with Jean, and might she have taken offence? But the problem is his to be borne. Touie never gives an indication that she finds anything amiss. And Jean – bless her – behaves with an ease and decorum which reassures him that nothing will go wrong. She never seeks him out in private, never slips a lover's note into his hand. At times, it is true, he thinks she is making a show of flirting with him. But when he considers it afterwards, he decides that she is deliberately behaving as she would do if they knew one another no better than they were pretending to. Perhaps the best way to show a wife that you have no designs on her husband is to flirt with him in front of her. If so, that is remarkably clever thinking.

And twice a year, they are able to escape to Masongill together. They arrive and leave by separate trains, like weekend guests who just happen to coincide. Arthur stays in his mother's cottage, while Jean is lodged with Mr and Mrs Denny at Parr Bank Farm. On the Saturday they sup at Masongill House. The Mam presides at Waller's table, as she always has, and presumably always will.

Except that things are no longer as simple as they were when the Mam first came here – not that they were ever simple then. For Waller has somehow managed to get himself married. Miss Ada Anderson, a clergyman's daughter from St Andrews, came to Thornton Vicarage as governess, and, so village gossip asserts, instantly set her cap at the master of Masongill House. She succeeded in marrying the man, only to find – and here gossip turned moralizing – that she could not change him. For the new husband had no intention of letting mere matrimony alter the way of life he had established. To be specific: he visits the Mam as often as he ever did; he dines with her *en tête-à-tête*; and he has a special bell installed at the back door of her cottage, which only he is allowed to ring. The Waller marriage does not bring forth children.

Mrs Waller never sets foot in Masongill Cottage, and absents herself when the Mam comes to sup at the House. If Waller desires that woman to preside, then so be it, but her authority at the table will not be recognized by the mistress of the house. Mrs Waller increasingly busies herself with her Siamese cats and a rose garden laid out with the rigour of a parade ground or vegetable plot. During a brief encounter with Arthur she showed herself both shy and stand-offish: the fact that he came from Edinburgh and she from St Andrews was no ground for intimacy, her manner suggested.

And so the four of them – Waller, the Mam, Arthur and Jean – sit round the supper table together. Food is brought and taken away, glasses shine in the candlelight, the talk is of books, and everyone behaves as if Waller were still a bachelor. From time to time, Arthur's eye is caught by the silhouette of a cat slipping along the wall and keeping well clear of Waller's boot. A sinuous form, easing its way through the shadows, like the memory of a wife discreetly absenting herself. Does every marriage have its own damn secret? Is there never anything straightforward at the heart of it all?

Still, Arthur long ago accepted that Waller would have to be endured. And since he cannot be with Jean all the time, he is content to golf with Waller. For a short and scholarly type, the master of Masongill House has a neat enough game. He lacks distance, of course, but is rather tidier, it has to be admitted, than Arthur, who still tends to despatch the ball in improbable directions. Apart from golf, there is decent shooting to be had in Waller's woods – partridge, grouse and rooks. The two men also go ferreting together. For five shillings the butcher's boy will arrive with his three ferrets and work them all morning to Waller's satisfaction, scaring up the contents of numerous rabbit pies.

But then there are the hours earned by such dutiful endeavour – the hours alone with Jean. They take the Mam's pony-and-dog cart and drive to nearby villages; they explore the range of wold and fell and sudden valleys north of Ingleton. Though Arthur's returns here are never uncomplicated – the taint of kidnap and betrayal will always linger – the role of tourist agent comes to him naturally and full-heartedly. He shows Jean the Twiss Valley and Pecca Falls, the gorge of the Doe and Beezley Falls. He watches her nerveless on a bridge sixty feet above Yew Tree Gorge. They climb Ingleborough together, and he cannot prevent himself feeling how good it is for a man to have a healthy young woman at his side. He is making no comparison, impugning nobody, just grateful that they do not have to make constant frustrating halts and rests. At the top, he plays archaeologist and points out the vestiges of the Brigantian stronghold; then topographer as they look west towards Morecambe, St George's Channel and the Isle of Man, while far to the north-west the Lake mountains and the Cumbrian ranges discreetly show themselves.

Inevitably, there are constraints and awkwardnesses. They may be far from home, but decorum cannot be abandoned; Arthur is, even here, a well-known figure, while the Mam has her position in local society. So a glance is sometimes required to rein in a certain tendency to candour and expressiveness on Jean's part. And though Arthur is more free to articulate his devotion, he cannot always feel as a lover should – like a man freshly invented. They are driving through Thornton one day, Jean's arm resting on his, the sun high in the sky and the prospect of an afternoon alone together, when she says,

'What a pretty church, Arthur. Stop, let us go in.'

He acts deaf for a moment, then replies, rather stiffly, 'It is not so pretty. Only the tower is original. Most of it is no more than thirty years old. It is all specious restoration.'

Jean does not press her interest, deferring to Arthur's gruff judgement as chief tourist agent. He snaps the reins against the idiosyncratic Mooi, and they drive on. It does not seem the moment to tell her that the church was no more than fifteen years restored when he walked down its aisle, a newly married man, with Touie's hand on his arm just where Jean's is now.

His return to Undershaw this time is not without guilt.

Arthur's way of being a father is to leave the children to their mother's care and then descend from time to time with sudden plans and presents. It seems to him that being a father is like being a slightly more responsible brother. You protect your children, you provide for them, you set an example; beyond that, you make them understand what they are, which is children, that is to say imperfect, even defective, adults. Yet he is also a generous man, and does not believe it necessary or morally improving for them to be deprived of what he was deprived of as a boy. At Hindhead, as at Norwood, there is a tennis ground; also a rifle range behind the house, where Kingsley and Mary are encouraged to improve their marksmanship. In the garden he installs a monorail, which skims and swoops through the hollows and rises of his four acres. Driven by electricity and stabilized by gyroscope, the monorail is the transport of the future. His friend Wells is certain of this, and Arthur agrees.

He buys himself a Roc motorbicycle, which proves mightily insubordinate, and which Touie will not allow the children near; then a chain-driven twelve-horse-power Wolseley, which is much applauded and does regular damage to the gateposts. This new motoring machine has rendered his carriage and horses redundant; though when he mentions this obvious fact to the Mam, she is outraged. You cannot put a family crest on a mere machine, she argues, let alone one which suffers the regular indignity of breaking down.

Kingsley and Mary are granted liberties not available to most of their friends. In summer they go barefoot, and may roam anywhere within a five-mile radius of Undershaw as long as they are home for meals, clean and tidy. Arthur has no objection when they make a pet of a hedgehog. On Sundays he will often announce that fresh air is better for the soul than liturgy, and enlist one of them as his caddie; a ride in the high dogcart to Hankley Golf Course, an erratic progress with a heavy golf bag, and then the reward of hot buttered toast in the club house. Their father will readily explain things to them, though not always the things they need or want to know; and he does so from a great height, even when he is on his knees beside them. He encourages self-sufficiency, sports, riding; he gives Kingsley books about great battles in world history, and warns him of the perils of military unpre-paredness.

Arthur's forte is solving things, but he cannot solve his children. None of their friends or schoolmates has a private monorail; yet Kingsley, with infuri-ating politeness, lets slip that it does not go fast enough, and perhaps the carriages should be bigger. Mary, meanwhile, climbs trees in a manner incompatible with female modesty. They are not bad children in any way; as far as he can assess the matter, they are good children. But even when they are well-mannered and properly behaved, what Arthur has not counted on is their relentlessness. It is as if they are always expectant – though of what, he cannot tell, and he doubts they can either. They are expectant of something he cannot provide.

Arthur privately thinks that Touie should have taught them more disci-pline; but this is a reproach he cannot make, except in the mildest terms. And so the children grow up between his erratic authoritarianism and her benign approving. When Arthur is in residence at Undershaw, he wants to work; and when he stops work, he wants to play golf or cricket, or have a quiet 200-up with Woodie on the billiards table. He has provided the family with comfort, security and money; in exchange he expects peace.

He does not get peace; still less from inside himself. When there is no chance of seeing Jean for a while, he tries to bring her close by doing what she would like doing. Because she is a keen horsewoman, he enlarges his stable at Undershaw from one horse to six, and begins riding to hounds. Because Jean is musical, Arthur decides to learn the banjo, a decision Touie greets with her normal indulgence. Arthur now plays the Bombardon tuba and the banjo, though neither instrument is famed for its ability to accompany a classically trained mezzo-soprano voice. Sometimes he and Jean arrange to read the same book while they are apart – Stevenson, Scott's poems, Meredith; each likes to imagine the other on the same page, sentence, phrase, word, syllable.

Touie's preferred reading is *The Imitation of Christ*. She has her faith, her children, her comfort, her quiet occupations. Arthur's guilt ensures that he behaves towards her with the utmost consideration and gentleness. Even when her saintly optimism seems to border on a monstrous complacency, and he feels a rage gathering within him, he knows he cannot inflict it upon her. To his shame, he inflicts it upon his children, upon servants, caddies, employees of the railway and idiot journalists. He remains utterly dutiful towards Touie, utterly in love with Jean; yet in other parts of his life he becomes harder and more irritable. *Patientia vincit* reads the admonition in stained glass. Yet he feels he is growing a stony carapace. His natural expression is turning into a prosecutor's stare. He looks through others accusingly, because he is so used to looking through himself.

He begins to think of himself geometrically, as being located at the centre of a triangle. Its points are the three women of his life, its sides the iron bars of duty. Naturally, he has placed Jean at the apex, with Touie and the Mam at the base. But sometimes the triangle seems to rotate around him, and then his head spins.

Jean never offers the slightest complaint or reproach. She tells him that she cannot, will not, ever love another person; that waiting for him is not a trial but a joy; that she is entirely happy; that their hours together are the central truth of her life.

'My darling,' he says, 'Do you think there was ever such a love story as ours since the world began?'

Jean feels her eyes fill with tears. At the same time, she is a little shocked. 'Arthur dearest, it is not a sporting competition.'

He accepts the rebuke. 'Even so, how many people have had their love tested as we have? I should think our case was about unique.'

'Does not every couple think their case unique?'

'It is a common delusion. Whereas with us –'

'Arthur!' Jean does not think boastfulness appropriate to love; she is inclined to find it vulgar.

'Even so,' he persists, 'even so I feel sometimes – no often – that there is a Guardian Spirit watching over us.'

'So do I,' Jean agrees.

Arthur does not find the notion of a Guardian Spirit fanciful, or even a banality. He finds it plausible and real.

Nevertheless, he needs an earthly witness to their love. He needs to offer proof. He takes to forwarding Jean's love letters to the Mam. He does not ask permission, or regard this as breaching a confidence. He needs it to be known that their feelings for one another are still as fresh as ever, and their trials not in vain. He tells the Mam to destroy the letters, and suggests a choice of method. She may either burn them, or – preferably – tear them into tiny pieces and scatter them among the flowers at Masongill Cottage.

Flowers. Each year, without fail, on the 15th of March, Jean receives a single snowdrop with a note from her beloved Arthur. A white flower once a year for Jean, and white lies all the year round for his wife.

And all the time, Arthur's fame increases. He is a clubman, a diner-out, a public figure. He becomes an authority on worlds beyond literature and medicine. He stands for Parliament as a Liberal Unionist in Edinburgh Central, where defeat is tempered by the recognition that much of politics is a mudbath. His views are canvassed, his support counted on. He is popular. He becomes more popular when he reluctantly submits to the joint will of the Mam and the British reading public: he resuscitates Sherlock Holmes and despatches him in the footprints of an enormous hound.

When the South African War breaks out, Arthur volunteers as a medical officer. The Mam does everything to dissuade him: she thinks his large frame a sure target for the Boer bullet; further, she judges the war nothing but a dishonourable scramble for gold. Arthur disagrees. It is his duty to go; he is acknowledged to have the strongest influence over young men – especially young sporting men – of anyone in England bar Kipling. He also thinks that this war is worth a white lie or two: the nation is getting into a fight which is a rightful one.

He leaves Tilbury on the *Oriental*. He is to be looked after on his adventure by Cleeve, the butler from Undershaw. Jean has filled his cabin with flowers, but will not come to say farewell; she cannot face a parting amid the thronged and thumping cheerfulness of a transport. As the whistle sounds for visitors to leave the ship the Mam bids him a tight-mouthed goodbye.

'I wish Jean had come,' he says, a small boy in a hulking suit.

'She is in the crowd,' the Mam replies. 'Somewhere. Hiding. She could not trust her feelings, she said.'

And with that she goes. Arthur rushes to the rail, furious and impotent; he watches his mother's white cap as if it will lead him to Jean. The gangplank is withdrawn, the ropes unslung; the *Oriental* pulls away, the hooter bellows and Arthur can see nothing and nobody through his tears. He lies down in his floral, fragrant cabin. The triangle, the triangle with iron bars, whirls inside his head, until it comes to rest with Touie at its apex. Touie, who instantly and devotedly approved this project, like every other he has ever undertaken; Touie, who asked him to write, but only if he has time, and who made no fuss. Dear Touie.

On the voyage out, his mood slowly lifts, as he begins to understand more fully why he has come. As a duty and example, of course; but also for selfish reasons. He has become a pampered and rewarded fellow, who needs some cleansing of the spirit. He has been safe too long, has lost muscle, and requires danger. He has been among women too long, and too confusingly, and yearns for the world of men. When the *Oriental* docks to take on coal at Cape de Verde, the Middlesex Yeomanry instantly organizes a cricket match on the first piece of flattened ground they can find. Arthur watches the game – against the staff of the telegraph station – with joy in his heart. There are rules for pleasure and rules for work. Rules, orders given and received, and a clear purpose. That is what he has come for.

At Bloemfontein the hospital tents are on the cricket field; the main ward is the pavilion. He sees much death; though more men are lost to enteric than to the Boer bullet. He takes five days' leave to follow the army's advance north, across the Vet river towards Pretoria. On his return, south of Brandfort, his party is stopped by a Basuto on a shaggy mount, who tells them of a British soldier lying wounded at some two hours' distance. They buy the fellow as a guide for a florin. There is a long ride through maize fields then out across the veldt. The wounded Englishman turns out to be a dead Australian: short, muscular, with a yellow waxen face. No. 410, New South Wales Mounted Infantry, now dismounted, his horse and his rifle gone. He has bled to death from a stomach wound. He lies with his pocket watch set up before him; he must have seen his life tick away by the minute. The watch has stopped at one o'clock in the morning. Beside him stands his empty water bottle, with a red ivory chessman balanced on the top of it. The other chessmen – more likely to be loot from a Boer farmstead than a soldier's pastime – are in his haversack. They gather his effects: a bandolier, a stylograph pen, a silk handkerchief, a clasp-knife, the Waterbury watch, plus £2 6s. 6d. in a frayed purse. The sticky body is slung over Arthur's horse, and a swarm of flies attends them on the two-mile ride to the nearest telegraph post. There they leave No. 410, New South Wales Mounted Infantry, for burial.

Arthur has seen all kinds of death in South Africa, but this is the one he will always remember. A fair fight, open air, and a great cause – he can imagine no better death.

On his return, his patriotic accounts of the war bring approval from the highest ranks of society. It is the interregnum between the old Queen's death and the new King's coronation. He is invited to dine with the future Edward VII and seated beside him. It is made clear that a knighthood is on offer in the Coronation Honours List if Dr Conan Doyle would care to accept it.

But Arthur does not care to. A knighthood is the badge of a provincial city mayor. The big men do not accept such baubles. Imagine Rhodes or Kipling or Chamberlain accepting such a thing. Not that he considers himself their equal; but why should his standards be lower than theirs? A knighthood is the sort of thing fellows like Alfred Austin and Hall Caine grab at – if they are lucky enough to be given the chance.

The Mam is both disbelieving and furious. What has it all been for, if not for this? Here is the boy who blazoned cardboard shields in her Edinburgh kitchen, who was taught each step of his ancestry back to the Plantagenets. Here is the man whose carriage harness bears the family crest, whose hallway celebrates his forebears in stained glass. Here is the boy who was taught the rules of chivalry and the man who practises them, who went to South Africa because of the fighting blood in him – the blood of Percy and Pack, Doyle and Conan. How dare he decline to become a knight of the realm, when his whole life has been aimed towards such a consummation?

The Mam bombards him with letters; to every argument, Arthur has a counter-argument. He insists that they drop the matter. The letters cease; he pronounces himself as relieved as Mafeking. And then she arrives at Undershaw. The whole house knows why she has come, this small, white-capped matriarch who is the more dominant for never raising her voice.

She lets him wait. She does not take him aside and suggest a walk. She does not knock on his study door. She leaves him alone for two days, knowing how the wait will operate on his nerves. Then, on the morning of her departure, she stands in the hallway with the light streaming through the glass escutcheons which shamefully omit the Foleys of Worcestershire, and asks a question.

'Has it not occurred to you that to refuse a knighthood would be an insult to the King?'

'I tell you, I cannot do it. As a matter of principle.'

'Well,' she says, looking up at him with those grey eyes which strip him of years and fame. 'If you wish to show your principles by an insult to the King, no doubt you can't.'

And so, with the week-long Coronation bells still echoing, Arthur is herded into a velvet-roped pen at Buckingham Palace. After the ceremony he finds himself next to Professor – now Sir – Oliver Lodge. They might discuss electromagnetic radiation, or the relative motion of matter and ether, or even their shared admiration for the new monarch. Instead, the two new Edwardian knights talk about telepathy, telekinesis and the reliability of mediums. Sir Oliver is convinced that the physical and the psychical are as close as the shared letters of the two words suggest. Indeed, having recently retired as president of the Physical Society, he is now president of the Psychical Society.

They debate the relative merits of Mrs Piper and Eusapia Paladino, and whether Florence Cook is more than just a skilful fraud. Lodge describes attending the Cambridge sittings, at which Paladino was put through her paces, under strictest conditions, in a sequence of nineteen seances. He has seen her produce ectoplasmic forms; also guitars playing themselves as they float through the air. He has watched a jar full of jonquils being conveyed from a table at the far end of the room, and being held, without any palpable means of support, beneath each of the sitters' noses in turn.

'If I were to play devil's advocate, Sir Oliver, and say that conjurers have offered to reproduce her exploits, and in some cases have succeeded in doing so, how would you reply?'

'I would reply that it is indeed possible that Paladino resorts to trickery on occasion. For instance, there are times when the expectation of the sitters is great and the spirits prove unforthcoming. The temptation is plain. But this does not mean that the spirits which do move through her are not genuine and true.' He pauses. 'You know what they say, Doyle, the scoffers? They say: from the study of protoplasm to the study of ectoplasm. And I reply: then remember all those who did not believe in protoplasm at the time.'

Arthur chuckles. 'And may I ask where you currently stand?'

'Where I stand? I have been researching and experimenting for nearly twenty years now. There is still much work to be done. But I would conclude, on the basis of my findings so far, that it is more than possible – indeed probable – that the mind survives the physical dissolution of the body.'

'You give me great heart.'

'We may soon be able to prove,' continues Lodge with a collusive twinkle, 'that it is not just Mr Sherlock Holmes who is able to escape evident and apparent death.'

Arthur smiles politely. That fellow is going to dog him to the gates of St Peter, or whatever the equivalent turns out to be in the new realm that is slowly being made palpable.

There is little *far niente* in Arthur's life. He is not a man to spend a summer's afternoon in a deckchair with a hat pulled down over his face, listening to the bees bothering the lupins. He would make as hopeless an invalid as Touie makes a successful one. His objection to inactivity is not so much moral – in his view, the Devil makes work for hands both idle and occupied – as temperamental. His life contains great bouts of mental activity, followed by great bouts of physical activity; in between he fits his social and family life, both of which he takes at a lick. He even sleeps as if it were part of life's business, rather than an interlude from it.

So he has few means of recourse when the machine overstrains itself. He is incapable of recuperating with an idle fortnight on the Italian lakes, or even a few days in the potting shed. He plunges instead into moods of depression and lassitude, which he seeks to hide from Touie and Jean. He shares them only with the Mam.

She suspects that he is more than usually troubled when he proposes a visit on his own account, rather than as a way of making a rendezvous with Jean. Arthur takes the 10.40 from St Pancras to Leeds. In the luncheon car, he finds himself thinking, as he increasingly does, about his father. He now acknowledges the harshness of his youthful judgement; perhaps age, or fame, has made him more forgiving. Or is it that there are times when Arthur feels on the edge of nervous collapse himself, when it seems that the normal human condition is to be on the edge of nervous collapse, and that it is mere good fortune, or some quirk of breeding, that keeps anyone from falling? Perhaps if he did not have his mother's blood in him, he might go – might already have gone – the way of Charles Doyle. And now Arthur begins to realize something for the first time: that the Mam has never criticized her husband, before or since his death. She does not need to, some might say. But even so: she, who always speaks her mind, has never been heard to say ill of the man who caused her so much embarrassment and suffering.

It is still light when he arrives at Ingleton. In the early evening they climb up through Bryan Waller's woodland and emerge on to the moor, gently scattering a few wild ponies. The large, erect, tweeded son aims words down at the red coat and neat white cap of his sure-footed mother. From time to time she picks up sticks for the fire. He finds this habit of hers vexing – as if he could not afford to buy her a cord of the finest firewood whenever she needs it.

'You see,' he says, 'there is a path here, and over there is Ingleborough, and we know that if we climb Ingleborough we can see across to Morecambe. And there are rivers whose course we can follow, which always flow in the same direction.'

The Mam does not know what to make of these topographical platitudes. They are most unlike Arthur.

'And were we to miss the path and get lost on the Wolds, we could use a compass and a map, which are easily obtainable. And even at night there are stars.'

'That is all true, Arthur.'

'No, it is banal. It is not worth saying.'

'Then tell me what you wish to say.'

'You brought me up,' he replies. 'There was never a son more devoted to his mother. I say that not as self-praise, merely as a statement of fact. You formed me, you gave me my sense of myself, you gave me my pride and what moral faculties I have. And there is still no son more devoted to his mother.

'I grew up surrounded by sisters. Annette, poor dear Annette, God rest her soul. Lottie, Connie, Ida, Dodo. I love them all in their different ways. I know them inside out. As a young man, I was not unfamiliar with female company. I did not debase myself as many another fellow did, but I was neither an ignoramus nor a prude.

'And yet . . . and yet I have come to think that women – other women – are like distant lands. Except that when I have been to distant lands – out on the veldt in Africa – I have always been able to find my bearings. Perhaps I am not making sense.'

He stops. He needs a reply. 'We are not so distant, Arthur. We are more like a neighbouring county which you have somehow forgotten to explore. And when you do, you are not sure if the place is much more advanced or much more primitive. Oh yes, I know how some men think. And perhaps it is both and perhaps it is neither. So tell me what you wish to say.'

'Jean is struck down with bouts of low spirits. Perhaps that is not the right way to describe them. It is physical – she has migraines – but it is more a kind of moral depression. She behaves, she talks as if she has done some awful thing. I never love her more than at such moments.' He attempts to take a deep breath of Yorkshire air, but it sounds more like a great sigh. 'And then I fall into black moods myself, but I merely loathe and despise myself for them.'

'And at such times no doubt she loves you just as much.'

'I never tell her. Perhaps she guesses. It is not my way.'

'I would not expect otherwise.'

'I think at times I shall run mad.' He says it calmly but bluntly, like a man giving a weather report. After a few paces, she reaches up and slips her arm through his. It is not one of her gestures, and it takes him by surprise.'

'Or if not run mad, die of a stroke. Explode like the boiler of a tramp steamer and just sink beneath the waves with all hands.'

The Mam does not answer. It is not necessary to refuse his simile, or even to ask if he has seen a doctor for chest pains.

'When the fit is on me, I doubt everything. I doubt I ever loved Touie. I doubt I love my children. I doubt my literary capability. I doubt Jean loves me.'

This does call for an answer. 'You do not doubt that you love her?'

'That, never. That, never. Which makes it worse. If I could doubt that, then I could doubt everything and sink happily into misery. No, that is always there, it has me in its monster grip.'

'Jean does love you, Arthur. I am quite certain of it. I know her. And I have read her letters that you send.'

'I think she does. I believe she does. How can I know she does? That's the question that tears at me when this mood descends. I think it, I believe it, but how can I ever know it? If only I could prove it, if either of us could prove it.'

They stop at a gate, and look down a tufted slope to the roof and chimneys of Masongill.

'But you are certain of your love for her, just as she is certain of her love for you?'

'Yes, but that is one-sided, that is not knowing, that is not proof.'

'Women often prove their love in a way that has been done many times.'

Arthur darts a glance down at his mother; but she is gazing resolutely ahead. All he can see is a curve of bonnet and the tip of her nose.

'But that is not proof either. That is just being desperate for evidence. If I made Jean my mistress it would not be proof that we loved one another.'

'I agree.'

'It might prove the opposite, that we are weakening in our love. It sometimes seems that honour and dishonour lie so close together, closer than I ever imagined.'

'I never taught you that honour was an easy path. What would it be worth if that was the case? And perhaps proof is impossible anyway. Perhaps the best we can manage is thinking and believing. Perhaps we only truly know in the hereafter.'

'Proof normally depends upon action. What is singular and damnable about our situation is that proof depends upon non-action. Our love is something separate, apart from the world, unknown to it. It is invisible, impalpable to the world, yet to me, to us, utterly visible, utterly palpable. It may not exist in a vacuum, but it does exist in a place where the atmosphere is different: lighter or heavier, I am never sure which. And somewhere outside of time. It has always been like this, from the beginning. That is what we immediately recognized. That we have this rare love, which sustains me – us – utterly.'

'And yet?'

'And yet. I scarcely dare voice the thought. It comes into my head when I am at the lowest. I find myself wondering . . . I find myself wondering: what if our love is not as I think, is not something existing outside time? What if everything I have believed about it is wrong? What if it is not special in any way, or at least, special only in the fact of being unadvertised and . . . unconsummated? And what if – what if Touie dies, and Jean and I are free, and our love can finally be advertised and sanctified, and brought out into the world, and what if at this point I discover that time has been quietly doing its work without my noticing, its work of gnawing and corroding and undermining? What if I then discover – what if we then discover – that I do not

190

love her as I thought, or that she does not love me as she thought? What would there be to be done then? What?'

Sensibly, the Mam does not reply.

Arthur confides everything to the Mam: his deepest fears, his greatest elations, and all the intermediate tribulations and joys of the material world. What he can never allude to is his deepening interest in spiritualism, or spiritism as he prefers it. The Mam, having left Catholic Edinburgh behind, has become, by a sheer process of attendance, a member of the Church of England. Three of her children have now been married at St Oswald's: Arthur himself, Ida and Dodo. She is instinctively opposed to the psychic world, which for her represents anarchy and mumbo-jumbo. She holds that people can only come to any understanding of their lives if society makes clear its truths to them; further, that its religious truths must be expressed through an established institution, be it Catholic or Anglican. And then there is the family to consider. Arthur is a knight of the realm; he has lunched and dined with the King; he is a public figure – she repeats back to him his boast that he is second only to Kipling in his influence on the healthy, sporting young men of the country. What if it came out that he was involved in seances and suchlike? It would dish all chance of a peerage.

In vain does he attempt to relate his conversation with Sir Oliver Lodge at Buckingham Palace. Surely the Mam must admit that Lodge is an entirely level-headed and scientifically reputable individual, as is proven by the fact that he has just been appointed first Principal of Birmingham University. But the Mam will not admit anything; in this area she refuses adamantinely to indulge her son.

Arthur fears to bring the matter up with Touie, in case it upsets the preternatural calm of her existence. She has, he knows, a simple trustingness in matters of faith. She presumes that after she dies she will go to a Heaven whose exact nature she cannot describe, and remain there in a condition she cannot imagine, until such time as Arthur comes to join her, followed in due course by their children, whereupon all of them will dwell together in a superior version of Southsea. Arthur thinks it unfair to disturb any of these presumptions.

It is harder still for him that he cannot talk to Jean, with whom he wants to share everything, from the last collar stud to the last semicolon. He has tried, but Jean is suspicious – or perhaps frightened – of anything touching the psychic world. Further, her dislike is expressed in ways Arthur finds untypical of her loving nature.

Once he tries recounting, with some tentativeness and a conscious suppression of zeal, his experience at a seance. Almost at once he notices a look of the sharpest disapproval come over those lovely features.

'What is it, my darling?'

'But Arthur,' she says, 'they are such common people.'

'Who are?'

'Those people. Like gypsy women who sit in fairground booths and tell your fortune with cards and tea leaves. They're just . . . common.'

Arthur finds such snobbery, especially in one he loves, unacceptable. He wants to say that it is the splendid lower-middle-class folk who have always been the spiritual peers of the nation: you need look no farther than the Puritans, whom many, of course, misprized. He wants to say that around the Sea of Galilee there were doubtless many who judged Our Lord Jesus Christ a little common. The Apostles, like most mediums, had little formal education. Naturally, he says none of this. He feels ashamed of his sudden irritation, and changes the subject.

And so he has to go outside his iron-sided triangle. He does not approach Lottie: he does not want to risk her love in any way, the more so as she helps nurse Touie. Instead, he goes to Connie. Connie, who only the other day, it seems, was wearing her hair down her back like the cable of a man-o'-war and breaking hearts across Continental Europe; Connie, who has settled all too solidly into the role of Kensington mother; Connie, moreover, who dared oppose him that day at Lord's. He has never solved the question of whether Connie changed Hornung's mind, or Hornung Connie's; but whichever way round, he has come to admire her for it.

He visits her one afternoon when Hornung is away; tea is served in her little upstairs sitting room, where once she heard him out about Jean. Strange to realize that his little sister is now nearer forty than thirty. But her age suits her. She is not quite as decorative as she once was, she is large, healthy and good-humoured. Jerome was not wrong to have called her a Brünnhilde when they were in Norway. It is as if, with the years, she has grown more robust in an attempt to counterbalance Hornung's ill-health.

'Connie,' he begins gently, 'Do you ever find yourself wondering what happens after we die?'

She looks at him sharply. Is there bad news about Touie? Is the Mam not well?

'It is a general enquiry,' he adds, sensing her alarm.

'No,' she replies. 'At least, very little. I worry about others dying. Not about myself. I did once, but it changes when you are a mother. I believe in the teachings of the Church. My Church. Our Church. The one you and the Mam left. I haven't the time to believe anything else.'

'Do you fear death?'

Connie reflects on this. She fears Willie's death — she knew the severity of his asthma when she married him, knew he would always be delicate — but that is fearing his absence, and the loss of his companionship. 'I can hardly like the idea,' she replies. 'But I'll cross that bridge when I come to it. You are sure you are not leading up to something?'

Arthur gives a brief shake of the head. 'So your position could be summed up as Wait and See?'

'I suppose so. Why?'

'Dear Connie — your attitude to the eternal is so English.'

'What a strange thought.'

Connie is smiling, and seems unlikely to shy away. Even so, Arthur doesn't know quite how to begin.

'When I was a lad at Stonyhurst, I had a friend called Partridge. He was a little younger than me. A fine catcher in the slips. He liked to bamboozle me with theological argument. He would choose examples of the Church's most illogical doctrines and ask me to justify them.'

'So he was an atheist?'

'Not at all. He was a stronger Catholic than I ever was. But he was trying to convince me of the truths of the Church by arguing against them. It turned out to be a misconceived tactic.'

'I wonder what has become of Partridge.'

Arthur smiles. 'As it happens, he is second cartoonist at *Punch*.'

He pauses. No, he must go directly at things. That is his way, after all.

'Many people — most people — are terrified of death, Connie. They're not like you in that respect. But they're like you in that they have English attitudes. Wait and see, cross that bridge when they come to it. But why should that reduce the fear? Why should uncertainty not increase it? And what is the point of life unless you know what happens afterwards? How can you make sense of the beginning if you don't know what the ending is?'

Connie wonders where Arthur is heading. She loves her large, generous, rumbustious brother. She thinks of him as Scottish practicality streaked with sudden fire.

'As I say, I believe what my Church teaches,' she replies. 'I see no alternative. Apart from atheism, which is mere emptiness and too depressing for words, and leads to socialism.'

'What do you think of spiritism?'

She knows that Arthur has been dabbling in psychic matters for years now. It is mentioned and half-mentioned behind his back.

'I suppose I mistrust it, Arthur.'

'Why?' He hopes Connie is not also going to prove a snob.

'Because I think it fraudulent.'

'You're right,' he answers, to her surprise. 'Much of it is. True prophets are always outnumbered by false – as Jesus Christ himself was. There is fraud, and trickery, even active criminal behaviour. There are some very dubious fellows muddying the water. Women too, I'm sorry to say.'

'Then that's what I think.'

'And it is not well explained at all. I sometimes think the world is divided into those who have psychic experiences but can't write, and those who can write but have no psychic experiences.'

Connie does not answer; she does not like the logical consequence of this sentence, which is sitting across from her, letting its tea go cold.

'But I said "much of it", Connie. Only "much of it" is fraudulent. If you visit a gold mine, do you find it filled with gold? No. Much of it – most of it – is base metal embedded in rock. You have to search for the gold.'

'I distrust metaphors, Arthur.'

'So do I. So do I. That is why I mistrust faith, which is the biggest metaphor of all. I have done with faith. I can only work with the clear white light of knowledge.'

Connie looks perplexed by this.

'The whole point of psychical research,' he explains, 'is to eliminate and expose fraud and deceit. To leave only what can be scientifically confirmed. If you eliminate the impossible, what is left, however improbable, must be the truth. Spiritism is not asking you to take a leap in the dark, or cross a bridge you have not yet come to.'

'So it is like Theosophy?' Connie is now nearing the extremity of her knowledge.

'Not like Theosophy. In the end, Theosophy is just another faith. As I say, I have done with faith.'

'And with Heaven and Hell?'

'You remember what the Mam told us – "Wear flannel next to your skin, and never believe in eternal punishment".'

'So everyone goes to Heaven? Sinners and the just alike? What incentive –'

Arthur cuts her off. He feels as if he is back arguing about the Tolley. 'Our spirits are not necessarily at peace after we pass over.'

'And God and Jesus? You do not believe in them?'

'Certainly. But not the God and the Jesus who are claimed by a Church which for centuries has been corrupt both spiritually and intellectually. And which demands of its followers the suspension of rational faculties.'

Connie now feels herself getting lost and also wonders if she should take offence. 'So what sort of Jesus do you believe in?'

'If you look at what it actually says in the Bible, if you ignore the way in which the text has been altered and misinterpreted to suit the will of the established churches, it's quite clear that Jesus was a highly trained psychic or medium. The inner circle of the Apostles, especially Peter, James and John, were clearly chosen for their spiritist capabilities. The "miracles" of the Bible are merely – well, not merely, wholly – examples of Jesus's psychic powers.'

'The raising of Lazarus? The feeding of the five thousand?'

'There are medical mediums who claim to see through the body's walls. There are apport mediums who claim to transport objects through time and space. And Pentecost, when the angel of the Lord came down and they all spoke in tongues. What is that but a seance? It's the most exact description of a seance I've read!'

'So you've become an early Christian, Arthur?'

'Not to mention Joan of Arc. She was clearly a great medium.'

'Her too?'

He suspects she is now mocking him – it would be just like her; and this makes it easier, not harder, for him to explain things.

'Think of it this way, Connie. Imagine there are a hundred mediums at work. Imagine ninety-nine of them are frauds. This means, does it not, that one is true? And if one is true, and the psychic phenomena channelled through that medium are authentic, we have proved our case. We need only prove it once and it is proved for everybody and for all time.'

'Prove what?' Connie has been thrown by her brother's sudden use of 'we'.

'The survival of the spirit after death. One case, and we prove it for all humanity. Let me tell you about something that happened twenty years ago in Melbourne. It was well documented at the time. Two young brothers went out into the bay in their boat with an experienced seaman at the tiller. Sailing conditions were good, but alas they never returned. Their father was a Spiritualist, and after two days with no news he called in a well-known sensitive – that's a medium – to try and trace them. The sensitive was given some of the brothers' belongings, and managed by psychometry to provide an account of their movements. The last he could make out was that their boat was in great difficulty and confusion reigned. It seemed that they were inevitably going to be lost.

'I see that look in your eye, Connie, and I know what you are thinking – that you would not have needed a psychic to tell you that. But wait. Two days later, another seance was held with the same sensitive, and the two lads, who had been trained in spiritual knowledge, came through at once. They apologized to their mother, who had not wanted them to set off, and gave an account of the capsizing and of their death by water. They reported that they were now in exactly the conditions of brightness and happiness that their father's preaching had promised. And they even brought the seaman who had perished with them to say a few words.

'Towards the end of the contact, one of the lads told how the other brother's arm had been torn off by a fish. The medium asked if it had been a shark, and the boy replied that it was not like any shark he had ever seen. Now, all this was written down at the time and some of it published in the newspapers. Mark the sequel. Some weeks later a large shark of a rare deep-sea species, one unfamiliar to the fishermen who caught it, and quite unknown in the waters off Melbourne, was taken some thirty miles away. Inside it was the bone of a human arm. Also, a watch, some coins, and other articles which belonged to the boy.' He paused. 'Now, Connie, what do you make of that?'

Connie reflects for a while. What she makes of it is that her brother is confusing religion with his love of fixing things. He sees a problem – death – and he looks for a way of solving it: such is his nature. She also thinks Arthur's spiritualism is connected, though quite how she cannot work out, with his love of chivalry and romance and the belief in a golden age. But she confines her objections to a narrower basis.

'What I make of it, my dear brother, is that it is a wonderful story, and you are a wonderful storyteller, as we all know. I also think that I was not in Melbourne twenty years ago, and neither were you.'

Arthur does not mind being rebuffed. 'Connie, you are a great rationalist, and that is the first step towards becoming a spiritist.'

'I doubt you will convert me, Arthur.' It seems to Connie that he has just told her a revised version of Jonah and the Whale – though one in which the victims were less fortunate – but that to base any beliefs upon such a story would be as much an act of faith as it was for those who first heard the story of Jonah. At least the Bible is proposing a metaphor. Arthur, because he dislikes metaphor, sees a parable and chooses to take it literally. As if the parable of the Wheat and the Tares were mere horticultural advice.

'Connie, what if someone you knew and loved were to die. And afterwards that person made contact with you, spoke to you, told you something only you knew, some chance intimate detail which could not have been discovered through anyone's trickery?'

'Arthur, I think that is another bridge I shall cross if ever I come to it.'

'Connie, you English Connie. Wait and see, wait and see what turns up. Not for me. I'm all for action now.'

'You always have been, Arthur.'

'We shall be laughed at. It is a great cause, but it will not be a fair fight. You must expect to see your brother laughed at. Still, always remember: one case is all we need. One case and the whole thing is proven. Proven beyond all reasonable doubt. Proven beyond all scientific refutation. Think of that, Connie.'

'Arthur, your tea is now quite cold.'

And so, gradually, the years accrue. It is ten years since Touie fell ill, six since he met Jean. It is eleven years since Touie fell ill, seven since he met Jean. It is twelve years since Touie fell ill, eight since he met Jean. Touie remains cheerful, free of pain, and ignorant, he is sure, of the gentle conspiracy surrounding her. Jean remains in her flat, practises her voice, rides to hounds, makes chaperoned visits to Undershaw and unchaperoned ones to Masongill; she never swerves from insisting that what she has is enough because it is all her heart desires, and she leaves one safe child-bearing year behind her after another. The Mam remains his rock, his confessor, his reassurance. Nothing moves. Perhaps nothing ever will move, until one day the strain attacks his heart and he simply explodes and expires. There is no way out, that is the beastliness of his position; or rather, each beckoning exit is marked Misery. In *Lasker's Chess Magazine* he reads of a position called *Zugzwang*, in which the player is unable to move any piece in any direction to any square without making his already imperilled state worse. This is what Arthur's life feels like.

Sir Arthur's life, on the other hand, which is all most people see, is in royal shape. Knight of the realm, friend of the King, champion of the Empire, and Deputy Lieutenant of Surrey. A man constantly in public demand. One year he is asked to judge a Strong Man competition organized by Mr Sandow the bodybuilder at the Albert Hall. He and Lawes the sculptor are the two assessors, with Sandow himself as referee. Eighty competitors display their muscles to a packed hall in batches of ten. Eighty bursting leopardskins are whittled down to twenty-four, to twelve, to six, and then a final three. Those remaining are wonderful specimens, but one is a little short, and another a little clumsy, so they award the title, and with it a valuable gold statue, to a man from Lancashire called Murray. The judges and some chosen company are then rewarded with a late champagne supper. Emerging into the midnight streets, Sir Arthur notices Murray walking ahead of him, the statuette tucked casually beneath one powerful arm. Sir Arthur joins him, congratulates him anew, and, perceiving that he is a very simple country fellow, asks where he is intending to stay the night. Murray confides that he has no money at all, merely his return ticket to Blackburn, and is planning to walk the deserted streets until his train leaves in the morning. So Arthur takes him to Morley's Hotel, and instructs the staff to look after him. The next morning he finds Murray cheerfully holding court from his bed to awed maids and waiters, his award glinting on the pillow beside him. It looks the very picture of a happy outcome, but this is not the image that stays in Sir Arthur's mind. It is that of a man walking ahead of him alone; a man who has won a great prize and been acclaimed, a man with a statuette of gold under his arm and yet no money in his pocket, a man planning to walk the gas-lit streets in solitude until daybreak.

Then there is Conan Doyle's life, which is also in fine fettle. He is too professional and too energetic ever to suffer from writer's block for more than a day or two. He identifies a story, researches and plans it, then writes it out. He is quite clear about the writer's responsibilities: they are firstly, to be intelligible, secondly, to be interesting, and thirdly, to be clever. He knows his own abilities, and he also knows that in the end the reader is king. That is why Mr Sherlock Holmes was brought back to life, allowed to have escaped the Reichenbach Falls thanks to a knowledge of esoteric Japanese wrestling holds and an ability to scramble up sheer rock faces. If the Americans insist on offering five thousand dollars for a mere half-dozen new stories – and in return only for American rights – then what can Dr Conan Doyle do except raise his hands in surrender and allow himself to be manacled to the consulting detective for the foreseeable future? And the fellow has brought other rewards: the University of Edinburgh has made him an Honorary Doctor of Letters. He may never be a big man like Kipling, but as he walked in parade through the city of his birth, he felt at ease in those academic robes; more so, he has to admit, than in the quaint garb of a Deputy Lieutenant of Surrey.

And then there is his fourth life, the one where he is neither Arthur, nor Sir Arthur, nor Dr Conan Doyle; the life in which name is irrelevant, as is wealth and rank and outward display and bodily carapace; the world of the spirit. The sense that he has been born for something else grows with each year. It is not easy; it will never be easy. It is not like signing up for one of the established religions. It is new, and dangerous, and utterly important. If you were to became a Hindoo, it would be regarded by society as an eccentricity rather than a derangement. But if you are prepared to open yourself to the world of Spiritism, then you must also be prepared to endure the jocosities and shallow paradoxes with which the Press misleads the public. Yet what are the scoffers and cynics and penny-a-liners when set beside Crookes and Myers and Lodge and Alfred Russel Wallace?

Science is leading the way, and will bring the scoffers low as it always does. For who would have believed in radio waves? Who would have believed in X-rays? Who would have believed in argon and helium and neon and xenon, all of which have been discovered in the last years? The invisible and the impalpable, which lie just below the surface of the real, just beneath the skin of things, are increasingly being made visible and palpable. The world and its purblind inhabitants are at last learning to see.

Take Crookes. What does Crookes say? 'It is incredible but it is true.' The man whose work in physics and chemistry is everywhere admired for its precision and truth. The man who discovered thallium, who spent years investigating the properties of rarefied gases and rare earths. Who better to pronounce on this equally rarefied world, this new territory inaccessible to duller minds and cabined spirits? It is incredible, but it is true.

And then Touie dies. It is thirteen years since she fell ill, nine since he met Jean. Now, in the springtime of the year 1906, she begins to lapse into mild delirium. Sir Douglas Powell is immediately in attendance; paler, balder, but still the courtliest messenger of death. This time, there is no chance of reprieve, and Arthur must prepare himself for what has been so long foretold. The vigil begins. Undershaw's clattering monorail is stilled, the rifle range placed out of bounds, the tennis net taken down for the season. Touie remains without pain, and easy in her mind, as the spring flowers in her room change to those of early summer. Gradually, she slips into longer periods of delirium. The tubercle has gone to her brain; there is partial paralysis of her left side and half her face. *The Imitation of Christ* lies unopened; Arthur is in constant attendance.

To the end, she recognizes him. She says, 'Bless you,' and 'Thank you, dear,' and when he raises her in the bed, she mumurs, 'That's the ticket.' As June turns to July, she is clearly dying. On the day itself, Arthur is at her side; Mary and Kingsley watch in awkward fear, half-embarrassed by their mother's paralysed face. In silence they wait. At three in the morning, Touie dies holding Arthur's hand. She is forty-nine, Arthur forty-seven. He is much in her room after her death; standing by her body, he tells himself that he has done his best. He also knows that this abandoned husk, laid out on the bed, is not all there remains of Touie. This white and waxen thing is just something she has left behind.

In the days that follow, Arthur feels, beneath the febrile exaltation of the bereaved, a solid sense of duty performed. Touie is buried as Lady Doyle beneath a marble cross at Grayshott. Messages of sympathy come from the great and the humble; from King and parlourmaid, from his fellow writers and his far-flung readers, from London clubs and imperial outposts. Arthur is at first touched and honoured by the condolences, and then, as they continue, increasingly disturbed. What exactly has he done to deserve such heartfelt sentiments, let alone the assumptions behind them?

These expressions of true feeling make him feel a hypocrite. Touie has been the gentlest companion a man could possibly have. He remembers showing her the military trophies on Clarence Esplanade; he sees her with a ship's biscuit between her lips at the Victualling Yard; he waltzes her round the kitchen table when heavily pregnant with Mary; he whisks her off to frozen Vienna; he tucks a blanket round her in Davos, and waves towards a recumbent figure on an Egyptian hotel verandah before launching a golf ball across the sands towards the nearest Pyramid. He remembers her smile, and her goodness; but he also remembers that it is years since he could put his hand upon his heart and swear that he loved her. Not just since Jean came along, but before that too. He has loved her as best a man can, given that he did not love her.

He knows that he should spend the next days and weeks with his children, because that is what a grieving parent does. Kingsley is thirteen and Mary seventeen: ages which now surprise him. Part of him has frozen time at the day and the year when he met Jean – the day his heart was utterly brought to life, and also placed in a state of suspended animation. He must accustom himself to the notion that his children will soon be adults.

If he needs any confirmation of this, Mary soon provides it. Over tea one afternoon a few days after the funeral, she says to him, in an alarmingly grown-up voice, 'Father, when Mother was dying, she said that you would remarry.'

Arthur almost chokes on his cake. He feels his colour rising, his chest tightening; perhaps this is the seizure he has been half-expecting. 'Did she, by God?' Touie certainly never mentioned the subject to him.

'Yes. No, not exactly. What she said was . . .' and Mary pauses while her father feels cacophony in his head, turmoil in his guts '. . . what she said was that I was not to be shocked if you were to remarry, because that is what she would want for you.'

Arthur does not know what to think. Has some trap been laid for him, or does no trap exist? Did Touie after all suspect? Did she confide in their daughter? Was it a general remark, or a specific one? He has lived with so much damned uncertainty over the last nine years that he doubts he can bear any more.

'And did she . . .' Arthur tries to sound jocular, while realizing that this is not the right tone – but then there is no right tone – 'And did she have any particular candidate in mind?'

'Father!' Mary is evidently shocked by the very notion, as well as by his tone.

The conversation passes to safer ground. But it stays with Arthur through the following days, as he takes flowers to Touie's grave, as he stands, distracted, in her empty room, as he avoids his desk, and finds he cannot face the letters of condolence, the letters of true feeling, which continue to arrive. He has spent nine years protecting Touie from the knowledge of Jean's existence; nine years trying never to give her a moment's unhappiness. But perhaps these two desires are – always were – incompatible. He readily admits that women are not his area of expertise. Does a woman know when you are in love with her? He thinks so, he believes so, he knows so, because that is what Jean recognized, in that sunlit garden, even before he himself was aware of it. And if so, then does a woman know when you are no longer in love with her? And does a woman also know when you are in love with someone else? Nine years ago he devised an elaborate plot to protect Touie, involving all those around her; but perhaps in the end it was only a scheme to protect himself and Jean. Perhaps it was entirely selfish, and Touie saw through its fraudulence; perhaps she knew all along. Mary cannot suspect the full burden of Touie's message about remarrying, but it gets through to Arthur now. Maybe she knew from the start, watched Arthur's squalid rearrangements of the truth from her sickbed, understood and smiled at every mean little lie her husband told her, imagined him downstairs busy at the adulterer's telephone. She would have felt helpless to protest, because she could no longer be a wife to him in the fullest sense. And what if – now his suspicions become darker still – what if she knew about Jean's importance from the start, and went on guessing? What if she found herself obliged to welcome Jean to Undershaw while imagining her Arthur's mistress?

Arthur's mind, being both powerful and intransigent, pursues the matter further. His conversation with Mary has further ramifications than those he first saw. Touie's death, he now realizes, will not put an end to his deceits. For Mary must never be allowed to know that he has been in love with Jean for these past nine long years. Nor must Kingsley. Boys, it is said, often take the betrayal of their mother even harder than girls do.

He imagines finding the right moment, practising the words, then clearing his throat and trying to sound – what? – as if he is barely able himself to credit what he is about to say.

'Mary dear, you know what your mother said before she died? About it being possible that I might one day remarry. Well, I must inform you that, to my own considerable surprise, she is going to be proved right.'

Will he find himself saying words like these? And if so, when? Before the year is out? No, of course not. But next year, the year after? How quickly is the grieving widower allowed to fall in love again? He knows how society feels on the matter, but what do children feel – his children in particular?

And then he imagines Mary's questions. Who is she, Father? Oh, Miss Leckie. I met her when I was quite little, didn't I? And then we kept running into her. And then she started coming to Undershaw. I always thought she would have been married by now. Lucky for you she's still free. How old is she? Thirty-one? So was she on the shelf, Papa? I'm surprised no one would have her. And when did you realize you loved her, Father?

Mary is not a child any more. She may not expect her father to lie, but she will notice the slightest incongruity in his story. What if he blunders? Arthur despises those fellows who are good liars, who organize their emotional lives – their marriages, even – on the basis of what they can get away with, who tell a half-truth here, a full lie there. Arthur has always thundered the importance of truth-telling at his children; now he must play the fullest hypocrite. He must smile, and look shyly pleased, and act surprised, and concoct a mendacious romance about how he came to love Jean Leckie, and tell that lie to his own children, and then maintain it for the rest of his life. And he must ask others to do the same on his behalf.

Jean. Quite properly, she did not come to the funeral; she sent a letter of condolence, and a week or so later Malcolm drove her over from Crowborough. It was not the easiest of meetings. When they arrived, Arthur found he could not embrace her in front of her brother and so, on an instinct, he kissed her hand. It was the wrong gesture – there was something almost facetious about it – and it set a tone of awkwardness that would not go away. She behaved impeccably, as he knew she would; but he was at a loss. When Malcolm tactfully decided to inspect the garden, Arthur found himself casting around hopelessly, expecting guidance. But from whom? From Touie installed behind her tea service? He did not know what to say, and so he used his grief as a disguise for his maladroitness, for his lack of joy at seeing Jean's face. He was glad when Malcolm returned from his bogus horticultural expedition. They left soon afterwards, and Arthur felt wretched.

The triangle within which he has lived – frettingly but safely – for so long is now broken, and the new geometry frightens him. His grieving exaltation fades, and lethargy overtakes him. He wanders the grounds of Undershaw as if they had been laid out by a stranger long ago. He visits his horses, but does not want them saddled. He goes daily to Touie's grave, and returns exhausted. He imagines her comforting him, reassuring him that wherever the truth lies, she has always loved him and now forgives him; but this seems a vain and selfish thing to demand of a dead woman. He sits in his study for long hours, smoking and looking at the glittering, hollow trophies acquired by a sportsman and successful writer. All his baubles seem meaningless beside the fact of Touie's death.

He leaves all his correspondence to Wood. His secretary has long since learned to reproduce his employer's signature, his inscriptions, his turns of phrase, even his opinions. Let him be Sir Arthur Conan Doyle for a while — the name's owner has no desire to be himself. Wood may open everything, and discard or answer as he wishes.

He has no energy; he eats little. To be hungry at such a time would be an obscenity. He lies down; he cannot sleep. He has no symptoms, only a general and intense weakness. He consults his old friend and medical adviser Charles Gibbs, who has attended him since his South African days. Gibbs tells him it is everything and nothing; in other words, it is nerves.

Soon, it is more than nerves. His guts give way. This at least Gibbs can identify, even if there is little he can do about it. Some microbe must have got into his system at Bloemfontein or on the veldt, and it remains there, waiting to break out when he is at his weakest. Gibbs prescribes a sleeping draught. But he can do nothing about the other microbe abroad in his patient's system, which is equally unkillable; the microbe of guilt.

He always imagined that Touie's long illness would somehow prepare him for her death. He always imagined that grief and guilt, if they followed, would be more clear-edged, more defined, more finite. Instead they seem like weather, like clouds constantly re-forming into new shapes, blown by nameless, unidentifiable winds.

He knows he must rouse himself, but feels incapable; after all, this will mean rousing himself to lie again. First, to perpetuate, to make historical, the old lie about his devoted love-marriage to Touie; afterwards, to organize and propagate the new lie, about Jean bringing unexpected solace to a grieving widower's heart. The thought of this new lie disgusts him. In lethargy there is at least truth: exhausted, gut-plagued, dragging from room to room, he is at least misleading no one. Except that he is: his condition is ascribed by everyone merely to grief.

He is a hypocrite; he is a fraud. In some ways, he has always felt a fraud, and the more famous he has become, the more fraudulent he has felt. He is lauded as a great man of the age, but though he takes an active part in the world, his heart feels out of kilter with it. Any normal man of the age would not have scrupled to make Jean his mistress. That is what men did nowadays, even in the highest ranks of society, as he has observed. But his moral life belongs more happily in the fourteenth century. And his spiritual life? Connie judged him an early Christian. He prefers to locate himself in the future. The twenty-first century, the twenty-second? It all depends how quickly slumbering humanity wakes up and learns to use its eyes.

And then his thoughts, already on a downward slope, tumble further. After nine years of wanting – of trying not to admit to wanting – the impossible, he is now free. He could marry Jean tomorrow morning and face only the bickering of village moralists. But wanting the impossible canonizes the wanting. Now that the impossible has become the possible, how much does he want? He cannot even tell this now. It is as if the muscles of the heart, overtaxed for so long, have turned to fraying rubber.

He once heard a story, narrated over port, of a married man who maintained a long-term mistress. This woman was of good social standing, certainly fit to marry him, which is what had always been anticipated and promised. Eventually, the wife died, and within weeks the widower duly remarried. But not his mistress; instead, a young woman of a lower social class whom he had met a few days after the funeral. At the time he had sounded to Arthur like a double cad: cad to the wife, then cad to the mistress.

Now, he realizes how easily such things happen. In the ragged months since Touie's death, he had scarcely entered society, and those to whom he has been introduced have left only the faintest impression. Yet even so – and allowing for the fact that he does not understand the other sex – some of its members were flirting with him. No, that is vulgar and unfair; but certainly, they were looking at him differently, at this famous author, this knight of the realm, who is now a widower. He can well imagine how the fraying rubber might suddenly break, how a young girl's simplicity, or even a coquette's scented smile, might suddenly pierce a heart grown temporarily impervious to a long and secret attachment. He understands the behaviour of the double cad. More than understands: he sees the advantage. If you allow yourself to succumb to such a *coup de foudre*, then it is, at least, the end to lying: you do not have to produce your long-secret love and introduce her as a new-met companion. You do not have to lie to your children for the rest of your life. As for your new wife: yes, you say, I know how she strikes you, and she could never replace the irreplaceable, but she has brought a little cheer and consolation into my heart. The forgiveness sought might not be immediately forthcoming, but at least the situation would be less complicated.

He sees Jean again, once in company and once alone, and on both occasions the awkwardness between them continues. He finds himself waiting for his heart to pulse again – no, he is instructing his heart to pulse again – and it refuses to do his bidding. He has been so used to forcing his thoughts, to pressing them and directing them where they have to go, that it comes as a shock that he is unable to do the same with the tender emotions. Jean looks as adorable as ever, except that her adorability does not set off the normal response. Some impotence of the heart appears to have struck him.

In the past, Arthur has eased the torments of thought by physical exertion; but he feels no desire to ride, to spar, to strike a ball at cricket, tennis or golf. Perhaps, if he were instantly transported to a high, snow-covered Alpine valley, an icy breeze might disperse the mephitic air which hangs around his soul. But it seems impossible. The person he once was, the *Sportesmann* who brought his Norwegian skis to Davos and crossed the Furka Pass with the Branger brothers, seems to him long departed, long out of sight on the other side of the mountain.

When, at length, his mind stops descending, when he feels less febrile of mind and gut, he tries to make a clearing in his head, to establish a little area of simple thought. If a man cannot tell what he wants to do, then he must find out what he ought to do. If desire has become complicated, then hold fast to duty. This is what he did with Touie, and what he must now do with Jean. He has loved her hopelessly and hopefully for nine years; such a feeling cannot simply disappear; so he must wait for its return. Until then, he must negotiate the great Grimpen Mire, where green-scummed pits and foul quagmires on every side threaten to pull a man down and swallow him for ever. To plot his course, he must call on everything he has learned up to now. In the Mire, there were hidden signs – bunches of reeds and strategically planted sticks – to guide the initiate to firmer ground; and it is the same when a man is morally lost. The path lies where honour directs. Honour has told him how to behave in the past years; now honour must tell him where he is to head. Honour binds him to Jean, as it bound him to Touie. He cannot tell at this distance if he will ever be truly happy again; but he knows that for him there can be no happiness where honour is absent.

The children are away at school; the house is silent; winds rip the trees bare; November turns to December. He feels a little steadier, as they suggested he would. One morning he wanders into Wood's office to look at his correspondence. On average he gets sixty letters a day. Over the last months Wood has been obliged to develop a system: he answers himself anything that can be dealt with immediately; items requiring Sir Arthur's opinion or decision are placed in a large wooden tray. If, by the end of the week, his employer has not had the heart or stomach to offer any guidance, Wood clears it off as best he can.

Today there is a small package on top of the tray. Arthur half-heartedly slides out the contents. There is a covering letter pinned to a file of cuttings from a newspaper called *The Umpire*. He has never heard of it. Perhaps it deals with cricket. No, from its pink newsprint he can tell it is a scandal sheet. He glances at the letter's signature. He reads a name that means absolutely nothing to him: George Edalji.

THREE
Ending with a Beginning

Arthur & George

Ever since Sherlock Holmes solved his first case, requests and demands have been coming in from all over the world. If persons or goods disappear in mysterious circumstances, if the police are more than usually baffled, if justice miscarries, then it appears that mankind's instinct is to appeal to Holmes and his creator. Letters addressed to 221B Baker Street are now automatically returned by the Post Office stamped ADDRESSEE UNKNOWN; those sent to Holmes c/o Sir Arthur are similarly dealt with. Over the years, Alfred Wood has often been struck by the way his employer is simultaneously proud of having created a character in whose true existence readers effortlessly believe, and irritated when they take such belief to its logical conclusion.

Then there are appeals directed to Sir Arthur Conan Doyle *in propria persona*, written on the presumption that anyone with the intelligence and guile to devise such complicated fictional crimes must therefore be equipped to solve real ones. Sir Arthur, if impressed or touched, will sometimes respond, though unfailingly in the negative. He will explain that he is, regrettably, no more a consulting detective than he is an English bowman of the fourteenth century or a debonair cavalry officer under the command of Napoleon Bonaparte.

So Wood has laid out the Edalji dossier with few expectations. Yet on this occasion Sir Arthur is back in his secretary's office within the hour, in mid-expostulation even as he barges through the door.

'It's as plain as a packstaff,' he is saying. 'The fellow's no more guilty than that typewriter of yours. I ask you, Woodie! It's a joke. The case of the locked room in reverse – not how does he get in but how does he get out? It's as shabby as shabby can be.'

Wood has not seen his employer so indignant for months. 'You wish me to reply?'

'Reply? I'm going to do more than reply. I'm going to stir things up. I'm going to knock some heads together. They'll rue the day they let this happen to an innocent man.'

Wood is as yet unsure who 'they' might be, or indeed what 'this' is that has 'happened'. In the supplicant's petition he observed little, apart from a strange surname, to distinguish it from dozens of other supposed miscar-riages of justice which Sir Arthur is expected single-handedly to overturn. But Wood does not at this moment care about the rights or wrongs of the Edalji case. He is only relieved that his employer seems, within the hour, to have shrugged off the lethargy and despondence that have afflicted him these past months.

In a covering letter George has explained the anomalous position in which he finds himself. The decision to free him on licence was taken by the previous Home Secretary, Mr Akers-Douglas, and implemented by the present one, Mr Herbert Gladstone; but neither has offered any official explanation of their reasons. George's conviction has not been cancelled, nor has any apology been tendered for his incarceration. One newspaper, doubtless briefed over a complicit luncheon by some nod-and-wink bureaucrat, shamelessly let it be known that the Home Office had no doubt as to the prisoner's guilt, but had released him because three years was considered the appropriate sentence for the crime in question. Sir Reginald Hardy, in deciding upon seven, had shown himself a touch over-zealous in the defence of Staffordshire's honour; and the Home Secretary was merely correcting this fit of enthusiasm.

All of which leaves George in moral despair and practical limbo. Do they think him guilty or not guilty? Are they apologizing for his conviction or reaffirming it? Unless and until the conviction is expunged, it is impossible for him to be readmitted to the Rolls. The Home Office perhaps expects George to display his relief by silence, and his gratitude by slinking away to another profession, preferably in the colonies. Yet George has survived prison only by the thought, the hope, of returning to work – somehow, somewhere – as a solicitor; and his supporters, having come thus far, have no intention of giving up either. One of Mr Yelverton's friends has given George temporary employment in his office as a clerk; but this is no solution. The solution can only come from the Home Office.

Arthur is late for his appointment with George Edalji at the Grand Hotel, Charing Cross; business with his bank has detained him. Now he enters the foyer at speed, and looks around. It is not difficult to spot his waiting guest: the only brown face is sitting about twelve feet away from him in profile. Arthur is about to step across and apologize when something makes him hold back. It is, perhaps, ungentlemanly to observe without permission; but not for nothing was he once the out-patient clerk of Dr Joseph Bell.

So: preliminary inspection reveals that the man he is about to meet is small and slight, of Oriental origin, with hair parted on the left and cropped close; he wears glasses, and the well-cut, discreet clothing of a provincial solicitor. All indisputably true, but this is hardly like identifying a French polisher or a left-handed cobbler from scratch. Yet still Arthur continues to observe, and is drawn back, not to the Edinburgh of Dr Bell, but to his own years of medical practice. Edalji, like many another men in the foyer, is barricaded between newspaper and high-winged armchair. Yet he is not sitting quite as others do: he holds the paper preternaturally close, and also a touch sideways, setting his head at an angle to the page. Dr Doyle, formerly of Southsea and Devonshire Place, is confident in his diagnosis. Myopia, possibly of quite a high degree. And who knows, perhaps a touch of astigmatism too.

'Mr Edalji.'

The newspaper is not flung down in excitement, but folded carefully. The young man does not leap to his feet and fall on the neck of his potential saviour. On the contrary, he stands up carefully, looks Sir Arthur in the eye, and extends his hand. There is no danger that this man is going to start babbling about Holmes. Instead, he holds himself in wait, polite and self-contained.

They withdraw to an unoccupied writing room, and Sir Arthur is able to examine his new acquaintance more closely. A broad face, fullish lips, a pronounced dimple in the middle of the chin; clean-shaven. For a man who has served three years in Lewes and Portland, and who must have been used to a softer life than most beforehand, he shows few signs of his ordeal. His black hair is shot with grey, but this rather gives him the aspect of a thinking, cultured person. He could very well still be a working solicitor, except that he is not.

'Do you know the exact value of your myopia? Six, seven dioptres? I am only guessing, of course.'

George is startled by this first question. He takes a pair of spectacles from his top pocket and hands them over. Arthur examines them, then turns his attention to the eyes whose defects they correct. These bulge somewhat, and give the solicitor a slightly vacant, staring appearance. Sir Arthur assesses his man with the judgement of a former ophthalmologist; but he is also familiar with the false moral inferences the general public is inclined to draw from ocular singularity.

'I am afraid I have no idea,' says George. I have only recently acquired spectacles, and did not enquire about their specifications. Nor do I always remember to wear them.'

'You did not have them as a child?'

'Indeed not. My eyesight was always poor, but when an oculist was consulted in Birmingham, he said it was unwise to prescribe them for a child. And then – well – I became too busy. But since my release I am, unfortunately, less busy.'

'As you explained in your letter. Now, Mr Edalji –'

'It's *Ayd*lji, actually, if you don't mind.' George says this instinctively.

'I apologize.'

'I am used to it. But since it is my name . . . You see, all Parsee names are stressed on the first syllable.'

Sir Arthur nods. 'Well, Mr *Ayd*lji, I should like you to be professionally examined by Mr Kenneth Scott of Manchester Square.'

'If you say so. But —'

'At my expense, of course.'

'Sir Arthur, I could not —'

'You can, and you will.' He says it softly, and George catches the Scottish burr for the first time. 'You are not employing me as a detective, Mr Edalji. I am offering — offering — my services. And when we have won you not only a free pardon but also a large sum in compensation for your wrongful imprisonment, I may send you Mr Scott's bill. But then again I may not.'

'Sir Arthur, I did not imagine for a moment when I wrote to you —'

'No, and nor did I when I received your letter. But there we are. And here we are.'

'The money is not important. I want my name back again. I want to be readmitted as a solicitor. That is all I want. To be allowed to practise again. To live a quiet, useful life. A normal life.'

'Of course. But I disagree. The money is very important. Not just as compensation for three years of your life. It is also symbolic. The British respect money. If you are given a free pardon, the public will know you are innocent. But if you are given money as well, the public will know you are completely innocent. There is a world of difference. Money will also prove that it is only the corrupt inertia of the Home Office that kept you in prison in the first place.'

George nods slowly to himself as he takes in the argument. Sir Arthur is impressed by the young man. He seems to have a calm and deliberate mind. From his Scottish mother or his clergyman father? Or a benign mixing of the two?

'Sir Arthur, may I ask if you are a Christian?'

Now it is Arthur's turn to be startled. He does not wish to offend this son of the manse, so he replies with his own question. 'Why do you ask?'

'I was brought up, as you know, in the Vicarage. I love and respect my parents, and naturally, when I was young, I shared their beliefs. How could I not? I would never have made a priest myself, but I accepted the teachings of the Bible as the best guide to living a true and honourable life.' He looks at Sir Arthur to see how he is responding; soft eyes and an inclination of the head encourage him. 'I still do think them the best guide. As I think the laws of England are the best guide for how society in general may live a true and honourable life together. But then my . . . my ordeal began. At first I viewed it all as an unfortunate example of maladministration of the law. The police made a mistake, but it would be corrected by the magistrates. The magistrates made a mistake, but it would be corrected by the Quarter Sessions. The Quarter Sessions made a mistake, but it would be corrected by the Home

Office. It will, I hope, still be corrected by the Home Office. It is a matter of great pain and, to say the least, inconvenience, that this has happened, but the process of the law will, in the end, deliver justice. That is what I believed, and what I still believe.

'However, it has been more complicated than I at first realized. I have lived my life within the law – that is to say, taking the law as my guide, while Christianity has been the moral support behind that. For my father, however –' and here George pauses, not, Arthur suspects, because he does not know what he is about to say, but because of its emotional weight – 'my father lives his life wholly within the Christian religion. As you would expect. So for him my ordeal must be comprehensible in those terms. For him there is – there must be – a religious justification for my suffering. He thinks it is God's purpose to strengthen my own faith and to act as an example for others. It is an embarrassment for me to say the word, but he imagines me a martyr.

'My father is elderly now, and becoming frail. Nor would I wish to contradict him. At Lewes and Portland I naturally attended chapel. I still go to church every Sunday. But I cannot claim that my faith has been strengthened by my imprisonment, nor' – he gives a cautious, wry smile – 'nor would my father be able to claim that congregations at St Mark's and neighbouring churches have increased in the last three years.'

Sir Arthur contemplates the odd formality of these opening remarks – as if they have been practised, even over-practised. No, that is too harsh. What else would a man do during three years of prison except turn his life – his messy, inchoate, half-understood life – into something resembling a witness statement?

'Your father, I imagine, would say that martyrs do not choose their lot, and may not even have an understanding of the matter.'

'Perhaps. But what I have just said is actually less than the truth. My incarceration did not strengthen my faith. Quite the contrary. It has, I think, destroyed it. My suffering has been quite purposeless, either for me or as any kind of example to others. Yet when I told my father that you had agreed to see me, his reaction was that it was all part of God's evident purpose in the world. Which is why, Sir Arthur, I asked if you were a Christian.'

'Whether I am or not would not affect your father's argument. God surely chooses any instrument to hand, whether Christian or heathen.'

'True. But you do not have to be soft with me.'

'No. And you will not find me a man to palter, Mr Edalji. For myself, I cannot see how your time in Lewes and Portland, and the loss of your profession and your place in society, can possibly serve God's purpose.'

'My father, you must understand, believes that this new century will bring in a more harmonious commingling of the races than in the past – that this is God's purpose, and I am intended to serve as some kind of messenger. Or victim. Or both.'

'Without in any way criticizing your father,' says Arthur carefully, 'I would have thought that if such had been God's intention, it would have been better served by making sure you had a gloriously successful career as a solicitor, and thus set an example to others for the commingling of the races.'

'You think as I do,' replies George. Arthur likes this answer. Others would have said, 'I agree with you.' But George has said it without vanity. It is simply that Arthur's words have confirmed what he has already thought.

'However, I agree with your father that this new century is likely to bring extraordinary developments in man's spiritual nature. Indeed, I believe that by the time the third millennium begins, the established churches will have withered, and all the wars and disharmonies their separate existences have brought into the world will also have disappeared.' George is about to protest that this is not what his father means at all; but Sir Arthur is forging on. 'Man is on the verge of elaborating the truths of psychical law as he has for centuries been elaborating the truths of physical law. When these truths come to be accepted, our whole way of living – and dying – will have to be rethought from first principles. We shall believe in more, not less. We shall understand more deeply the processes of life. We shall realize that death is not a door closed in our face, but a door left ajar. And by the time that new millennium begins, I believe we shall have a greater capacity for happiness and fellow-feeling than ever before in mankind's frequently miserable existence.' Sir Arthur suddenly catches himself, an orator on a damn soapbox. 'I apologize. It is a hobby horse. No, it is a great deal more than that. But you did ask.'

'There is no need to apologize.'

'There is. I have allowed us to stray far from the matter in hand. To business again. May I ask if there is anyone you suspect of the crime?'

'Which one?'

'All of them. The persecutions. The forged letters. The rippings – not just of the Colliery pony, but all the others.'

'To be perfectly honest, Sir Arthur, for the last three years I and those who have supported me have been more concerned with proving my innocence than anyone else's guilt.'

'Understandably. But a connection inevitably exists. So is there anyone you might suspect?'

'No. No one. Everything was done anonymously. And I cannot imagine who would take pleasure in mutilating animals.'

'You had enemies in Great Wyrley?'

'Evidently. But unseen ones. I had few acquaintances there, whether friend or foe. We did not go out into local society.'

'Why not?'

'I have only recently begun to understand why not. At the time, as a child, I assumed it to be normal. The truth is, my parents had very little money, and what they had, they spent on their children's education. I did not miss going to other boys' houses. I was a happy child, I think.'

'Yes.' This seems less than the full answer. 'But, I presume, given your father's origins –'

'Sir Arthur, I should like to make one thing quite clear. I do not believe that race prejudice has anything to do with my case.'

'I have to say that you surprise me.'

'My father believes that I would not have suffered as I did if I had been, for instance, the son of Captain Anson. That is certainly true. But in my view the matter is a red herring. Go to Wyrley and ask the villagers if you do not believe me. At all events, if any prejudice exists, it is confined to a very small section of the community. There has been an occasional slight, but what man does not suffer that, in some form or another?'

'I understand your desire not to play the martyr –'

'No, it is not that, Sir Arthur.' George stops, and looks momentarily embarrassed. 'Is that what I should be calling you, by the way?'

'You may call me that. Or Doyle if you prefer.'

'I think I prefer Sir Arthur. As you may imagine, I have thought a great deal about this matter. I was brought up as an Englishman. I went to school, I studied the law, I did my articles, I became a solicitor. Did anyone try to hold me back from this progress? On the contrary. My schoolmasters encouraged me, the partners at Sangster, Vickery & Speight took notice of me, my father's congregation uttered words of praise when I qualified. No clients refused my advice at Newhall Street on the grounds of my origin.'

'No, but –'

'Let me continue. There have been, as I said, occasional slights. There were teasings and jokes. I am not so naive as to be unaware that some people look at me differently. But I am a lawyer, Sir Arthur. What evidence do I have that anyone has acted against me because of race prejudice? Sergeant Upton used to try and frighten me, but no doubt he frightened other boys as well. Captain Anson clearly took a dislike to me, without ever having met me. What concerned me more about the police was their lack of competence. For example, they themselves, despite covering the district with special constables, never discovered a single mutilated animal. These events were always reported to them by the farmers, or by men going to work. I was not the only person to conclude that the police were afraid of the so-called Gang, even if they were quite unable to prove its existence.

'So if you are proposing that my ordeal has been caused by race prejudice, then I must ask you for your evidence. I do not recall Mr Disturnal ever alluding to the subject. Or Sir Reginald Hardy. Did the jury find me guilty because of my skin? That is too easy an answer. And I might add that during my years in prison I was fairly treated by the staff and the other inmates.'

'If I may make a suggestion,' replied Sir Arthur. 'Perhaps you should try occasionally not to think like a lawyer. The fact that no evidence of a phenomenon can be adduced does not mean that it does not exist.'

'Agreed.'

'So, when the persecutions began against your family, did you believe – do you believe – you were random victims?'

'Probably not. But others were victims too.'

'Only of the letter writing. None suffered as you did.'

'True. But it would be quite unsound to deduce from this the purpose and motive of those involved. Perhaps my father – who can be severe in person – rebuked some farm boy for stealing apples, or blaspheming.'

'You think something like that to be the start of it?'

'I have no idea. But I will not, I am afraid, stop thinking like a lawyer. It is what I am. And as a lawyer I require evidence.'

'Perhaps others can see what you cannot.'

'No doubt. But it is also a question of what is useful. It is not useful to me as a general principle of life to assume that those with whom I have dealings have a secret dislike of me. And at the present juncture, it is no use imagining that if only the Home Secretary were to become convinced that race prejudice lies at the heart of the case, then I shall have my pardon and the compensation to which you allude. Or perhaps, Sir Arthur, you believe Mr Gladstone himself to be afflicted with that prejudice?'

'I have absolutely no . . . evidence of that. Indeed, I very much doubt it.'

'Then please let us drop the subject.'

'Very well.' Arthur is impressed by such firmness – indeed, stubbornness. 'I should like to meet your parents. Also your sister. Discreetly, however. My instinct is always to go directly at things, but there are times when tactics and even bluff are necessary. As Lionel Amery likes to say, if you fight with a rhinoceros, you don't want to tie a horn to your nose.' George is baffled by this analogy, but Arthur does not notice. 'I doubt it would help our cause if I were to be seen tramping the district with you or a member of your family. I need a contact, an acquaintance in the village. Perhaps you can suggest one.'

'Harry Charlesworth,' replies George automatically, just as if facing Great-Aunt Stoneham, or Greenway and Stentson. 'Well, we sat next to one another at school. I pretended he was my friend. We were the two clever boys. My father used to rebuke me for not being friendlier with the farm boys, but frankly there was little contact possible. Harry Charlesworth has taken over the running of his father's dairy. He has an honest reputation.'

'You say you had little society with the village?'

'And they little with me. In truth, Sir Arthur, I always intended, after qualifying, to live in Birmingham. I found Wyrley – between ourselves – a dull and backward place. At first I continued living at home, fearing to break the news to my parents, ignoring the village except for necessities. Having boots repaired, for example. And then gradually I found myself, not exactly trapped, but living so much within my family that it was becoming harder and harder to even think of leaving. And I am very attached to my sister Maud. So that was my position until . . . all that you know was done to me. After I was released from prison, it was naturally impossible for me to return to Staffordshire. So now I am in London. I have lodgings in Mecklenburgh Square, with Miss Goode. My mother was with me in the first weeks after my release. But Father needs her at home. She comes down when she can be spared to see how I am faring. My life –' George pauses for a moment, 'my life, as you can see, is in abeyance.'

Arthur notes again how cautious and exact George is, whether describing large matters or small, emotions or facts. His man is a first-class witness. It is not his fault if he is unable to see what others can.

'Mr Edalji –'

'George, please.' Sir Arthur's pronunciation has been slipping back to Ee-dal-jee, and his new patron must be spared embarrassment.

'You and I, George, you and I, we are . . . unofficial Englishmen.'

George is taken aback by this remark. He regards Sir Arthur as a very official Englishman indeed: his name, his manner, his fame, his air of being absolutely at ease in this grand London hotel, even down to the time he kept George waiting. If Sir Arthur had not appeared to be part of official England, George would probably not have written to him in the first place. But it seems impolite to question a man's categorization of himself.

Instead, he reflects upon his own status. How is he less than a full Englishman? He is one by birth, by citizenship, by education, by religion, by profession. Does Sir Arthur mean that when they took away his freedom and struck him off the Rolls, they also struck him off the roll of Englishmen? If so, he has no other land. He cannot go back two generations. He can hardly return to India, a place he has never visited and has little desire to.

'Sir Arthur, when my . . . troubles began, my father would sometimes take me into his study and instruct me about the achievements of famous Parsees. How this one became a successful businessman, that one a Member of Parliament. Once – though I have not the slightest interest in sports – he told me about a Parsee cricket team which had come from Bombay and made a tour of England. Apparently they were the first team from India to visit these shores.'

'1886, I believe. Played about thirty, won only a single match, I'm afraid. Forgive me – in my idle hours I am a student of Wisden. They returned a couple of years later, with better results, I seem to remember.'

'You see, Sir Arthur, you are more knowledgeable than I am. And I am unable to pretend to be something I am not. My father brought me up an Englishman, and he cannot, when things become difficult, attempt to console me with matters he has never previously stressed.'

'Your father came from . . . ?'

'Bombay. He was converted by missionaries. They were Scottish, in fact. As my mother is.'

'I understand your father,' says Sir Arthur. It is a phrase, George realizes, that he has never in his life heard before. 'The truths of one's race and the truths of one's religion do not always lie in the same valley. Sometimes it is necessary to cross a high ridge in winter snow to find the greater truth.'

George ponders this remark as if it is part of a sworn affidavit. 'But then your heart is divided and you are cut off from your people?'

'No – then it is your duty to tell your people about the valley over the ridge. You look back down to the village whence you have come, and you observe that they have dipped the flags in salute, because they imagine that getting to the ridge itself is the triumph. But it is not. And so you raise your ski stick to them and point. Down there, you indicate, down there is the truth, down there in the next valley. Follow me over the ridge.'

George came to the Grand Hotel anticipating a concentrated examination of the evidence in his case. The conversation has taken several unexpected turns. Now he is feeling somewhat lost. Arthur senses a certain dismay in his new young friend. He feels responsible; he has meant to be encouraging. Enough reflection, then; it is time for action. Also, for anger.

'George, those who have supported you so far – Mr Yelverton and all the rest – have done sterling work. They have been utterly diligent and correct. If the British state were a rational institution, you would even now be back at your desk in Newhall Street. But it is not. So my plan is not to repeat the work of Mr Yelverton, to express the same reasonable doubts and make the same reasonable requests. I am going to do something different. I am going to make a great deal of *noise*. The English – the official English – do not like noise. They think it vulgar; it embarrasses them. But if calm reason has not worked, I shall give them noisy reason. I shall not use the back stairs but the front steps. I shall bang a big drum. I intend to shake more than a few trees, George, and we shall see what rotten fruit falls down.'

Sir Arthur stands to say goodbye. Now he towers over the little law clerk. Yet he has not done this in their conversation. George is surprised that such a famous man can listen as well as fulminate, be gentle as well as forceful. Despite this last declaration, however, he feels the need for some basic verification.

'Sir Arthur, may I ask . . . to put it simply . . . you think me innocent?'

Arthur looks down with a clear, steady gaze. 'George, I have read your newspaper articles, and now I have met you in person. So my reply is, No, I do not think you are innocent. No, I do not believe you are innocent. I *know* you are innocent.' Then he extends a large, athletic hand, toughened by numerous sports of which George is entirely ignorant.

Arthur

As soon as Wood had familiarized himself with the dossier, he was sent ahead in a scouting capacity. He was to survey the area, assess the temper of the locals, drink moderately in the public houses, and make contact with Harry Charlesworth. He was not, however, to play the detective, and was to stay away from the Vicarage. Arthur had not yet decided his plan of campaign, but knew that the best way to cut off sources of information would be to set up public stall and announce that he and Woodie had come to prove the innocence of George Edalji. And, by implication, the guilt of some other local resident. He did not want to alarm the interests of untruth.

In the library at Undershaw, he bent himself to research. He established that the parish of Great Wyrley contained a number of well-built residences and farmhouses; that its soil was light loam, with a subsoil of clay and gravel; that its chief crops were wheat, barley, turnips and mangolds. The station, a quarter of a mile to the north-west, was on the Walsall, Cannock & Rugeley branch of the London & North Western Railway. The Vicarage, with a net yearly value of £265, including residence, had been held since 1876 by the Reverend Shapurji Edalji of St Augustine's College, Canterbury. The Working Men's Institute, nearby at Landywood, seated 250 for lectures or concerts, and was well supplied with daily and weekly newspapers. The Public Elementary School, built in 1882, had Samuel John Mason as its master. The

Post Office was held by William Henry Brookes, who was also grocer, draper and ironmonger; the Station by Albert Ernest Merriman, who had evidently inherited the stationmaster's cap from his father, Samuel Merriman. There were three beer retailers in the village: Henry Badger, Mrs Ann Corbett and Thomas Yates. The butcher was Bernard Greensill. The manager of the Great Wyrley Colliery Company was William Browell and its secretary John Boult. William Wynn was the plumber, decorator, gas-fitter and general dealer. So normal, all of it sounded; so ordered, so English.

He decided, with regret, not to drive: the arrival of a twelve-horse-power, chain-driven, one-ton Wolseley in the lanes of Staffordshire would not exactly render him inconspicuous. A pity, since it was to Birmingham that he had gone, only two years previously, to collect the machine. A journey with a lighter purpose, that had been. He remembered wearing his peaked yachting cap, which had recently become the badge of fashion for the motorist. A fact perhaps not widely recognized among the local citizenry, for as he was pacing the platform of New Street waiting for the Wolseley salesman, a peremptory young woman had accosted him, demanding to know how the trains were running to Walsall.

He left the motor in the stables and took the Waterloo train from Haslemere. He would break his journey in London and see Jean for only the fourth time as a widower and free man. He had written and told her to expect him that afternoon; he had closed with the tenderest of farewells; yet as the train pulled out of Haslemere he found himself wishing, more than anything, that he was in his Wolseley, yachting cap crammed down over his ears, goggles tight against his eyes, roaring up through the heart of England towards Staffordshire. He could not understand this reaction, which made him feel both guilty and irritated. He knew that he loved Jean, that he would marry her, and make her the second Lady Doyle; yet he was not looking forward to seeing her in the way he would wish. If only human beings were as simple as machinery.

Arthur found something near a groan about to break from him, which he suppressed for the sake of the other first-class passengers. And that was all part of it – the way you were obliged to live. You stifled a groan, you lied about your love, you deceived your legal wife, and all in the name of honour. That was the damned paradox of it: in order to behave well, you had to behave badly. Why could he not bundle Jean into the Wolseley, drive her up to Staffordshire, register at an hotel as man and wife, and give his sergeant-major's stare to anyone who raised an eyebrow? Because he couldn't, because it wouldn't work, because it looked simple but wasn't, because, because . . . As the train passed the outskirts of Woking, he thought again with quiet envy of that Australian soldier out on the veldt. No. 410, New South Wales Mounted Infantry, lying inert with a red chess pawn balanced in his water bottle. A fair fight, open air, a great cause: no better death. Life should be more like that.

He goes to her flat; she is wearing blue silk; they embrace wholeheartedly. There is no requirement to pull back, and yet also, he realizes, no need; he remains unstirred by their reunion. They sit down; there is tea; he enquires after her family; she asks why he is going to Birmingham.

An hour later, when he has still reached no further than the committal proceedings at Cannock, she takes his hand and says,

'It is wonderful, dear Arthur, to see you in such spirits again.'

'You too, my darling,' he replies, and continues his narrative. As she would expect, the story he tells is full of colour and suspense; she is also both moved and relieved that the man she loves is shaking off the cares of recent months. Even so, by the time his story is finished, his purpose explained, his watch consulted, and the railway timetable re-examined, her disappointment lies close to the surface.

'I wish, Arthur, that I was coming with you.'

'How quite extraordinary,' he replies, and his eyes seem to focus on her properly for the first time. 'You know, as I was sitting on the train, I imagined driving up to Staffordshire with you at my side, the two of us, like man and wife.'

He shakes his head at this coincidence, which is perhaps explicable by the capacity for thought-transference between two hearts that are so close. Then he gets to his feet, collects his hat and coat, and departs.

Jean is not hurt by Arthur's behaviour – she is too indelibly in love with him for that – but as she rests her hands on the lukewarm teapot, she realizes that her position, and her future position, will require some practical thought. It has been difficult, so difficult, these past years; there have been so many arrangements and concessions and concealments. Why did she assume that Touie's death would change everything, and that there would be instant embraces in full sunshine to the applause of friends, while a distant band-stand played English tunes? There can be no such sudden transition; and the small amount of additional freedom they have been granted may prove more rather than less hazardous.

She finds herself thinking differently about Touie. No longer as the untouchable other whose honour must be protected, the self-effacing hostess, the simple, gentle, loving wife and mother who took so long to die. Touie's great quality, Arthur once told her, was that she always said Yes to anything he proposed. If they were to pack up instantly and depart for Austria, she said Yes; if they were to buy a new house, she said Yes; if he were to go off to London for a few days, or South Africa for several months, she said Yes. This was her nature; she trusted Arthur entirely, trusted him to make the correct decisions for her as well as him.

Jean trusts Arthur too; she knows he is a man of honour. She also knows – and this is another reason she loves and admires him – that he is constantly in motion, whether writing a new book, championing some cause, dashing around the world or hurling himself into his latest enthusiasm. He is never going to be the sort of man whose ambition is a suburban villa, a pair of slippers and a garden spade; who longs to hang over the front gate and wait for the paper boy to bring him news from distant lands.

And so something which it is too early to call a decision – more a kind of warning awareness – begins to form in Jean's mind. She has been Arthur's waiting girl since March the fifteenth, 1897; in a few months it will be the tenth anniversary of their meeting. Ten years, ten treasured snowdrops. She would rather wait for Arthur than be contentedly married to any other man on the globe. Yet, having been his waiting girl, she has no desire to be a waiting wife. She imagines them married, and Arthur announcing his impending departure – whether to Stoke Poges or Timbuctoo – in order to right a great wrong; and she imagines herself replying that she will ask Woodie to arrange their tickets. Their tickets, she will say quietly. She will be at his side. She will travel with him; she will sit in the front row when he gives a lecture; she will smooth his path and make sure of proper service in hotels and trains and liners. She will ride with him flank to flank, if not – given her superior control of a horse – a little ahead. She may even learn golf if he continues golfing. She will not be one of those harridan wives who pursue their mates even to the steps of the club; but she will be there at his side, and she will indicate, by word and constant deed, that this will remain her place until death do them part. This is the kind of wife she intends to be.

Meanwhile, Arthur sat on the Birmingham train, reminding himself of his only previous experience of playing detective. The Society for Psychical Research had asked him to assist in the investigation of a haunted house at Charmouth in Dorsetshire. He had travelled down with Dr Scott and a certain Mr Podmore, a professional skilled in such inquiries. They had taken all the usual steps to outwit fraud: bolting doors and windows, laying worsted threads across the stairs. Then they had sat up with their host for two successive nights. On the first, he had refilled his pipe a lot and fought narcolepsy; but in the middle of the second night, just as they were giving up hope, they were startled – and, for the instant, terrified – by the sound of furniture being violently cudgelled close at hand. The noise appeared to be coming from the kitchen, but when they rushed there the room was empty and everything in its place. They searched the house from cellar to attic, hunting for hidden spaces; they found nothing. And the doors were still locked, the windows barred, the threads unbroken.

Podmore had been surprisingly negative about this haunting; he suspected that some associate of their host's had lain concealed behind the panelling. At the time, Arthur acceded to this view. However, some years later, the house had burned to the ground; and – more significantly still – the skeleton of a child no more than ten years old had been dug up in the garden. For Arthur, this had changed everything. In cases where a young life is violently taken, a store of unused vitality often becomes available. At such times the unknown and the marvellous press upon us from all sides; they loom in fluc-tuating shapes, warning us of the limitations of what we call matter. This seemed the irrefutable explanation to Arthur; but Podmore had declined to amend his report retrospectively. In fact, the fellow had behaved all along more like a damned materialist sceptic than an expert charged with authen-ticating psychic phenomena. Still, why concern yourself with the Podmores of this world when you have Crookes and Myers and Lodge and Alfred Russel Wallace? Arthur repeated to himself the formula: it is incredible, but it is true. When he first heard the words, they had sounded like a flexible paradox; now they were hardening into an iron certainty.

Arthur made his rendezvous with Wood at the Imperial Family Hotel in Temple Street. He was less likely to be recognized here than at the Grand, where he might normally stop. They had to minimize the chance of some teasing headline on the society page of the *Gazette* or the *Post*: **WHAT IS SHERLOCK HOLMES UP TO IN BIRMINGHAM?**

Their first foray out to Great Wyrley was planned for late the following afternoon. Profiting from the December dusk, they would make their way to the Vicarage as anonymously as possible, and return to Birmingham as soon as their business was done. Arthur was keen to visit a theatrical costumier and equip himself with a false beard for the expedition; but Wood was discouraging. He thought this would draw more rather than less atten-tion to them; indeed, any visit to a costumier would guarantee unwelcome paragraphs in the local press. A turned-up collar and a muffler, together with a raised newspaper in the train, would be enough to get them unscathed to Wyrley; then they would just stroll along to the Vicarage by the badly lit lane as if –

'As if we are what?' asked Arthur.

'Do we need to pretend?' Wood did not understand why his employer was so insistent upon disguise; first material, then psychological. In his view it was an Englishman's inalienable right to tell others, especially those of a nosy inclination, to mind their own business.

'Certainly. We need it for ourselves. We must think of ourselves as . . . hmmm . . . I have it – emissaries from the Church Commissioners, come to respond to the Vicar's report on the fabric of St Mark's.'

'It is a relatively new and sturdily built church,' replied Wood. Then he caught his employer's glance. 'Well, if you insist, Sir Arthur.'

At New Street, late the next afternoon, they chose a carriage which would deposit them, at Wyrley & Churchbridge, as far from the station building as possible. By this stratagem they planned to escape the intrusive gaze of other alighting passengers. But in the event, no one else got off the train, and as a consequence the ecclesiastical imposters received extra scrutiny from the stationmaster. Pulling his muffler defensively up around his moustache, Arthur felt almost larky. You do not know me, he thought, but I know you: Albert Ernest Merriman, the son of Samuel. What an adventure!

He followed Wood along a darkened lane; at one point they skirted a public house, but the sole sign of activity was a man lolling on the front step, studiously chewing his cap. After eight or nine minutes, with only an occasional gas lamp to trouble them, they came upon the dull bulk of St Mark's with its high, double-pitched roof. Wood led his employer along its southern wall, so close that Arthur could note the greyish stone streaked with purply-red. As they passed the porch, two buildings came into view some thirty yards beyond the west end of the church: to the right, a schoolroom of dark brick, with a faint diamond pattern picked out in lighter brick; to the left, the more substantial Vicarage. A few moments later, Arthur found himself looking down at the broad doorstep where, fifteen years previously, the key to Walsall School had been laid. As he raised the knocker and calculated how gently he should make it fall, he imagined the more thunderous arrival of Inspector Campbell with his band of specials, and the turmoil it had brought to that quiet household.

The Vicar, his wife and daughter were waiting for them. Sir Arthur could immediately recognize the source of George's simple good manners, and also of his self-containment. The family was glad of his arrival, but not effusive; conscious of his fame, yet not overawed. He was relieved for once to find himself in the presence of three people, none of whom, he was prepared to wager, had ever read a single one of his books.

The Vicar was paler-skinned than his son, with a flat-topped head balding at the front, and a strong, bulldoggy aspect to him. He shared the same mouth with George, but to Arthur's eye looked both more handsome and more Occidental.

Two thick files were produced. Arthur took out an item at random: a letter folded from a single sheet, making four closely written pages.

'My dear Shapurji', he read, 'I have great pleasure in informing you that it is now our intention to review the persecution of the Vicar!!! (shame of Great Wyrley).' It was a competent hand, he thought, rather than a neat one. '. . . a certain lunatic asylum not a hundred miles distant from your thrice cursed home . . . and that you will be forcibly removed in case you give way to any strong expressions of opinion.' No spelling mistakes either, so far. 'I shall send a double number of the most hellish postcards in your name and Charlotte's at the earliest opportunity.' Charlotte was presumably the Vicar's wife. 'Revenge on you and Brookes . . .' That name was familiar from his researches. '. . . have sent a letter in his name to the Courier that he will not be responsible for his wife's debts . . . I repeat that there will be no need for the lunacy act to take you in charge as these persons are sure to have you arrested.' And then, in four descending lines, a mocking farewell:

> Wishing you a Merry Christmas and New Year,
> I am ever
> Yours Satan
> God Satan

'Poisonous,' said Sir Arthur.
'Which one is that?'
'One from Satan.'
'Yes,' said the Vicar. 'A prolific correspondent.'

Arthur inspected a few more items. It was one thing to hear about anonymous letters, even to read extracts from them in the Press. Then they sounded like childish pranks. But to hold one in your hand, and to be sitting with its recipients, was, he realized, quite different. That first one was filthy stuff, with its caddish reference to the Vicar's wife by her Christian name. The work of a lunatic, perhaps; though a lunatic with a clear, well-formed hand, able lucidly to express his twisted hatreds and mad plans. Arthur was not surprised that the Edaljis had taken to locking their doors at night.

'Merry Christmas,' Arthur read out, still half in disbelief. 'And you have no suspicion who might have written any of these noxious effusions?'
'Suspicion? None.'
'That servant you were obliged to dismiss?'
'She left the district. She is long gone.'
'Her family?'

'Her family are decent folk. Sir Arthur, as you may imagine, we have given this much thought from the beginning. But I have no suspicions. I do not listen to gossip and rumour, and if I did, what help would that be? Gossip and rumour were the cause of my son's imprisonment. I would scarcely wish done to another what has been done to him.'

'Unless he were the culprit.'

'Indeed.'

'And this Brookes. He is the grocer and ironmonger?'

'Yes. He too received poison letters for a while. He was more phlegmatic about it. Or more idle. At any rate, unwilling to go to the police. There had been some incident on the railway involving his son and another boy – I no longer remember the details. Brookes was never going to make common cause with us. There is little respect for the police in the district, I have to tell you. It is an irony that of all the local inhabitants we were the family that was most inclined to trust the police.'

'Except for the Chief Constable.'

'His attitude was . . . unhelpful.'

'Mr *Ay*dlji' – Arthur made a specific effort with the pronunciation – 'I plan to find out why. I intend to go back to the very beginnings of the case. Tell me, apart from the direct persecutions, have you suffered any other hostility since you came here?'

The Vicar looked questioningly at his wife. 'The Election,' she replied.

'Yes, that is true. I have, on more than one occasion, lent the schoolroom for political meetings. There was a problem for Liberals in obtaining halls. I am a Liberal myself . . . There were complaints from some of the more conservative parishioners.

'More than complaints?'

'One or two ceased coming to St Mark's, it is true.'

'And you continued lending the hall?'

'Certainly. But I do not want to exaggerate. I am talking of protests, strongly worded but civil. I am not talking of threats.'

Sir Arthur admired the Vicar's precision; also his lack of self-pity. He had noted the same qualities in George. 'Was Captain Anson involved?'

'Anson? No, it was much more local that that. He only became involved later. I have included his letters for you to see.'

Arthur then took the family through the events of August to October 1903, alert for any inconsistency, overlooked detail, or conflict of evidence. 'In retrospect, it's a pity you did not send Inspector Campbell and his men away until they had equipped themselves with a search warrant, and prepared yourself for their return with the presence of a solicitor.'

'But that would have been the behaviour of guilty people. We had nothing to hide. We knew George to be innocent. The sooner the police searched, the sooner they would be able to redirect their investigations more profitably. Inspector Campbell and his men were, in any case, quite correct in their behaviour.'

Not all of the time, thought Arthur. There was something missing in his understanding of the case, something to do with that police visit.

'Sir Arthur.' It was Mrs Edalji, slender, white-haired, quiet-voiced. 'May I say two things to you? First, how pleasant it is to hear a Scottish voice again in these parts. Do I detect Edinburgh on your tongue?'

'You do indeed, Ma'am.'

'And the second thing concerns my son. You have met George.'

'I was much impressed by him. I can think of many who would not have remained so strong in mind and body after three years in Lewes and Portland. He is a credit to you.'

Mrs Edalji smiled briefly at the compliment. 'What George wants more than anything is to be allowed to return to his work as a solicitor. That is all he has ever wanted. It is perhaps worse for him now than when he was in prison. Then things were clearer. Now he is in a state of limbo. The Incorporated Law Society cannot readmit him until the taint is washed from his name.'

There was nothing which galvanized Arthur more than being appealed to by a gentle, elderly, female Scottish voice.

'Rest assured, Ma'am, I am planning to make a tremendous noise. I am going to stir things up. There will be a few people sleeping less soundly in their beds by the time I have finished with them.'

But this did not seem to be the promise Mrs Edalji required. 'I expect so, Sir Arthur, and we thank you for it. What I am saying is rather different. George is, as you have observed, a boy – a young man, rather – of some resilience. To be honest, his resilience has surprised both of us. We imagined him frailer. He is determined to overthrow this injustice. But that is all he wants. He does not wish for the limelight. He does not want to become an advocate for any particular cause. He is not a representative of anything. He wishes to return to work. He wishes for an ordinary life.'

'He wishes to get married,' put in the daughter, who until this moment had been quite silent.

'Maud!' The Vicar was more surprised than rebuking. 'How can he? Since when? Charlotte – did you know anything of this?'

'Father, don't be alarmed. I mean, he wants to be married in general.'

'Married in general,' repeated the Vicar. He looked at his distinguished guest. 'Do you think that is possible, Sir Arthur?'

'I myself,' replied Arthur with a chuckle, 'have only ever been married in particular. It is the system I understand, and the one I would recommend.'

'In that case,' – and here the Vicar smiled for the first time – 'we must forbid George from getting married in general.'

Back at the Imperial Family Hotel, Arthur and his secretary took a late supper and retired to an unoccupied smoking room. Arthur fired up his pipe and watched Wood ignite some low brand of cigarette.

'A fine family,' said Sir Arthur. 'Modest, impressive.'

'Indeed.'

Arthur had a sudden apprehension, set off by Mrs Edalji's words. What if their arrival on the scene provoked fresh persecutions? After all, Satan – indeed, God Satan – was still out there sharpening both his pen and his curved instrument with concave sides. God Satan: how peculiarly repellent were the perversions of an institutional religion once it began its irreversible decline. The sooner the whole edifice was swept away the better.

'Woodie, let me use you as a sounding board, if I may.' He did not wait for an answer; nor did his secretary think one was expected. 'There are three aspects of this case which I at present fail to understand. They are blanks waiting to be filled. And the first of them is why Anson took against George Edalji. You've seen the letters he wrote to the Vicar. Threatening a schoolboy with penal servitude.'

'Indeed.'

'He is a person of distinction. I researched him. The second son of the Second Earl of Lichfield. Late Royal Artillery. Chief Constable since 1888. Why should such a man write such a letter?'

Wood merely cleared his throat.

'Well?'

'I am not an investigator, Sir Arthur. I have heard you say that in the detective business you must eliminate the impossible and what is left, however improbable, must be the truth.'

'Not my own formulation, alas. But one I endorse.'

'So that is why I would not make an investigator. If someone asks me a question, I just look for the obvious answer.'

'And what would be your obvious answer in the case of Captain Anson and George Edalji?'

'That he dislikes people who are coloured.'

'Now that is indeed very obvious, Alfred. So obvious it cannot be the case. Whatever his faults, Anson is an English gentleman and a Chief Constable.'

'I told you I was not an investigator.'

'Let us not abandon hope so quickly. We'll see what you can do with my second blank. Which is this. Leaving aside that early episode with the maid-servant, the persecution of the Edaljis takes place in two separate outbursts. The first runs from 1892 to the very beginning of 1896. It is intense and increasing. All of a sudden it stops. Nothing happens for seven years. Then it starts up again, and the first horse is ripped. February 1903. Why the gap, that's what I can't understand, why the gap? Investigator Wood, what is your view?'

The secretary did not enjoy this game very much; it seemed to be constructed so that he could only lose. 'Perhaps because whoever was responsible wasn't there.'

'Where?'

'In Wyrley.'

'Where was he?'

'He'd gone away.'

'Where to?'

'I don't know, Sir Arthur. Perhaps he was in prison. Perhaps he'd gone to Birmingham. Perhaps he'd run away to sea.'

'I rather doubt it. Again, it's too obvious. People in the district would have noticed. There'd have been talk.'

'The Edaljis said they didn't listen to talk.'

'Hmm. Let's see if Harry Charlesworth does. Now, the third area I don't understand is the matter of the hairs on the clothing. If we could eliminate the obvious on this one –'

'Thank you, Sir Arthur.'

'Oh, for Heaven's sake, Woodie, don't take offence. You're much too useful to take offence.'

Wood reflected that he had always had a deal of sympathy for the character of Dr Watson. 'What is the problem, sir?'

'The problem is this. The police examined George's clothing at the Vicarage and said there were hairs on it. The Vicar, his wife and his daughter examined the clothing and said there were no hairs on it. The police surgeon, Dr Butter – and police surgeons in my experience are the most scrupulous fellows – gave evidence that he found twenty-nine hairs "similar in length, colour and structure" to those of the mutilated pony. So there is a clear conflict. Were the Edaljis perjuring themselves to protect George? That would appear to be what the jury believed. George's explanation was that he might have leaned against a gate into a field in which cows were paddocked. I'm not surprised the jury didn't believe him. It sounds like a statement you are panicked into, not a description of something that happened. Besides, it still leaves the family as perjurers. If the hairs were on his clothing, they'd have seen them, wouldn't they?'

Wood took his time over this. Ever since entering Sir Arthur's employ, he had been acquiring new functions. Secretary, amanuensis, signature-forger, motoring assistant, golf partner, billiards opponent; now sounding board and stater of the obvious. Also, one who must be prepared for ridicule. Well, so be it. 'If the hairs weren't on his coat when the Edaljis examined it . . .'

'Yes . . .'

'And if they weren't there beforehand because George didn't lean on any gate . . .'

'Yes . . .'

'Then they must have got there afterwards.'

'After what?'

'After the clothing left the Vicarage.'

'You mean Dr Butter put them there?'

'No. I don't know. But if you want the obvious answer, it's that they got there afterwards. Somehow. And if so, then only the police are lying. Or some of the police.'

'A not impossible occurrence. You know, Alfred, you're not necessarily wrong, I'll say that for you.'

A compliment, Wood reflected, that Dr Watson might have been proud to receive.

The next day they returned to Wyrley with less pretence of concealment, and called on Harry Charlesworth in his milking parlour. They squelched through the consequences of a herd of cows to a small office attached to the back of the farmhouse. There were three rickety chairs, a small desk, a muddy raffia mat, and a calendar for the previous month at an angle on the wall. Harry was a blond, open-faced young man who seemed to welcome this interruption to his work.

'So you've come about George?'

Arthur looked crossly at Wood, who shook his head in denial.

'How did you know?'

'You went to the Vicarage last night.'

'Did we?'

'Well, at any rate two strangers were seen going to the Vicarage after dark, one of them a tall gentleman pulling his muffler up to hide his moustache, and the other a shorter one in a bowler hat.'

'Oh dear,' said Arthur. Perhaps he should have gone to the theatrical costumier after all.

'And now the same two gentlemen, if disguising themselves less obviously, have come to see me on business I was told was confidential but was soon to be revealed.' Harry Charlesworth was enjoying himself greatly. He was also happy to reminisce.

'Yes, we were at school together, when we were littl'uns. George was always very quiet. Never got into trouble, not like the rest of us. Clever too. Cleverer than me, and I was clever back then. Not that you'd know it now. Staring up the backside of a cow all day does rub away at your intelligence, you know.'

Arthur ignored this diversion into vulgar autobiography. 'But did George have any enemies? Was he disliked – on account of his colour, for instance?'

Harry thought about this for a while. 'Not as far as I can recall. But you know what it is with boys – they have likes and dislikes different from grown-ups. And different from month to month. If George was disliked, it was more for being clever. Or because his father was the Vicar and disapproved of the sort of things boys got up to. Or because he was shortsighted. The master put him up the front so he could see the blackboard. Maybe that looked like favouritism. More of a reason to dislike him than being coloured.'

Harry's analysis of the Wyrley Outrages was not complex. The case against George was daft. The police were daft. And the notion that there was a mysterious Gang flitting around after nightfall under the orders of some mysterious Captain was daftest of all.

'Harry, we shall need to interview Trooper Green. Given that he's the only person hereabouts who actually admits to ripping a horse.'

'Fancy a long trip, do you?'

'Where to?'

'South Africa. Ah, you didn't know. Harry Green got himself a ticket to South Africa just a couple of weeks after the trial was over. It wasn't a return ticket either.'

'Interesting. Any idea who paid for it?'

'Well, not Harry Green, that's for certain. Someone interested in keeping him out of harm's way.'

'The police?'

'Possible. Not that they were too thrilled with him by the time he left. He went back on his confession. Said he'd never done the ripping, and the police had bullied the confession out of him.'

'Did he, by Jove? What do you make of that, Woodie?'

Wood dutifully stated the obvious. 'Well, I'd say he was lying either the first time or the second. Or,' he added with a touch of mischief, 'possibly both.'

'Harry, can you find out if Mr Green has an address for his son in South Africa?'

'I can certainly try.'

'And another thing. Was there talk in Wyrley about who might have done it, given that George didn't?'

'There's always talk. It's the same price as rain. All I'd say is, it's got to be someone who knows how to handle animals. You can't just go up to a horse or a sheep or a cow and say, Hold still my lovely while I rip your guts out. I'd like to see George Edalji go into the parlour and try and milk one of my cows . . .' Harry lost himself briefly in the amusement of this notion. 'He'd be kicked to death or fall in the shit before he'd got his stool under her.'

Arthur leaned forward. 'Harry, would you be prepared to help us clear your friend and old schoolfellow's name?'

Harry Charlesworth noted the lowered voice and cajoling tone, but was suspicious of it. 'He was never exactly my friend.' Then his face brightened. 'Of course, I'd have to take time off from the dairy . . .'

Arthur had initially ascribed a more chivalrous nature to Harry Charlesworth, but decided not to be disappointed. Once a retainer and fee structure had been agreed, Harry, in his new capacity as assistant consulting detective, showed them the route George was supposed to have taken that drenching August night three and a half years previously. They set off across the field behind the Vicarage, climbed a fence, forced their way through a hedge, crossed the railway by a subterranean passage, climbed another fence, crossed another field, braved a clinging, thorny hedge, crossed another paddock, and found themselves on the edge of the Colliery field. Three-quarters of a mile at a rough guess.

Wood took out his pocket watch. 'Eighteen and a half minutes.'

'And we are fit men,' commented Arthur, still plucking thorns from his overcoat and wiping mud from his shoes. 'And it is daylight, and it is not raining, and we have excellent eyesight.'

Back at the dairy, after money had changed hands, Arthur asked about the general pattern of crime in the neighbourhood. It sounded routine: theft of livestock, public drunkenness, firing of hayricks. Had there been any violent incidents apart from the attacks on farmstock? Harry half-remembered something from around the time George was sentenced. An attack on a mother and her little girl. Two fellows with a knife. Caused a bit of a stir, but never went to court. Yes, he would be happy to look into the matter.

They shook hands, and Harry walked them to the ironmonger's, which also served as the grocery, the drapery and the Post Office.

William Brookes was a small, rotund man, with bushy white whiskers counterbalancing his bald cranium; he wore a green apron stained by the years. He was neither overtly welcoming nor overtly suspicious. He was about to take them into a back room when Sir Arthur, nudging his secretary, announced that he was in great need of a bootscraper. He took an intense interest in the choice on offer, and when purchase and wrapping were complete, acted as if the rest of their visit was just a happy afterthought.

In the storeroom, Brookes spent so long digging around in drawers and muttering to himself that Sir Arthur wondered if he might have to buy a zinc bath and a couple of mops to expedite matters. But the ironmonger eventually located a small packet of heavily creased letters bound with twine. Arthur immediately recognized the paper on which they were written; the same cheap notebook had served for the letters to the Vicarage.

Brookes recalled, as best he could, the failed attempt at blackmail all those years ago. His boy Frederick and another boy were meant to have spat upon some old woman at Walsall Station, and he had been instructed to send money to the Post Office there if he wanted to avoid his son being prosecuted.

'You did nothing about it?'

'Course not. Look at the letters for yourself. Look at the handwriting. It was just a prank.'

'You never thought of paying?'

'No.'

'Did you think of going to the police?'

Brookes gave a scornful puff of the cheeks. 'Not for a moment. Less than a tenth of a moment. I ignored it, and it went away. Now the Vicar, he was all of a pother. Went around complaining, writing to the Chief Constable and all that, and where did it get him? Just made it all worse, didn't it? For him and his lad. Not that I'm blaming him for what happened, you understand. Just that he's never understood this sort of village. He's a bit too . . . cut and dried for it, if you know what I mean.'

Arthur did not comment. 'And why do you think the blackmailer picked on your son and the other boy?'

Brookes puffed his cheeks again. 'It's years now, sir, as I say. Ten? Maybe more. You should ask my boy, well, he's a man now.'

'Do you remember who this other boy was?'

'It's not something I've needed to remember.'

'Does your boy still live locally?'

'Fred? No, Fred's long left. He's in Birmingham now. Works on the canal. Doesn't want to take on the shop.' The ironmonger paused, then added with sudden vehemence, 'Little bastard.'

'And might you have an address for him?'

'I might. And might you want anything to go with that bootscraper?'

Arthur was in high good humour on the train back to Birmingham. Every so often he glanced at the three parcels beside Wood, each of them wrapped in oiled brown paper and tied with string, and smiled at the way the world was.

'So what do you think of the day's work, Alfred?'

What did he think? What was the obvious answer? Well, what was the true answer? 'To be perfectly honest, I think we've made not very much progress.'

'No, it's better than that. We've made not very much progress in several different directions. And we did need a bootscraper.'

'Did we? I thought we had one at Undershaw.'

'Don't be a spoilsport, Woodie. A house can never have too many bootscrapers. In later years we shall remember it as the Edalji Scraper, and each time we wipe our boots on it we shall think of this adventure.'

'If you say so.'

Arthur left Wood to whatever mood he was in, and gazed out at the passing fields and hedgerows. He tried to imagine George Edalji on this train, going up to Mason College, then to Sangster, Vickery & Speight, then to his own practice in Newhall Street. He tried to imagine George Edalji in the village of Great Wyrley, walking the lanes, going to the bootmaker, doing business with Brookes. The young solicitor – well-spoken and well-dressed though he was – would cut a queer figure even in Hindhead, and no doubt a queerer one in the wilds of Staffordshire. He was evidently an admirable fellow, with a lucid brain and a resilient character. But if you merely looked at him – looked at him, moreover, with the eye of an ill-educated farm-hand, a dimwit village policeman, a narrow-minded English juror, or a suspicious chairman of Quarter Sessions – you might not get beyond a brown skin and an ocular peculiarity. He would seem queer. And then, if some queer things started happening, what passed for logic in an unenlightened village would glibly ascribe the events to the person.

And once reason – true reason – is left behind, the farther it is left behind the better, for those who do the leaving. A man's virtues are turned into his faults. Self-control presents itself as secretiveness, intelligence as cunning. And so a respectable lawyer, bat-blind and of slight physique, becomes a degenerate who flits across fields at dead of night, evading the watch of twenty special constables, in order to wade through the blood of mutilated animals. It is so utterly topsy-turvy that it seems logical. And in Arthur's judgement, it all boiled down to that singular optical defect he had immediately observed in the foyer of the Grand Hotel, Charing Cross. Therein lay the moral certainty of George Edalji's innocence, and the reason why he should have become a scapegoat.

In Birmingham, they tracked Frederick Brookes down to his lodgings near the canal. He assessed the two gentlemen, who to him smelt of London, recognized the wrapping of the three parcels under the shorter gentleman's arm, and announced that his price for information was half a crown. Sir Arthur, accustoming himself to the ways of the natives, offered a sliding scale, rising from one shilling and threepence to two and sixpence, depending on the usefulness of the answers. Brookes agreed.

Fred Wynn, he said, had been the name of his companion. Yes, he was some relation to the plumber and gas-fitter in Wyrley. Nephew perhaps, or second cousin. Wynn lived two stops down the line and they went to school together at Walsall. No, he'd quite lost touch with him. As for that incident all those years ago, the letter and the spitting business – he and Wynn had been pretty sure at the time it was the work of the boy who broke the carriage window and then tried to blame it on them. They'd blamed it back on him, and the officers from the railway company had interviewed all three of them, also Wynn's father and Brookes's father. But they couldn't work out who was telling the truth so in the end just gave everyone a warning. And that was the end of it. The other boy's name had been Speck. He'd lived somewhere near Wyrley. But no, Brookes hadn't seen him for years.

Arthur noted all this with his silver propelling pencil. He judged the information worth two shillings and threepence. Frederick Brookes did not demur.

Back at the Imperial Family Hotel, Arthur was handed a note from Jean.

> My Dearest Arthur,
>   I write to find out how your great investigations are
> proceeding. I wish I were by your side as your gather
> evidence and interview suspects. Everything that you do is as
> important to me as my own life. I miss your presence but have
> joy in thinking of what you are seeking to achieve for your
> young friend. Hasten to report all you have discovered to
>   Your loving and adoring
>   Jean

Arthur found himself taken aback. It seemed uncharacteristically direct for a love letter. Perhaps it wasn't a love letter. Yes, of course it was. But somehow different. Well, Jean was different – different from what he had ever known before. She surprised him, even after ten years. He was proud of her, and proud of being surprised.

Later, as Arthur was rereading the note for a final time that night, Alfred Wood lay awake in a smaller bedroom on a higher floor. In the darkness, he could just make out, on his dressing table, the three wrapped parcels sold them by that sly ironmonger. Brookes had also made Sir Arthur pay him a 'deposit' for the loan of the anonymous letters in his possession. Wood had deliberately made no comment either at the time or afterwards, which was probably why his employer had accused him on the train of sulking.

Today his role had been that of assistant investigator: partner, almost friend to Sir Arthur. After supper, on the hotel billiards table, competitiveness had made equals of the two men. Tomorrow, he would revert to his usual position of secretary and amanuensis, taking dictation like any female stenographer. This variety of function and mental register did not bother him. He was devoted to his employer, serving him with diligence and efficiency in whatever capacity was necessary. If Sir Arthur required him to state the obvious, he would do so. If Sir Arthur required him not to state the obvious, he was mute.

He was also expected not to notice the obvious. When a clerk had rushed up to them in the foyer with a letter, he had not noticed the way Sir Arthur's hand trembled as he accepted it, nor the schoolboyish way he stuffed it into his pocket. Nor did he notice his employer's eagerness to get to his room before supper, or his subsequent cheerfulness throughout the meal. It was an important professional skill – to observe without noticing – and over the last years its usefulness had increased.

He thought it might take him a while to adjust himself to Miss Leckie – though he doubted she would still be using her maiden name by the end of the next twelvemonth. He would serve the second Lady Conan Doyle as assiduously as he had served the first one; though with less immediate wholeheartedness. He was not sure how much he liked Jean Leckie. This was, he knew, quite unimportant. You did not, as a schoolmaster, have to like the headmaster's wife. And he would never be required to give his opinion. So it did not matter. But over the eight or nine years she had been coming to Undershaw, he had often caught himself wondering if there was not something a little false about her. At a certain moment she had become aware of his importance in the daily running of Sir Arthur's life; whereupon she made a point of being agreeable to him. More than agreeable. A hand had been placed upon his arm, and she had even, in imitation of Sir Arthur, called him Woodie. He thought this an intimacy she had failed to earn. Even Mrs Doyle – as he always thought of her – would not call him that. Miss Leckie made considerable play of being natural, of seeming at times to be reining in with difficulty a great instinctive warmth; but it struck Wood as being a kind of coquetry. He would lay anyone a hundred-point start that Sir Arthur did not see it as such. His employer liked to maintain that the game of golf was a coquette; though it seemed to Wood that sports played you a lot straighter than most women.

Again, it did not matter. If Sir Arthur got what he wanted, and Jean Leckie did too, and they were happy together, where was the harm? But it made Alfred Wood a little more relieved that he had never himself come near to marrying. He did not see the benefit of the arrangement, except from a hygienic point of view. You married a true woman, and became bored with her; you married a false one, and did not notice rings were being run around you. Those seemed to be the two choices available to a man.

Sir Arthur sometimes accused him of having moods. It was rather, he felt, that he had his silences – and his obvious thoughts. For instance, about Mrs Doyle: about happy Southsea days, busy London ones, and those long sad months at the end. Thoughts too about the future Lady Conan Doyle, and the influence she might have upon Sir Arthur and the household. Thoughts about Kingsley and Mary, and how they would react to a stepmother – or rather, to this particular stepmother. Kingsley would doubtless survive: he had his father's cheerful manliness already. But Wood feared a little for Mary, who was such an awkward, yearning girl.

Well, that would do for tonight. Except: he thought that in the morning he might accidentally leave the bootscraper and the other parcels behind.

At Undershaw, Arthur retreated to his study, filled his pipe and began to consider strategy. It was clear there would have to be a two-pronged attack. The first thrust would establish, once and for all, that George Edalji was innocent; not just wrongly convicted on misleading evidence, but wholly innocent, one-hundred-per-cent innocent. The second thrust would identify the true culprit, oblige the Home Office to admit its errors, and result in a fresh prosecution.

As he set to work, Arthur felt back on familiar ground. It was like starting a book: you had the story but not all of it, most of the characters but not all of them some but not all of the causal links. You had your beginning, and you had your ending. There would be a great number of topics to be kept in the head at the same time. Some would be in motion, some static; some racing away, others resisting all the mental energy you could throw at them. Well, he was used to that. And so, as with a novel, he tabulated the key matters and annotated them briefly.

1. TRIAL

Yelverton. Use dossier (with perm.), build, sharpen. Cautious – lawyer.
   Vachell? No – avoid reit. defence case. Pity no official transcript
   (campaign for this?). Reliable newspaper accounts? (besides
   Umpire).

Hairs/Butter. W. probably right!! Not before (o/wise Edaljis perjurers) ∴ after. Unintentional, intentional? Who? When? How? Butter?? Interview. Also: hairs found, any latitude/ambiguity? Or *must* be pony?

Letters. Examine: paper/materials, orthography, style, content, psychology. Gurrin, fraudulence of. Beck case. Propose better expert (good/bad tactic?). Who? Dreyfus fellow? Also: one writer, more? Also, Writer = Ripper? Writer X Ripper? Connection/overlap?

Eyesight. Scott's report. Enough? Others? Mother's evidence. Effect of dark/night on GE's vision?

Green. Who bullied? Who paid? Trace/interview.

Anson. Interview. Prejudice? Evidence w/held? Influence on Constab. See Campbell. Ask for police records?

One of the advantages of celebrity, Arthur admitted, was that his name opened doors. Whether he needed a lepidopterist or an expert on the history of the longbow, a police surgeon or a chief constable, his requests for an interview would normally be smiled upon. It was largely thanks to Holmes – although thanking Holmes did not come easily to Arthur. Little had he known, when he invented the fellow, how his consulting detective would turn into a skeleton key.

He relit his pipe, and moved on to the second part of his thematic table.

2. CULPRIT

Letters. see prec.

Animals. Slaughtermen? Butchers? Farmers? Cf. cases elsewhere. Method typical/untypical? Expert – who? Gossip/suspicion (Harry C).

Instrument. Not razor (trial) ∴ what? Butter? Lewis? 'curved with conc. sides'. Knife? Agricultural instr.? purpose? Adapted instr.?

Gap. 7yr silence 96–03. Why?? Intentional/unintentional/enforced? Who absent? Who wd know?

Walsall. Key. School. Greatorex. Other boys. Window/spitting. Brookes. Wynn. Speck. Connected? Unconnected? Normal? Any GE business/connection there (ask). Headmaster?

Previous/subsequent. Other maimings. Farrington.

And that was about it for the moment. Arthur puffed his pipe and let his eye wander up and down the lists, wondering which items were strong, and which weak. Farrington, for instance. Farrington was a rough miner who worked for the Wyrley Colliery and had been convicted in the spring of '04 – just about the time George was being moved from Lewes to Portland – of mutilating a horse, two sheep and a lamb. The police naturally maintained that the fellow, despite being a rude, illiterate loafer in public houses, was an associate of the known criminal Edalji. Obvious soulmates, thought Arthur sarcastically. Would Farrington lead him somewhere or nowhere? Was his crime merely emulative?

Perhaps the mercenary Brookes and the mysterious Speck would yield something. That was an odd name, Speck – though the only direction it was leading his brain at the moment was to South Africa. When he'd been down there he'd eaten a great deal of speck, as they called their colonial form of bacon. Unlike the British version, it could be derived from any number of animals – indeed, he recalled that he had once eaten hippopotamus speck. Now where had that been? Bloemfontein, or on the journey north?

The mind was wandering now. And in Arthur's experience, the only way to concentrate it was first to clear it. Holmes might have played his violin, or perhaps succumbed to that indulgence his creator was nowadays embarrassed to have awarded him. No cocaine syringe for Arthur: he put his trust in a bagful of hickory-shafted golf clubs.

He had always regarded the game as being, in theory, perfectly made for him. It required a combination of eye, brain and body: apt enough for an ophthalmologist turned writer who still retained his physical vigour. That, at least, was the theory. In practice, golf was always luring you on and then evading you. What a dance she had led him across the globe.

As he drove to the Hankley clubhouse, he remembered the rudimentary links in front of the Mena House Hotel. If you sliced your drive you might find your ball bunkered in the grave of some Rameses or Thothmes of old. One afternoon a passerby, assessing Arthur's vigorous yet erratic game, had cuttingly remarked that he understood there was a special tax for excavating in Egypt. But even this round had been outdone in oddity by the golf played from Kipling's house in Vermont. It had been Thanksgiving time, with snow already thick on the ground, and a ball was no sooner struck than it became invisible. Happily, one of them – and they still disputed which – had the notion of painting the balls red. The oddity didn't stop there, however, because the snow's icy crust imparted a fantastical run to the slightest decent hit. At one point he and Rudyard had launched their drives on a downward slope; there was no reason for the garish balls ever to stop, and they skidded a full two miles into the Connecticut River. Two miles: that is what he and Rudyard always believed, and damn the scepticism of certain clubhouses.

The coquette was kind to him that day, and he found himself on the eighteenth fairway still in with a chance of breaking 80. If he could get his niblick
pitch to within putting distance . . . As he contemplated the shot, he suddenly
became aware that he would not play this course many more times. For the
simple reason that he would have to leave Undershaw. Leave Undershaw?
Impossible, he answered automatically. Yes, but nevertheless inevitable. He
had built the house for Touie, who had been its first and only mistress. How
could he bring Jean back there as his bride? It would be not just dishonourable,
but positively indecent. It was one thing for Touie, in all her saintliness, to
hint that he might marry again; quite another to bring a second wife back
to the house, there to enjoy with her the very delights forbidden to him and
Touie for every single night of their lives together under that roof.

Of course, it was out of the question. Yet how tactful, and how intelligent, of Jean not to have pointed this out, but to have let him find his own
way to that conclusion. She really was an extraordinary woman. And it
further touched him that she was involving herself in the Edalji case. It was
ungentlemanly to make comparisons, but Touie, while approving his mission,
would have been equally happy whether he had failed or succeeded. So,
doubtless, would Jean; yet her interest changed matters. It made him determined to succeed for George, for the sake of justice, for – to put it higher
still – the honour of his country; but also for his darling girl. It would be a
trophy to lay at her feet.

Rampant with these emotions, Arthur charged his first putt fifteen feet
past the hole, left the next one six feet short, and managed to miss that too.
An 82 instead of a 79: yes indeed, they ought to keep women off the golf
course. Not simply off the fairways and putting greens, but out of the heads
of the players, otherwise chaos would ensue, as it had just done. Jean had
once mooted taking up golf, and at the time he had replied with moderate
enthusiasm. But it was clearly a bad idea. It was not just the polling booth
from which the fair sex should be barred in the interests of civic harmony.

Back at Undershaw, he found that the afternoon mail had brought a communication from Mr Kenneth Scott of Manchester Square.

'There we have it!' he was shouting as he kicked open Wood's office door.
'There we have it!'

His secretary looked at the paper laid in front of him. He read:

Right eye: 8.75 Diop Spher.
            1.75 Diop cylind axis 90°
Left eye: 8.25 Diop Spher.

'You see, I told Scott to paralyse the accommodation with atropine, so that the results were entirely independent of the patient. Just in case somebody tried claiming that George was feigning blindness. This is exactly what I would have hoped for. Rock solid! Incontrovertible!'

'May I ask,' said Wood, who was finding the part of Watson easier that day, 'what exactly it means?'

'It means, it means . . . in all my years practising as an oculist, I never once remember correcting so high a degree of astygmatic myopia. Here, listen to what Scott writes.' He seized the letter back. '"Like all myopics, Mr Edalji must find it at all times difficult to see clearly any objects more than a few inches off, and in dusk it would be practically impossible for him to find his way about any place with which he was not perfectly familiar."'

'In other words, Alfred, in other words, gentlemen of the jury, he's as blind as the proverbial bat. Except of course that the bat would be able to find its way to a field on a dark night, unlike our friend. I know what I shall do. I shall issue a challenge. I shall offer to have glasses made up to this prescription, and if any defender of the police will put them on at night, I will guarantee that he will not be able to make his way from the Vicarage to the field and back in under an hour. I will wager my reputation on that. Why are you looking dubious, gentleman of the jury?'

'I was just listening, Sir Arthur.'

'No, you were looking dubious. I can recognize dubiety when I see it. Come on, give me the obvious question.'

Wood sighed. 'I was only wondering whether George's eyesight might not have deteriorated in the course of three years' penal servitude.'

'Aha! I guessed you might be thinking that. Absolutely not the case. George's blindness is a permanent structural condition. That's official. So it was just as bad in 1903 as it is now. And he didn't even have glasses then. Any further questions?'

'No, Sir Arthur.' Although there was a lurking observation he did not think fit to raise. His employer might indeed never have met with such a degree of astygmatic myopia in all his days as an oculist. On the other hand, Wood had many times heard him regale a dinner table with the story of how he boasted the emptiest waiting room in Devonshire Place, and how his phenom-enal lack of patients had given him time to write his books.

'I think I shall ask for three thousand.'

'Three thousand what?'

'Pounds, man, pounds. I base my calculation on the Beck Case.'

Wood's expression was as good as any question.

'The Beck Case, surely you remember the Beck Case? Really not?'

Sir Arthur shook his head in mock disapproval. 'Adolf Beck. Of Norwegian origin as I recall. Convicted of frauds against women. They believed him to be an ex-convict by the name of – would you believe it? – John Smith, who had previously served time for similar offences. Beck got seven years' penal servitude. Released on licence about five years ago. Three years on, rearrested again. Convicted again. Judge had misgivings, postponed sentence, and in the meantime who should turn up but the original fraudster Mr Smith. One detail of the case I do recall. How did they know Beck and Smith were not one and the same person? One was circumcised and the other wasn't. On such details does justice sometimes hang.

'Ah. You are looking even more puzzled than at the beginning. Quite understandable. The point. Two points. One, Beck was convicted on the mistaken identification of numerous female witnesses. Ten or eleven of them, in fact. I make no comment. But he was also convicted on the clear evidence of a certain expert in forged and anonymous handwriting. Our old friend Thomas Gurrin. Obliged to present himself to the Beck Committee of Inquiry and admit that his testimony had twice condemned an innocent man. And scarcely a year before this confession of incompetence he had been swearing himself black and blue against George Edalji. In my view he should be barred from the witness box and every case in which he has been involved should be re-examined.

'Anyway, point two. After the Committee's report, Beck was pardoned and awarded five thousand pounds by the Treasury. Five thousand pounds for five years. You can work out the tariff. I shall be asking for three thousand.'

The campaign was advancing. He would write to Dr Butter requesting an interview; to the Headmaster of Walsall School to enquire about the boy Speck; to Captain Anson for the police records in the case; and to George to check if he had ever had any contentious business in Walsall. He would look up the Beck Report to confirm the extent of Gurrin's humiliation, and formally demand of the Home Secretary a new and final investigation into the entire matter.

He planned to devote the next couple of days to the anonymous letters, trying to make them less anonymous, seeking to progress from graphology to psychology to possible identity. Then he would turn the dossier over to Dr Lindsay Johnson for professional comparison with examples of George's handwriting. Johnson was the top man in Europe, having been called by Maître Labori in the Dreyfus Case. Yes, he thought: by the time I have finished I shall make the Edalji Case into as big a stir as they did with Dreyfus over there in France.

He sat at his desk with the bundles of letters, a magnifying glass, a notebook and his propelling pencil. He took a deep breath and then slowly, cautiously, as if watching for some evil spirit to escape, he undid the ribbons on the Vicar's parcels and the twine on Brookes's. The Vicar's letters were dated in pencil and numbered in order of receipt; those of the ironmonger were in no evident sequence.

He read them through in all their poisonous hatred and leering familiarity, their boastfulness and their near insanity, their grand claims and their triviality. *I am God I am God Almighty I am a fool a liar a slanderer a sneak Oh I am going to make it hot for the postman.* It was risible, yet risibility on risibility amounted to cruelty of a diabolical kind, under which the very minds of the victims might have broken down. As Arthur read on, his anger and disgust began to quieten, and he tried to let the phrases soak into him. *You dirty sneaks you want twelve months penal servitude . . . I am as sharp as sharp can be . . . You great hulking blackguard I have got you fixed you dirty Cad you bloody monkey . . . I know all the toffs and if I have got a dare devil face it is no worse than yours . . . Who pinched those eggs on Wednesday night why you did or your man but I don't think they would hang me . . .*

He read and reread, sorted and re-sorted, analysed, compared, annotated. Gradually, hints turned to suspicions and then to hypotheses. For a start, whether or not there was a gang of rippers, there certainly appeared to be a gang of writers. Three, he posited: two young adults and a boy. The two adults seemed at times to run into one another, but there was, he judged, a distinction to be made. One was solely malicious; while the other had outbursts of religious mania which veered from hysterical piety to outrageous blasphemy. This was the one who signed himself Satan, God and their theological conjoining, God Satan. As for the boy, he was exceedingly foul-mouthed, and Arthur put his age at between twelve and sixteen. The adults also bragged of their powers of forgery. 'Do you think we could not imitate your kid's writing?' one of them had written to the Vicar in 1892. And to prove it, there was a whole page elaborately covered with the plausible signatures of the entire Edalji family, of the Brookes family, and of others in the neighbourhood.

A large proportion of the letters were on the same paper, and had arrived in similar envelopes. Sometimes one writer would begin and then give way to another: the effusions of God Satan would be followed on the same page by the rough scrawl and rude drawings – rude in every sense – of the lad. This would strongly suggest that all three of them lived under the same roof. Where might this roof be? Since a number of the letters had been hand-delivered to their victims in Wyrley, it was reasonable to assume a proximity of not much more than a mile or two.

Next, what sort of roof might shelter three such scribes? Some establishment housing young males of different ages? A cramming school, perhaps? Arthur consulted educational directories, but could find nothing within any plausible distance. Could the malefactors be three clerks in an office, or three assistants in a business? The more he considered the matter, the more he was driven to conclude that they were members of the same family, two older brothers and a younger one. Some of the letters were extremely long, which argued for a household of idlers with time on their hands.

He needed more specifics. For instance, Walsall School seemed to be a constant factor in the case, yet how important a factor? And then, what about this letter? The religious maniac was quite evidently alluding to Milton. *Paradise Lost*, Book One: the fall of Satan and the burning lake of Hell, which the writer announced as his own final destination. It certainly would be if Arthur had his way. So, here was a further question for the Headmaster: had *Paradise Lost* ever been on the syllabus at the school, if so when, and how many boys had studied it, and did any of them take it especially to heart? Was this clutching at straws, or exploring every possibility? It was hard to tell.

He read the letters forwards; he read them backwards; he read them in a random sequence; he shuffled them like a pack of cards. And then his eye caught something, and five minutes later he was thumping his secretary's door back on its hinges.

'Alfred, I congratulate you. You hit the nail squarely on the head.'

'I did?'

Arthur thrust a letter on to Wood's desk. 'Look, there. And there, and there.' The secretary followed Arthur's stabbing finger without enlightenment.

'Which nail did I hit?'

'Look, man, there: *boy must be sent away to sea.* And here: *waves come over you.* This is the first Greatorex letter, don't you see? And here too: *I don't think they would hang me but send me to sea.*'

Wood's expression made it clear that the obvious was escaping him.

'The gap, Woodie, the gap. The seven years. Why the gap, I asked, why the gap? And you replied, Because he wasn't there. And I said, Where'd he gone, and you replied, Perhaps he'd run away to sea. And this is the first anonymous letter after that seven-year interval. I'll double-check, but I'll wager your salary there isn't a single reference to the sea in all the letters of the earlier persecution.'

'Well,' said Wood, allowing himself a touch of complacency, 'it did seem like a possible explanation.'

'And what clinches it, in case you have the slightest doubt,' – though the secretary, having just been congratulated on his brilliance, was not inclined immediately to doubt it – 'is where the final hoax came from.'

'You'll have to remind me, I'm afraid, Sir Arthur.'

'December 1895, remember? An advertisement in a Blackpool newspaper offering the entire contents of the Vicarage for sale by auction.'

'Yes?'

'Come on, man, come on. Blackpool, what is Blackpool? The pleasure resort for Liverpool. That's where he took ship from, Liverpool. It's as plain as a packstaff.'

Alfred Wood was kept busy that afternoon. There was a letter to the Headmaster of Walsall School enquiring about the teaching of Milton; one to Harry Charlesworth instructing him to trace any local inhabitants who had been away to sea between the years 1896 and 1903, and also to trace a boy or man called Speck; and one to Dr Lindsay Johnson requesting an urgent comparison between the letters in the accompanying dossier and those in George Edalji's hand already supplied. Meanwhile Arthur wrote to the Mam and Jean informing them of his progress in the case.

The next morning's post included a letter in a familiar envelope. The post-mark was Cannock:

> Honoured Sir,
> A line to tell you we are narks of the detectives and know
> Edalji killed the horse and wrote those letters. No use trying
> to lay it on others. It is Edalji and it will be proven for he is
> not a right sort nor . . .

Arthur turned the page, read on, and let out a roar:

> . . . there was no education to be got at Walsall when that
> bloody swine Aldis was high school boss. He got the bloody
> bullet after the governors were sent letters about him. Ha, ha.

A supplementary request was despatched to the Headmaster of Walsall School, asking about the circumstances of his predecessor's departure; then this latest piece of evidence was forwarded to Dr Lindsay Johnson.

Undershaw felt quiet. Both children were away: Kingsley in his first half at Eton, Mary at Prior's Field, Godalming. The weather was gloomy; Arthur took solitary meals by a blazing fire; in the evenings he played billiards with Woodie. He could see his fiftieth birthday on the horizon – if a horizon could be as close as a mere two years away. He still turned out at cricket, and every so often his cover drive proved a thing of beauty, on which opposing captains were kind enough to comment. But all too often he would stand at the crease, watch a disrespectful bowler arrive in a whirl of arms, feel a thud on his pads, glare down the pitch at the umpire, and hear, from twenty-two yards away, the regretful judgment, 'Very sorry, Sir Arthur.' A decision against which there was no appeal.

It was time to admit that his glory days were over. Seven for 61 against Cambridgeshire one season, and the wicket of W.G. Grace the next. Admittedly the great man had already scored a century when Arthur came on as fifth-change bowler and dismissed him with off-theory, that duffer's trick. But even so: W.G. Grace c W. Storer b A.I. Conan Doyle 110. In celebration he had written a mock-heroic poem in nineteen stanzas; but neither his verse nor the deed it recorded were enough to get him into Wisden. Captain of England, as Partridge had once predicted? Captain of Authors v Actors at Lord's last summer was more his mark. On that June day, he had opened the batting with Wodehouse, who got himself comically bowled for a duck. Arthur himself made two, and Hornung didn't even get an innings. Horace Bleakley had made fifty-four. Perhaps the better the writer, the worse the cricketer.

And it was the same with golf, where the gap between dream and reality grew wider with every year. But billiards . . . now billiards was a game where decline was not automatically the order of the day. Players continued without any obvious falling-away into their fifties, their sixties, even their seventies. Strength was not paramount; experience and tactics were the thing. Kiss cannons, ricochet cannons, postman's knock, nursery cannons along the top cushions – what a game. Was there any reason why, with a little more practice and perhaps some advice from a professional, he should not enter the English Amateur Championship? He would need to improve his long jennies, of course. He had to tell himself each time: spot the ball in baulk for a plain half-ball into the top pocket, and then play it as a steady half-ball with as much pocket side as you can manage. Wood had little trouble with long jennies; though he still had a devil of a distance to go with his double-baulks, as Arthur constantly pointed out to him.

Nearing fifty: the second half of his life about to begin, if tardily. He had lost Touie and found Jean. He had abandoned the scientific materialism he had been inducted into, and found a way to open the great door into the beyond just a crack. Wits liked to repeat that the English, since they lacked any spiritual instinct, had invented cricket in order to give themselves a sense of eternity. Purblind observers imagined that billards was the same shot played over and over again. Poppycock, both notions. The English were not a demonstrative race, it was true – they were not Italians – but they had as much of a spiritual nature as the next tribe. And no two billiards shots were alike, any more than any two human souls were alike.

He visited Touie's grave at Grayshott. He laid flowers, he wept, and as he turned to go, he caught himself wondering when he would come next. Would it be the following week, or would it be in two weeks' time? And after that? And after that? At a certain point the flowers would cease, and his visits would become rarer. He would start a new life with Jean, perhaps over at Crowborough, near her parents. It would become . . . inconvenient to visit Touie. He would tell himself that thinking of her was sufficient. Jean would – God willing – be able to bear his children. Who would visit Touie then? He shook his head to clear away this thought. There was no point anticipating future guilt. You must act according to your best principles, and then deal with what came later on its own terms.

Even so, back at Undershaw – back in Touie's empty house – he found himself drawn to her bedroom. He had given no instructions for it to be rearranged or redecorated – how could he? So there was the bed on which she had died at three o'clock in the morning with the scent of violets in the air and her fragile hand resting in his great clumsy paw. Mary and Kingsley sitting in exhausted and frightened politeness. Touie raising herself with almost her last breath and telling Mary to take care of Kingsley . . . Sighing, Arthur crossed to the window. Ten years ago he had chosen this room for her as having the best view, down into the garden and the private narrowing valley where the woods converged. Her bedroom, her sick-room, her death-room – he had always tried to make it as pleasant and as painless as he could.

That is what he had told himself – told himself and others so often that he had ended up believing it. Had he always been fooling himself? For this was the very room where, a few weeks before her death, Touie had told their daughter that her father would marry again. When Mary reported the conversation, he had tried to make light of the matter – a foolish decision, he now realized. He should have taken the opportunity to praise Touie, and also to prepare the ground; instead he had been panicked into jocularity and asked something like, 'Did she have any particular candidate in mind?' To which Mary had said, 'Father!' And there was no doubting the disapproval with which that word had been pronounced.

He continued looking out of the bedroom window, down past the neglected tennis ground to the valley which once, in a moment of whimsy, he had found reminiscent of a German folk tale. Now it looked no more than the part of Surrey that it was. He could hardly reopen the conversation with Mary. But one thing was certain: if Touie knew, then he was destroyed. If Touie knew and Mary knew, then he was doubly destroyed. If Touie knew, then Hornung was right. If Touie knew, then the Mam was wrong. If Touie knew, then he had played the grossest hypocrite with Connie and shamefully manipulated old Mrs Hawkins. If Touie knew, then his whole concept of honourable behaviour was a sham. On the wold above Masongill, he had said to the Mam that honour and dishonour lay so close to one another that it was hard to tell them apart, and the Mam had replied that this was what made honour so important. What if he had been paddling in dishonour the whole time, fooling himself yet nobody else? What if the world took him for a common adulterer – and even though he was not, he might as well have been? What if Hornung had been right and there was no difference between guilt and innocence?

He sat heavily on the bed and thought of those illicit journeys to Yorkshire: how he and Jean would arrive by different trains, and leave by different ones, so that they could pretend to innocence. Ingleton was two hundred and fifty miles from Hindhead; there they were safe. But he had confused safety with honour. Over the years, it must have become perfectly plain to everyone. What were English villages but vortices of gossip? However Jean might be chaperoned, however clearly he and Jean never stayed under the same roof, here was the famous Arthur Conan Doyle, who married in the parish church, striding over wold and fell with another woman at his side.

And then there was Waller. All that time, in his blithe smugness, he had never asked himself what Waller made of it all. The Mam had approved his course of action, and this had been sufficient. It did not matter what Waller thought. And Waller, being a smooth and easy fellow, had never been crude. He had behaved as if he entirely believed whatever story was put in front of him. The Leckies being old friends of the Doyles; the Mam having always been fond of the Leckie girl. Waller had never said more nor less than common courtesy and common prudence enjoined. He did not try to put Arthur off his golf swing with some comment about Jean Leckie being a handsome young woman. But Waller would have seen the subterfuge immediately. Perhaps – God forbid – he had discussed it with the Mam behind Arthur's back. No, he could not bear to think as much. But in any case, Waller would have seen, Waller would have known. And – which was the hardest part, Arthur now realized – Waller would have been able to look at him with immense self-satisfaction. While they shot partridge together and went out ferreting, he would have been remembering that schoolboy back from Austria, who had viewed him as a cuckoo in the nest, who stood there galumphingly ignorant yet full of violent speculation and violent embarrassment. And then the years had passed, and Arthur began coming to Masongill for a few stolen hours alone with Jean. And now Waller was able silently, without the slightest murmur – which made it all the worse, of course, and all the more superior – Waller was able to take his moral revenge. You dared to look at me and disapprove? You dared to think you understood life? You dared impugn your mother's honour? And now you come here and use your mother and myself and the whole village as camouflage for a rendezvous? You take your mother's pony cart and drive past St Oswald's with your inamorata at your side. You think the village does not notice? You imagine your best man an amnesiac? You tell yourself – and others – that your behaviour is honourable?

No, he must stop. He knew this spiral too well already, he knew its descending temptations, and exactly where it led: to lethargy, despair and self-contempt. No, he must stick to known facts. The Mam had approved his actions. So had everyone except Hornung. Waller had said nothing. Touie had merely warned Mary not to be shocked if he remarried – the words of a loving and considerate wife and mother. Touie had said nothing more and therefore known nothing more. Mary knew nothing. Neither the living nor the dead would benefit from him torturing himself. And life must go on. Touie knew that and Touie had not resented it. Life must go on.

Dr Butter agreed to meet him in London; but other correspondents were less encouraging. George had never done business of any kind in Walsall. Mr Mitchell, the Headmaster of Walsall School, informed him that no pupil by the name of Speck had been on their roll in the last twenty years: further, that his predecessor Mr Aldis had served with distinction for sixteen years, and the notion that he was either denounced or dismissed was plain nonsense. The Home Secretary, Mr Herbert Gladstone, presented his compliments and respects to Sir Arthur, and after several paragraphs of flummery and twaddle regretfully declined any further review of the already much-reviewed Edalji case. The final letter was on the writing paper of the Staffordshire County Police. 'Dear Sir,' it began, 'I shall be much interested to note what Sherlock Holmes has to say about a case in real life . . .' But jocularity did not signal cooperativeness: Captain Anson was not inclined to assist Sir Arthur in any respect. There was no precedent for turning over police records to a member of the public, however distinguished he might be; no precedent either for permitting such a member to interview officers of the force under the Captain's command. Indeed, since Sir Arthur's evident intention was to discredit the Staffordshire Constabulary, its Chief Constable could not see that cooperation with the enemy was strategically or tactically advisable.

Arthur preferred the combative bluntness of the former artillery officer to the mealy-mouthedness of the politician. It might be possible to win Anson round; though his use of military metaphor made Arthur wonder if rather than civilly answering his opponents shot for shot – his expert against their expert – he should not lay down an artillery barrage and blast their position to smithereens. Yes, why not? If they had one handwriting expert, he would produce several in return: not just Dr Lindsay Johnson but perhaps Mr Gobert and Mr Douglas Blackburn as well. And in case anyone doubted Mr Kenneth Scott of Manchester Square, he would send George to several more eye specialists. Yelverton had favoured attrition, which had produced satisfactory results until the final stalemate; now Arthur would switch to maximum force and an advance on all fronts.

He met Dr Butter at the Grand Hotel, Charing Cross. This time he was not late as he turned in from Northumberland Avenue; nor did he linger surreptitiously to observe the police surgeon. In any case, he could have deduced the man's character in advance from his evidence: it was measured, cautious, and not given to wild or frivolous speculation. At the trial he had never claimed more than his observations could support: this had been advantageous to the defence over the bloodstains, disadvantageous over the hairs. It had been Butter's evidence, even more than that of the charlatan Gurrin, which had condemned George to Lewes and Portland.

'It is good of you to spare me the time, Dr Butter.' They were in the same writing room where only a couple of weeks previously he had obtained his first impressions of George Edalji.

The surgeon smiled. He was a handsome, grey-haired man about a decade older than Arthur. 'I am happy to. I am glad to have the opportunity of thanking the man who wrote' – and here there seemed to be a microscopic pause, unless it was only within Arthur's own brain – '*The White Company*.'

Arthur smiled in reply. He had always found the company of police surgeons to be as agreeable as it was instructive.

'Dr Butter, I wonder if you would agree to talk on a frank basis. That is to say, I have great regard for your evidence, but I have various questions and indeed speculations to put before you. Everything you say will be treated in confidence, and I shall not repeat a single word without giving you the opportunity to endorse it, correct it, or withdraw it completely. Would that be acceptable?'

Dr Butter agreed, and Arthur led him, to begin with, through the parts of his evidence which were the least controversial, or at any rate irrefutable by the defence. The razors, the boots, the stains of various kinds.

'Did it surprise you, Dr Butter, that there was so little blood on the clothing, given what George Edalji was accused of doing?'

'No. Or rather, you are asking too large a question. If Edalji had said, Yes, I mutilated the pony, this is the instrument I did it with, these were the clothes I was wearing, and I acted by myself, then I would be competent to offer an opinion. And in those circumstances I would have to say to you that yes, I would be very surprised, indeed astonished.'

'But?'

'But my evidence was, as it always is, about what I found: this amount of mammalian blood on this garment, and so on. That was my evidence. If I cannot tell how or when it got there, I am unable to comment further.'

'In the witness box, of course not. But between ourselves . . .'

'Between ourselves, I would think that if a man rips a horse, there would be a lot of blood, and he would be unable to control where it fell, especially if the deed is done on a dark night.'

'So you are with me? He cannot have done it?'

'No, Sir Arthur, I am not with you. I am very far from with you. There is a wide expanse between the two positions. For instance, anyone going out deliberately to rip a horse would know to wear some kind of apron, just as slaughtermen do. It would be an obvious precaution. But a few spots might fall elsewhere, and escape notice.'

'No evidence of any apron was given in court.'

'That is not my point. I am merely giving you a different explanation from your own. Another might be that there were others present. If there were a gang, as has been suggested, then the young man might not have done the ripping himself, but might have been standing by, and a few drops of blood might have fallen on his clothes in the process.'

'Again, no such evidence was given.'

'But there was a strong suggestion of a gang, was there not?'

'There was deliberate mention of a gang. But not a shred of proof.'

'The other man who ripped his horse?'

'Green. But even Green did not claim there was a gang.'

'Sir Arthur, I quite follow your argument, and your desire for evidence to support it. I merely say, there are other possibilities, whether or not they were brought out in court.'

'You are quite right.' Arthur decided not to press further on this. 'May we talk instead about the hairs? You said in your evidence that you picked twenty-nine hairs from the clothing, and that when you examined them under the microscope they were – if I remember your words correctly – "similar in length, colour and structure" to those from the piece of skin cut from the Colliery pony.'

'That is correct.'

'"Similar". You did not say "exactly the same as".'

'No.'

'Because they were not exactly the same as?'

'No, because that is a conclusion rather than an observation. But to say that they were similar in length, colour and structure is, in layman's terms, to say that they were exactly the same.'

'No doubt in your mind?'

'Sir Arthur, in the witness box I always err on the side of caution. Between ourselves, and under the conditions you have proposed for this interview, I would assure you that the hairs on the clothing were from the same animal whose skin I examined under the microscope.'

'And from exactly the same part too?'

'I do not follow you.'

'The same beast, but also the same part of the beast, namely the belly?'

'Yes, that is true.'

'Now, the hairs on different parts of a horse or pony would vary in length, and perhaps thickness and perhaps structure. Hairs from the tail or mane, for example, would be different?'

'That is also true.'

'Yet all of the twenty-nine hairs you examined were exactly the same, and from exactly the same part of the pony?'

'Indeed.'

'Can we imagine something together, Dr Butter? Again, in complete confidence, within these anonymous walls. Let us imagine – distasteful as it might be – that you or I go out to disembowel a horse.'

'If I may correct you, the pony was not disembowelled.'

'No?'

'The evidence given was that it had been ripped, and was bleeding, and had to be shot. But the bowels were not hanging from the cut as they would have been had it been attacked differently.'

'Thank you. So, imagine we wish to rip a pony. We would have to approach it, calm it down. Stroke its muzzle, perhaps, talk to it, stroke its flank. Then imagine how we might hold it while we rip it. If we are to rip the belly, we might stand against its flank, perhaps put an arm over its back, holding it there while we reached underneath with whatever instrument we were using.'

'I do not know. I have never attended such a gruesome scene.'

'But you do not dispute that this is how you might do it? I have horses myself, they are nervous creatures at the best of times.'

'We were not in the field. And this was not a horse from your stables, Sir Arthur. This was a pit pony. Are not pit ponies notorious for their docility? Are they not used to being handled by miners? Do they not trust those who approach them?'

'You are right, we were not in the field. But indulge me for the moment. Imagine that the act was done as I described it.'

'Very well. Though of course it might have been done quite differently. If there was more than one person present, for example.'

'I grant you that, Dr Butter. And you must grant me in return that if the deed were done roughly as I described it, then it is inconceivable that the only hairs which ended up on the individual's clothing were all from the same place, namely the belly, which in any case is not where you would touch the animal to calm it. And further, the same hairs are found on different parts of the clothing – on both the sleeve and the left breast of the jacket. Would you not expect, at the very minimum, some hairs from another part of the pony?'

'Perhaps. If your description of events is the true one. But as before you offer only two possible explanations – that of the prosecution, and your own. There is a wide expanse between them. For instance, there might have been some longer hairs on the clothing, but they were noticed by the culprit and removed. That would not be surprising, would it? Or they might have blown away in the wind. Or again, there might have been a gang . . .'

Arthur then moved, very cautiously, towards the 'obvious' solution proposed by Wood.

'You work at Cannock, I believe?'

'Yes.'

'The piece of skin was not cut by you?'

'No, by Mr Lewis who attended the animal.'

'And it was delivered to you at Cannock?'

'Yes.'

'And the clothing was also delivered?'

'Yes.'

'Before or afterwards?'

'What do you mean?'

'Did the clothing arrive before the skin, or the skin before the clothing?'

'Oh, I see. No, they arrived together.'

'At the same time?'

'Yes.'

'By the same police officer?'

'Yes.'

'In the same parcel?'

'Yes.'

'Who was the police officer?'

'I have no idea. I see so many. Besides, they all look young to me nowadays, so they all look the same.'

253

'Do you remember what he said?'

'Sir Arthur, this was over three years ago. There is not the slightest reason why I should remember a word he said. He would merely have told me that the parcel came from Inspector Campbell. He might have said what was in it. He might have said the items were for examination, but I hardly needed to be told that, did I?'

'And during the time these items were in your possession, they were kept scrupulously apart, the skin and the clothing? I do not intend to sound like counsel.'

'You do a very good likeness, if I may say so. And naturally I see where you are heading. There was no possibility of contamination in my laboratory, I can assure you.'

'I was not for a moment suggesting it, Dr Butter. I was heading in a different direction. Can you describe to me the parcel you received?'

'Sir Arthur, I can see exactly where you are heading. I have not stood cross-examination by defence counsel for these last twenty years without recognizing such an approach, or without having to answer for the procedures of the police. You were hoping I might say that the skin and the clothing were all rolled up together in some old piece of sacking into which the police had incompetently stuffed them. In which case you impugn my integrity as well as theirs.'

There was a steeliness now overlaying Dr Butter's civility. This was a witness you would always prefer to have on your side.

'I would not do such a thing,' said Arthur mollifyingly.

'You just have, Sir Arthur. You implied that I might have ignored the possibility of contamination. The items were separately wrapped and sealed, and no amount of shaking them around could have made the hairs escape from one package into the other.'

'I am obliged to you, Dr Butter, for eliminating this possibility.' And thus leaving it down to a choice of two: police incompetence before the items were packed separately, or police malice while this was happening. Well, he had pressed Butter far enough. Except . . . 'May I ask one more question? It is purely factual.'

'Of course. Forgive my irritation.'

'It is understandable. I was behaving too much like a defence counsel, as you observed.'

'It was not so much that. It is this. I have worked with the Staffordshire Constabulary for twenty years and more. Twenty years of going to court and having to answer sly questions based on assumptions I know to be false. Twenty years of seeing a jury's ignorance being played to. Twenty years of presenting evidence which is as clear and unambiguous as I can make it, which is based on rigorous scientific analysis, and then being treated, if not as a fraud, then as someone who is merely giving an opinion, that opinion being no more valuable than the next man's. Except that the next man does not have a microscope and if he did would not be competent to focus it. I state what I have observed – what I know – and find myself being told disdainfully that this is merely what I happen to think.'

'I entirely sympathize,' said Sir Arthur.

'I wonder. In any case, your question.'

'At what time of day did you receive the police parcel?'

'What time? About nine o'clock.'

Arthur was amazed by such despatch. The pony had been discovered at about 6.20, Campbell was still in the field at the time George was leaving home to catch the 7.39, he arrived at the Vicarage with Parsons and his band of specials some time before eight. Then they had to search the place, argue with the Edaljis . . .

'I'm sorry, Dr Butter, without sounding like counsel again, surely it was later than that?'

'Later? Certainly not. I know what time the parcel arrived. I remember complaining. They insisted on putting the parcel into my hands that day. I told them I could not possibly stay till after nine. I had my watch out when it arrived. Nine o'clock.'

'The mistake is entirely mine. I thought you meant nine o'clock in the morning.'

Now it is the surgeon's turn to look surprised. 'Sir Arthur, the police are, in my experience, both competent and industrious. Also honest. But they are not miracle-workers.'

Sir Arthur agreed, and the two men parted on friendly terms. But afterwards he found himself thinking exactly that: the police *are* miracle-workers. They are able to make twenty-nine horse hairs pass from one sealed package to another merely by the power of thought. Perhaps he should write them up for the Society of Psychical Research.

Yes, he might compare them to apport mediums, who were supposedly able to dematerialize objects and then rematerialize them, making showers of ancient coins fall upon the seance table, not to mention small Assyrian tablets and semi-precious stones. This was one branch of spiritism about which Arthur remained deeply sceptical; indeed, the most amateur detective was usually able to trace the ancient coins to the nearest numismatist's. As for the fellows who dealt in snakes and tortoises and live birds: Arthur thought they belonged more in the circus or the conjuror's booth. Or the Staffordshire Constabulary.

He was getting skittish. But that was just exhilaration. Twelve hours – therein lay his answer. The police had the evidence in their possession for twelve hours before delivering it to Dr Butter. Where had it been, who had charge of it, how had it been handled? Was there casual contamination, or a particular act done with the specific intention of incriminating George Edalji? Almost certainly, they would never find out, not without a deathbed confession – and Arthur had always been dubious of deathbed confessions.

His exhilaration mounted further when Dr Lindsay Johnson's report arrived at Undershaw. It was backed by two notebooks full of Johnson's detailed graphological analysis. The top man in Europe judged that none of the letters submitted to him, whether penned by malevolent schemer, religious maniac or degenerate boy, had any significant consonance with genuine documents written by George Edalji. In certain examples there was a kind of specious resemblance; but this was no more than you would expect from a forger who admitted trying to counterfeit another's handwriting. You would expect him capable of achieving occasionally a plausible facsimile; yet there were always giveaway signs to prove that George had – literally – no hand in it.

The first part of Arthur's list was now more than half ticked off: *Yelverton – Hairs – Letters – Eyesight*. Then there was *Green* – still work to do on him – and *Anson*. He would beard the Chief Constable directly. 'I shall be much interested to note what Sherlock Holmes has to say about a case in real life . . .' had been Anson's sarcastic response. Well, then, Arthur would take him at his word; he would write up his findings so far, send them off to Anson, and invite his comments.

As he sat down at his desk to begin his draft, he felt, for the first time since Touie's death, a sense of the properness of things. After the depression and guilt and lethargy, after the challenge and the call to action, he was where he belonged: a man at a desk with a pen in his hand, eager to tell a story and to make people see things differently; while out there, up in London, waiting for him – although not for too much longer – was the woman who, from now on, would be his first reader and the first witness of his life. He felt charged with energy; the material teemed in his head; and his purpose was clear. He began with a sentence he had been working on in trains and hotels and taxicabs, something both dramatic and declaratory:

> The first sight which I ever had of Mr. George Edalji was enough
> in itself both to convince me of the extreme improbability of
> his being guilty of the crime for which he was condemned, and
> to suggest some at least of the reasons which had led to his being
> suspected.

And from there the narrative sped out of him, like a great unrolling chain, its links as hard-forged as he could make them. In two days he wrote fifteen thousand words. There might still be things to add, when the additional reports came in from oculists and handwriting experts. He also dealt lightly with what he took to be Anson's role in the affair: no point expecting a useful response from a fellow if you went hard at him before you had even met him. Then Wood typed up the report, and a copy was sent by registered post to the Chief Constable.

Two days later a reply arrived from Green Hall, Stafford, inviting Sir Arthur to dine with Captain and Mrs Anson on any day of the following week. He would, naturally, be welcome to stay overnight. There was no comment at all on Arthur's report, only a whimsical postscript: 'You may bring Mr Sherlock Holmes with you if you wish. Mrs Anson would be delighted to meet him. Let me know if he too requires accommodation.'

Sir Arthur handed the letter to his secretary. 'Keeping his powder dry by the looks of it.'

Wood nodded in agreement, and knew not to comment on the P.S.

'I suppose, Woodie, you don't fancy coming as Holmes?'

'I shall accompany you if you wish, Sir Arthur, but you know my thoughts on dressing up.' He also felt that, having already been cast as Watson, playing Holmes as well would be beyond his dramatic elasticity. 'I may be more use to you practising my billards.'

'Quite right, Alfred. You hold the fort. And don't neglect your double-baulks. I'll see what Anson's made of.'

While Arthur is planning his trip to Staffordshire, Jean is thinking further ahead. It is time to address her transition from waiting girl to non-waiting wife. It is now the month of January. Touie died the previous July; clearly, Arthur cannot marry within the twelvemonth. They have not yet talked about a date, but an autumn wedding is not an impossible thought. Fifteen months – few could be shocked by such an interval. The sentimental prefer a spring wedding; but the autumn suits a second marriage, in Jean's opinion. And then a Continental honeymoon. Italy, of course, and, well, she has always felt a yen for Constantinople.

A wedding means bridesmaids, but this has long been settled: Leslie Rose and Lily Loder-Symonds are marked for the task. But a wedding also means a church, and a church means religion. The Mam brought Arthur up a Catholic, but both have since deserted the faith: the Mam for Anglicanism, Arthur for Sunday golf. Arthur has even become covert about his middle name, Ignatius. There is little chance then, that she, a Catholic from the cradle, will marry as one. This may distress her parents, especially her mother; but if that is the price, Jean will pay it.

Might there be a further price? If she is going to be at Arthur's side in all things, then she must face what up till now she has run from. On the few occasions that Arthur has mentioned his interest in psychical matters, she has turned away. Inwardly, she has shuddered at the vulgarity and stupidity of that world: at silly old men pretending to go into trances, at old crones in frightful wigs gazing into crystal balls, at people holding hands in the darkness and making one another jump. And it has nothing to do with religion, which means morality. And the notion that this . . . mumbo-jumbo appeals to her beloved Arthur is both upsetting and barely credible. How can someone like Arthur, whose reasoning power is second to none, allow himself to associate with such people?

It is true that her great friend Lily Loder-Symonds is an enthusiast for table-turning, but Jean regards this as a whimsicality. She discourages talk of seances, even though Lily assures her they are full of respectable people. Perhaps she should talk the matter through with Lily first, as a way of conquering her distaste. No, that would be pusillanimous. She is marrying Arthur, after all, not Lily.

So when he arrives on his way north, she sits him down, listens dutifully to news of the investigation, and then says, to his evident surprise, 'I should very much like to meet this young man of yours.'

'Would you, my darling? He is a very decent fellow, horribly traduced. I am sure he would be honoured and delighted.'

'He is a Parsee, I think you said?'

'Well, not exactly. His father –'

'What do Parsees believe, Arthur? Are they Hindoos?'

'No, they are Zoroastrians.' Arthur enjoys requests like this. The fundamental mystery of women can, he thinks, be encompassed and held at bay as long as he is allowed to explain things to them. He describes, with settled confidence, the historical origins of the Parsees, their characteristic appearance, their headgear, their liberal attitude to women, their tradition of being born on the ground floor of the house. He passes over the ceremony of purification, since this involves ablution with cow urine; but is expatiating upon the central position of astrology in Parsee life, and heading towards the towers of silence and the posthumous attention of vultures, when Jean raises her hand to stop him. She realizes that this is not the way to do things. The history of Zoroastrianism is not helping make the smooth transition she has somehow hoped for. Also, it feels dishonest, against her view of herself.

'Arthur, my dear,' she interrupts. 'There is something I wish to talk about.'

He looks surprised, and slightly alarmed. If he has always valued her directness, there is a residual suspicion within him that whenever a woman says something must be talked about, it is rarely something to a man's comfort or advantage.

'I want you to explain to me your involvement in ... do you call it spiritism or spiritualism?'

'Spiritism is the term I prefer, but it seems to be losing currency. However, I thought you disliked the entire subject.' He means more than this: that she fears and despises the whole subject – and, *a fortiori*, its adherents.

'Arthur, I could not dislike anything you are interested in.' She means less than this: that she hopes she cannot dislike anything he is interested in.

And so he begins to explain his involvement, from experiments in thought-transference with the future architect of Undershaw to conversations inside Buckingham Palace with Sir Oliver Lodge. At all points he stresses the scientific origins and procedures of psychical research. He goes very carefully, making it sound as respectable and unthreatening as he can. His tone as much as his words begins to reassure her a little.

'It is true, Arthur, that Lily has talked to me a little about table-turning, but I suppose I have always considered it against Church teaching. Is it not heresy?'

'It goes against Church institutions, that is true. Not least because it cuts out the middleman.'

'Arthur! That is hardly a proper way to speak about the clergy.'

'But it is what, historically, they have been. Middlemen, intermediaries. Conveyors of the truth at first, but increasingly controllers of the truth, obfuscators, politicians. The Cathars were on the right line, that of direct access to God untrammelled by layers of hierarchy. Naturally they were wiped out by Rome.'

'So your – do I call them beliefs or not? – make you hostile to my Church?' And therefore, she means, to all its members. To one specific member.

'No, my dearest. And I would never seek to dissuade you from going to your Church. But we are moving beyond all religions. Soon – very soon in historical terms – they will be things of the past. Look at it this way. Is religion the only domain of thought which is non-progressive? Wouldn't that be a strange thing? Are we forever to be referred to a standard set two thousand years ago? Cannot people see that as the human brain evolves, it must take a wider outlook? A half-formed brain makes a half-formed God, and who shall say our brains are even half-formed yet?'

Jean is silent. She thinks that the standards set two thousand years ago are true ones which should be obeyed; and that while the brain might develop, and produce all sorts of scientific advances, the soul, which is the spark of the divine, is something quite separate and immutable, and not subject to evolution.

'Do you remember when I judged the Strong Man competition? At the Albert Hall? He was called Murray, the winner. I followed him out into the night. He had a gold statue under his arm, he was the strongest man in Britain. Yet he was lost in the fog . . .'

No, metaphor was the wrong approach. Metaphors were for the institutional religions. Metaphors paltered.

'What we are doing, Jean, is a simple thing. We are taking the essence of the great religions, which is the life of the spirit, and rendering it more visible and thus more understandable.'

These sound like tempter's words to her, and her tone is crisp. 'By seances and table-turning?'

'Which look strange to the outsider, I freely admit. As the ceremonies of your Church would look strange to a visiting Zoroastrian. The body and blood of Christ on a plate and in a cup – he might think that was sheer hocus-pocus. Religions – all religions – have become mired in ritual and despotism. We do not say, Come and pray in our church and follow our instructions and perhaps one day you will be rewarded in the afterlife. That is like the bargaining of carpet salesmen. Rather, we will show you now, as you live, the reality of certain psychic phenomena, which will prove to you the physical abolition of death.'

'So you do not believe in the resurrection of the body?'

'That we go into the ground and rot, then at some future time are put back together whole? No. The body is a mere husk, a container which we shed. It is true that some souls wander in darkness for a while after death, but that is only because they are unprepared for the transition to the farther side. A true spiritist who understands the process will pass easily and without anguish. And will also be able to communicate more quickly with the world he has left behind.'

'You have witnessed this?'

'Oh yes. And hope to do so more frequently as I understand more.'

A sudden chill goes through Jean. 'You are not, I hope, going to become a medium, dear Arthur.' She has a picture of her beloved husband as an aged huckster going into trances and talking in funny voices. And of the new Lady Doyle being known as a huckster's wife.

'Oh no, I have no such powers. True mediums are very, very rare. They are often simple, humble people. Like Jesus Christ, for instance.'

Jean ignores this comparison. 'And what about morality, Arthur?'

'Morality is unchanged. True morality, that is – which comes from the individual conscience and the love of God.'

'I do not mean for you, Arthur. You know what I mean. If people –

ordinary people – do not have the Church to tell them how to behave, then they will relapse into brutish squalor and self-interest.'

'I do not see that as the alternative. Spiritists, true spiritists, are men and women of high moral calibre. I could name you several. And their morality is the higher because they are closer to an understanding of spiritual truth. If the ordinary person to whom you allude were to see proof of the spirit world at first hand, if he were to realize how close it is to us at all times, then brutishness and self-interest will lose their appeal. Make the truth apparent, and morality will take care of itself.'

'Arthur, you are going too fast for me.' More to the point, Jean feels a headache coming on; indeed, she fears, a migraine.

'Of course. We have all our lives ahead of us. And then all of eternity together.'

Jean smiles. She wonders what Touie will be doing for all of the eternity she and Arthur have together. Though of course the same problem will present itself, whether her Church turns out to be telling the truth, or those low-born mediums who so impress her husband-to-be.

Arthur himself is far from getting a headache. Life is on the move again: first the Edalji case, and now Jean's sudden interest in the things beneath that truly matter. He will soon be back to full gusto. On the doorstep he embraces his waiting girl and, for the first time since Touie's death, finds himself reacting like a prospective bridegroom.

Anson

Arthur told the cabby to drop him at the old lock-up next to the White Lion Hotel. The inn lay directly opposite the gates of Green Hall. It was an instinctive tactic, to arrive on foot. Overnight bag in hand, he followed the gently rising drive from the Lichfield Road, trying to make his shoeleather discreet on the gravel. As the house, slantingly lit by the frail late-afternoon sun, became plain before him, he stopped in a tree's shade. Why should the methods of Dr Joseph Bell not persuade architecture to yield secrets, just as physiology did? So: 1820s, he guessed; white stucco; a pseudo-Greek façade; a solid portico with two pairs of unfluted Ionic columns; three windows on either side. Three storeys – and yet to his enquiring eye there was something suspicious about the third. Yes, he would bet Wood a forty-point start that there was not a single attic room behind that row of seven windows: a mere architectural trick to make the house taller and more impressive. Not that this fakery could be blamed on the current occupant. Peering beyond the house, across to the right, Doyle could make out a sunken rose garden, a tennis ground, a summer house flanked by a pair of young grafted hornbeams.

What story did it all tell? One of money, breeding, taste, history, power. The family's name had been made in the eighteenth century by Anson the circumnavigator, who had also laid down its first fortune – prize money from the capture of a Spanish galleon. His nephew had been raised to the viscountcy in 1806; promotion to the earldom followed in 1831. If this was the second son's residence, and his elder brother held Shugborough, then the Ansons knew how to foster their inheritance.

A few feet back from a second-floor window, Captain Anson called softly to his wife.

'Blanche, the Great Detective is almost upon us. He is studying the driveway for the footprints of an enormous hound.' Mrs Anson had rarely heard him so skittish. 'Now, when he arrives, you are not to burble about his books.'

'I, burble?' She pretended more offence than she took.

'He has already been burbled at across the length and breadth of the country. His supporters have burbled him to death. We are to be hospitable but not ingratiating.'

Mrs Anson had been married long enough to know that this was a sign of nerves rather than any true apprehension over her behaviour. 'I have ordered clear soup, baked whiting and mutton cutlets.'

'Accompanied by?'

'Brussels sprouts and potato croquets, of course. You did not need to ask. Then semolina soufflé and anchovy eggs.'

'Perfection.'

'For breakfast, would you prefer fried bacon and brawn, or grilled herrings and beef roll?'

'In this weather – the latter, I believe, would suit. And remember, Blanche, no discussion of the case over dinner.'

'That will be no hardship to me, George.'

In any case, Doyle proved himself a punctilious guest, keen to be shown his room, equally keen to descend from it in time for a tour of the grounds before the light faded. As one property owner to another, he showed concern over the frequency with which the River Sow flooded the water meadows, and then asked about the curious earthen mound which lay half-concealed by the summer house. Anson explained that it was an old ice house, now put out of business by refrigeration; he wondered if he might not turn it over to the storage of wine. Next they considered how the turf of the tennis ground was surviving the winter, and jointly regretted the brevity of season that the English climate imposed. Anson accepted Doyle's praise and appreciation, all of which assumed that he was the owner of Green Hall. In truth, he merely leased it; but why should he tell the Great Detective that?

'I see those young hornbeams have been grafted.'

'You do not miss a trick, Doyle,' replied the Chief Constable with a smile. It was the lightest of references to what lay ahead.

'I have had planting years myself.'

At dinner, the Ansons occupied either end of the table, with Doyle granted the view through the central window out on to the dormant rose garden. He showed himself properly attentive to Mrs Anson's questions; at times, she thought, excessively so.

'You are well acquainted with Staffordshire, Sir Arthur?'

'Not as well as I should be. But there is a connection with my father's family. The original Doyle was a cadet-branch of the Staffordshire Doyles, which, as you may know, produced Sir Francis Hastings Doyle and other distinguished men. This cadet took part in the invasion of Ireland and was granted estates in County Wexford.'

Mrs Anson smiled encouragingly, not that it seemed necessary. 'And on your mother's side?'

'Ah, now that is of considerable interest. My mother is great on archaeology, and with the help of Sir Arthur Vicars – the Ulster King of Arms, and himself a relative – has been able to work out her descent over a period of five centuries. It is her boast – our boast – that we have a family tree on which many of the great ones of the earth have roosted. My grandmother's uncle was Sir Denis Pack, who led the Scottish Brigade at Waterloo.'

'Indeed.' Mrs Anson was a firm believer in class, also in its duties and obligations. But it was nature and bearing, rather than documentation, that proved a gentleman.

'However, the real romance of the family is traced from the marriage in the mid-seventeenth century of the Reverend Richard Pack to Mary Percy, heir to the Irish branch of the Percys of Northumberland. From this moment we connect up to three separate marriages with the Plantagenets. One has, therefore, some strange strains in one's blood which are noble in origin, and, one can but hope, are noble in tendency.'

'One can but hope,' repeated Mrs Anson. She herself was the daughter of Mr G. Miller of Brentry, Gloucester, and had little curiosity about her distant ancestors. It seemed to her that if you paid an investigator to elaborate your family tree, you would always end up being connected to some great family. Genealogical detectives did not, on the whole, send in bills attached to confirmation that you were descended from swineherds on one side of the family and pedlars on the other.

'Although,' Sir Arthur continued, 'by the time Katherine Pack – the niece of Sir Denis – was widowed in Edinburgh, the family fortunes had fallen into a parlous condition. Indeed, she was obliged to take in a paying guest. Which was how my father – the paying guest – came to meet my mother.'

'Charming,' commented Mrs Anson. 'Altogether charming. And now you are busy restoring the family fortunes.'

'When I was a small boy, I was much pained by the poverty to which my mother was reduced. I sensed that it was against the grain of her nature. That memory is part of what has always driven me on.'

'Charming,' repeated Mrs Anson, meaning it rather less this time. Noble blood, hard times, restored fortunes. She was happy enough to believe such themes in a library novel, but when confronted by a living version was inclined to find them implausible and sentimental. She wondered how long the family's ascendancy would last this time round. What did they say about quick money? One generation to make it, one to enjoy it, one to lose it.

But Sir Arthur, if more than a touch vainglorious about his ancestry, was a diligent table-companion. He showed abundant appetite, even if he ate without the slightest comment on what was put in front of him. Mrs Anson could not decide whether he believed it vulgar to applaud food, or whether he simply lacked taste buds. Also unmentioned at table were the Edalji case, the state of criminal justice, the administration of Sir Henry Campbell-Bannerman, and the exploits of Sherlock Holmes. But they managed to steer a course, like three scullers without a cox, Sir Arthur pulling vigorously on one side, and the Ansons dipping their blades sufficiently on the other to keep the boat straight.

The anchovy eggs were despatched, and Blanche Anson could sense male restiveness farther down the table. They were eager for the curtained study, the poked fire, the lit cigar, the glass of brandy, and the opportunity, in as civilized a way as possible, to tear great lumps out of one another. She could scent, above the odours of the table, something primitive and brutal in the air. She rose, and bade the combatants goodnight.

The gentlemen passed into Captain Anson's study, where a fire was in full spate. Doyle took in the glisten of fresh coal in the brass bucket, the polished spines of bound periodicals, a sparkling three-bottle tantalus, the lacquered belly of a bloated fish in a glass case. Everything gleamed: even that pair of antlers from a non-native species – a Scandinavian elk of some kind, he assumed – had attracted the housemaid's attention.

He eased a cigar from the offered box and rolled it between his fingers. Anson passed him a penknife and a box of cigar matches.

'I deprecate the use of the cigar-cutter,' he announced. 'I shall always prefer the nice conduct of the knife.'

Doyle nodded, and bent to his task, then flicked the cut stub into the fire.

'I understand that the advancement of science has now brought us the invention of an electric cigar-lighter?'

'If so, it has not reached Hindhead,' replied Doyle. He declined any billing as the metropolis come to patronize the provinces. But he identified a need in his host to assert mastery in his own study. Well, if so, he would help him.

'The elk,' he proposed, 'is perhaps from Southern Canada?'

'Sweden,' replied the Chief Constable almost too quickly. 'Not a mistake your detective would have made.'

Ah, so we shall have that one first, shall we? Doyle watched Anson light his own cigar. In the match's flare the Stafford knot of his tiepin briefly gleamed.

'Blanche reads your books,' said the Chief Constable, nodding a little, as if this settled the matter. 'She is also very partial to Mrs Braddon.'

Doyle felt a sudden pain, the literary equivalent of gout. And there was a further stab as Anson continued, 'I am more for Stanley Weyman myself.'

'Capital,' Doyle answered, 'Capital.' By which he meant, It is capital that you prefer him as far as I am concerned.

'You see, Doyle – I'm sure you don't mind if I speak frankly? – I may not be what you would call a literary fellow, but as Chief Constable I inevitably take a more professional view of matters than I imagine most of your readers do. That the police officers you introduce into your tales are inadequate to their task is something which is, I quite understand, necessary to the logic of your inventions. How else would your scientific detective shine if not surrounded by boobies?'

It was not worth arguing the toss. 'Boobies' hardly described Lestrade and Gregson and Hopkins and . . . oh, it wasn't –

'No, I fully understand your reasons, Doyle. But in the real world . . .'

At this point Doyle more or less stopped listening. In any case, his mind had snagged on the phrase 'the real world'. How easily everyone understood what was real and what was not. The world in which a benighted young solicitor was sentenced to penal servitude in Portland . . . the world in which Holmes unravelled another mystery beyond the powers of Lestrade and his colleagues . . . or the world beyond, the world behind the closed door, through which Touie had effortlessly slipped. Some people believed in only one of these worlds, some in two, a few in all three. Why did people imagine that progress consisted of believing in less, rather than believing in more, in opening yourself to more of the universe?

'. . . which is why, my good fellow, I shall not, without orders from the Home Office, be issuing my inspectors with cocaine syringes and my sergeants and constables with violins.'

Doyle inclined his head, as if acknowledging a palpable hit. But that was enough play-acting and guestliness.

'To the case at hand. You have read my analysis.'

'I have read your . . . story,' replied Anson. 'A deplorable business, it has to be said. A series of mistakes. It could all have been nipped in the bud so much earlier.'

Anson's candour surprised Doyle. "I'm glad to hear you say that. Which mistakes did you have in mind?'

'The family's. That's where it all went wrong. The wife's family. What took it into their heads? Whatever took it into their heads? Doyle, really: your niece insists upon marrying a Parsee – can't be persuaded out of it – and what do you do? You give the fellow a living . . . *here*. In Great Wyrley. You might as well appoint a Fenian to be Chief Constable of Staffordshire and have done with it.'

'I'm inclined to agree with you,' replied Doyle. 'No doubt his patron sought to demonstrate the universality of the Anglican Church. The Vicar is, in my judgement, both an amiable and a devoted man, who has served the parish to the best of his ability. But the introduction of a coloured clergyman into such a rude and unrefined parish was bound to cause a regrettable situation. It is certainly an experiment that should not be repeated.'

Anson looked across at his guest with sudden respect – even allowing for that gibe about 'rude and unrefined'. There was more common ground here than he had expected. He ought to have known that Sir Arthur was unlikely to prove an out-and-out radical.

'And then to introduce three half-caste children into the neighbourhood.'

'George, Horace and Maud.'

'Three half-caste children,' repeated Anson.

'George, Horace and Maud,' repeated Doyle.

'George, Horace and Maud Ee-dal-jee.'

'You have read my analysis?'

'I have read your . . . analysis' – Anson decided to concede the word this time – 'and I admire, Sir Arthur, both your tenacity and your passion. I promise to keep your amateur speculations to myself. To broadcast them would do your reputation no good.'

'I think you must allow me to be the judge of that.'

'As you wish, as you wish. Blanche was reading to me the other day. An interview you gave in the *Strand* some years ago, about your methods. I trust you were not grossly misrepresented?'

'I have no memory of being so. But I am not in the habit of reading through in a spirit of verification.'

'You described how, when you wrote your tales, that it was always the conclusion which first preoccupied you.'

'Beginning with an ending. You cannot know which path to travel unless you first know the destination.'

'Exactly. And you have described in your . . . analysis how when you met young Edalji for the first time – in the lobby of an hotel, I believe – you observed him for a while, and even before meeting him were convinced of his innocence?'

'Indeed, For the reasons clearly stated.'

'For the reasons clearly *felt*, I would prefer to say. Everything you have written proceeds from that feeling. Once you became convinced of the wretched youth's innocence, everything fell into place.'

'Whereas once you became convinced of the youth's guilt, everything fell into place.'

'My conclusion was not based upon some intuition in the lobby of an hotel, but upon the consequences of police observations and reports over a number of years.'

'You made the boy a target from the beginning. You wrote threatening him with penal servitude.'

'I tried to warn both the boy and his father of the consequences of persisting in the criminal path on which he had manifestly set out. I am not wrong, I think, to take the view that police work is not just punitive but also prophylactic.'

Doyle nodded at a phrase which had, he suspected, been prepared especially for him. 'You forget that before meeting George I had read his excellent articles in *The Umpire*.'

'I have yet to meet anyone detained at His Majesty's pleasure who did not have a persuasive explanation of why he was not guilty.'

'In your view George Edalji sent letters denouncing himself?'

'Among a great variety of other letters. Yes.'

'In your view he was the ringleader of a gang who dismembered beasts?'

'Who can tell? Gang is a newspaper word. I have no doubt there were others involved. I also have no doubt that the solicitor was the cleverest of them.'

'In your view, his father, a minister of the Church of England, perjured himself to give his son an alibi?'

'Doyle, a personal question, if I may. Do you have a son?'

'I do. He is fourteen.'

'And if he fell into trouble, you would help him.'

'Yes. But if he committed a crime, I would not perjure myself.'

'But you would still help and protect him, short of that.'

'Yes.'

'Then perhaps, with your imagination, you can picture someone else doing more.'

'I cannot picture a priest of the Church of England placing his hand on the Bible and knowingly committing perjury.'

'Then try to imagine this instead. Imagine a Parsee father putting loyalty to his Parsee family above loyalty to a land not his own, even if it has given him shelter and encouragement. He wants to save his son's skin, Doyle. Skin.'

'And in your view the mother and sister also perjured themselves?'

'Doyle, you keep saying *in my view*. "My view", as you call it, is the view not just of myself, but of the Staffordshire Constabulary, prosecuting counsel, a properly sworn English jury, and the justices of the Quarter Sessions. I attended every day of the trial, and I can assure you of one thing, which will be painful to you but which you cannot avoid. The jury did not believe the evidence of the Edalji family – certainly not of the father and daughter. The mother's evidence was perhaps less important. That is not something lightly done. An English jury sitting round a table considering its verdict is a solemn business. They weigh evidence. They examine character. They do not sit there waiting for a sign from above like . . . table-turners at a seance.'

Doyle looked across sharply. Was this a random phrase, or a knowing attempt to unsettle him? Well, it would take more than that.

'We are talking, Anson, not of some butcher's boy, but of a professional Englishman, a solicitor in his late twenties, already known as the author of a book on railway law.'

'Then the greater his misdemeanour. If you imagine the criminal courts entertain only the criminal classes, you are more naive than I took you for. Even authors sometimes stand in the dock, as you must be aware. And the sentence doubtless reflected the gravity of a case in which one sworn to uphold and interpret the law so grievously flouted it.'

'Seven years' penal servitude. Even Wilde only received two.'

'That is why sentencing is for the court, rather than for you or me. I might not have given Edalji less, though I would certainly have given Wilde more. He was thoroughly guilty – and of perjury too.'

'I dined with him once,' said Doyle. Antagonism was now rising like mist from the River Sow, and all his instincts told him to pull back a little. 'It would have been in '89, I think. A golden evening for me. I had expected a monologuist and an egotist, but I found him a gentleman of perfect manners. There were four of us, and though he towered over the other three, he never let it show. Your monologue man, however clever, can never be a gentleman at heart. With Wilde it was give and take, and he had the art of seeming interested in everything that we might say. He had even read my *Micah Clarke*.

'I recall that we were discussing how the good fortune of friends may sometimes make us strangely discontented. Wilde told us the story of the Devil in the Libyan Desert. Do you know that one? No? Well, the Devil was about his business, going the rounds of his empire, when he came across a number of small fiends tormenting a holy hermit. They were employing temptations and provocations of a routine nature, which the sainted man was resisting without much difficulty. "That is not how it is done," said their Master. "I will show you. Watch carefully." Whereupon the Devil approached the holy hermit from behind, and in a honeyed tone whispered in his ear, "Your brother has just been appointed Bishop of Alexandria." And immediately a scowl of furious jealousy crossed the hermit's face. "*That*," said the Devil, "is how it is best done."'

Anson joined in Doyle's laughter, though less than full-heartedly. The shallow cynicisms of a metropolitan sodomite were not to his taste. 'Be that as it may,' he said, 'the Devil certainly found Wilde himself easy prey.'

'I must add,' Doyle went on, 'that never in Wilde's conversation did I observe one trace of coarseness of thought, nor could I at that time associate him with such an idea.'

'In other words, a professional gentleman.'

Doyle ignored the gibe. 'I met him again, some years later, in a London street, you know, and he appeared to me to have gone quite mad. He asked if I had gone to see a play of his. I told him regrettably not. "Oh, you must go," he said to me with the gravest of expressions. "It is wonderful! It is genius!" Nothing could have been farther from his previous gentlemanly instincts. I thought at the time, and I still think, that the monstrous development which ruined him was pathological, and that a hospital rather than a police court was the place for its consideration.'

'Your liberalism would empty the gaols,' remarked Anson drily.

'You mistake me, sir. I have twice engaged in the vile business of electioneering, but I am not a party man. I pride myself on being an unofficial Englishman.'

The phrase – which struck Anson as self-satisfied – wafted between them like a skein of cigar smoke. He decided it was time to make a push.

'That young man whose case you have so honourably taken up, Sir Arthur

– he is not, I should warn you, entirely what you think. There were various matters which did not come out in court . . .'

'No doubt for the very good reason that they were forbidden by the rules of evidence. Or else were allegations so flimsy that they would have been destroyed by the defence.'

'Between ourselves, Doyle, there were rumours . . .'

'There are always rumours.'

'Rumours of gambling debts, rumours of the misuse of clients' funds. You might ask your young friend if, in the months leading up to the case, he was in any serious trouble.'

'I have no intention of doing any such thing.'

Anson rose slowly, walked to his desk, took a key from one drawer, unlocked another, and extracted a folder.

'I show you this in strictest confidence. It is addressed to Sir Benjamin Stone. It was doubtless one of many.'

The letter was dated 29th December 1902. At the top left were printed George Edalji's professional and telegrammic addresses; at the top right, 'Great Wyrley, Walsall.' It did not require testimony from that rogue Gurrin to convince Doyle that the handwriting was George's.

> Dear Sir, I am reduced from a fairly comfortable position to absolute poverty, primarily through having had to pay a large sum of money (nearly £220) for a friend for whom I was surety. I borrowed from three moneylenders in the hope of righting myself, but their exorbitant interest only made matters worse, & two of them have now <u>presented a bankruptcy petition</u> against me, but are willing to withdraw if I can raise £115 at once. I have no such friends to whom I can appeal, & as bankruptcy would ruin me and prevent me practising for a long time during which I should lose all my clients, I am, as a last resource, appealing to a few strangers.
>
> My friends can only find me £30, I have about £21 myself, & shall be most thankful for <u>any aid</u>, no matter how small as it will all help me to meet my heavy liability.
>
> Apologizing for troubling you and trusting you may assist me as far as you can.
>
> I am,
>
> Yours respectfully,
>
> G.E. Edalji

Anson watched Doyle as he read the letter. No need to point out that it was written five weeks before the first maiming. The ball was in his court now. Doyle flicked the letter over and reread some of its phrases. Eventually he said,

'You doubtless investigated?'

'Certainly not. This is not a police matter. Begging on the public highway is an offence, but begging among the professional classes is no concern of ours.'

'I see no reference here to gambling debts or misuse of clients' funds.'

'Which would hardly have been the way to Sir Benjamin Stone's heart. Try reading between the lines.'

'I decline to. This seems to me the desperate appeal of an honourable young man let down by his generosity to a friend. The Parsees are known for their charity.'

'Ah, so suddenly he's a Parsee?'

'What do you mean?'

'You cannot have him a professional Englishman one moment and a Parsee the next, just as it suits you. Is it prudent for an honourable young man to pledge such a large sum, and to put himself in the hands of three separate moneylenders? How many solicitors have you known do this? Read between the lines, Doyle. Ask your friend about it.'

'I have no intention of asking him about it. And clearly, he did not go bankrupt.'

'Indeed. I suspect the mother helped out.'

'Or perhaps there were others in Birmingham who showed him the same confidence he had shown the friend for whom he stood surety.'

Anson found Doyle as stubborn as he was naive. 'I applaud your . . . romantic streak, Sir Arthur. It does you credit. But forgive me if I find it unrealistic. As I do your campaign. Your fellow has been released from prison. He is a free man. What is the point of seeking to whip up popular opinion? You want the Home Office to look at the case again? The Home Office has looked at it countless times. You want a committee? What makes you sure it will give you what you want?'

'We shall get a committee. We shall get a free pardon. We shall get compensation. And furthermore we shall establish the identity of the true criminal in whose place George Edalji has suffered.'

'Oh, that too?' Anson was now becoming seriously irritated. It could so easily have been a pleasant evening: two men of the world, each approaching fifty, one the son of an earl and the other a knight of the realm, both of them, as it happened, Deputy Lieutenants of their respective counties. They had far more in common than was setting them apart . . . and instead it was turning rancorous.

'Doyle, let me make two points to you, if I may. You clearly imagine that there was some continuous line of persecution stretching back years – the letters, the hoaxes, the mutilations, the additional threats. You further think the police blame all of it on your friend. Whereas you blame all of it on criminals known or unknown, but the same criminals. Where is the logic in either approach? We only charged Edalji with two offences, and the second charge was in any case not proceeded with. I expect he is innocent of numerous matters. A criminal spree such as this rarely has single authorship. He might be the ringleader, he might be a mere follower. He might have seen the effect of an anonymous letter and decided to try it for himself. Might have seen the effect of a hoax and decided to play hoaxer. Heard of a gang cutting animals, and decided to join it.

'My second point is this. In my time I've seen people who were probably guilty found innocent, and people who were probably innocent found guilty. Don't look so surprised. I've known examples of wrongful accusation and wrongful conviction. But in such cases the victim is rarely as straightforward as his defenders would like. For instance, let me make a suggestion. You came across George Edalji for the first time in a hotel foyer. You were late for the meeting, I understand. You saw him in a particular posture, from which you deduced his innocence. Let me put this to you. George Edalji was there before you. He was expecting you. He know you would observe him. He arranged himself accordingly.'

Doyle did not reply to this, just stuck out his chin and pulled on his cigar. Anson was finding him a damned stubborn fellow, this Scotsman or Irishman or whatever he claimed to be.

'You want him to be completely innocent, don't you? Not just innocent, but completely innocent? In my experience, Doyle, no one is completely innocent. They may be found not guilty, but that's different from being innocent. Almost no one's completely innocent.'

'How about Jesus Christ?'

Oh, for God's sake, thought Anson. And I'm not Pontius Pilate either. 'Well, from a purely legal point of view,' he said in a mild, after-dinner manner, 'you could argue that Our Lord helped bring the prosecution upon Himself.'

Now it was Doyle who felt they were straying from the matter in hand.

'Then let me ask you this. What, in your opinion, really happened?'

Anson laughed, rather too openly. 'That I'm afraid, is a question from detective fiction. It is what your readers beg, and what you so winningly provide. *Tell us what really happened.*

'Most crimes, Doyle – almost all crimes, in fact – occur without witnesses.

The burglar waits for the house to be empty. The murderer waits until his victim is alone. The man who slashes the horse waits for the cover of night. If there is a witness, it is often an accomplice, another criminal. You catch a criminal, he lies. Always. You separate two accomplices, they tell separate lies. You get one to turn King's evidence, he tells a new sort of lie. The entire resources of the Staffordshire Constabulary could be assigned to a case, and we would never end up knowing *what really happened*, as you put it. I am not making some philosophical argument, I am being practical. What we know, what we end up knowing, is – enough to secure a conviction. Forgive me for lecturing you about the real world.'

Doyle wondered if he would ever cease being punished for having invented Sherlock Holmes. Corrected, advised, lectured, patronized – when would it ever stop? Still, he must press on. He must keep his temper whatever the provocation.

'But leaving all that aside, Anson. And admitting – as I fear we must admit – that by the end of the evening we may not have shifted one another's position by one jot or one tittle. What I am asking is this. You believe that a respectable young solicitor, having shown no previous sign of a violent nature, suddenly goes out one night and attacks a pit pony in a most wicked and violent fashion. I ask you simply, Why?'

Anson groaned inwardly. Motive. The criminal mind. Here we go again. He rose and refilled their glasses.

'You are the one with the paid imagination, Doyle.'

'Yet I believe him innocent. And am unable to make the leap that you have made. You are not in the witness box. We are two English gentlemen sitting over fine brandy and, if I may say so, even finer cigars, in a handsome house in the middle of this splendid county. Whatever you say will remain within these four walls, I give you my word on that. I merely ask: according to you, Why?'

'Very well. Let us start with known facts. The case of Elizabeth Foster, the maid-of-all-work. Where you allege it all began. Naturally, we looked at the case but there simply wasn't enough evidence to prosecute.'

Doyle looked at the Chief Constable blankly. 'I don't understand. There was a prosecution. She pleaded guilty.'

'There was a private prosection – by the Vicar. And the girl was bullied by lawyers into pleading guilty. Not the sort of gesture to endear you to your parishioners.'

'So the police failed to support the family even then?'

'Doyle, we prosecute when the evidence is there. As we prosecuted when the solicitor himself was victim of an assault. Ah, I see he didn't tell you that.'

'He does not seek pity.'

'That's by the by.' Anson picked a paper from his file. 'November 1900. Assault by two Wyrley youths. Pushed him through a hedge in Landywood, and one of them also damaged his umbrella. Both pleaded guilty. Fined with costs. Cannock magistrates. You didn't know he'd been there before?'

'May I see that?'

'Afraid not. Police records.'

'Then at least give me the names of those convicted.' When Anson hesitated, he added, 'I can always get my bloodhounds on to the matter.'

Anson, to Doyle's surprise, gave a kind of humorous bark. 'So you're a bloodhound man too? Oh, very well, they were called Walker and Gladwin.' He saw that they meant nothing to Doyle. 'Anyway, we might presume that this was not an isolated occurrence. He was probably assaulted before or after, more mildly perhaps. Doubtless insulted too. The young men of Staffordshire are far from saints.'

'It may surprise you to know that George Edalji specifically rejects race prejudice as the basis of his misfortune.'

'So much the better. Then we may happily leave it on one side.'

'Though of course,' added Doyle, 'I do not agree with his analysis.'

'Well, that is your prerogative,' replied Anson complacently.

'And why is this assault relevant?'

'Because, Doyle, you cannot understand the ending until you know the beginning.' Anson was now starting to enjoy himself. His blows were hitting home, one by one. 'George Edalji had good reason to hate the district of Wyrley. Or thought he did.'

'So he took revenge by killing livestock? Where's the connection?'

'I see you are from the city, Doyle. A cow, a horse, a sheep, a pig is more than livestock. It is livelihood. Call it – an economic target.'

'Can you demonstrate a link between either of George's assailants in Landywood and any of the livestock subsequently mutilated?'

'No, I can't. But you should not expect criminals to follow logic.'

'Not even intelligent ones?'

'Even less so, in my experience. Anyway, we have a young man who is his parents' pet, still stuck at home when his younger brother has flown the coop. A young man with a grudge against the district, to which he feels superior. He finds himself in catastrophic debt. The moneylenders are threatening him with the bankruptcy court, professional ruin is staring him in the face. Everything he has ever worked for in his life is about to disappear . . .'

'And so?'

'So . . . perhaps he ran mad like your friend Mr Wilde.'

'Wilde was corrupted by his success, in my view. One may hardly compare the effect of nightly applause in the West End with the critical reception to a treatise on railway law.'

'You said Wilde's case was a pathological development. Why not Edalji's too? I believe the solicitor was at his wits' end for months. The strain must have been considerable, even unbearable. You yourself called his begging letter "desperate". Some pathological development might occur, some tendency to evil in the blood might inevitably emerge.'

'Half his blood is Scottish.'

'Indeed.'

'And the other half is Parsee. The most highly educated and commercially successful of Indian sects.'

'I do not doubt it. They are not called the Jews of Bombay for nothing. And equally I do not doubt that it is the mixing of the blood that is partly the cause of all this.'

'My own blood is mixed Scottish and Irish,' said Doyle. 'Does this make me cut cattle?'

'You make my argument for me. What Englishman – what Scotsman – what half Scotsman – would take a blade to a horse, a cow, a sheep?'

'You forget the miner Farrington, who did just that while George was in prison. But I ask you in return: what Indian would do the same? Do they not venerate cattle as gods there?'

'Indeed. But when the blood is mixed, that is where the trouble starts. An irreconcilable division is set up. Why does human society everywhere abhor the half-caste? Because his soul is torn between the impulse to civilization and the pull of barbarism.'

'And is it the Scottish or the Parsee blood you hold responsible for barbarism?'

'You are facetious, Doyle. You yourself believe in blood. You believe in race. You told me over dinner how your mother had proudly traced her ancestry back five centuries. Forgive me if I misquote you, but I recall that many of the great ones of the earth have roosted in your family tree.'

'You do not misquote me. Are you saying that George Edalji slit the bellies of horses because that's what his ancestors did five centuries ago in Persia or wherever they were then?'

'I have no idea whether barbaric or ritual practices were involved. Perhaps so. It may well be that Edalji himself did not know what impelled him to act as he did. An urge from centuries back, brought to the surface by this sudden and deplorable miscegenation.'

'You truly believe that this is what happened?'

'Something like it, yes.'

'Then what about Horace?'

'Horace?'

'Horace Edalji. Born of the same mixture of bloods. Currently a respected employee of His Majesty's Government. In the tax inspectorate. You are not suggesting Horace was part of the gang?'

'I am not.'

'Why not? He has as good credentials.'

'Again, you are being facetious. Horace Edalji lives in Manchester, for a start. Besides, I am merely proposing that a mixing of the blood produces a tendency, a susceptibility under certain extreme circumstances to revert to barbarism. To be sure, many half-castes live perfectly respectable lives.'

'Unless something triggers them . . .'

'As the full moon may trigger lunacy in some gypsies and Irish.'

'It has never had that effect on me.'

'Low-born Irish, my dear Doyle. Nothing personal intended.'

'So what is the difference between George and Horace? Why, in your belief, has one resorted to barbarism and the other not – or not as yet?'

'Do you have a brother, Doyle?'

'I do indeed. A younger one. Innes. He's a career officer.'

'Why has he not written detective stories?'

'I am not tonight's theorist.'

'Because circumstances, even between brothers, vary.'

'Again, why not Horace?'

'The evidence has been staring you in the face, Doyle. It was all brought out in court, by the family itself. I'm surprised you overlooked it.'

It was a pity, Doyle thought, that he had not booked into the White Lion Hotel over the road. He might have the need to kick some furniture before the evening was finished.

'Cases like this, which seem baffling as well as repugnant to the outsider often turn, in my experience, on matters which are not discussed in court, for obvious reasons. Matters which are normally confined to the smoking room. But you are, as you have indicated with your tales of Mr Oscar Wilde, a man of the world. You have a medical training too, as I recall. And you have travelled in support of our army in the South African War, I believe.'

'All that is true.' Where was the fellow leading him?

'Your friend Mr Edalji is thirty years old. He is unmarried.'

'As are many young men of his age.'

'And is likely to remain so.'

'Especially given his prison sentence.'

'No, Doyle, that's not the problem. There's always a certain low sort of woman attracted by the whiff of Portland. The hindrance is other. The hindrance is that your man's a goggling half-caste. Not many takers for that, not in Staffordshire.'

'Your point?'

But Anson did not seem especially keen to reach his point.

'The accused, as was noted at the Quarter Sessions, did not have any friends.'

'I thought he was a member of the famous Wyrley Gang?'

Anson ignored this riposte. 'Neither male comrades nor, for that matter, friends of the fairer sex. He has never been seen with a girl on his arm. Not even a parlourmaid.'

'I did not realize you had him followed quite so closely.'

'He does not engage in sporting activities either. Had you noticed that? The great manly English games – cricket, football, golf, tennis, boxing – are all quite foreign to him. Archery,' the Chief Constable added; and then, as an afterthought, 'Gymnastics.'

'You expect a man with a myopia of eight dioptres to enter the boxing ring, otherwise you'll send him to gaol?'

'Ah, his eyesight, the answer to everything.' Anson could feel Doyle's exasperation building, and sought to incite it further. 'Yes, a poor, bookish, solitary boy with bulging eyes.'

'So?'

'You trained, I think, as an ophthalmologist?'

'I had consulting rooms in Devonshire Place for a short while.'

'And did you examine many cases of exophthalmus?'

'Not a great number. To tell the truth, I had few patients. They neglected me to such an extent that I was able to give my time there to literary composition. So their absence was to prove unexpectedly beneficial.'

Anson noted the ritual display of self-satisfaction, but pressed ahead. 'And what condition do you associate with exophthalmus?'

'It sometimes occurs as a consequence of whooping cough. And, of course, as a side-effect of strangulation.'

'Exophthalmus is commonly associated with an unhealthy degree of sexual desire.'

'Balderdash!'

'No doubt, Sir Arthur, your Devonshire Place patients were altogether too refined.'

'It's absurd.' Had they descended into folk traditions and old wives' tales? This from a Chief Constable?

'It is not, of course, an observation that would be put up in evidence. But it is generally reported among those who deal with a certain class of criminal.'

'It's still balderdash.'

'As you wish. Further, we need to consider the curious sleeping arrangements at the Vicarage.'

'Which are absolute proof of the young man's innocence.'

'We have agreed we shall not change each other's minds one jot or one tittle tonight. But even so, let us consider those sleeping arrangements. The boy is – what? ten? – when his little sister falls ill. From that moment, mother and daughter sleep in the same room, while father and elder son also share a common dormitory. Lucky Horace has a room of his own.'

'Are you suggesting – are you suggesting that something dastardly happened in that room?' Where on earth was Anson heading? Was he completely off his head?

'No, Doyle. The opposite. I am absolutely certain that nothing whatever happened in that room. Nothing except sleep and prayers. Nothing happened. Nothing. The dog did not bark, if you will excuse me.'

'Then . . . ?'

'As I said, all the evidence is in front of you. From the age of ten, a boy sleeps in the same locked room as his father. Through the age of puberty and into early manhood, night after night after night. His brother leaves home – and what happens? Does he inherit his brother's bedroom? No, this extraordinary arrangement continues. He is a solitary boy, and then a solitary young man, with a grotesque appearance. He is never seen in the company of the opposite sex. Yet he has, we may presume, normal urges and appetites. And if, despite your scepticism, we believe the evidence of his exophthalmus, he was prey to urges and appetites stronger than customary. We are men, Doyle, who understand this side of things. We are familiar with the perils of adolescence and young manhood. How the choice often lies between carnal self-indulgence which leads to moral and physical enfeeblement, even to criminal behaviour, and a healthy diversion from base urges into manly sporting activities. Edalji, by his circumstances, was happily prevented from taking the former path, and chose not to divert himself with the latter. And while I admit that boxing would hardly have been his forte, there were, for instance, gymnastics, and physical culture, and the new American science of body-building.'

'Are you suggesting that on the night of the outrage there was . . . some sexual purpose or manifestation?'

'Not directly, no. But you are asking me what I believe happened and why.

Let us admit, for the moment, much of what you claim about the young man. He was a good student, a son who honoured his parents, who prayed in his father's church, who did not smoke or drink, who worked hard at his practice. And yet you in return must accept the likelihood of another side to him. How could there not be, given the peculiarity of his breeding, his intense isolation and confinement, his excessive urges? By day he is a diligent member of society. And then by night, every so often, he yields to something barbaric, something buried deep within his dark soul, something even he probably does not understand.'

'It's pure speculation,' said Doyle, though there was something about his voice – something quieter and less confident – that struck Anson.

'You instructed me to speculate. You will admit that I have seen more examples of criminal behaviour and criminal purpose than you. I speculate on that basis. You have insisted on the fact that Edalji is of the professional class. How often, you implicitly asked, did the professional classes commit crimes? More often than you would believe, was my answer. However, I would return the question to you in a different form, Sir Arthur. How often do you find happily married men, whose happiness naturally involves regular sexual fulfilment, committing crimes of a violent and perverted nature? Do we believe that Jack the Ripper was a happily married man?

'No, we do not. I would go further. I would suggest that if a normal healthy man is continually deprived of sexual fulfilment, for whatever reason and under whatever circumstances, it may – I only say may, I put it no stronger – it may begin to affect the cast of his mind. I think this is what happened with Edalji. He felt himself in a terrible cage surrounded by iron bars. When would he ever escape? When would he ever achieve any kind of sexual fulfilment? In my view, a continuous period of sexual frustration, year after year after year, can start to turn a man's mind, Doyle. He can end up worshipping strange gods, and performing strange rites.'

There was no reply from his famous guest. Indeed, Doyle seemed quite puce in the face. Perhaps it was the effect of the brandy. Perhaps for all his worldly airs the man was a prude. Or perhaps – and this seemed the most likely – he saw the overwhelming force of the argument ranged against him. In any case, his eyes were trained on the ashtray as he crushed out the perfectly smokeable length of a very decent cigar. Anson waited, but his guest had now transferred his gaze to the fire, unwilling or unable to reply. Well, that seemed to be the end of that. Time to move to more practical matters.

'I trust you sleep soundly tonight, Doyle. But be warned that some believe Green Hall to be haunted.'

'Really,' came the reply. But Anson could tell Doyle's mind was far away.

'There is supposedly a headless horseman. Also the crunching of coach wheels in the gravel of the drive, and yet no coach. Also the ringing of mysterious bells, and yet no bells have ever been found. Tommyrot, of course, sheer tommyrot.' Anson found himself feeling positively blithe. 'But I doubt you are susceptible to phantoms and zombies and poltergeists.'

'The spirits of the dead do not trouble me,' said Doyle in a flat, tired voice. 'Indeed, I welcome them.'

'Breakfast is at eight, if that suits you.'

As Doyle retired in what Anson took to be defeat, the Chief Constable swept the cigar butts into the fire and watched them briefly flare. When he got to bed, Blanche was still awake, rereading Mrs Braddon. In the side dressing room her husband tossed his jacket across the clothes horse and shouted through to her, 'Sherlock Holmes baffled! Scotland Yard solves mystery!'

'George, don't bellow so.'

Captain Anson came tiptoeing through in his braided dressing gown with a vast grin on his face. 'I do not care if the Great Detective is crouching with his ear to the keyhole. I have taught him a thing or two about the real world tonight.'

Blanche Anson had rarely seen her husband so light-headed, and decided to confiscate the key to the tantalus for the rest of the week.

Arthur

Arthur's rage had been building since the moment the door of Green Hall closed behind him. The first leg of his journey back to Hindhead did little to alleviate it. The Walsall, Cannock & Rugeley line of the London & North Western Railway amounted to a constant series of provocations: from Stafford, where George was condemned, through Rugeley where he went to school, Hednesford where he supposedly threatened to shoot Sergeant Robinson in the head, Cannock where those fools of magistrates committed him, Wyrley & Churchbridge where it all began, then past fields grazed by what could be Blewitt's livestock, via Walsall where the source of the conspiracy must surely be found, to Birmingham where George had been arrested. Each station on the line had its message, and it was the same message, written by Anson: I and my kind own the land around here, and the people, and the justice.

Jean has never seen Arthur in such a temper. It is mid-afternoon, and he bangs the tea service around as he tells his story.

'And do you know what else he said? He dared to assert that it would do my reputation no good if my . . . my amateur speculations were to be broad-

cast. I have not been treated with such condescension since I was an impe-
cunious doctor in Southsea attempting to persuade a rich patient that he was
entirely healthy when he insisted on being at death's door.'

'And what did you do? In Southsea, I mean.'

'What did I do? I repeated that he was as fit as a fiddle, he replied that
he didn't pay a doctor to tell him that, so I told him to find a different specialist
who would diagnose whatever ailment he found it convenient to imagine.'

Jean laughs at the scene, her amusement tinged with a little regret that she
was not there, could never have been there. The future lies ahead of them,
it is true, but suddenly she minds not having had a little of the past as well.

'So what will you do?'

'I know exactly what I shall do. Anson thinks that I have prepared this
report with the intention of sending it to the Home Office, where it will
gather dust and be slightingly referred to in some internal review which may
finally see the light of day when we are all dead. I have no intention of
playing that game. I shall publish my findings as widely as it is possible to
do. I thought of it on the train. I shall offer my report to the *Daily Telegraph*,
who I daresay will be happy to print it. But I shall do more than that. I shall
ask them to head it "No Copyright", so that other papers – and especially
the Midland ones – may reproduce it *in extenso* and free of charge.'

'Wonderful. And so generous.'

'That's by the by. It's a matter of what's most effective. And furthermore,
I shall now make Captain Anson's position in the case, his prejudiced involvement from the very beginning, as clear as a bell. If he wants my *amateur speculations* on his activities, he shall have them. He shall have them in the libel
court if he wishes. And he may very well find that his professional future is
not as he imagines after I've finished with him.'

'Arthur, if I may . . .'

'Yes, my dear?'

'It might be advisable not to turn this into a personal vendetta against
Captain Anson.'

'I don't see why not. Much of the evil has its origins with him.'

'I mean, Arthur dear, that you must not let Captain Anson distract you
from your primary purpose. Because if he did, then Captain Anson would
be the first to be contented.'

Arthur looks at her with pride as well as pleasure. Not just a useful suggestion, but a damned intelligent one into the bargain.

'You are quite right. I shall not scourge Anson more than will serve George's
interests. But he shall not remain unscourged either. And I shall put him and
his entire police force to shame with the second part of my investigation.

Things are becoming clearer as to the culprit, and if I can demonstrate that he was under Anson's nose since the beginning of the affair, and that he did nothing about it, what course will be left to him but resignation? I shall have the Staffordshire Constabulary reorganized from end to end by the time I'm finished with this business. Full steam ahead!'

He notices Jean's smile, which seems to him both admiring and indulgent, a powerful combination.

'And talking of which, my darling, I really do think we should set a wedding date. Otherwise people might take you for an unconscionable flirt.'

'Me, Arthur? Me?'

He chuckles, and reaches for her hand. Full steam ahead, he thinks, otherwise the whole boiler room might just explode.

Back at Undershaw, Arthur took up his pen and settled Anson's hash. That letter to the Vicar – 'I trust to be able to obtain a dose of penal servitude for the offender' – had there ever been such a gross prejudging by a responsible official? Arthur felt his temper rising as he recopied the words; felt also the coolth of Jean's advice. He must do what was most effective for George; he must avoid libel; equally, he must make the verdict on Anson absolute. It had been a long time since he had been so condescended to. Well, Anson would find out what that felt like.

> Now, [he began] I have no doubt that Captain Anson was quite honest in his dislike of George Edalji, and unconscious of his own prejudice. It would be folly to think otherwise. But men in his position have no right to such feelings. They are too powerful, others are too weak, and the consequences are too terrible. As I trace the course of events, this dislike of their chief's filtered down until it came to imbue the whole force, and when they had George Edalji they did not give him the most elementary justice.

Before the case, during it, but also afterwards: Anson's arrogance had been as boundless as his prejudice.

> I do not know what subsequent reports from Captain Anson prevented justice being done at the Home Office, but this I do know, that instead of leaving the fallen man alone, every possible effort was made after the conviction to blacken his character, and that of his father, so as to frighten off anyone who might be inclined to investigate the case. When Mr Yelverton first took it up, he had a letter over Captain Anson's signature, saying,

under date Nov. 8, 1903: 'It is right to tell you that you will find it a simple waste of time to attempt to prove that George Edalji could not, owing to his position and alleged good character, have been guilty of writing offensive and abominable letters. His father is as well aware as I am of his proclivities in the direction of anonymous writing, and several other people have personal knowledge on the same subject.'

Now, both Edalji and his father declare on oath that the former never wrote an anonymous letter in his life, and on being applied to by Mr Yelverton for the names of the 'several other people' no answer was received. Consider that this letter was written immediately after the conviction, and that it was intended to nip in the bud the movement in the direction of mercy. It is certainly a little like kicking a man when he is down.

If that doesn't dish Anson, Arthur thought, nothing will. He imagined newspaper editorials, questions in Parliament, a mealy-mouthed statement from the Home Office, and perhaps a lengthy foreign tour before some comfortable yet distant billet was found for the former Chief Constable. The West Indies might be the place. It would be a sadness for Mrs Anson, whom Arthur had found a spirited table-companion. But she would doubtless survive her husband's rightful humiliation better than George's mother had been able to withstand her son's wrongful humiliation.

The *Daily Telegraph* published Arthur's findings over two days, the 11th and 12th of January. The newspaper laid it out well, and the compositors were on their best behaviour. Arthur read his words through again, all the way to their thundering conclusion:

> The door is shut in our faces. Now we turn to the last tribunal of all, a tribunal which never errs when the facts are fairly laid before them, and we ask the public of Great Britain whether this thing is to go on.

The response to the articles was tremendous. Soon the telegram boy could have found his way to Undershaw blindfold. There was support from Barrie, Meredith, and others in the writing profession. The correspondence page of the *Telegraph* was filled with debate about George's eyesight and the defence's dereliction in failing to introduce it. George's mother added her own testimony:

I always spoke to the solicitor employed for the defence of the extreme short sight of my son, which has been from a child. I considered that sufficient proof at once, if there had been no other, that he could not have gone to the field, with a so-called 'road' impossible even to people with good sight, at night. I felt this so much that I was distressed that no opportunity was given me when giving evidence to speak on his defective sight. The time allowed me was very short, and I suppose people were tired of the case . . . My son's sight was always so defective that he bent very close to the paper in writing, and held a book or paper very close to his eyes, and when out walking he did not recognize people easily. When I met him anywhere I always felt I must look for him, not he for me.

Other letters demanded a search for Elizabeth Foster, anatomized the character of Colonel Anson, and dilated upon the prevalence of gangs in Staffordshire. One correspondent explained how easily horse hairs might work themselves loose from inside the lining of a coat. There were letters from one of George's fellow passengers on the Wyrley train, from Onlooker of Hampstead NW and from A Friend to Parsees. Mr Aroon Chunder Dutt MD (Cantab.) wished to point out that cattle maiming was a crime entirely foreign to the Eastern nature. Chowry Muthu MD of New Cavendish Street reminded readers that all India was watching the case, and that the name and honour of England were at stake.

Three days after the second *Telegraph* article appeared, Arthur and Mr Yelverton were received at the Home Office by Mr Gladstone, Sir Mackenzie Chambers and Mr Blackwell. It was agreed that the proceedings should be considered private. The conversation lasted an hour. Afterwards, Sir A. Conan Doyle stated that he and Mr Yelverton had met with a *courteous and sympathetic reception*, and that he was *confident* the Home Office would do all it could to clear the matter up.

The waiving of copyright helped spread the story not just to the Midlands, but across the world. Arthur's cuttings agency was overburdened, and he grew used to the repeated headline, which taught him the same verb in many different languages: SHERLOCK HOLMES INVESTIGATES. Expressions of support – and occasional dissent – arrived by every post. Fantastical solutions to the case were proposed: for instance, that the persecution of the Edaljis had been conducted by other Parsees as punishment for Shapurji's apostasy. And of course there was another letter in a handwriting which had now become very familiar:

> I know from a detective of Scotland Yard that if you write to
> Gladstone and say you find Edalji is guilty after all they will
> make you a lord next year. Is it not better to be a lord than to
> run the risk of losing kidneys and liver. Think of all the
> ghoolish murders that are committed why then should you
> escape?

Arthur noted the spelling mistake, judged that he had got his man on the run, and flipped the page:

> The proof of what I tell you is in the writing he put in the
> papers when they loosed him out of prison where he ought to
> have been kept along with his dad and all the black and
> yellow-faced Jews. Nobody could copy his writing like that,
> you blind fool.

Such crude provocation merely confirmed the need to push forward on all fronts. There must be no slackening of effort. Mr Mitchell wrote to confirm that Milton had indeed been on the syllabus at Walsall School during the period that interested Sir Arthur; though begged to add that the great poet had been taught in the schools of Staffordshire for as long as the oldest master could recall, and indeed was still being taught. Harry Charlesworth reported that he had traced Fred Wynn, once the schoolfellow of the Brookes boy, now a house painter of Cheslyn Bay, and would ask him about Speck. Three days later a telegram with an agreed formula arrived: INVITED DINNER HEDNES-FORD TUESDAY CHARLESWORTH STOP.

Harry Charlesworth met Sir Arthur and Mr Wood at Hednesford station and walked them to the Rising Sun public house. In the saloon bar they were introduced to a lanky young man with a celluloid collar and frayed cuffs. There were some whitish stains on one sleeve of his jacket, which Arthur thought unlikely to be either horse's saliva or even bread and milk.

'Tell them what you told me,' said Harry.

Wynn looked at the strangers slowly and tapped his glass. Arthur sent Wood off for the necessary encouragement to their informant's voice box.

'I was at school with Speck,' he began. 'He was always at the bottom of the class. Always in trouble. Set a rick on fire one summer. Liked to chew tobacco. One evening I was on the train with Brookes when Speck came running into the same compartment, straight to the end of the carriage and stuck his head through the window smashing it to bits. Just started laughing at what he'd done. Then we all moved to another carriage.

'A couple of days later some railway police arrived and said we are to be charged with breaking the window. We both said Speck did it, so he had to pay for it, and they caught him cutting the straps of the window as well, and he had to pay for that too. Then Brookes's Pa started getting letters saying Brookes and me had been spitting on an old lady at Walsall Station. He was always in mischief, Speck. Then the school had him taken away. I don't recall he was exactly expelled, but as good as.'

'And what became of him?' asked Arthur.

'A year or two later I heard he'd been sent to sea.'

'To sea? You're sure? Absolutely sure?'

'Well, that's what they said. Anyway, he disappeared.'

'When would this have been?'

'As I say, a year or two later. He probably fired the rick in about '92, I'd say.

'So he would have gone to sea at the end of '95, beginning of '96?'

'That I couldn't say.'

'Roughly?'

'I couldn't say nearer than I've said already.'

'Do you remember which port he departed from?'

Wynn shook his head.

'Or when he returned? If he did return?'

Wynn shook his head again. 'Charlesworth said you'd be interested.' He tapped his glass once more. This time Arthur ignored the gesture.

'I am interested, Mr Wynn, but you'll forgive me if I say there's a problem with your story.'

'Is there just?'

'You went to Walsall School?'

'Yes.'

'And so did Brookes?'

'Yes.'

'And so did Speck?'

'Yes.'

'Then how do you account for the fact that Mr Mitchell, the current Headmaster, assures me that there has been no boy of that name at the school in the past twenty years?'

'Oh, I see,' said Wynn. 'Speck was just what we called him. He was a little fellow, like a speck. That's probably why. No, his real name was Sharp.'

'Sharp?'

'Royden Sharp.'

Arthur picked up Mr Wynn's glass and handed it to his secretary. Anything with that, Mr Wynn? A chaser of whisky, perhaps?'

'Now that would be very noble of you, Sir Arthur. Very noble. And I was wondering if in return I might request a favour of you.' He reached down to a small haversack, and Arthur left the Rising Sun with half a dozen narrative sketches of local life – 'I thought of calling them "Vignettes"' – on whose literary merit he had promised to adjudicate.

'Royden Sharp. Now that's a new name in the case. How would we set about tracing him? Any ideas, Harry?'

'Oh yes,' said Harry. 'I didn't want to mention it in front of Wynn in case he drank the house dry. I can give you a lead on him. He used to be the ward of Mr Greatorex.'

'Greatorex!'

'There were two Sharp brothers, Wallie and Royden. One of them was at school with George and me, though I can't remember which at this distance. But Mr Greatorex can tell you about them.'

They took the train two stops back up the line to Wyrley & Churchbridge, then walked to Littleworth Farm. Mr and Mrs Greatorex were a comfortable, easy couple in late middle age, hospitable and direct. For once, Arthur felt, it would not be a matter of beer and bootscrapers, of calculating whether the correct price of information was two shillings and threepence or two shillings and fourpence.

'Wallie and Royden Sharp were the sons of my tenant farmer Peter Sharp,' Mr Greatorex began. 'They were rather wild boys. No, that's perhaps unfair. Royden was a wild boy. I remember his father once had to pay for a rick he set on fire. Wallie was more strange than wild.

'Royden was expelled from school – from Walsall. Both boys went there. Royden was idle and destructive, I gathered, though I never had the full story. Peter sent him next to Wisbech School, but that didn't take any better. So he had him apprenticed to a butcher, by the name of Meldon I think, in Cannock. Then, towards the end of '93, I became involved. The boys' father was dying, and he asked me if I would become Royden's trustee. It was the least I could do, and naturally I made what promises I could to Peter. I did my best, but Royden was simply uncontrollable. Nothing but trouble. Thieving, smashing things, lying constantly . . . wouldn't stick at any job. In the end I said he had two choices. Either I would stop his allowance and report him to the police, or he could go to sea.'

'We are aware of which alternative he chose.'

'So I got him a passage as an apprentice on the *General Roberts*, belonging to Lewis Davies & Co.'

'This would be when?'

'At the end of 1895. The very end. I think she sailed on the 30th of December.'

'And from which port, Mr Greatorex?' Arthur knew the answer already, but still leaned forward in anticipation.

'Liverpool.'

'And how long did he stay with the *General Roberts*?'

'Well, for once he stuck at something. He finished his apprenticeship about four years later, and got a third mate's certificate. Then he came home.'

'Does that take us to 1903?'

'No, no. Earlier. '01, I'm sure. But he was only home briefly, Then he got a billet on a cattle boat between Liverpool and America. He served ten months on it. And after that he came home permanently. That would have been in '03.'

'A cattle ship, indeed. And where is he now?'

'In the same house his father had. But he's much changed. He's married, for a start.'

'Did you ever suspect him or his brothers of writing the letters in your son's name?'

'No.'

'Why not?'

'There were no grounds. And I would have judged him too idle, and perhaps not imaginative enough.'

'And – let me guess – did they have a younger brother – perhaps a rather foul-mouthed boy, I would guess?'

'No, no. There were just the two of them.'

'Or a young companion of that kind, who was often with them?'

'No. Not at all.'

'I see. And did Royden Sharp resent your trusteeship?'

'Frequently, yes. He didn't understand why I refused to hand over all the money his father had left him. Not that there was much. A fact which made me all the more determined not to let him squander it.'

'The other boy – Wallie – he was the elder?'

'Yes, he'd be about thirty now.'

'So that's the one you were at school with, Harry?' Charlesworth nodded. 'You said he was strange. In what way?'

'Strange. Not quite of this world. I can't be more precise.'

'Any signs of religious mania?'

'Not that I was aware of. He was clever, Wallie. Brainy.'

'Did he study Milton at Walsall School?'

'Not that I was aware of.'

'And after school?'

'He was apprenticed to an electrical engineer for a while.'

'Which would permit him to travel to the neighbouring towns?'

Mr Greatorex looked puzzled by the question. 'Certainly. Like many another man.'

'And . . . do the brothers still live together?'

'No, Wallie left the country a year or two back.'

'Where did he go?'

'South Africa.'

Arthur turned to his secretary. 'Why is everyone going to South Africa all of a sudden? Would you have an address for him there, Mr Greatorex?'

'I might have done. Except that we heard he died. Recently. November last.'

'Ah. A pity. And the house where they lived together, where Royden still lives . . .'

'I can take you there.'

'No, not yet. My question is . . . is it isolated?'

'Fairly. Like many another house.'

'So that you could enter or leave without neighbours observing you?'

'Oh yes.'

'And it is easy of access to the country?'

'Indeed. It backs on to open fields. But so do many houses.'

'Sir Arthur.' It was the first time Mrs Greatorex had spoken. As he turned to her, he noticed that her colour had risen, and she was more agitated that when they arrived. 'You suspect him, don't you? Or both of them?'

'The evidence is accumulating, to say the least, ma'am.'

Arthur prepared himself for some loyal protestation from Mrs Greatorex, a refusal to countenance his suspicions and slanders.

'Then I had better tell you what I know. About three and a half years ago – it was in July, I remember, the July before they arrested George Edalji – I was passing the Sharps' house one afternoon and called in. Wallie was out but Royden was there. We started talking about the maimings – that's what everyone was talking about at the time. After a while Royden went over to a cupboard in the kitchen and showed me . . . an instrument. Held it in front of me. He said, "This is what they kill the cattle with." It made me feel sick just to look at it, so I told him to put it away. I said, "You don't want them to think you are the man, do you?" And then he put it back in the cupboard.'

'Why didn't you tell me?' asked her husband.

'I thought there were enough rumours flying around without wanting to add to them. And I just wanted to forget the whole incident.'

Arthur contained his reaction and asked neutrally, 'You didn't think of telling the police?'

'No. After I got over the shock I went for a walk and thought about it. And I decided Royden was just boasting. Pretending to know something. He would hardly show me the thing if he'd done it himself, would he? And then he's a lad I've known all my life. He'd been a bit wild, as my husband explained, but since he came back from sea he settled down. He'd got himself engaged and was planning to be married. Well, he is married now. But he was known to the police and I thought that if I went and told them, they'd just make out a case against him whatever the evidence was.'

Yes, thought Arthur; and because of your silence, they went and made a case out against George instead.

'I still don't understand why you didn't tell me,' said Mr Greatorex.

'Because – because you were always harder on the boy than me. And I knew you'd jump to conclusions.'

'Conclusions which would probably have been quite correct,' he replied with a certain tartness.

Arthur pushed on. They could have their marital disagreement later. 'Mrs Greatorex, what sort of an . . . instrument was it?'

'The blade was about so long.' She gestured: a foot or so, then. 'And it folded into a casing, like a giant pocket knife. It's not a farm instrument. But it was the blade that was the frightening thing. It had a curve in it.'

'You mean, like a scimitar? Or a sickle?'

'No, no, the blade itself was straight, and its edge wasn't sharp at all. But towards the end there was a part that curved outwards, which looked extremely sharp.'

'Could you draw it for us?'

'Certainly.' Mrs Greatorex pulled out a kitchen drawer, and on a piece of lined paper made a confident freehand outline:

'This is blunt, along here, and here as well, where it's straight. And there, where it curves, it's horribly sharp.'

Arthur looked at the others. Mr Greatorex and Harry shook their heads. Alfred Wood turned the drawing round so that it faced him and said, 'Two to one it's a horse lancet. Of the larger sort. I expect he stole it from the cattle ship.'

'You see,' said Mrs Greaterex, 'Your friend is jumping to conclusions immediately. Just as the police would have done.'

This time Arthur could not hold back. 'Whereas instead they jumped to conclusions about George Edalji.' Mrs Greatorex's high colour returned at this remark. 'And forgive my asking, ma'am, but did you not think of telling the police about the instrument later – at the time they charged George?'

'I thought about it, yes.'

'But did nothing.'

'Sir Arthur,' replied Mrs Greatorex, 'I do not recall your presence in the district at the time of the maimings. There was widespread hysteria. Rumours about this person and that person. Rumours about a Great Wyrley Gang. Rumours that they were going to move on from animals to young women. Talk about pagan sacrifices. It was all to do with the new moon, some said. Indeed, now I recall, Royden's wife once told me he reacted strangely to the new moon.'

'That's true,' said her husband ruminatively. 'I noticed it too. He used to laugh like a maniac when the moon was new. I thought at first he was just putting it on, but I caught him doing it when no one was about.'

'But don't you see –' Arthur began.

Mrs Greatorex cut him off. 'Laughing is not a crime. Even laughing like a maniac.'

'But didn't you think . . . ?'

'Sir Arthur, I have no great regard for the intelligence or the efficiency of the Staffordshire Constabulary. I think that is one thing we might be agreed upon. And if you are concerned about your young friend's wrongful imprisonment, then I was concerned about the same thing happening to Royden Sharp. It might not have ended with your friend escaping gaol, but rather with both of them behind bars for belonging to the same gang, whether it existed or not.'

Arthur decided to accept the rebuke. 'And what about the weapon? Did you tell him to destroy it?'

'Certainly not. We haven't mentioned it from that day to this.'

'Then may I ask you, Mrs Greatorex, to continue in that silence for a few days more? And a final question. Do the names Walker or Gladwin mean anything to you – in connection with the Sharps?'

The couple shook their heads.

'Harry?'

'I think I remember Gladwin. Worked for a drayman. Haven't seen him in years, though.'

Harry was told to await instructions, while Arthur and his secretary returned to Birmingham for the night. More convenient accommodation at Cannock had been proposed; but Arthur liked to be confident of a decent glass of burgundy at the end of a hard day's work. Over dinner at the Imperial Family Hotel, he suddenly remembered a phrase from one of the letters. He threw his knife and fork down with a clatter.

'When the ripper was boasting of how nobody could catch him. He wrote, "I am as sharp as sharp can be."'

'"As Sharp as Sharp can be",' repeated Wood.

'Exactly.'

'But who was the foul-mouthed boy?'

'I don't know.' Arthur was rather downcast that this particular intuition had not been confirmed. 'Perhaps a neighbour's boy. Or perhaps one of the Sharps invented him.'

'So what do we do now?'

'We continue.'

'But I thought we'd – you'd – solved it. Royden Sharp is the ripper. Royden Sharp and Wallie Sharp together wrote the letters.'

'I agree, Woodie. Now tell me why it was Royden Sharp.'

Wood answered, counting off his fingers as he did so. 'Because he showed the horse lancet to Mrs Greatorex. Because the wounds the animals suffered, cutting the skin and muscle but not penetrating the gut, could only have been inflicted by such an unusual instrument. Because he had worked as a butcher and also on a cattle ship, and therefore knew about handling animals and cutting them up. Because he could have stolen the lancet from the ship. Because the pattern of the letters and the slashings matches the pattern of his presence and absence from Wyrley. Because there are clear hints in the letters about his movements and activities. Because he has a record of mischief. Because he is affected by the new moon.'

'Excellent, Woodie, excellent. A full case, well presented, and dependent on inference and circumstantial evidence.'

'Oh,' said the secretary, disappointed. 'Have I missed something?'

'No, nothing. Royden Sharp is our man, there's not the slightest doubt about it in my mind. But we need more concrete proof. In particular, we need the horse lancet. We need to secure it. Sharp knows we're in the district, and if he's any sense it will already have been thrown into the deepest lake he knows.'

'And if it hasn't?'

'If it hasn't, then you and Harry Charlesworth are going to stumble across it and secure it.'

'Stumble?'

'Stumble.'

'And secure it?'

'Indeed.'

'Have you any suggestions about our modus operandi?'

'Frankly, I think it would be better if I didn't know too much. But I imagine that it is still the custom in these parts of the country for people to leave their doors unlocked. And if it turns out to be a matter of negotiation, then I would suggest that the sum involved appear in the accounts for Undershaw in whichever column you choose to put it.'

Wood was rather irritated by this high-mindedness. 'Sharp is hardly likely to hand it over if we knock on his door and say, Excuse us, may we please buy the lancet you ripped the animals with, so that we can show it to the police?'

'No, I agree,' said Arthur with a chuckle. 'That would never do. You will need to be more imaginative, the two of you. A little more subtlety. Or, for that matter, a little more directness. One of you might distract him, perhaps in a public house, while the other . . . She did mention a cupboard in the kitchen, did she not? But really, I must leave it to you.'

'You will stand bail for me if required?'

'I will even give you a character witness.'

Wood shook his head slowly. 'I still can't get over it. This time last night we knew almost nothing. Or rather, we had a few suspicions. Now we know everything. All in a day. Wynn, Greatorex, Mrs Greatorex – and that's it. We may not be able to prove it, but we know it. And all in a day.'

'It's not meant to happen like this,' said Arthur. 'I should know. I've written it enough times. It's not meant to happen by following simple steps. It's meant to seem utterly insoluble right up until the end. And then you unravel the knot with one glorious piece of deduction, something entirely logical yet quite astounding, and then you feel a great sense of triumph.'

'Which you don't?'

'Now? No, I feel almost disappointed. Indeed, I do feel disappointed.'

'Well,' said Wood, 'you must permit a simpler soul a sense of triumph.'

'Willingly.'

Later, when Arthur had smoked his final pipe and turned in, he lay in bed reflecting on this. He had set himself a challenge, and today he had overcome it; yet he felt no exultation. Pride, perhaps, and that certain warmth when you take a rest from labour, but not happiness, let alone triumph.

He remembered the day he had married Touie. He had loved her, of course, and in that early stage doted on her entirely and could not wait for the marriage's consummation. But when they wed, at Thornton-in-Lonsdale with that fellow Waller at his elbow, he had felt a sense of . . . how could he put it without being disrespectful to her memory? He was happy only insofar as she had looked happy. That was the truth. Of course, later, as little as a day or two later, he began to experience the happiness he had hoped for. But at the moment itself, much less than he had anticipated.

Perhaps this was why, at every turn in his life, he had always sought a new challenge. A new cause, a new campaign – because he was only capable of brief joy at the success of the previous one. At moments like this, he envied Woodie's simplicity; he envied those capable of resting on their laurels. But this had never been his way.

And so, what remained to be done now? The lancet must be secured. A specimen of Royden Sharp's handwriting must be obtained – perhaps from Mr and Mrs Greatorex. He must see if Walker and Gladwin had any further relevance. There was the matter of the woman and child who were attacked. Royden Sharp's scholastic career at Walsall must be investigated. He must try to match Wallie Sharp's movements more specifically to places from which letters had been posted. He must show the horse lancet, once secured, to veterinary surgeons who had attended the injured animals, and ask for their professional evaluation. He must ask George what, if anything, he remembered of the Sharps.

He must write to the Mam. He must write to Jean.

Now that his head was full of tasks, he descended into untroubled sleep.

Back at Undershaw, Arthur felt as he did when nearing the end of a book: most of it was in place, the main thrill of creation was past, now it was just a matter of work, of making the thing as watertight as possible. Over the next days the results of his instructions, queries and proddings began to arrive. The first came in the form of a waxed brown-paper parcel tied with string, like a purchase from Brookes's ironmongery. But he knew what it was before he opened it; he knew from Wood's face.

He unwrapped the parcel, and slowly opened the horse lancet out to its full length. It was a vicious instrument, made the more so by the contrast between the bluntness of the straight section and the honed edge on the lethal curve – which was indeed as sharp as sharp could be.

'Bestial,' said Arthur. 'May I ask –'

But his secretary cut off the enquiry with a shake of the head. Sir Arthur couldn't have it both ways, first not knowing and then choosing to know.

George Edalji wrote to say that he had no memory of the Sharp brothers, either at school or subsequently; nor could he think of a reason why they might bear any animus against himself or his father.

More satisfactory was a letter from Mr Mitchell detailing Royden Sharp's scholastic record:

Xmas, 1890.	Lower 1. Order, 23rd out of 23. Very backward and weak. French and Latin not attempted.
Easter, 1891.	Lower 1. Order, 20th out of 20. Dull, homework neglected, begins to improve in Drawing.
Midsummer, 1891.	Lower 1. Order, 18th out of 18. Beginning to progress, caned for misbehaviour in class, tobacco chewing, prevarication, and nicknaming.
Xmas, 1891.	Lower 1. Order, 16th out of 16. Unsatisfactory, often untruthful. Always complaining or being complained of. Detected cheating, and frequently absent without leave. Drawing improved.
Easter, 1892.	Form 1. Order, 8th out of 8. Idle and mischievous, caned daily, wrote to father, falsified school-fellows' marks, and lied deliberately about it. Caned 20 times this term.
Midsummer, 1892.	Played truant, forged letters and initials, removed by his father.

There we are, thought Arthur: forging, cheating, lying, nicknaming, general mischief. And further, note the date of the expulsion or removal, whichever you prefer: Midsummer 1892. That was when the campaign had begun, against the Edaljis, against Brookes and against Walsall School. Arthur felt his irritation rising – that he could find such things out by a normal process of logical inquiry, whereas those dunderheads . . . He would like to set the Staffordshire Constabulary up against a wall, from the Chief Constable and Superintendent Barrett through Inspector Campbell and Sergeants Parsons and Upton down to the humblest novice in the force, and ask them a simple question. In December 1892 a large key belonging to Walsall School was stolen from the premises and transported to Great Wyrley. Who might be the more plausible suspect: a boy who a few months previously had been ignominiously removed from the school after a career there of stupidity and malice; or the studious and academically promising son of a Vicar, who had never attended Walsall School, never visited its premises, and bore no more grudge against the establishment than did the Man in the Moon? Answer me that, Chief Constable, Superintendent, Inspector, Sergeant and PC Cooper. Answer me that, you twelve good men and true at the Court of Quarter Sessions.

Harry Charlesworth sent an account of an incident which had taken place in Great Wyrley in the late autumn or early winter of 1903. Mrs Jarius Handley was coming from Wyrley Station one evening, having gone there to buy some papers for sale. She was accompanied by her young daughter. They were accosted in the road by two men. One of them caught the girl by the throat, and held something in his hand which gleamed. Both mother and child screamed, whereupon the man ran away, crying to his comrade who had gone on, 'All right, Jack, I am coming.' The girl declared that her mother had been stopped once before by the same man. He was described as having a round face, no moustache, about 5ft 8ins in height, a dark suit, a shiny peaked cap. This description fitted that of Royden Sharp, who at the time wore a sailor-like costume, which he had subsequently abandoned. It was further suggested that 'Jack' was Jack Hart, a dissolute butcher and known companion of Sharp's. The police had been informed, but there was no arrest made in the case.

Harry added in a post-scriptum that Fred Wynn had been in touch with him again and that in exchange for a pint of stout recalled something which had previously escaped him. When he and Brookes and Speck had all attended Walsall School, one thing generally known about Royden Sharp was that he could not be left in a railway carriage without turning up the cushion and slitting it on the underside with a knife, so as to let the horsehair out. Then he would laugh wildly and turn the cushion back again.

On Friday March 1st, after a six-week delay intended perhaps to show that the Home Secretary was not responding to pressure from any one known source, a Committee of Inquiry was announced. Its purpose was to consider various matters in the Edalji Case which had given rise to public disquiet. The Home Office wished to emphasize, however, that the Committee's deliberations in no wise amounted to a re-trial of the case. Witnesses would not be called, nor would Mr Edalji's presence be required. The Committee would examine such materials as were in the possession of the Home Office and adjudicate on certain procedural matters. Sir Arthur Wilson KCIE, the Right Hon. John Lloyd Wharton, Chairman of the Quarter Sessions for the County of Durham, and Sir Albert de Rutzen, the Chief Magistrate in London, would report to Mr Gladstone as speedily as possible.

Arthur decided that these gentlemen should not be left to jaw at one another complacently about 'certain procedural matters'. To his reworked *Telegraph* articles – which would themselves prove George's innocence – he would append a private memorandum setting out the case against Royden Sharp. He would describe his investigation, summarize his evidence, and list those from whom further testimony might be obtained: specifically the butcher Jack Hart of Bridgetown, and Harry Green, now of South Africa. Also Mrs Royden Sharp, who could confirm the effect of the new moon upon her husband.

He would send George a copy of the memorandum, inviting his comments. He would also keep Anson on the hop. Every so often, as he remembered that long wrangle over brandy and cigars, an unstoppable growl would rise in his throat. Their exchange had been noisy but largely futile – like that of two Scandinavian elks locking antlers in the forest. Even so, he had been shocked by the complacency and prejudice of a man who ought to have known better. And then, at the last, for Anson to try scaring him with stories of ghosts. How very little the Chief Constable knew his man. In his study, Arthur took out the horse lancet, opened it up and drew round the blade's outline on a sheet of tracing paper. He would send the drawing – marked 'life size' – to the Chief Constable, asking for his views.

'Well, you have your Committee,' said Wood, as they pulled their cues from the rack that evening.

'I would rather say that *they* have *their* Committee.'

'By which you indicate that you are less than satisfied?'

'I have some hope that even these gentlemen cannot fail to acknowledge what is staring them in the face.'

'But?'

'But – you know who Albert de Rutzen is?'

'The Chief Magistrate of London, my newspaper informs me.'

'He is that, he is that. He is also the cousin of Captain Anson.'

George & Arthur

George had read the *Telegraph* articles several times before writing to thank Sir Arthur; and he read them once again before their second meeting at the Grand Hotel, Charing Cross. It was most disconcerting to see oneself described not by some provincial penny-a-liner but by the most famous writer of the day. It made him feel like several overlapping people at the same time: a victim seeking redress; a solicitor facing the highest tribunal in the country; and a character in a novel.

Here was Sir Arthur explaining why he, George, could not possibly have been involved with the supposed band of Wyrley ruffians: 'In the first place, he is a total abstainer, which in itself hardly seems to commend him to such a gang. He does not smoke. He is very shy and nervous. He is a most distinguished student.' This was all true, and yet untrue; flattering, yet unflattering; believable, yet unbelievable. He was not a *most* distinguished student; merely a good, hard-working one. He had received second-class honours, not first, the bronze medal, not silver or gold, from the Birmingham Law Society. He was certainly a capable solicitor, more so than Greenway or Stentson were likely to become, but he would never be eminent. Equally, he was not, by his own estimation, *very* shy. And if he had been judged nervous on the basis of that previous meeting at the hotel, then there were mitigating circumstances. He had been sitting in the foyer reading his newspaper, beginning to worry if he were mistaken about the time or even the day, when he had become aware of a large, overcoated figure standing a few yards away and scrutinizing him intently. How would anyone else react to being stared at by a great novelist? George thought this estimation of him as shy and nervous had probably been confirmed, if not propagated, by his parents. He did not know how it was in other families, but at the Vicarage the parental view of children had not evolved at the same speed as the children themselves. George was not just thinking of himself; his parents did not seem to take account of Maud's development, of how she was becoming stronger and more capable. And now that he came to reflect upon it further, he didn't believe he *had* been so nervous with Sir Arthur. On an occasion far more likely to provoke nerves *he faced the crowded court with perfect composure* – wasn't that what the Birmingham *Daily Post* had written?

He did not smoke. This was true. He judged it a pointless, unpleasant and costly habit. But also one unconnected with criminal behaviour. Sherlock Holmes famously smoked a pipe – and Sir Arthur, he understood, did likewise – but this did not make either of them candidates for membership of a gang. It was also true that he was a total abstainer: the consequence of his upbringing, not of some principled act of renunciation. But he acknowledged that any juryman, or any committee, might interpret the fact in more than one way. Abstention could be taken as proof either of moderation or extremity. It might be a sign of a fellow able to control his human urges; or equally of someone who resisted vice in order to concentrate his mind on other, more essential things – someone a touch inhuman, even fanatical.

He in no way minimized the value and quality of Sir Arthur's work. The articles described with rare skill *a chain of circumstances which seem so extraordinary that they are far beyond the invention of the writer of fiction*. George had read and reread with pride and gratitude such declarations as *Until each and all of these questions is settled a dark stain will remain upon the administrative annals of this country*. Sir Arthur had promised to make a noise, and the noise he had made had echoed far beyond Staffordshire, far beyond London, far beyond England itself. Without Sir Arthur shaking the trees, as he had put it, the Home Office would almost certainly not have appointed a Committee; though how the Committee itself would respond to the noise and the tree-shaking was another matter. It seemed to George that Sir Arthur had gone very hard on the Home Office's handling of Mr Yelverton's memorial, when he wrote that he *cannot imagine anything more absurd and unjust in an Oriental despotism*. To denounce someone as despotic might not be the best way to persuade them to be less despotic in the future. And then there was the Statement of the Case against Royden Sharp . . .

'George! I'm so sorry. We were detained.'

He is standing there, and not alone. There is a handsome young woman beside him; she looks dashing and self-confident in a shade of green George could not possibly name. The sort of colour women knew about. She is smiling a little and extending her hand.

'This is Miss Jean Leckie. We were . . . shopping.' He sounds uneasy.

'No, Arthur, you were talking.' Her tone is affable yet firm.

'Well, I was talking to a shopkeeper. He had done service in South Africa, and it was only civil to ask him –'

'That is still talking, not shopping.'

George is bewildered by this exchange.

'As you can see, George, we are preparing for marriage.'

'I am very happy to meet you,' says Miss Jean Leckie, smiling more widely, so that George notices she has rather large front teeth. 'And now I must go.' She shakes her head teasingly at Arthur and skips away.

'Marriage,' says Arthur as he sinks into a chair in the writing room. The word barely amounts to a question. Even so, George answers – and with a strange precision.

'It is a condition that I aspire to.'

'Well, it can be a puzzling condition, I warn you. Bliss, of course. But damned puzzling bliss more often than not.'

George nods. He does not agree, while admitting he has little evidence to go on. Certainly he would not describe his parents' marriage as damned puzzling bliss. None of those three words could in any way be reasonably applied to life at the Vicarage.

'To business, anyway.'

They discuss the *Telegraph* articles, the response they have elicited, the

Gladstone Committee, its terms of reference and membership. Arthur wonders if he personally should expose Sir Albert de Rutzen's cousinage, or drop a hint to a newspaper editor at his club, or simply leave the whole matter alone. He looks across at George, expecting an instant opinion. But George does not have an instant opinion. This may be because he is *very shy and nervous*; or because he is a solicitor; or because he finds it difficult to switch from being Sir Arthur's cause to Sir Arthur's tactical adviser.

'I think Mr Yelverton is perhaps the person to consult on that.'

'But I am consulting *you*,' replies Arthur, as if George is shilly-shallying.

George's opinion, as far as he can call it one when it feels no more than an instinct, is that the first option would be too provoking, the third too passive, and so on the whole he might be inclined to advise the middle course. Unless, of course . . . and as he is starting to reconsider, he is aware of Sir Arthur's impatience. This does, admittedly, make him a little nervous.

'I will make one prediction, George. They will not be straightforward about the Committee's report.'

George wonders if Arthur still requires his view of the previous matter. He assumes not. 'But they must publish it.'

'Oh, they must, and they will. But I know how governments operate, especially when they have been embarrassed or shamed. They will hide it away somehow. They will bury it if they can.'

'How could they do that?'

'Well, for a start they could publish it on a Friday afternoon, when people have left for the weekend. Or during the recess. There are all sorts of tricks.'

'But if it is a good report, it will reflect well upon them.'

'It can't be a good report,' says Arthur firmly. 'Not from their point of view. If they confirm your innocence, as they must, it means that the Home Office has for the past three years knowingly obstructed justice despite all the information laid before it. And in the extremely unlikely – I would say impossible – case of them finding you still guilty – which is the only other option – there will be such an almighty stink that careers will be at stake.'

'Yes, I see.'

They have now been talking for half an hour or so, and Arthur is puzzled that George has made no reference at all to his Statement of the Case against Royden Sharp. No, more than puzzled; irritated, on the way to being insulted. It half crosses his mind to ask George about that begging letter he was shown at Green Hall. But no, that would be playing Anson's game for him. Perhaps George just assumes it is up to the host to set the agenda. That must be it.

'So,' he says. 'Royden Sharp.'

'Yes,' replies George. 'I never knew him, as I said when I wrote to you.

It must have been his brother I was at school with when I was little. Though I have no memory of him either.'

Arthur nods. Come on, man, is what he thinks. I have not just exonerated you, I have produced the criminal bound hand and foot for arrest and trial. Is this not, at the very least, news to you? Against all his temperament, he waits.

'I am surprised,' George finally says. 'Why should he wish to harm me?'

Arthur does not reply. He has already offered his replies. He thinks it is time George did some work on his own behalf.

'I am aware that you consider race prejudice to be a factor in the case, Sir Arthur. But as I have already said, I cannot agree. Sharp and I do not know one another. To dislike someone you have to know them. And then you find the reason for disliking them. And then, perhaps, if you cannot find a satisfactory reason, you blame your dislike on some oddity of theirs, such as the colour of their skin. But as I say, Sharp does not know me. I have been trying to think of some action of mine that he might have taken as a slight or an injury. Perhaps he is related to someone to whom I gave professional advice . . .' Arthur does not comment; he thinks that you can only point out the obvious so many times. 'And I do not understand why he should wish to maim cattle and horses in this way. Or why anyone should. Do you, Sir Arthur?'

'As I said in my Statement,' replies Arthur, who is getting more dissatisfied by the minute, 'I suspect that he was strangely affected by the new moon.'

'Possibly,' replies George. 'Though not all the cases took place at the same point on the lunar cycle.'

'That is correct. But most did.'

'Yes.'

'So might you not reasonably conclude that those extraneous mutilations were performed in order deliberately to mislead investigators?'

'Yes, you might.'

'Mr Edalji, I do not appear to have convinced you.'

'Forgive me, Sir Arthur, it is not that I am, or wish to seem, in any way, less than immensely grateful to you. It is, perhaps, that I am a solicitor.'

'True.' Maybe he is being too hard on the fellow. But it is strange: as if he has brought him a bag of gold from the farthest ends of the earth, and received the reply, But frankly, I would have preferred silver.

'The instrument,' says George. 'The horse lancet.'

'Yes?'

'May I ask how you know what it looks like?'

'Indeed. By two methods. First, I asked Mrs Greatorex to draw it for me.

Whereupon Mr Wood recognized it as a horse lancet. And secondly –' Arthur leaves a pause for effect, 'I have it in my possession.'

'You have it?'

Arthur nods. 'I could show you it if you like.' George looks alarmed. 'Not here. Don't worry, I haven't brought it with me. It's at Undershaw.'

'May I ask how you obtained it?'

Arthur rubs a finger up the side of his nose. Then he relents. 'Wood and Harry Charlesworth stumbled upon it.'

'Stumbled?'

'It was clear that the weapon had to be secured before Sharp could dispose of it. He knew I was in the district and on his trail. He even started sending me the sort of letters he used to send you. Threatening me with the removal of vital organs. If he had two cerebral hemispheres to rub together, he'd have buried the instrument where no one would find it for a hundred years. So I instructed Wood and Harry to stumble across it.'

'I see.' George feels as he does when a client begins confidentially telling him things no client should ever tell a solicitor, not even his own – especially not his own. 'And have you interviewed Sharp?'

'No. I think that's plain from my Statement.'

'Yes, of course. Forgive me.'

'So, unless you have any objection, I shall include my Statement against Sharp with my other submissions to the Home Office.'

'Sir Arthur, I cannot possibly express the gratitude I feel –'

'I do not want you to. I did not do it for your blasted gratitude, which you have already sufficiently expressed. I did it because you are innocent, and I am ashamed of the way the judicial and bureaucratic machinery of this country operates.'

'Nevertheless, no one else could have done what you have done. And in so comparatively short a time as well.'

He is as good as saying I botched it, thinks Arthur. No, don't be absurd – it's merely that he's far more interested in his own vindication, and in making absolutely sure of that, than in Sharp's prosecution. Which is perfectly understandable. Finish item one before proceeding to item two – what else would you expect of a cautious lawyer? Whereas I attack on all fronts simultaneously. He's just worrying that I might take my eye off the ball.

But later, when they had parted and Arthur sat in a cab on the way to Jean's flat, he began to wonder. What was that dictum? People will forgive you anything except the help you give them? Something like that. And maybe such a response was exaggerated in a case like this. When he had read up about Dreyfus it had struck him that many of those who came to help the

Frenchman, who worked for him out of a deep passion, who saw his case not just as a great battle between Truth and Lies, between Justice and Injustice, but as a matter which explained and even defined the country they lived in – that many of them were not at all impressed by Colonel Alfred Dreyfus. They had found him rather a dry stick, cold and correct, and not exactly flowing with the juices of gratitude and human sympathy. Someone had written that the victim was usually not up to the mystique of his own affair. That was a rather French thing to say, but not necessarily wide of the mark.

Or maybe that was just as unfair. When he had first met George Edalji, he had been impressed by how this rather frail and delicate young man could have withstood three years of penal servitude. In his surprise, he had doubt-less failed to appreciate what it must have cost George. Perhaps the only way to survive was to concentrate utterly, from dawn to dusk, on the minutiae of your own case, to have nothing else in your head, to have all the facts and arguments marshalled for whenever they might be needed. Only then could you survive monstrous injustice and the squalid reversal in your habits of living. So it might be expecting too much of George Edalji to expect him to react as a free man might. Until he was pardoned and compensated, he could not go back to being the man he had been before.

Save your irritation for others, thought Arthur. George is a good fellow, and an innocent man, but there is no point wishing sanctity upon him. Wanting more gratitude than he can offer is like wanting every reviewer to declare each new book of yours a work of genius. Yes, save your irritation for others. Captain Anson for a start, whose letter this morning contained a fresh piece of insolence: the blunt refusal to admit that the mutilations could have been caused by a horse lancet. And to cap it, the dismissive line, 'What you drew was an ordinary fleam.' Indeed! Arthur had not bothered George with this latest provocation.

And as well as Anson, he was finding himself irritated by Willie Hornung. His brother-in-law had a new joke, which Connie had passed on to him over lunch. 'What do Arthur Conan Doyle and George Edalji have in common?' No? Give up? "Sentences."' Arthur growled to himself. Sentences – he thought that witty? Objectively, Arthur could see that some might find it so. But really . . . Unless he was beginning to lose his sense of humour. They said it happened to people in middle age. No – poppycock. And now he was starting to irritate himself. Another trait of middle age, no doubt.

George, meanwhile, was still in the writing room at the Grand Hotel. He was in low spirits. He had been disgracefully impolite and ungrateful towards Sir Arthur. And after the months and months of work he had put into the case. George was ashamed of himself. He must write to apologize. And yet . . . and yet . . . it would have been dishonest to say more than he did. Or rather, if he had said more, he would have been obliged to be honest.

He had read the Statement of the Case against Royden Sharp that Arthur was sending to the Home Office. He had read it several times, naturally. And each time his impression had hardened. His conclusion – his inevitable, professional conclusion – was that it would not help his own position. Further, his judgement – which he would never have dared utter at their meeting – was that Sir Arthur's case against Sharp strangely resembled the Staffordshire Constabulary's case against himself.

It was based, to begin with, and in exactly the same way, upon the letters. Sir Reginald Hardy had said in his summing-up at Stafford that the person who wrote the letters must also have been the person who maimed the livestock. This connection was explicit, and rightly criticized by Mr Yelverton and those who had taken up his case. Yet here was Sir Arthur making exactly the same connection. The letters were his starting point, and through them he had traced Royden Sharp's hand, and his comings and goings, at every turn. The letters incriminated Sharp, just as they had previously incriminated George. And while it was now concluded that the letters had been deliberately written by Sharp and his brother to pull George into the affair, why could they not equally have been written by someone else to pull Sharp into the affair? If they had been false the first time, why should they be true the second?

Likewise, all Sir Arthur's evidence was circumstantial, and much of it hearsay. A woman and a child were assaulted by someone who might have been Royden Sharp, except that his name had not been raised at the time and no police action had been taken. A statement had been made to Mrs Greatorex three or more years ago, which she had not seen fit to pass on to anyone at the time, but which she now brought up when Royden Sharp's name was mentioned. She also remembered some hearsay – or a piece of washing line gossip – from Sharp's wife. Royden Sharp had an exceedingly poor scholastic record: yet if that were sufficient proof of criminal intent, the gaols would be full. Royden Sharp was supposed to be strangely influenced by the moon – except on those occasions when he was not. Further, Sharp lived in a house from which it was easy to escape unobserved at night: just like the Vicarage, and any number of other houses in the district.

And if this wasn't enough to make a solicitor's heart sink, there was worse, far worse. Sir Arthur's only piece of solid evidence was the horse lancet, which he had now taken possession of. And what exactly was the

304

legal value of such an item so obtained? A third party, namely Sir Arthur, had incited a fourth party, namely Mr Wood, to enter illegally the property of yet another party, Royden Sharp, and steal an item which he had then transported halfway across the kingdom. It was understandable that he had not handed it over to the Staffordshire Constabulary, but it could have been lodged with a proper legal official. A solicitor-at-law, for instance. Whereas Sir Arthur's actions had contaminated the evidence. Even the police knew that they had to obtain either a search warrant, or the express and un-ambiguous permission of the householder, before entering premises. George admitted that criminal law was not his speciality, but it seemed to him that Sir Arthur had incited an associate to commit burglary and in the process rendered valueless a vital piece of evidence. And he might even be lucky to escape a charge of conspiracy to commit theft.

This was where Sir Arthur's excess of enthusiasm had led him. And it was all, George decided, the fault of Sherlock Holmes. Sir Arthur had been too influenced by his own creation. Holmes performed his brilliant acts of deduc-tion and then handed villains over to the authorities with their unambiguous guilt written all over them. But Holmes had never once been obliged to stand in the witness box and have his suppositions and intuitions and immaculate theories ground to very fine dust over a period of several hours by the likes of Mr Disturnal. What Sir Arthur had done was the equivalent of go into a field where the criminal's footprints might be found and trample all over it wearing several different pairs of boots. He had, in his eagerness, destroyed the legal case against Royden Sharp even as he was trying to make it. And it was all the fault of Mr Sherlock Holmes.

Arthur & George

As he holds a copy of the Report of the Gladstone Committee in his hand, Arthur is relieved that he has twice failed to be elected to Parliament. He need feel no direct shame. This is how they do things, how they bury bad news. They have released the Report without the slightest warning on the Friday before the Whitsun holiday. Who will want to read about a miscarriage of justice while taking the train to the seaside? Who will be available to provide informed comment? Who will care, by the time Whit Sunday and Whit Monday have passed and work begins again? The Edalji Case – wasn't that settled months ago?

George also holds a copy in his hand. He looks at the title page:

PAPERS

relating to the

CASE OF GEORGE EDALJI

presented to both Houses of Parliament
by Command of His Majesty

and then, at the bottom:

London: printed for His Majesty's Stationery Office
by Eyre and Spottiswoode,
Printers to the King's Most Excellent Majesty
[Cd. 3503.] Price 1½d.   1907

It sounds substantial, but the price seems to give it away. A penny halfpenny to learn the truth about his case, his life . . . He opens the pamphlet warily. Four pages of Report, then two brief appendices. A penny halfpenny. His breath is coming short. His life summed up for him yet again. And this time not for readers of the *Cannock Chase Courier*, the Birmingham *Daily Gazette* or the Birmingham *Daily Post*, the *Daily Telegraph* or *The Times*, but for both Houses of Parliament and the King's Most Excellent Majesty . . .

Arthur has taken the Report, unread, to Jean's flat. This is only right. Just as the Report itself is laid before Parliament, so the consequences of his venture should be laid before her. She has taken an interest in the matter which far exceeded his expectations. In truth, he had no expectations at all. But she was always at his side, if not literally, then metaphorically. So she must be there at the conclusion.

George takes a glass of water and sits in an armchair. His mother has returned to Wyrley and he is currently alone in Miss Goode's lodgings, whose address is registered with Scotland Yard. He places a notebook on the arm of the chair, as he does not want to mark the Report itself. Perhaps he is not yet cured of the regulations governing the use of library books in Lewes and Portland. Arthur stands with his back to the fireplace while Jean sews, her head already half-cocked for the extracts Arthur will read to her. She wonders if they should have done more on this day for George Edalji, perhaps invited him for a glass of champagne, except that he does not drink; although since it was only this morning they heard the Report was due to be released . . .

George Edalji was tried on the charge of feloniously wounding . . .

'Hah!' says Arthur, barely half a paragraph in. 'Listen to this. *The Assistant Chairman of Quarter Sessions, who presided at the trial, when consulted about the conviction, reported that he and his colleagues were strongly of the opinion that the conviction was right.* Amateurs. Rank amateurs. Not a lawyer among them. I sometimes feel, my dear Jean, that the entire country is run by amateurs. Listen to them. *These circumstances make us hesitate very seriously before expressing dissent from a conviction so arrived at, and so approved.*'

George is less concerned by this opening; he is enough of a lawyer to know when a *however* is round the corner. And here it comes – not one, but three of them. However, there was considerable feeling in the neighbour- hood of Wyrley at the time; however, the police, so long baffled, were *natu- rally extremely anxious* to arrest someone; however, the police had both begun and carried on the investigation *for the purpose of finding evidence against Edalji.* There, it was said, quite openly and now quite officially. The police were prejudiced against him from the start.

Both Arthur and George read: *The case is also one of great inherent diffi- culty, because there is no possible view that can be taken of it, which does not involve extreme improbabilities.* Poppycock, Arthur thinks. What on earth are the extreme improbabilities in George's being innocent? George thinks, this is just an elaborate form of words; they are saying there is no middle ground; which is true, because either I am completely innocent or I am completely guilty, and since there are *extreme improbabilities* in the prosecution case, therefore it must and will be dismissed.

The *defects* in the trial . . . the prosecution case changed in two substantial regards as it went along. Indeed. First in the matter of when the crime was supposed to have been committed. Police evidence *inconsistent, and indeed contra- dictory.* Similar discrepancies about the razor . . . The footprints. *We think the value of the footprints as evidence is practically nothing.* The razor as weapon. *Not very easy to reconcile with the evidence of the veterinary surgeon.* The blood not fresh. The hairs. *Dr Butter, who is a witness quite above suspicion.*

Dr Butter was always the stumbling block, thinks George. But this is very fair so far. Next, the letters. The Greatorex letters are the key, and the jury examined them at length. *They considered their verdict for a considerable time, and we think they must be taken to have held that Edalji was the writer of those letters. We have ourselves carefully examined the letters, and compared them with the admitted handwriting of Edalji, and we are not prepared to dissent from the finding at which the jury arrived.*

George feels himself going faint. He is only relieved his parents are not with him. He reads the words again. *we are not prepared to dissent.* They think he wrote the letters! The Committee is telling the world he wrote the Greatorex letters! He takes a gulp of water. He lays the Report down on his knee until he can recover himself.

Arthur, meanwhile, reads on, his anger rising. However, the fact that Edalji wrote the letters doesn't mean he also committed the outrages. 'Oh, that's very white of them,' he exclaims. They are not the letters of a guilty man trying to throw the blame on others. How in the name of all earthly and unearthly powers could they be, Arthur growls to himself, since the man they throw most blame on is George himself. *We think it quite likely that they are the letters of an innocent man, but a wrong-headed and malicious man, indulging in a piece of impish mischief, pretending to know what he may know nothing of, in order to puzzle the police, and increase their difficulties in a very difficult investigation.*

'Balderdash!' shouts Arthur. 'Bal-der-dash.'

'Arthur.'

'Balderdash, balderdash,' he repeats. 'I have met no one in my entire life who is a more sober and straightforward man than George Edalji. *impish mischief* – did the fools not read all those testimonials to his character supplied by Yelverton? *wrong-headed and malicious man.* Is this, this . . . novella' – he slaps it on the mantelpiece – 'protected by Parliamentary privilege? If not, I'll have them in the libel court. I'll have the lot of them there. I'll fund it myself.'

George feels he is hallucinating. He feels as if the world has gone mad. He is back at Portland having a dry bath. They have ordered him stripped to his shirt, they have made him lift his legs and open his mouth. They have pulled up his tongue and – what's this, D462? What's this you've been hiding under your tongue? I do believe it's a crowbar. Don't you think this is a crowbar the prisoner has hidden under his tongue, officer? We'd better report this to the Governor. You're in serious trouble, D462, I'd better warn you. And you with all your talk about being the last prisoner in the gaol who might want to escape. You with your sainted airs and your library books. We've got your number, George Edalji, and it's D462.

He stops again. Arthur continues. The second defect of the prosecution's case lay in whether or not Edalji was meant to have acted alone; they changed their mind as the evidence suited them. Well, at least the officially appointed dunderheads couldn't miss that. The key question of eyesight. *much stress has been laid on this in some of the communications addressed to the Home Office.* Yes indeed: stress laid by the leading men of Harley Street and Manchester Square. *We have carefully considered the report of the eminent expert who examined Edalji in prison and the opinion of oculists that have been laid before us; and the materials now collected appear to us entirely insufficient to establish the alleged impossibility.*

'Imbeciles! *entirely insufficient.* Dunderheads and imbeciles!'

Jean keeps her head lowered. This was, she remembers, the very starting point of Arthur's campaign: the reason he did not just think George Edalji was innocent, he knew it. How disrespectful can they be, to treat Arthur's work and judgement so lightly!

But he is reading on, rushing ahead as if to forget this point. '*In our opinion, the conviction was unsatisfactory and . . . we cannot agree with the verdict of the jury.* Ha!'

'That means you've won, Arthur. They have cleared his name.'

'Ha!' Arthur does not even acknowledge the interjection. 'Now listen to this. *Our view of the case means that it would not have been warranted for the Home Office previously to interfere.* Hypocrites. Liars. Wholesale purveyors of whitewash.'

'What does that mean, Arthur?'

'It means, my dearest Jean, that no one has done anything wrong. It means that the great British solution to everything has been applied. Something terrible has happened, but nobody has done anything wrong. It ought to be retrospectively enshrined in the Bill of Rights. Nothing shall be anybody's fault, and especially not ours.'

'But they admit the verdict was wrong.'

'They said that George was innocent, but the fact that he has enjoyed three years of penal servitude is nobody's fault. Time after time the defects were pointed out to the Home Office and time after time the Home Office declined to reconsider. Nobody did anything wrong. Hurrah, hurrah.'

'Arthur, calm down a little, please. Take a little brandy and soda or something. You may even smoke your pipe if you wish.'

'Never in front of a lady.'

'Well, I would happily make an exception. But do calm down a little. And then we shall see how they justify such a statement.'

But George gets there first. *suggestions . . . prerogative of mercy . . . grant of a free pardon . . . On the one hand, we think the conviction ought not to have taken place, for the reasons we have stated . . . total ruin of his professional position and prospects . . . police supervisions . . . difficult if not impossible for him to recover anything like the position he has lost.* George stops at this moment, and takes a drink of water. He knows that *on the one hand* is always followed by *on the other hand*, and is not sure he is able to face what that hand might be.

'*On the other hand,*' roars Arthur. 'My God, the Home Office will find as many hands as that Indian god, what's his name –'

'Shiva, dear.'

'Shiva, when they want to find a reason why nothing is their fault. *On the other hand, being unable to disagree with what we take to be the finding of the jury, that Edalji was the writer of the letters of 1903, we cannot but see that, assuming him to be an innocent man, he has to some extent brought his troubles upon himself.* No, no, no no, NO.'

'Arthur, please. People will think we are having an argument.'

'I'm sorry. It's just that . . . aaah, *Appendix One*, yes, yes, petitions, reasons why the Home Office never does anything. *Appendix Two*, let's see how the Solomon of the Home Office thanks the Committee. *careful and exhaustive report*. Exhaustive! Four whole pages, with not a single mention of Anson or Royden Sharp! Blether . . . *brought his troubles upon himself* . . . blether blether . . . *accept the conclusions* . . . *however* . . . *exceptional case* . . . I'll say so . . . *permanent disqualifications* . . . Oh, I see, what they're most afraid of is the legal profession, all of which knows this is the greatest miscarriage of justice since, since . . . yes, so if they allow him to be reinstated . . . blether, blether . . . *fullest and most anxious considerations* . . . *free pardon.*'

'Free pardon,' repeats Jean, looking up. So victory is theirs.

'*Free pardon*,' reads George, aware that there is one sentence of the Report left to come.

'*Free pardon*,' repeats Arthur. He and George read the last sentence together. '*But I have also come to the conclusion that the case is not one in which any grant of compensation can be made.*'

George lays down the Report and puts his head in his hands. Arthur, in a tone of sardonic funereality, reads its final words, '*I am, yours very truly, H.J. Gladstone.*'

'Arthur dear, you were rather rushing things towards the end.' She has never seen him in such a mood before; she finds it alarming. She would not like such feelings ever turned against her.

'They should erect new signs at the Home Office. Instead of Entrance and Exit, they should read On the One Hand and On the Other Hand.'

'Arthur, could you try to be a little less obscure and just tell me what this means, exactly.'

'It means, it means, my darling Jean, that this Home Office, this Government, this country, this England of ours has discovered a new legal concept. In the old days, you were either innocent or guilty. If you were not innocent, you were guilty, and if you were not guilty, you were innocent. A simple enough system, tried and tested down many centuries, grasped by judges, juries and the populace at large. As from today, we have a new concept in English law – guilty *and* innocent. George Edalji is a pioneer in this regard. The only man to be granted a free pardon for a crime he never committed, and yet to be told at the same time that it was quite right he served three years' penal servitude.'

'So it's a compromise?'

'Compromise! No, it's a hypocrisy. It's what this country does best. The bureaucrats and the politicians have spent centuries perfecting it. It's called a Government Report. It's called Blether, it's called –'

'Arthur, light your pipe.'

'Never. I once caught a fellow smoking in front of a lady. I took the pipe from his mouth, snapped it in two and threw the pieces at his feet.'

'But Mr Edalji will be able to return to his work as a solicitor.'

'He will. And every potential client of his who can read a newspaper will think they are consulting a man mad enough to write anonymous letters denouncing himself for a heinous crime which even the Home Secretary and the cousin of the blessed Anson admit he had absolutely nothing to do with.'

'But perhaps it will be forgotten. You said that they were burying bad news by producing it over Whitsun. So perhaps people will only remember that Mr Edalji was granted a free pardon.'

'Not if I have anything to do with it.'

'You mean you are continuing?'

'They haven't seen the back of me yet. I'm not going to let them get away with *this*. I gave George my word. I gave you my word.'

'No, Arthur. You said what you were going to do, and you did it, and you have obtained a free pardon, and George can go back to work, which is what his mother said was all he wanted. It has been a great success, Arthur.'

'Jean, please stop being reasonable with me.'

'You wish me to be unreasonable with you?'

'I would shed blood to avoid that.'

'On the other hand?' asks Jean teasingly.

'With you,' says Arthur, 'there is no other hand. There is only one hand. It is simple. It is the only thing in my life that ever seems simple. At last. At long last.'

George has no one to console him, no one to tease him, no one to stop the words rolling back and forth in his skull. *A wrong-headed and malicious man, indulging in a piece of impish mischief, pretending to know what he may know nothing of, in order to puzzle the police, and increase their difficulties in a very difficult investigation.* A judgment presented to both Houses of Parliament and to the King's Most Excellent Majesty.

That evening George was asked by a representative of the Press for his response to the Report. He pronounced himself *profoundly dissatisfied with the result*. He called it *merely a step in the right direction*, but the allegation that he had written the Greatorex letters was *a slander – an insult . . . a baseless insinuation, and I shall not rest until it is withdrawn and an apology tendered.*

Further, *no compensation has been offered*. They admitted he had been wrongly convicted, so *it is only just that I should be compensated for the three years' penal servitude that I suffered. I shall not let matters rest as they are. I want compensation for my wrongs*.

Arthur wrote to the *Daily Telegraph*, calling the Committee's position *absolutely illogical and untenable*. He asked if anything *meaner or more un-English* could be imagined than a free pardon without reparation. He offered to demonstrate *in half an hour* that George Edalji could not have written the anonymous letters. He proposed that since it was unfair to ask the taxpayer to fund George Edalji's compensation, *it might well be levied in equal parts from the Staffordshire police, the Quarter Sessions Court and the Home Office, since it is these three groups of men who are guilty among them of this fiasco*.

The Vicar of Great Wyrley also wrote to the *Daily Telegraph*, pointing out that the jury itself had made no pronouncement on the authorship of the letters, and that any false deductions were the fault of Sir Reginald Hardy, who had been *rash and illogical* enough to tell the jury that *he who wrote the letters also committed the crime*. A distinguished barrister who had attended the trial had called the Chairman's summing-up *a regrettable performance*. The Vicar described his son's treatment, by both the police and the Home Office, as *most shocking and heartless*. As for the conduct and conclusions of the Home Secretary and his Committee: *This may be diplomacy, statecraft, but it is not what they would have done if he had been the son of an English squire or an English nobleman*.

Also dissatisfied with the Report was Captain Anson. Interviewed by the Staffordshire *Sentinel*, he replied to criticisms involving *the honour of the police*. The Committee, in identifying so-called *contradictions* of evidence, had simply not understood the police case. It was also *untrue* that the police began from a certainty of Edalji's guilt, and then sought evidence to support that view. On the contrary, Edalji was not suspected *until some months after* the outrages began. *Various persons were indicated as being conceivably implicated in the offences*, but were gradually eliminated. Suspicion only *finally became excited against Edalji owing to his commonly-talked-of habits of wandering abroad late at night*.

This interview was reported in the *Daily Telegraph*, to which George wrote in rebuttal. The *flimsy foundation* on which the case against him had been built was now clear. *As a fact*, he never did *once* 'wander abroad', and unless returning late from Birmingham or from some evening entertainment in the district, was *invariably in by about 9.30*. There was *no person in the district* less likely to be out at night, and apparently *the police took seriously* something intended *as a joke*. Further, if he had been out late habitually, this fact would have been known to the *large body of police* patrolling the district.

It had been a cold and unseasonal Whitsun. A Millionaire's Son had been Killed in a Motor Racing Tragedy while Driving his 200 H.P. Car. Foreign Princes had arrived in Madrid for a Royal Christening. Wine Growers had Rioted in Béziers, where the Town Hall had been Sacked and Burnt by Peasants. But there was nothing – there had now been nothing for years – about Miss Hickman the Lady Doctor.

Sir Arthur offered to fund any libel suit George cared to bring against Captain Anson, the Home Secretary, or members of the Gladstone Committee, either separately or jointly. George, while renewing his expressions of gratitude, politely declined. Such redress as he had just obtained had been achieved thanks to Sir Arthur's commitment, hard work, logic, and love of making a noise. But noise, George thought, was not the best solution to everything. Heat did not always produce light, and noise did not always produce locomotion. The *Daily Telegraph* was calling for a public inquiry into all aspects of the case; this, in George's view, was what they should now be pressing for. The newspaper had also launched a monetary appeal on his behalf.

Arthur, meanwhile, continued his campaign. No one had taken up his offer to demonstrate *in half an hour* that George Edalji could not have written the letters – not even Gladstone, who had publicly asserted the contrary. So Arthur would demonstrate the matter to Gladstone, the Committee, Anson, Gurrin and all readers of the *Daily Telegraph*. He devoted three lengthy articles to the matter, with copious holographic illustration. He demonstrated how the letters were obviously written by someone of *an entirely different class* to Edalji, *a foul-mouthed boor*, *a blackguard*, someone with *neither grammar nor decency*. He further declared himself personally slighted by the Gladstone Committee, given that in their Report *there is not a word which leads me to think that my evidence was considered*. In the matter of Edalji's eyesight, the Committee quoted the opinion of *some unnamed prison doctor* while ignoring the views of fifteen experts, *some of them the first oculists in the country*, which he had submitted. The members of the Committee had merely added themselves to *that long line of policemen, officials and politicians* who owed a *very abject apology* to *this ill-used man*. But until such an apology was offered, and reparation made, *no mutual daubings of complimentary whitewash will ever get them clean*.

Throughout May and June there were constant questions in Parliament. Sir Gilbert Parker asked if there were any precedent for compensation not being paid to someone wrongly convicted and subsequently granted a free pardon. Mr Gladstone: 'I know of no analagous case.' Mr Ashley asked if the Home Secretary considered George Edalji to be innocent. Mr Gladstone: 'I can hardly think that is a proper Question to ask me. It is a matter of opinion.' Mr Pike Pease asked what character Mr Edalji had borne in prison. Mr Gladstone: 'His prison character was good.' Mr Mitchell-Thompson asked the Home Secretary to set up a new inquiry to consider the matter of the handwriting. Mr Gladstone declined. Captain Craig asked for any notes taken during the trial for the use of the Court to be laid before Parliament. Mr Gladstone declined. Mr F.E. Smith asked if it was the case that Mr Edalji would have received compensation had it not been for the doubt as to his authorship of the letters. Mr Gladstone: 'I am afraid I am unable to answer that question.' Mr Ashley asked why this man had been released if his innocence was not completely established. Mr Gladstone: 'That is a Question which really does not concern me. The release was consequent on a decision by my predecessor, with which, however, I agree.' Mr Harmood-Banner asked for details of similar outrages against farmstock committed while George Edalji was in prison. Mr Gladstone replied that there had been three in the Great Wyrley neighbourhood, in September 1903, November 1903 and March 1904. Mr F.E. Smith asked in how many cases over the last twenty years compensation had been paid after convictions had been shown to be unsatisfactory, and what amounts were involved. Mr Gladstone replied that there had been twelve such cases in the previous twenty years, two involving substantial sums: 'In one case the sum of £5,000 was paid, and in the other the sum of £1,600 was divided between two persons. In the remaining ten cases the compensation paid varied from £1 to £40.' Mr Pike Pease asked if free pardons were granted in all these cases. Mr Gladstone: 'I am not sure.' Captain Faber asked for all police reports and communications addressed to the Home Office on the subject of the Edalji Case to be printed. Mr Gladstone declined. And finally, on 27th June, Mr Vincent Kennedy asked: 'Is Edalji being thus treated because he is not an Englishman?' In the words of *Hansard*: '[No answer was returned.]'

Arthur continued to receive anonymous letters and abusive cards, the letters in coarse yellow envelopes gummed up with stamp paper. They were postmarked London NW, but the creases in the documents indicated to him that they may have been carried under cover, or possibly in somebody's pocket – that of a railway guard, for instance – from the Midlands to London for posting. He offered a reward of £20 to anyone who helped trace them back to their writer.

Arthur requested further interviews with the Home Secretary and his Under Secretary Mr Blackwell. In the *Daily Telegraph* he described being treated with *courtesy* but also with a *chilly want of sympathy*. Further, they took *an obvious side with impeached officialdom* and made him feel a *hostile atmosphere* around him. There was to be no rise in temperature, no change in atmosphere; the officials regretted that henceforth they would be too occupied with the business of state to afford Sir Arthur Conan Doyle any more of their time.

The Incorporated Law Society voted to restore George Edalji to its Rolls.

The *Daily Telegraph* paid out the contents of its appeal fund, which amounted to some £300.

Thereafter, with no new events, no disputes, no libel suits, no government action, no further Questions in Parliament, no public inquiry, no apology and no compensation, there was little for the Press to report.

Jean says to Arthur, 'There is one more thing we can do for your friend.'

'What is that, my dear?'

'We can invite him to our wedding.'

Arthur is rather confused by this suggestion. 'But I thought we had decided that only our families and our closest friends would be present?'

'That is the wedding itself, Arthur. Afterwards there is the reception.'

The unofficial Englishman looks at his unofficial fiancée. 'Did anyone ever tell you that apart from being the most adorable of women, you are also pre-eminently wise, and much more able to see what is right and necessary than the poor oaf you will be taking as a husband?'

'I shall be at your side, Arthur, always at your side. And therefore looking in the same direction. Whatever that direction may prove to be.'

George & Arthur

As the summer began to pass, as conversation turned to cricket or the Indian crisis, as Scotland Yard no longer required monthly confirmation by registered post of George's address, as the Home Office remained silent, as even the indefatigable Mr Yelverton failed to come up with a new stratagem, as George was informed that an office awaited him at 2 Mecklenburgh Street until such time as he found his own premises, as Sir Arthur's communications diminished to brief notes of encouragement or rage, as his father returned more full-mindedly to parish work, as his mother judged it safe to leave her elder son and only daughter in one another's care, as Captain the Honourable George Anson failed to announce any renewed investigation into the Great Wyrley Outrages despite their now having no official author, as George learned to read a newspaper again without one eye constantly snagging at a mention of his name, as yet another animal was mutilated in the Wyrley district, as interest nevertheless dribbled away and even the anonymous letter writer grew weary of his abuse, George realized that the final, official verdict on his case had been given, and was unlikely ever to be changed.

Innocent yet guilty: so said the Gladstone Committee, and so said the British Government through its Home Secretary. Innocent yet guilty. Innocent yet wrong-headed and malicious. Innocent yet indulging in impish mischief. Innocent yet deliberately seeking to interfere with the proper investigations of the police. Innocent yet bringing his troubles upon himself. Innocent yet undeserving of compensation. Innocent yet undeserving of an apology. Innocent yet fully deserving of three years' penal servitude.

But that was not the only verdict. Much of the Press had been on his side: the *Daily Telegraph* had called the Committee's and the Home Secretary's position *weak, illogical and inconclusive*. The public's attitude, as far as he could gauge it, was that he *never once had fair play*. The legal profession, in great numbers, had supported him. And finally, one of the greatest writers of the age had loudly and continually asserted his innocence. Would these verdicts in time come to outweigh the official one?

George also sought to take a wider view of his own case, and the lessons it contained. If you could not expect the police to be more efficient, or witnesses more honest, then you must at least improve the tribunals where their words were tested. A case like his should never have been conducted by a Chairman with no legal training; you would have to improve the qualifications of those on the bench. And even if the Quarter Sessions and the Assize Courts could be made to function better, there must still be recourse to finer and wiser legal minds: in other words, to a court of appeal. It was an absurdity that the only way to overturn a wrongful conviction such as his was by petitioning the Home Secretary, that petition to arrive with hundreds – no, thousands – of others each year, most of them from manifestly guilty occupants of His Majesty's prisons, who had little better to occupy their time with than confecting memorials for the Home Office. Obviously, futile and frivolous appeals to any new Court should be weeded out; but where there had been a serious dispute of law or fact, or where the conduct of the lower court had been prejudicial or incompetent, then a higher court must reconsider the case.

George's father had hinted to him on various occasions that his sufferings had a higher purpose to them. George had never wanted to be a martyr, and still saw no Christian explanation of his travails. But the Beck Case and the Edalji Case had between them produced great stirrings among his profession, and it was entirely possible that he might turn out to have been a kind of martyr after all, if of a simpler, more practical kind – a legal martyr whose sufferings brought about progress in the administration of justice. Nothing, in George's view, could possibly make up for the years stolen in Lewes and Portland, and the year of limbo following his release; and yet, might it not be some consolation if this terrible fracture in his life led to some ultimate good for his profession?

Cautiously, as if aware of the sin of pride, George began to imagine a legal textbook written a hundred years thence. 'The Court of Appeal was originally set up as the result of numerous miscarriages of justice which aroused public discontent. Not the least of these was the Edalji case, whose details need no longer concern us, but whose victim, it should be noted in passing, was the author of *Railway Law for the "Man in the Train"*, one of the first works to clarify this often confusing subject, and a book which is still referred to . . .' There were worse fates, George decided, than to be a footnote in legal history.

One morning, a tall oblong card arrived for him. It was printed in silver copperplate hand:

Mr & Mrs Leckie

request the pleasure of

Mr George Edalji's

Company

at the Whitehall Rooms

Hotel Metropole

on Wednesday September 18th

at 2.45 o'clock

on the occasion of

the marriage of their daughter

Jean

with Sir Arthur Conan Doyle

Glebe House,
Blackheath   *R.S.V.P.*

George was touched beyond expression. He set the card on his mantelpiece, and replied immediately. The Incorporated Law Society had readmitted him to the Rolls, and now Sir Arthur had readmitted him to human society. Not that he had any social ambitions – not to such high reaches anyway; but he recognized the invitation as a noble and symbolic gesture to one who just a year previously had been keeping himself sane in Portland Gaol with the novels of Tobias Smollett. George thought for a long time as to what might be a suitable wedding present, and eventually decided on well-bound, one-volume editions of Shakespeare and Tennyson.

Arthur is determined to throw any damn reporters off the scent. There is no announcement of where he and Jean are to be married; his wedding-eve dinner at The Gaiety is a discreet affair; and at St Margaret's Westminster the striped awning is put out at the very last minute. Only a few passers-by gather at this drowsy, sun-dusted corner beside the Abbey to see who might be getting married on a discreet Wednesday rather than an ostentatious Saturday.

Arthur wears a frock coat and white waistcoat, with a large white gardenia in his buttonhole. His brother Innes, on special leave from autumn manoeuvres, makes a nervous best man. Cyril Angell, husband of Arthur's youngest sister Dodo, will officiate. The Mam, whose seventieth birthday has recently been celebrated, wears grey brocade; Connie and Willie are there, and Lottie and Ida and Kingsley and Mary. Arthur's dream of gathering his family around him under one roof has never come to pass; but here, for a brief while, they are all assembled. And for once Mr Waller is not of the party.

The chancel is decorated with tall palms; groups of white flowers are arranged at their base. The service is to be fully choral, and Arthur, given his Sunday preference for golf over church, has allowed Jean to choose the hymns: 'Praise the Lord, ye Heavens adore Him' and 'O, Perfect Love, all human thought transcending'. He stands in the front pew, remembering her last words to him. 'I shall not keep you waiting, Arthur. I have made that quite clear to my father.' He knows she will be as good as her word. Some might say that since they have waited ten years for one another, an extra ten or twenty minutes will do no harm, and may even improve the drama of the event. But Jean, to his delight, is quite devoid of that supposedly appealing bridal coquetry. They are to be married at a quarter to two; therefore she will be at the church at a quarter to two. This is a sound basis for a marriage, he thinks. As he stands looking at the altar, he reflects that he does not always understand women, but he recognizes those who play with a straight bat and those who don't.

Jean Leckie arrives on the arm of her father at one forty-five precisely.

She is met at the porch by her bridesmaids, Lily Loder-Symonds of spiritualist leanings, and Leslie Rose. Jean's page is Master Bransford Angell, son
of Cyril and Dodo, dressed in a blue and cream silk Court suit. Jean's dress,
semi-Empire style with a Princess front, is made of ivory silk Spanish lace,
its designs outlined with fine pearl embroidery. The underdress is of silver
tissue; the train, edged with white crêpe de Chine, falls from a chiffon true-
lovers' knot caught in with a horseshoe of white heather; the veil is worn
over a wreath of orange blossom.

Arthur takes very little of this in as Jean arrives beside him. He is not
much of a frock man, and thus perfectly complacent about the superstition
that the wedding dress shall remain unglimpsed by the groom until it arrives
with the bride. He thinks Jean looks damned handsome, and he has an overall
impression of cream and pearls and a long train. The truth is, he would be
just as happy to see her in riding clothes. He gives his responses lustily; hers
are barely audible.

At the Hotel Metropole there is a grand staircase leading to the Whitehall
Rooms. The train is proving an almighty nuisance; the bridesmaids and little
Bransford are fussing interminably over it when Arthur becomes impatient.
He sweeps his bride from her feet and carries her effortlessly up the stairs.
He smells orange blossom, feels the imprint of pearls against his cheek, and
hears his bride's quiet laughter for the first time that day. There is a cheer
from the marriage party below and a louder, answering cheer from the recep-
tion party gathered above.

George is acutely aware that he will know no one there except Sir Arthur,
whom he has met only twice, and the bride, who briefly shook his hand at
the Grand Hotel, Charing Cross. He very much doubts Mr Yelverton will be
invited, let alone Harry Charlesworth. He has handed in his present and
declined the alcoholic drinks everyone else is holding. He looks around the
Whitehall Rooms: chefs are busying themselves at a long buffet table, the
Metropole orchestra is tuning up, and everywhere there are tall palm trees
with ferns and foliage and clumps of white flowers at their base. More white
flowers decorate the little tables set round the edge of the room.

To George's surprise and considerable relief, people come up and speak to
him; they seem to know who he is, and greet him as if they are almost his
familiars. Alfred Wood introduces himself, and talks of visiting Wyrley Vicarage
and having had the great pleasure of meeting George's family. Mr Jerome the
comic writer congratulates him on his successful fight for justice, introduces
him to Miss Jerome, and points out other celebrities: J.M. Barrie over there,
and Bram Stoker, and Max Pemberton. Sir Gilbert Parker, who has several
times embarrassed the Home Secretary in the House of Commons, comes

across to shake George's hand. George realizes that all of them are treating him as a deeply wronged man; not one of them looks at him as if he were the private author of a series of insane and obscene letters. There is nothing directly said; just an implicit assumption that he is the sort of fellow who generally understands things in the way they also generally understand things.

While the orchestra plays quietly, three basketfuls of telegrams and cables are brought in, opened, and read out by Sir Arthur's brother. Then there is food, and more champagne than George has ever seen poured in his life, and speeches and toasts, and when the bridegroom gives his speech it contains words which might as well be champagne, for they bubble up into George's brain and make him giddy with excitement.

'. . . and among us this afternoon I am delighted to welcome my young friend *George Edalji. There is no one I am prouder to see here than him . . .*' and faces turn towards George, and smiles are given, and glasses half-raised, and he has no idea where to look, but realizes that it doesn't matter anyway.

Bride and groom take a ceremonial turn on the dance floor, to much happy whooping, and then begin to circulate among their guests, at first together, then separately. George finds himself beside Mr Wood, who is half backed into a palm tree and has ferns up to his knees.

'Sir Arthur always advises concealment,' he says with a wink. Together they look out at the throng.

'A happy day,' George observes.

'And the end of a very long road,' replies Mr Wood.

George does not know what to make of this remark, so contents himself with a nod of agreement. 'Have you worked for Sir Arthur for many years?'

'Southsea, Norwood, Hindhead. Next stop Timbuctoo I shouldn't wonder.'

'Really?' says George. 'Is that the honeymoon destination?'

Mr Wood frowns at this, as if unable to follow the question. He takes another pull at his champagne glass. 'I understand you're keen to get married in general. Sir Arthur thinks you should get married in per-tick-er-ler.' He pronounces this last word with a staccato effect which for some reason amuses him. 'Or is that stating the obvious?'

George feels alarmed by this turn in the conversation, and also somewhat embarrassed. Mr Wood is sliding his forefinger up and down the side of his nose. 'Your sister's the nark,' he adds. 'Couldn't stand up to a pair of part-time consulting detectives.'

'Maud?'

'That's her name. Nice young lady. Quiet, nothing wrong with that. Not that I intend to marry myself, either in general, or in per-tick-er-ler.' He smiles to himself. George decides that Mr Wood is being agreeable rather than malicious. However, he suspects the fellow might be a little inebriated. 'Bit of a palaver, if you ask me. And then there's the expense.' Mr Wood waves his glass at the band, the flowers, the waiters. One of the latter takes his gesture as a command and refills his glass.

George is beginning to wonder where the exchange might lead when he sees, over Mr Wood's shoulder, Lady Conan Doyle bearing down on them.

'Woodie,' she says, and it seems to George that a strange look comes over his companion. But before he can assess it, the secretary has somehow disappeared.

'Mr Edalji,' Lady Conan Doyle pronounces his name with just the right stress, and rests a gloved hand on his forearm. 'I am so pleased you could come.'

George is taken aback: it is not as if he has been obliged to turn down many other engagements to be here.

'I wish you every happiness,' he replies. He looks at her dress. He has never seen anything like it before. None of the Staffordshire villagers his father has married has ever worn a dress remotely like this. He thinks he ought to praise it, but does not know how to do so. But it does not matter, because she is speaking to him again.

'Mr Edalji, I would like to thank you.'

Again, he is taken aback. Have they opened their wedding presents already? Surely not. But what else could she be referring to?

'Well, I wasn't sure what you might require –'

'No,' she says, 'I do not mean that, whatever it might be.' She smiles at him. Her eyes are a sort of grey-green, he thinks, her hair golden. Is he staring at her? 'I mean, it is partly thanks to you that this happy day has occurred when it has and how it has.'

Now George is completely baffled. Further, he is staring, he knows he is.

'I expect we shall be interrupted at any moment, and in any case I was not intending to explain. You may never know what I mean. But I am grateful to you in a way you cannot guess. And so it is quite right that you are here.'

George is still pondering these words as a swirl of noise takes the new Lady Conan Doyle away. *I am grateful to you in a way you cannot guess.* A few moments later, Sir Arthur shakes his hand, tells him he meant every word of his speech, claps him on the shoulder, and moves on to his next guest. The bride disappears and then reappears in different clothes. A final toast is drunk, glasses are drained, cheers are raised, the couple depart. There is nothing left for George to do except bid farewell to his temporary friends.

The next morning he bought *The Times* and the *Daily Telegraph*. One paper listed his name between those of Mr Frank Bullen and Mr Hornung, the other had him between Mr Bullen and Mr Hunter. He discovered that the white flowers he had been unable to identify were called *lilium Harrisii*. Also that Sir Arthur and Lady Conan Doyle had afterwards left for Paris, en route to Dresden and Venice. 'The bride,' he read, 'travelled in a dress of ivory white cloth, trimmed with white Boutache braid, and having a bodice and sleeves of lace, with cloth over-sleeves. At the back the coat was caught into the waist with gold embroidered buttons. In front, folds of the cloth fell softly at either side of a lace chemisette. The dresses were by Maison Dupree, Lee, B.M.'

He scarcely understood a word of this. It was as mysterious to him as the words the dress's wearer had uttered the day before.

He wondered if he would ever marry himself. In the past, when idly imagining the possibility, the scene would always taken place at St Mark's, his father officiating, his mother gazing at him proudly. He had never been able to picture his bride's face, but that had never bothered him. Since his ordeal, however, the location no longer struck him as plausible, and this seemed to undermine the likelihood of the whole event. He wondered if Maud would ever marry. And Horace? He knew little of his brother's present life. Horace had declined to attend the trial, and had never visited him in gaol. He managed an inappropriate postcard from time to time. Horace had not been home in several years. Perhaps he was married already.

George wondered if he would ever see Sir Arthur and the new Lady Conan Doyle again. He would spend the next months and years attempting to regain in London the sort of life he had once begun to have in Birmingham; while they would go off to whatever existence world-famous authors and their young brides enjoyed. He was not sure how things would go between them if a common cause was lacking. Perhaps this was being over-sensitive on his part, or over-timid. But he tried to imagine visiting them in Sussex, or dining with Sir Arthur at his London club, or receiving them in whatever modest accommodation he might be able to afford. No, that was another implausible scene from a life he would not have. In all probability they would never meet again. Still, for three-quarters of a year their paths had crossed, and if yesterday had marked the end of that crossing point, perhaps George did not mind so very much. Indeed, part of him preferred it that way.

FOUR

Endings

George

On the Tuesday, Maud passed her *Daily Herald* silently across the breakfast table. Sir Arthur had died at 9.15 the previous morning at Windlesham, his home in Sussex. **DIES PRAISING HIS WIFE** announced the headline; and then **'YOU ARE WONDERFUL!' SAYS SHERLOCK HOLMES' CREATOR** and then **NO MOURNING**. George read how there was 'no gloom' in the house at Crowborough; the blinds had deliberately not been drawn; and only Mary, Sir Arthur's daughter by his first marriage, was 'showing grief'.

Mr Denis Conan Doyle talked freely to the *Herald*'s Special Correspondent, 'not in a hushed voice, but normally, glad and proud to talk about him. "He was the most wonderful husband and father that ever lived," he said, "and one of the greatest men. He was greater than most people knew, because he was so modest."' Two paragraphs of proper filial praise followed. But the next paragraph made George embarrassed; he almost wanted to hide the paper from Maud. Should a son speak like this about his parents – especially to a newspaper? 'He and my mother were lovers to the end. When she heard him coming she would jump up like a girl and pat her hair and run to meet him. There had never been greater lovers than these two.' Apart from the impropriety, George disapproved of the boasting – the more so as it followed close upon the assertion of Sir Arthur's own modesty. He, surely, would never have made such claims for himself. The son continued: 'If it had not been for our knowledge that we have not lost him, I am certain that my mother would have been dead within an hour.'

Denis's younger brother Adrian corroborated their father's continuing presence in their lives. 'I know perfectly well that I am going to have conversations with him. My father fully believed that when he passed over he would continue to keep in touch with us. All his family believe so, too. There is no question that my father will often speak to us, just as he did before he passed over.' Not that it would be entirely straightforward: 'We shall always know when he is speaking, but one has to be careful, because there are practical jokers on the other side as there are here. It is quite possible that they may attempt to impersonate him. But there are tests which my mother knows, such as little mannerisms of speech which cannot be impersonated.'

George was confused. The instant sadness he felt at the news – as if, somehow, he had lost a third parent – was deemed to be impermissible: **NO MOURNING**. Sir Arthur had died happily; his family – with one exception – was resisting grief. The blinds were not drawn; there was no gloom. Who was he, then, to pronounce himself bereft? He wondered whether to express this quandary to Maud, who would be able to think more clearly about such matters; but judged it might seem egotistical. The dead man's own modesty perhaps compelled a modesty of grief among those who had known him.

Sir Arthur had been seventy-one. The obituaries were substantial and affectionate. George followed the news all week, and discovered to his slight discomfort that Maud's *Herald* gave him rather more information than his own *Telegraph*. There was to be a GARDEN FUNERAL which was JUST A FAMILY FAREWELL. George wondered if he would be invited; he hoped that those who had celebrated Sir Arthur's marriage might also be allowed to bear witness to his . . . he was going to say death, but the word was not in use at Crowborough. His passing over; his promotion, as some termed it. No, this was an inappropriate expectation – he was not in any sense a member of the family. Having settled the matter in his mind, George felt slightly piqued to discover from the next day's paper that a crowd of three hundred would attend the funeral.

Sir Arthur's brother-in-law, the Revd Cyril Angell, who had buried the first Lady Conan Doyle and married the second one, took the service in the rose garden at Windlesham. He was assisted by the Revd C. Drayton Thomas. There was little black in the congregation; Jean wore a flowered summer dress. Sir Arthur was laid to rest near the garden hut which had served him so long as a study. Telegrams arrived from all over the world, and a special train had to be run to carry all the flowers. When laid out on the burial field, they looked, according to one witness, as if a fanciful Dutch garden had grown as high as a man's head. Jean had ordered a headboard made of British oak, inscribed with the words BLADE STRAIGHT, STEEL TRUE. A sportsman and a chivalrous knight to the end.

George felt that all had been done properly, if unconventionally; his benefactor had been honoured as he would have wished. But Friday's *Daily Herald* announced that the story was not yet complete. CONAN DOYLE'S EMPTY CHAIR read the four-column headline, and beneath it an explanation which jumped from type-size to type-size. CLAIRVOYANT to attend GREAT MEETING. 6,000 Spiritualists at Memorial Meeting. WIFE'S WISH. Medium Who Will be Quite Frank.

This public farewell would take place at the Albert Hall on Sunday July 13th 1930 at 7 p.m. The service was to be organized by Mr Frank Hawken, secretary of the Marylebone Spiritualist Association. Lady Conan Doyle, who would attend with other family members, said that she looked upon it as the last public demonstration she would attend with her husband. An empty chair would be placed on the stage to symbolize Sir Arthur's presence, and she would sit to the left of it – the position she had occupied tirelessly over the last two decades.

But there was more. Lady Conan Doyle had asked that there be a demonstration of clairvoyance in the course of the meeting. This would be performed by Mrs Estelle Roberts, who had always been Sir Arthur's favourite medium. Mr Hawken favoured the *Herald* with an interview: 'Whether Sir Arthur Conan Doyle will be able to demonstrate sufficiently yet awhile for a medium to describe him is problematical,' he stated. 'I should imagine that he would be quite capable of demonstrating already. He was quite prepared for his passing.' Further: 'If he did demonstrate it is doubtful whether the evidence would be accepted by the sceptics, but we who know Mrs Roberts as a medium would have no doubt on the matter at all. We know that if she cannot see him she will be quite frank about it.' There was no mention here, George noted, of any threat from practical jokers.

Maud watched her brother finish the story. 'You will have to go,' she said. 'You think so?'

'Definitely. He called you his friend. You must say your farewell, even if the circumstances are unusual. You had better go to the Marylebone Association for your ticket. This afternoon or tomorrow – otherwise you will be anxious.'

It was strange, but agreeable, how decisive Maud could be. Whether at his desk or not, George was in the habit of chasing one argument after another before coming to a decision. Maud refused to waste such time; she saw more clearly – or at least more quickly – and he handed over household decisions to her just as he handed over whatever money he did not require for clothing and office expenses. She looked after their living costs, placed a certain amount each month in a savings account, and gave the remainder to charity.

'You do not think Father would disapprove of . . . of this sort of thing?'

'Father has been dead for twelve years,' replied Maud. 'And I always like to think that those who are in God's presence find themselves somewhat changed from how they were on earth.'

It still took him by surprise that Maud could be so forthright; her statement verged on the critical. George decided not to discuss it, but to consider it later in private. He returned to the newspaper. His knowledge of spiritualism was mostly based on a few dozen pages written by Sir Arthur, and he could not say they had received his fullest concentration. The notion of six thousand people waiting for their lost leader to address them through a medium struck him as an alarming proposition.

He had an aversion to large numbers of people gathered in one spot. He thought of the crowds at Cannock and Stafford, of the rough loiterers besieging the Vicarage after his arrest. He remembered men thumping violently on the cab door and waving their sticks; he remembered the crush of men in Lewes and Portland, and how it sharpened the pleasures of solitary confinement. In certain circumstances he might attend a public lecture, or a large meeting of solicitors; but as a general rule he regarded the tendency of human beings to agglomerate in one place as the beginning of unreason. It was true that he lived in London, a most populous city, but he was able largely to control his contact with his fellow men and women. He preferred them to come into his office one by one; he felt protected by his desk and by his knowledge of the law. It was safe here at 79 Borough High Street: the office downstairs, and upstairs the rooms he shared with Maud.

It had been an excellent notion that they should live together, though he could no longer recall who proposed it. When Sir Arthur was helping vindicate him, Mother had stayed some part of the time with him at Miss Goode's lodgings in Mecklenburgh Square. But it became evident that she must return to Wyrley, and the idea of exchanging the women of the household had seemed logical. Maud, to their parents' great surprise, though much less to his, had proved immensely capable. She organized the house for him, cooked, acted as secretary when his own was away, and listened to his stories of the day's work with as much enthusiasm as if she were back in the old schoolroom. She had become more outgoing and more opinionated since moving to London; she had also learned how to tease him, which gave him rare pleasure.

'But what shall I wear?'

Her speed of reply meant that she must have foreseen the question. 'Your blue business suit. It is not a funeral, and in any case they do not believe in black. But it is important to show respect.'

'It is a vast arena by the sound of it. I doubt I shall be able to get a ticket near the stage.'

It had become part of their living together that George habitually looked for objections to plans that had already been decided. And in return, Maud indulged such prevarication. Now she disappeared, and he heard the sound of objects being dragged around the attic room above his head. A few minutes later she placed before him something that caused a sudden frisson: his binoculars in their dust-laden case. She fetched a cloth, and wiped the dust away; the leather, long unpolished, shone dully with damp.

Instantly, brother and sister are standing once more in Castle Gardens, Aberystwyth, on the last entirely happy day of his life. A passer-by points out Mount Snowdon; but all George can see is the delight on his sister's face. She turns and promises to buy him a pair of binoculars. Two weeks later his ordeal began, and afterwards, when he was free and they moved to Borough High Street, on their first Christmas together she had given him this present which had made him come close to weeping for himself.

He had been grateful, but also puzzled, since they were now far from Snowdon, and he doubted they would ever return to Aberystwyth. Maud had anticipated this response, and suggested he take up birdwatching. This had immediately struck him, like all Maud's proposals, as eminently sensible, and so for several Sunday afternoons he had gone off to the marshes and wood- lands surrounding London. She thought he needed a hobby; he thought she needed him out of the house from time to time. He stuck at it dutifully for a few months, but in truth he had trouble following a bird in flight, and the ones at rest seemed to take pleasure in being camouflaged. Additionally and alternatively, many of the places from which it was deemed best to watch birds struck him as cold and damp. If you had spent three years in prison, you did not need any more cold and damp in your life until you were placed in your coffin and lowered into the coldest, dampest place of all. That had been George's considered view of birdwatching.

'I felt so sorry for you that day.'

George looked up, the picture in his head of a twenty-one-year-old girl by the disappointing ruins of a Welsh castle replaced by a greying, middle- aged woman behind a teapot. She spotted some more dust on the binocular case and gave it another wipe. George gazed at his sister. Sometimes he could not tell which of them was taking care of the other.

'It was a happy day,' he said firmly, holding to the memory he had made into certainty by repetition. 'The Belle Vue Hotel. The tramway. Roast chicken. Not going to pick up pebbles. The railway journey. It was a happy day.'

'I was pretending for most of it.'

George was not sure he wanted his memories disturbed. 'I could never tell how much you knew,' he said.

'George, I was not a child. I might have been a child when it all began, but not then. What else did I have to do except work it out? You cannot keep things from someone of twenty-one who rarely leaves the house. You are only keeping things from yourself, pretending to yourself, and hoping she will go along with it.'

George thought his way back from the Maud he knew now, and realized there must have been a lot more of this woman in that girl than he was aware of at the time. But he had no desire to pursue the complications of this. He had decided long ago what had happened; he knew his own story. He might be willing to accept a general correction of the kind just made; but the last thing he wanted was fresh detail.

Maud sensed this. And if, back then, he had kept things from her, she had also kept things from him. She would never tell him of the morning Father had called her into his study and announced that he feared greatly for the mental stability of her brother. He said George had been under much strain and was refusing to take the slightest holiday; so he would propose over dinner that brother and sister take a day trip to Aberystwyth, and whether she wanted to or not she was to concur and insist that they must, absolutely must go. And this was what had happened. George had politely yet stubbornly refused his father, then yielded to the pleas of his sister.

It had been a piece of scheming quite untypical of the Vicarage. But more shocking to Maud had been Father's assessment of George's condition. To her he had always been the reliable, conscientious brother; while Horace was the frivolous one, who lived life on a whim, who lacked stolidity. And as it turned out, she had been right and Father wrong. For how could George have survived his ordeal if he had not possessed much greater mental fortitude than Father ever attributed to him? But these were thoughts Maud would always keep to herself.

'There was one matter on which Sir Arthur was profoundly wrong,' George declared suddenly. 'He opposed votes for women.' Since her brother had always supported female suffrage during the time it had been an issue, this opinion came as no surprise to Maud. Rather, it was the fierceness in his voice that was unaccountable. George was now looking away from his sister in embarrassment. The trail of memory, and all that came with it, had set off in him the tenderest of emotions towards Maud, and a realization that these had been, and would continue to be, the strongest feelings of his life. But George was neither skilled nor easy at conveying such thoughts, and even this most indirect of confessions disturbed him. So he rose, folded the *Herald* unnecessarily, handed it back, and went downstairs to his office.

There was work to be done, but instead he sat at his desk thinking about Sir Arthur. They had last met twenty-three years ago; still, the link between them had somehow never been broken. He had followed Sir Arthur's writings and doings, his travels and campaigns, his interventions in the public life of the nation. George often agreed with his pronouncements – on divorce reform, the threat from Germany, the need for a Channel Tunnel, the moral necessity of returning Gibraltar to Spain. He permitted himself, however, to be frankly dubious about one of Sir Arthur's lesser-known contributions to penal reform: the proposal that hardened recidivists in His Majesty's gaols should all be transported to the Scottish island of Tiree. George had cut articles from the newspapers, followed Sherlock Holmes's continuing exploits in *The Strand Magazine*, and borrowed Sir Arthur's latest books from the library. Twice he had taken Maud to the cinema to watch Mr Eille Norwood's remarkable impersonation of the consulting detective.

He remembered, the year they first came to Borough High Street, buying the *Daily Mail* solely to read Sir Arthur's special despatch on the marathon race at the London Olympics. George could not have been less interested in athletic endeavour, but he was rewarded by a further insight – if any more were needed – into the nature of his benefactor. Sir Arthur's description had been so vivid that George read it again and again until he could picture it in his head like a newsreel. The vast stadium – the expectant crowd – a small figure enters ahead of all the others – an Italian in a state of near collapse – he falls, he rises, he falls again, he rises again, he staggers – then an American enters the stadium and begins to catch him up – the plucky Italian is twenty yards from the tape – the crowd is hypnotized – he falls again – he is helped up – willing arms propel him through the tape before the American can catch him. But the Italian has, of course, broken the rules by accepting assistance and the American is declared the winner.

Any other writer would have left it at that, pleased with his success at evoking the drama of the moment. But Sir Arthur was not any other writer, and had been so touched by the Italian's bravery that he started a subscription for the man. Three hundred pounds had been contributed, which enabled the runner to open a baker's shop in his native village – something a gold medal would never have been able to effect. This was typical of Sir Arthur: generous and practical in equal parts.

After his success with the Edalji Case, Sir Arthur had involved himself in other judicial protests. George was rather ashamed to admit that his feelings towards subsequent victims consisted of envy verging occasionally on disapproval. There was Oscar Slater, for instance, whose case took up years and years of Sir Arthur's life. The man had, it was true, been wrongly accused of murder, and nearly executed, and Sir Arthur's intervention had spared him the gallows and eventually gained his release; but Slater was a very low sort of fellow, a professional criminal who had shown not an ounce of gratitude towards those who had helped him.

Sir Arthur had also continued to play the detective. Only three or four years ago there had been the curious case of the woman writer who disappeared. Christie, that was her name. Apparently a rising star of detective fiction, though George had not the slightest interest in rising stars, as long as Holmes was still compiling his casebook. Mrs Christie had vanished from her home in Berkshire, and her car was found abandoned some five miles from Guildford. When three police forces could find no trace of her, the Chief Constable of Surrey had called in Sir Arthur – who had, in his time, been Deputy Lieutenant of the county. What happened next surprised many people. Did Sir Arthur interview witnesses, scour the trampled ground for footprints, or cross-examine the police, as he had done in the famous Edalji

Case? Not a bit of it. He had contacted Christie's husband, borrowed one of the missing woman's gloves, and taken it off to a psychic who had laid it against his forehead in an attempt to locate the woman. Well, it was one thing – as George had proposed to the Staffordshire Constabulary – to use real bloodhounds to sniff out a trail, quite another to employ psychic ones who merely stayed at home and sniffed gloves. George, on reading of Sir Arthur's novel investigative techniques, had felt quite relieved that more orthodox ones had been applied in his own case.

However, it would take a great deal more than a few such eccentricities to dent George's utter respect for Sir Arthur. He had it as a young man of thirty, newly released from prison; and he had it still as a fifty-four-year old solicitor, his moustache and hair now quite grey. The only reason he was able to sit here at his desk on a Friday morning was because of Sir Arthur's high principles, and his willingness to convert them into action. George's life had been returned to him. He had a full set of law books, a satisfactory practice, a choice of hats, and a splendid – some might even say gaudy – fob chain strung across a waistcoat that each year felt a little tighter. He was a householder, and a man who had his opinions about matters of the day. He did not have a wife, it was true; nor did he have long lunches with colleagues who cried 'Good old George!' as he reached for the bill. Instead, he had a curious kind of fame, or half-fame, or, as the years had passed, quarter-fame. He had wanted to be known as a lawyer, and he had ended up being known as a miscarriage of justice. His case had led to the setting-up of the Court of Criminal Appeal, whose decisions over the last two decades had elaborated the common law of crime to an extent widely recognized as revolutionary. George was proud of his association – however unintentional it had been – with this event. But who was aware of it? A few people would respond to his name by shaking his hand warmly, treating him as a man who once, long ago, had been famously wronged; others looked at him with the eyes of farm boys or special constables in country lanes; but most nowadays had never heard of him.

At times he resented this, and felt ashamed of his resentment. He knew that in all his years of suffering, there had been nothing he longed for more than anonymity. The Chaplain at Lewes had asked him what he missed, and he had replied that he missed his life. Now he had it back; he had work, enough money, people to nod to in the street. But he was occasionally nudged by the thought that he deserved more; that his ordeal should have led to more reward. From villain to martyr to nobody very much – was this not unfair? His supporters had assured him that his case was as significant as that of Dreyfus, that it revealed as much about England as the Frenchman's did about

France, and just as there had been Dreyfusards and anti-Dreyfusards so there were those for and against Edalji. They further insisted that in Sir Arthur Conan Doyle he had as great a defender, and a better writer, than the Frenchman Émile Zola, whose books were reportedly vulgar and who had run away to England when threatened in his turn with gaol. Imagine Sir Arthur scuttling off to Paris to evade the whim of some politician or prosecutor. He would have stayed and fought and made a great noise and shaken the bars of his cell until the prison collapsed.

And yet, for all this, the name of Dreyfus had constantly increased in fame, and was known around the globe, while that of Edalji was scarcely recognized in Wolverhampton. This was partly his own doing – or lack of doing. After his release he was frequently asked to address meetings, to write newspaper articles, and give interviews. He invariably declined. He did not wish to be a spokesman, or the representative of a cause; he did not have the temperament for the public platform; and having once recounted his sufferings for *The Umpire*, he felt it immodest to do so again whenever invited. He had considered preparing a revised edition of his book on railway law, yet felt that this too might be exploiting his notoriety.

But more than this, he suspected that his obscurity was something to do with England itself. France, as he understood it, was a country of extremes, of violent opinion, violent principles and long memories. England was a quieter place, just as principled, but less keen on making a fuss about its principles; a place where the common law was trusted more than government statute; where people got on with their own business and did not seek to interfere with that of others; where great public eruptions took place from time to time, eruptions of feeling which might even tip over into violence and injustice, but which soon faded in the memory, and were rarely built into the history of the country. This has happened, now let us forget about it and carry on as before: such was the English way. Something was wrong, something was broken, but now it has been repaired, so let us pretend that nothing much was wrong in the first place. The Edalji Case would not have arisen if there had been a Court of Appeal? Very well, then: pardon Edalji, establish a Court of Appeal before the year is out – and what more remains to be said about the matter? This was England, and George could understand England's point of view, because George was English himself.

He had written twice to Sir Arthur since the wedding. In the last year of the war father had died; on a chilly May morning he was buried close to Uncle Compson, a dozen yards from the church where he had officiated for more than forty years. George felt that Sir Arthur – having met his father – would wish to know; in reply he had received a brief note of condolence.

But then, a few months later, he read in the newspaper that Sir Arthur's son Kingsley, having been wounded on the Somme and left in a weakened state, had like so many others been carried off by influenza. A mere fortnight before the Armistice was signed. He wrote again, a son who had lost a father to a father who had lost a son. This time he received a longer letter. Kingsley had been the last name of a bitter roll-call. Sir Arthur's wife had lost her brother Malcolm in the first week of the war. His nephew Oscar Hornung had been killed at Ypres, along with another of his nephews. His sister Lottie's husband had died on his first day in the trenches. And so on, and so on. Sir Arthur listed those known to himself and his wife. But in closing he expressed the certainty that they were not lost, merely waiting on the farther side.

George no longer counted himself a religious person. If he was any sort of Christian at all, it was not down to the vestiges of filial piety; it was down to fraternal love. He went to church because it gave Maud pleasure that he did so. As far as the afterlife went, he thought he would wait and see. He was suspicious of zeal. He had been somewhat alarmed at the Grand Hotel when Sir Arthur had talked so intensely about his religious feelings, which were scarcely germane to the matter in hand. But this had at least prepared George for the subsequent news that his benefactor had become a fully-fledged Spiritualist and was planning to devote his remaining years and energies to the movement. Many right-thinking people were grossly shocked by the announcement. If Sir Arthur, the very ideal of an English gentleman, had restricted himself to a little genteel Sunday-afternoon table-turning among friends, they might not have minded. But this had never been Sir Arthur's way. If he believed something, he wanted everyone else to believe it as well. This had always been his strength and sometimes his weakness. So there had been mockery from every direction, with impertinent newspaper headlines asking **HAS SHERLOCK HOLMES GONE MAD?** Wherever Sir Arthur lectured, there were counter-lectures from opponents of every stripe – Jesuits, Plymouth Brethren, angry materialists. Only the other week Bishop Barnes of Birmingham had attacked the 'fantastic types of belief' currently proliferating. Christian Science and Spiritualism were false creeds which 'drove the simple to resuscitate moribund ideas', George had read. Yet neither mockery nor clerical rebuke could ever deter Sir Arthur.

Though George was instinctively sceptical about Spiritualism, he declined to side with the attacks on it. While he did not think himself competent to judge such matters, he knew how to choose between Bishop Barnes of Birmingham and Sir Arthur Conan Doyle. He remembered – and it was one of his great memories, one he had always imagined sharing with a wife – the conclusion of that first meeting at the Grand Hotel. They had stood to say goodbye, and Sir Arthur had naturally towered over him, and this large, forceful, gentle man had looked him in the eye and said, 'I do not think you are innocent. I do not believe you are innocent. I *know* you are innocent.' The words were more than a poem, more than a prayer, they were the expression of a truth against which lies would break. If Sir Arthur said he knew a thing, then the burden of proof, to George's legal mind, shifted to the other fellow.

He took down *Memories and Adventures*, Sir Arthur's autobiography, a stout, midnight-blue volume, published six years previously. It fell open where it always did, at page 215. 'In 1906,' he read yet again, 'my wife passed away after a long illness . . . For some time after these days of darkness I was unable to settle to work until the Edalji case came suddenly to turn my energies into an entirely unexpected channel.' George always felt a little uneasy at this beginning. It seemed to imply that his case had come along at a convenient moment, its peculiar nature being just what was required to drag Sir Arthur from a slough of despond; as if he might have reacted differently – indeed, not at all – had the first Lady Conan Doyle not recently died. Was this being unfair? Was he scrutinizing a simple sentence too closely? But that was what he did, each day of his professional life: he read carefully. And Sir Arthur had presumably written for careful readers.

There were many other sentences which George had underlined with pencil and annotated in the margin. This, of his father, for a start: 'How the Vicar came to be a Parsee, or how a Parsee came to be the Vicar, I have no idea.' Well, Sir Arthur did once have an idea, and a very precise and correct idea, because George had explained his father's journey at the Grand Hotel, Charing Cross. And then this: 'Perhaps some Catholic-minded patron wished to demonstrate the universality of the Anglican Church. The experiment will not, I hope, be repeated, for though the Vicar was an amiable and devoted man, the appearance of a coloured clergyman with a half-caste son in a rude, unrefined parish was bound to cause some regrettable situation.' George found this unfair; it practically blamed his mother's family, in whose gift the parish had been, for the events that occurred. Nor did he like being characterized as a 'half-caste son'. It was doubtless true in a technical sense, but he no more thought of himself in those terms than he thought of Maud as his half-caste sister, or Horace as his half-caste brother. Was there not a better way of putting it? Perhaps his father, who believed that the world's future depended upon the harmonious commingling of the races, could have come up with a better expression.

'What aroused my indignation and gave me the driving force to carry the thing through was the utter helplessness of this forlorn little group of people, the coloured clergyman in his strange position, the brave, blue-eyed, grey-haired mother, the young daughter, baited by brutal boors.' Utter helplessness? You would not think from this that Father had published his own analysis of the case before Sir Arthur had even appeared on the scene; nor that Mother and Maud were constantly writing letters, rallying support and obtaining testimonials. It seemed to George that Sir Arthur, while deserving of much credit and thanks, was rather too determined to annex for himself the whole credit and thanks. He certainly diminished the long campaign by Mr Voules of *Truth*, not to mention Mr Yelverton, and the memorials, and the petition of signatures. Even Sir Arthur's account of how he first became aware of the case was manifestly faulty. 'It was late in 1906 that I chanced to pick up an obscure paper called *The Umpire*, and my eye caught an article which was a statement of his case, made by himself.' But Sir Arthur had only 'chanced to pick up' this 'obscure paper' because George had sent him all his articles with a long covering letter. As Sir Arthur must have very well known.

No, George thought, this was ungracious of him. Sir Arthur was doubtless working from memory, from the version of events he had himself told and retold down the years. George knew from taking witness statements how the constant recounting of events smoothed the edges of stories, rendered the speaker more self-important, made everything more certain than it had seemed at the time. His eye now sped through Sir Arthur's account, not wishing to find any more fault. The words 'travesty of Justice' near the end were followed by: 'The *Daily Telegraph* got up a subscription for him which ran to some £300.' George allowed himself a slightly taut smile: it was the very sum that had been raised the following year by Sir Arthur's appeal on behalf of the Italian marathon runner. The two events had touched the heart of the British public to exactly the same measurable degree: three years' false imprisonment with penal servitude, and falling over at the end of an athletic race. Well, it was no doubt salutary to have your case put in true perspective.

But two lines later there was the sentence which George had read more than any other in the book, which made up for any inaccuracies and false emphases, which offered balm to one whose suffering had been so humiliatingly quantified. Here it was: 'He came to my wedding reception, and there was no guest I was prouder to see.' Yes. George decided to take *Memories and Adventures* with him to the service, in case anyone objected to his presence. He did not know what Spiritualists looked like – let alone six thousand of them – but he doubted he looked like one himself. The book would be his passport in case of difficulty. You see, here on page 215, this is me, I am come to bid him farewell, I am proud to be his guest once more.

On Sunday afternoon, shortly after four o'clock, he turned out of No. 79

Borough High Street and headed for London Bridge: a small brown man in a blue business suit, with a dark blue book tucked under his left arm and a pair of binoculars over his right shoulder. A casual observer might think he was going to a race meeting – except that none was held on a Sunday. Or could that be a birdwatching book under his arm – yet who went birdwatching in a business suit? He would have made a strange sight in Staffordshire, and even in Birmingham they might have put him down for an eccentric; but nobody would do so in London, which contained more than enough eccentrics already.

When he first moved here, he had been apprehensive. About his future life, of course; about how he and Maud would manage together; about the magnitude of the city, its crowds and its noise; and beyond this, about how people would treat him. Whether there would be lurking ruffians like those who had pushed him through a hedge in Landywood and damaged his umbrella, or lunatic policemen like Upton threatening to do him harm; whether he would encounter the race prejudice Sir Arthur was convinced lay at the bottom of his case. But as he crossed London Bridge, which he had been doing now for more than twenty years, he felt quite at his ease. People generally left you alone, either from courtesy or indifference, and George was grateful for either motive.

It was true that inaccurate assumptions were habitually made: that he and his sister had recently arrived in the country; that he was a Hindoo; that he was a trader in spices. And of course he was still asked where he came from; though when he replied – to avoid discussing the finer points of geography – that he was from Birmingham, his interlocutors mostly nodded in an un-surprised way, as if they had always expected the inhabitants of Birmingham to look like George Edalji. Naturally there were the kind of humorous allusions that Greenway and Stentson went in for – though few to Bechuana Land – but he regarded this as some inevitable normality, like rain or fog. And there were even some people who, on learning that you came from Birmingham, expressed disappointment, because they had been hoping for news from distant lands which you were quite unable to supply.

He took the Underground from Bank to High Street Kensington, then walked east until the Albert Hall bulged into view. His cautiousness over time – about which Maud liked to tease him – had made him arrive almost two hours before the service was due to begin. He decided to take a stroll in the park.

It was just after five on a fine Sunday afternoon in July, and a bandstand was blaring away. The park was full of families, trippers, soldiers – though at no point did they form a dense crowd, so George was not made anxious.

Nor did he look at young couples flirting with one another, or at sober parents organizing young children, with the same envy he might once have done. When he first came to London, he had not yet given up hope of getting married; indeed, he used to worry about how his future wife and Maud might get on. For it was clear that he could not abandon Maud; nor would he wish to. But then a few years passed, and he realized that Maud's good opinion of his future wife mattered more to him than the other way round. And then a few more years passed, and the general disadvantages of a wife became even more apparent. A wife might appear agreeable but turn out to be a scold; a wife might not understand thrift; a wife would certainly wish for children, and George thought he probably could not bear the noise, or the disturbance it would bring to his work. And then, of course, there were sexual matters, which often did not lead to harmony. George did not handle divorce cases, but as a lawyer he had seen evidence enough of the misery that could be inflicted by marriage. Sir Arthur had long campaigned against the oppressiveness of the divorce laws, and been president of the Reform Union for many years, before handing over to Lord Birkenhead. From one name on the roll of honour to another: it had been Lord Birkenhead, as F.E. Smith, who had asked Gladstone searching questions in the House about the Edalji Case.

But that was by the by. He was fifty-four years old, living in adequate comfort and largely philosophical about his unmarried condition. His brother Horace was now lost to the family: he had married, moved to Ireland and changed his name. Quite in which order he had done these three things George was not sure, but they were all clearly linked, and the undesirability of each action bled into the others. Well, there were different ways of living; and the truth was, neither he nor Maud had ever been very likely to marry. They were similar in their shyness, and in seeming to fend off those who approached them. But the world contained enough marriages, and was certainly not threatened with underpopulation. Brother and sister could live as harmoniously as husband and wife; in some instances, more so.

In their early days together, he and Maud would make the journey back to Wyrley two or three times a year; but they were rarely happy visits. For George they brought back too many specific memories. The door-knocker still made him jump, and in the evening, as he looked out into the darkened garden, he would often glimpse beneath the trees shifting outlines which he knew to be nothing and yet still feared. With Maud it was different. Devoted as she was to Father and Mother, when she stepped back inside the Vicarage she became withdrawn and tentative; she had few opinions and her laugh was never heard. George could almost swear that she was beginning to ail. But he always knew the cure: it was called New Street Station and the London train.

At first, when he and Maud went out together, people sometimes mistook them for husband and wife; and George, who did not want anyone to think he was incapable of marriage, would say, rather precisely, 'No, this is my dear sister Maud.' But as time passed, he would occasionally not bother to make the correction, and afterwards Maud would take his arm and give a little laugh. Soon, he supposed, when her hair was as grey as his, they would be taken for an old married couple, and he might not even care to dispute that assumption.

He had been wandering randomly, and now found himself approaching the Albert Memorial. The Prince was sitting in his gilded, glittering surround, with all the famous men of the world in attendance on him. George extracted his binoculars from their case and started practising. He swept slowly up the Memorial, above the levels at which art and science and industry held sway, above the seated figure of the pensive Consort, up to a higher realm. The burred knob was hard to control, and sometimes there was a mass of un-focused foliage filling the lens, but eventually he emerged at the plain vision of a chunky Christian cross. From there he tracked slowly down the spire, which seemed as heavily populated as the lower reaches of the monument. There were tiers of angels and then – just lower than the angels – a cluster of more human figures, classically draped. He circled the Memorial, frequently losing focus, trying to work out who they might be: a woman with a book in one hand and a snake in the other, a man in a bearskin with a big club, a woman with an anchor, a hooded figure with a long candle in its hand . . . Were they saints, perhaps, or symbolic figures? Ah, here at last was one he recognized, standing on a corner pedestal: she had a sword in one hand, a pair of scales in the other. George was pleased to note that the sculptor had not given her a blindfold. That detail had often drawn his disapproval: not because he didn't understand its significance, but because others failed to. The blindfold permitted the ignorant to make gibes at his profession. That George would not allow.

He returned the binoculars to their case, and moved his attention from the monochrome, frozen figures to the colourful, moving ones all around him, from the sculpted frieze to the living one. And in that moment, George was struck by the realization that everybody was going to be dead. He occasion-ally pondered his own death; he had grieved for his parents – his father twelve years ago, his mother six; he had read obituaries in the newspapers and gone to the funerals of colleagues; and he was here for the great farewell to Sir Arthur. But never before had he understood – though it was more a visceral awareness than a mental comprehension – that everybody was going to be dead. He had surely been informed of this as a child, although only in the context of everyone – like Uncle Compson – continuing to live thereafter, either in the bosom of Christ or, if they were wicked, elsewhere. But now he looked about him. Prince Albert was dead already, of course, and so was the Widow of Windsor who had mourned him; but that woman with a parasol would be dead, and her mother next to her dead sooner, and those small children dead later, although if there was another war the boys might be dead sooner, and those two dogs with them would also be dead, and the distant bandsmen, and the baby in the perambulator, even the baby in the perambulator, even if it lived to be as old as the oldest inhabitant on the planet, a hundred and five, a hundred and ten, whatever it was, that baby would be dead too.

And though George was now nearing the limit of his imagination, he continued a little further. If you knew someone who had died, then you could think about them in one of two ways: as being dead, extinguished utterly, with the death of the body the test and proof that their self, their essence, their individuality, no longer existed; or you could believe that somewhere, somehow, according to whatever religion you held, and how fervently or tepidly you held it, they were still alive, either in a way predicted by sacred texts, or in some way we had yet to comprehend. It was one or the other; there was no position of compromise; and George was privately inclined to think extinction the more probable. But when you stood in Hyde Park on a warm summer's afternoon among thousands of other human beings, few of whom were probably thinking about being dead, it was less easy to believe that this intense and complex thing called life was merely some chance happening on an obscure planet, a brief moment of light between two eternities of darkness. At such a moment it was possible to feel that all this vitality must continue somehow, somewhere. George knew he was not about to succumb to any uprush of religious sentiment – he was not going to ask the Marylebone Spiritualist Association for some of the books and brochures they had offered him when he had taken his ticket. He also knew that he would doubtless go on living as he had done, observing like the rest of the country – and mainly because of Maud – the general rituals of the Church of England, observing them in a kind of half-hearted, imprecisely hopeful way until such time as he died, when he would discover what the truth of the matter was, or, more likely, not discover anything at all. But just today – as that horse and rider trotted past him – that horse and rider as doomed as Prince Albert – he thought he saw a little of what Sir Arthur had come to see.

It all made him feel breathless and panicky; he sat on a bench to calm himself. He looked at the passers-by but saw only dead people walking – prisoners released on licence but likely to be recalled at any moment. He

340

opened *Memories and Adventures* and began flipping its pages in an attempt to distract himself. And instantly two words presented themselves to his eyes. They were in normal type, but they struck him like capitals: 'Albert Hall'. A more superstitious or credulous mind might have found significance in the moment; George declined to view it as anything more than a coincidence. Even so, he read, and was distracted. He read how, nearly thirty years previously, Sir Arthur had been invited to judge a Strong Man competition in the Hall; and how, after a champagne supper, he had walked out into the empty night and found himself a few steps behind the victor, a simple fellow preparing to walk the London streets until it was time to catch the morning train back to Lancashire. George feels himself in a sudden, vivid dreamland. There is fog, and people's breath is white, and a strong man with a gold statue has no money for a bed. He sees the fellow from behind, as Sir Arthur had; he sees a hat at an angle, the cloth of a jacket pulled tight by powerful shoulders, a statue clamped casually under one arm, its feet pointing backwards. Lost in the fog, but with a large, gentle, Scottish-voiced rescuer padding up behind, and never afraid to act. What will happen to them all – the wrongly accused lawyer, the collapsed marathon runner, the disoriented strong man – now that Sir Arthur has left them?

There was still an hour to go, but people had already started moving towards the Hall, so he joined them to avoid a later crush. His ticket was for a second-tier box. He was directed up some back steps and emerged into a curving corridor. A door was opened, and he found himself in the narrow funnel of a box. There were five seats, all currently empty: one at the back, two side by side, and another pair at the front by the brass rail. George hesitated for a moment, then took a breath and stepped forwards.

Lights blaze at him from all around this gilt and red-plush Colosseum. It is less a building than an oval canyon; he looks far across, far below, far above. How many does it hold – eight thousand, ten thousand? Almost dizzy, he takes a seat at the front. He is glad Maud suggested bringing the binoculars: he scours the arena and the sloping stalls, the three tiers of boxes, the great pipe organ behind the stage, then the higher slope of the circle, the row of arches supported by brown marble columns, and above them the beginnings of a soaring dome cut off from view by a floating canopy of linen duck, like a cloudscape over their heads. He examines the people arriving below – some in full evening dress, but most obedient to Sir Arthur's wish that he be not mourned. George sweeps the binoculars back to the platform: there are banks of what he takes to be hydrangeas, and large drooping ferns of some kind. A line of square-backed chairs has been set up for the family. The middle one has an oblong of cardboard set up across it. George focuses his glasses on this chair. The sign reads SIR ARTHUR CONAN DOYLE.

As the hall fills up, George stows his binoculars back in their case. Neighbours arrive in the box on his left; he is only a padded armrest away. They greet him in a friendly manner, as if the occasion, while serious, is also informal. He wonders if he is the only person present who is not a spiritualist. A family of four arrives to complete his box; he offers to take the single seat at the back, but they will not hear of it. They seem to him like ordinary Londoners: a couple, with two children approaching adulthood. The wife unselfconsciously takes the seat next to him: she is a woman in her late thirties, he judges, dressed in dark blue, with a broad, clear face and flowing auburn hair.

'Halfway to Heaven already, up here, aren't we?' she says pleasantly. He nods politely. 'And where are you from?'

For once, George decides to respond precisely. 'Great Wyrley,' he says. 'It's near Cannock in Staffordshire.' He half expects her to say, like Greenway and Stentson, 'No, where are you really from?' But instead she just waits, perhaps for him to mention which spiritualist association he belongs to. George is tempted to say, 'Sir Arthur was a friend of mine,' and to add, 'Indeed, I was at his wedding,' and then, if she doubts him, to prove it from his copy of *Memories and Adventures*. But he thinks this might appear presumptuous. Besides, she might wonder why, if he was a friend of Sir Arthur's, he is sitting so far away from the stage among ordinary folk who did not have that luck.

When the hall is full, the lights are dimmed and the official party walks out on stage. George wonders if they are meant to stand up, perhaps even applaud; he is so used to the rituals of the Church, of knowing when to stand, to kneel, to remain seated, that he feels rather lost. If this were a theatre and they played the National Anthem, that would solve the problem. He feels everyone ought to be on their feet, in tribute to Sir Arthur and in deference to his widow; but there is no instruction, and so all remain seated. Lady Conan Doyle is wearing grey rather than mourning black; her two tall sons, Denis and Adrian, are in evening dress and carry top hats; they are followed by their sister Jean, and half-sister Mary, the surviving child of Sir Arthur's first marriage. Lady Conan Doyle takes her seat at the left hand of the empty chair. One son sits next to her, the other on the far side of the placard; the two young men rather self-consciously place their top hats on the floor. George cannot see their faces at all distinctly, and wants to reach for his binoculars, but doubts the gesture would be held appropriate. Instead, he looks down at his watch. It is seven o'clock precisely. He is impressed by the punctuality; he somehow expected spiritualists to be more lax in their timekeeping.

Mr George Craze of the Marylebone Spiritualist Association introduces himself as chairman of the meeting. He begins by reading a statement on behalf of Lady Conan Doyle:

> At every meeting all over the world, I have sat at my beloved husband's side, and at this great meeting, where people have come with respect and love in their hearts to do him honour, his chair is placed beside me, and I know that in the spiritual presence he will be close to me. Although our earthly eyes cannot see beyond the earth's vibrations, those with the God-given extra sight called clairvoyance will be able to see the dear form in our midst.
>
> I want in my children's, and my own, and my beloved husband's name, to thank you all from my heart for the love for him which brought you here tonight.

There is a murmur round the hall; George is unable to tell if it indicates sympathy for the widow, or disappointment that Sir Arthur will not be miraculously appearing before them on stage. Mr Craze confirms that, contrary to the more foolish speculation in the press, there is no question of some physical representation of Sir Arthur manifesting itself as if by magic trick. For those unacquainted with the truths of Spiritualism, and especially for journalists present, he explains that when someone passes over, there is often a period of confusion for the spirit, which may not be able to demonstrate immediately. Sir Arthur, however, was quite prepared for his passing, which he faced with a smiling tranquillity, leaving his family like one going on a long journey yet confident they would all meet again soon. In such conditions it is expected that the spirit will find its place and its powers quicker than most.

George remembers something Sir Arthur's son Adrian told the *Daily Herald*. The family, he said, would miss the patriarch's footsteps and his physical presence, but that was all: 'Otherwise, he might only have gone to Australia.' George knows that his champion once visited that distant continent, because a few years ago he borrowed *The Wanderings of a Spiritualist* from the library. In truth, he found its travel information of greater interest than its theological disquisitions. But he remembers that when Sir Arthur and his family – along with the indefatigable Mr Wood – were propagandizing in Australia, they were christened The Pilgrims. Now Sir Arthur is back there, or at least in the spiritualist equivalent, whatever that might be.

A telegram from Sir Oliver Lodge is read out. 'Our great-hearted champion will still be continuing his campaign on the Other Side, with added wisdom and knowledge. *Sursum corda.*' Then Mrs St Clair Stobart reads from Corinthians, and declares that St Paul's words are fitting to the occasion, since Sir Arthur was often in his life described as the St Paul of Spiritualism. Miss Gladys Ripley sings Liddle's solo 'Abide With Me'. The Revd G. Vale Owen speaks of Sir Arthur's literary work and agrees with the author's ownview that *The White Company* and its sequel *Sir Nigel* were his best writings; indeed, he judges that the description in the latter work of a Christian knight and man of high devotion may serve as the very picture of Sir Arthur himself. The Revd C. Drayton Thomas, who took half the funeral service at Crowborough, praises Sir Arthur's tireless activity as Spiritualism's mouthpiece.

Next they all stand for the movement's favourite hymn, 'Lead, Kindly Light'. George notices something different about the singing, which he cannot at first identify. 'Keep thou my feet; I do not ask to see/The distant scene; one step enough for me.' For a moment he is distracted by the words, which do not seem especially appropriate to Spiritualism: as far as George understands it, the movement's adherents have their eyes on the distant scene all the time, and have precisely laid down the steps it takes to get there. Then he shifts his attention from matter to manner. The singing *is* different. In church people sing hymns as if reacquainting themselves with lines familiar from months and years ago – lines containing truths so established that they need neither proving, nor thinking about. Here there is directness and freshness in the voices; also a kind of cheerfulness verging on passion which most Vicars would find worrisome. Each word is enunciated as if it contains a brand new truth, one which needs to be celebrated and urgently conveyed to others. It all strikes George as highly unEnglish. Cautiously, he finds it rather admirable. 'till/The night is gone,/And with the morn those angel faces smile,/Which I have loved long since, and lost awhile.'

As the hymn ends and they takes their seats again, George gives his neighbour a small, indeterminate greeting – modest enough, yet even so, something he would never do in church. She responds with a smile that fills every surface of her face. There is nothing forward in it, nor anything of the missionary either. Nor is there any evident complacency. Her smile merely says: yes, this is certain, this is right, this is joyful.

George is impressed, but also slightly shocked: he is suspicious of joy. He has come across little of it in his life. In his childhood there was something called pleasure, usually accompanied by the adjectives guilty, furtive or illicit. The only pleasures allowed were those modified by the word simple. As for joy, it was something associated with angels blowing trumpets, and its true place was in Heaven not on Earth. Let joy be unconfined – that was what

344

people said, wasn't it? But in George's experience, joy has always been closely confined. As for pleasure, he has known the pleasure of doing one's duty – to family, to clients, and occasionally to God. But he has never done most of the things that afford his compatriots pleasure: drinking beer, dancing, playing football and cricket; not to mention things that might have come if marriage had come. He will never know a woman who jumps up like a girl, pats her hair, and runs to meet him.

Mr E. W. Oaten, who once proudly chaired the first large meeting Sir Arthur addressed on Spiritualism, says that no man better combined within himself all the virtues we associate with the British character: courage, optimism, loyalty, sympathy, magnanimity, love of truth and devotion to God. Next Mr Hannen Swaffer recalls how less than a fortnight ago, Sir Arthur, though mortally ill, struggled up the steps of the Home Office to plead for the repeal of the Witchcraft Act, which those of malevolent intent sought to invoke against mediums. It was his last duty, and in his devotion to duty he never faltered. This showed itself in every aspect of his life. Many people knew Doyle the writer, Doyle the dramatist, Doyle the traveller, Doyle the boxer, Doyle the cricketer who once dismissed the great W.G. Grace. But greater than any of these was the Doyle who pleaded for justice when the innocent were made to suffer. It was due to his influence that the law of Criminal Appeal was carried. It was this Doyle who so triumphantly took up the causes of Edalji and Slater.

George instinctively looks down at the mention of his name, then proudly up, then surreptitiously sideways. A pity he has been coupled yet again with that low and ungrateful criminal; but he may, he thinks, take honourable pleasure in having his name spoken at this great occasion. Maud will be pleased too. He glances more openly at his neighbours, but his moment has passed. They have eyes only for Mr Swaffer, who has moved on to celebrate another Doyle, and an even greater one than Doyle the bringer of justice. This greatest of all Doyles was and is the man who in the hours of the War's despair carried to the women of the country the comforting proof that their loved ones were not dead.

They are now asked to stand in silence for two minutes to honour the memory of their great champion. Lady Conan Doyle, as she rises, looks briefly down at the empty chair next to her, and then stands, with one tall son on either side of her, gazing out at the hall. Six – eight? ten? – thousand gaze back, from gallery, from balcony, from tiered boxes, from the great curve of stalls, and from the arena. In church, people would lower their heads and close their eyes to remember the departed. Here there is no such discretion or inwardness: frank sympathy is conveyed with a direct look. It also seems to George that the silence is of a different nature to any he has felt before. Official silences are respectful, grave, often deliberately saddening; this silence is active, filled with anticipation and even passion. If a silence can be like suppressed noise, then this is such a silence. When it ends, George realizes that it has held such a strange power over him that he has almost forgotten about Sir Arthur.

Mr Craze is back at the microphone. 'This evening,' he announces as the many thousand take their seats again, 'we are going to make a very daring experiment with the courage implanted in us by our late leader. We have with us a spirit sensitive who is going to try to give impressions from this platform. One reason why we hesitate to do it in such a colossal meeting is that it places a terrific strain on the sensitive. In an assembly of ten thousand people a tremendous force is centred upon the medium. Tonight, Mrs Roberts will try to describe some particular friends, but it will be the first time this has been attempted in such a tremendous gathering. You can help with your vibrations as you sing the next hymn, "Open My Eyes That I May See Glimpses of Truth".'

George has never been to a seance. He has never, for that matter, crossed a gypsy's palm with silver, or paid twopence to sit before a crystal ball at a funfair. He believes it is all hocus-pocus. Only a fool or a backward tribesman would believe that the lines on a hand or the tea leaves in a cup reveal anything. He is willing to respect Sir Arthur's certainty that the spirit survives death; perhaps, too, that under certain circumstances such a spirit might be able to communicate with the living. He is also prepared to admit that there might be something in the telepathic experiments Sir Arthur described in his autobiography. But there comes a point where George draws the line. He draws it, for instance, when people make the furniture jump around, when bells are mysteriously rung and fluorescent faces of the dead appear out of the darkness, when spirit hands leave their supposed imprint on soft wax. George finds this all too obviously a conjuring trick. How can it not be suspicious that the best conditions for spirit communication – drawn curtains, extinguished lights, people joining hands so that they cannot get up and verify what is happening – are precisely the best conditions in which charlatanry can flourish? Regretfully, he judges Sir Arthur credulous. He has read that the American illusionist Mr Harry Houdini, whose acquaintance Sir Arthur made in the United States, offered to reproduce every single effect known to professional mediums. On numerous occasions he had been tied up securely by honest men, but once the lights were out always managed to free himself sufficiently to ring bells, set off noises, shift the furniture around and even engender ectoplasm. Sir Arthur declined Mr Houdini's challenge. He did not deny that the illusionist might be able to produce such effects, but preferred his own interpretation of that ability: Mr Houdini was in fact the possessor of spiritual powers, whose existence he perversely chose to deny.

As the singing of 'Open My Eyes' comes to an end, a slim woman with short dark hair, dressed in flowing black satin, comes forward to the microphone. This is Mrs Estelle Roberts, Sir Arthur's favourite medium. The atmosphere in the hall is now even more intense than during the two-minute silence. Mrs Roberts stands there, slightly swaying, hands clasped together, head cast down. Every eye is upon her. Slowly, very slowly, she begins to lift her head; then her hands are unclasped and her arms begin to spread, while the slow sway continues. Finally, she speaks.

'There are vast numbers of spirits here with us,' she begins. 'They are pushing behind me like anything.'

It does indeed seem like this: as if she is holding herself upright despite great pressure from several directions.

Nothing happens for a while, except more swaying, more unseen buffeting. The woman on George's right whispers, 'She is waiting for Red Cloud to appear.'

George nods.

'That's her spirit guide,' the neighbour adds.

George does not know what to say. This is not his world at all.

'Many of the guides are Indians.' The woman pauses, then smiles and adds, without the slightest embarrassment, 'Red Indians, I mean.'

The waiting is as active as the silence was; as if those in the hall are pressing upon the slim figure of Mrs Roberts much as any invisible spirits are. The waiting builds and the swaying figure plants her feet wider as if to hold her balance.

'They are pushing, they are pushing, many of them are unhappy, the hall, the lights, the world they prefer – a young man, dark hair brushed back, in uniform, a Sam Browne belt, he has a message – a woman, a mother, three children, one of them passed and is with her now – elderly gentleman bald head was a doctor not far from here a dark grey suit passed suddenly after a dreadful accident – a baby, yes, a little girl taken away by influenza she misses her two brothers Bob is one of them and her parents – Stop it! Stop it!' – Mrs Roberts suddenly shouts, and with her arms outstretched seems to push back at the spirits crowding behind her – 'There are too many of them, their voices are confused, a middle-aged man in a dark overcoat who spent much of his life in Africa – he has a message – there is a white-haired grandmother who shares your anxiety and wants you to know –'

George listens to the crowd of spirits being given fleeting description. The impression is that they are all clamouring for attention, fighting to convey their messages. A facetious if logical question comes into George's mind, from where he cannot tell, unless as a reaction to all this unwonted intensity. If these are indeed the spirits of Englishmen and Englishwomen who have passed over into the next world, surely they would know how to form a proper queue? If they have been promoted to a higher state, why have they been reduced to such an importunate rabble? He does not think he will share this thought with his immediate neighbours, who are now leaning forwards and gripping the brass rail.

'– a man in a double-breasted suit between twenty-five and thirty who has a message – a girl, no, sisters, who suddenly passed – an elderly gentleman, over seventy, who lived in Hertfordshire –'

The roll-call continues, and sometimes a brief description will draw a gasp from a distant part of the hall. The sense of anticipation around him is feverish and overwrought; there is also something fearful to it. George wonders what it must be like to be picked out in the presence of thousands by a departed member of your family. He wonders if most would not prefer it to happen in the privacy of a dark and curtained seance room. Or, possibly, not at all.

Mrs Roberts goes quiet again. It is as if the competing babble behind and around her has also subsided for the moment. Then suddenly the medium flings out her right arm and points to the back of the stalls, on the other side of the hall to George. 'Yes, there! I see him! I see the spirit form of a young soldier. He is looking for someone. He is looking for a gentleman with hardly any hair.'

George, like everyone else with a view across the hall, peers intently, half expecting the spirit form to be visible, half trying to identify the man with little hair. Mrs Roberts raises her hand to shelter her eyes, as if the arc lights are interfering with her perception of the spirit form.

'He looks to be about twenty-four. In khaki uniform. Upright, well built, a small moustache. Mouth droops a little at the corners. He passed suddenly.'

Mrs Roberts pauses, and tilts her head downwards, rather as counsel might do when taking a note from the solicitor at his side.

'He gives 1916 as the year of his passing. He distinctly calls you "Uncle". Yes, "Uncle Fred".'

A bald-headed man at the back of the stalls rises to his feet, nods, and just as suddenly sits down, as if he is not sure of the etiquette.

'He speaks of a brother Charles,' the medium continues. 'Is that correct? He wants to know if you have Aunt Lillian with you. Do you understand?'

The man stays in his seat this time, nodding vigorously.

'He tells me that there was an anniversary, the birthday of a brother. Some anxiety in the home. There is no need for it. The message continues –' and then Mrs Roberts suddenly lurches forward, as if violently propelled from behind. She spins round and cries, 'All *right!*' She seems to be pushing back. 'All *right!* I say.'

But when she turns to face the arena again, it is clear that contact with the soldier has been broken. The medium places her hands over her face, fingers pressed against forehead, thumbs beneath her ears, as if trying to recover the necessary equilibrium. Finally, she takes her hands away and stretches her arms out.

This time the spirit is of a woman, aged between twenty-five and thirty, whose name begins with a J. She was promoted while giving birth to a little girl, who passed over at the same time. Mrs Roberts is scanning the front of the arena, following the progress of a mother with a spirit infant in her arms, as she tries to locate her forsaken husband. 'Yes, she says her name is June – and she is looking for – R, yes R – is it Richard?' At which a man rises straight up from his seat and shouts, 'Where is she? Where are you, June? June, speak to me. Show me our child!' He is quite distraught and staring all around him, until an elderly couple, looking embarrassed, pull him back down.

Mrs Roberts, as if the interruption has never taken place, so total has been her concentration on the spirit voice, says, 'The message is that she and the child are watching over you and taking care of you in your present trouble. They are waiting for you on the farther side. They are happy, and they wish you to be happy until you all meet again.'

The spirits are now becoming more orderly, it seems. Identifications are made and messages passed. A man is seeking his daughter. She is interested in music. He is holding an open score. Initials are established, then names. Mrs Roberts gives the message: the spirit of one of the great musicians is helping the man's daughter; if she continues to work hard, the spirit will continue with his influence.

George is beginning to discern a pattern. The messages conveyed, whether of consolation or encouragement or both, are of a very general nature. So too are most of the identifications, at least to begin with. But then comes some clinching detail, which the medium will often take time searching for. George thinks it highly unlikely that these spirits, if they exist, can be so surprisingly incapable of conveying their identity without a lot of guessing games from Mrs Roberts. Is the supposed problem of transmission between the two worlds no more than a ploy to raise the drama – indeed, the melo-drama – until the culminating moment when someone in the audience nods, or raises an arm, or stands up as if summoned, or puts their hands to their face in disbelief and joy?

It could be just a clever guessing game: there is surely a statistical probability that someone with the correct initial, and then the correct name, will be present in an audience of this size, and a medium might cleverly organize her words to lead her to this candidate. Or it could all be a straightforward hoax, with accomplices planted in the audience to impress and perhaps convert the credulous. And then there is a third possibility: that those in the audience who nod and raise an arm and stand up and cry out are genuinely taken by surprise, and genuinely believe contact has been made; but this is because someone in their circle – perhaps a fervent Spiritualist determined to spread belief by however cynical a means – has passed on private details to the organizers. This, George concludes, is probably how it is done. As with perjury, it works best when there is a clever mixture of the true and the false.

'And now there is a message from a gentleman, a very proper and distinguished gentleman, who passed ten years ago, twelve years ago. Yes, I have it, he passed in 1918, he tells me.' The year Father died, thinks George. 'He was about seventy-five years of age.' Strange, Father was seventy-six. A longish pause, and then: 'He was a very spiritual man.' At which point, George feels his flesh begin to prickle, all along his arms and up into his neck. No, no, surely not. He feels frozen in his seat; his shoulders lock solid; he stares rigidly at the stage, waiting for the medium's next move.

She raises her head, and starts looking at the higher parts of the hall, between the upper boxes and the gallery. 'He says he spent his first years in India.'

George is now utterly terrified. No one knew he was coming here except Maud. Perhaps it is a wild guess – or rather, an exactly accurate guess – by someone who worked out that various people connected with Sir Arthur would probably be here. But no – because many of the most famous and respectable, like Sir Oliver Lodge, have merely sent telegrams. Could someone have recognized him when he arrived? This was just about possible – but then how could they have discovered the very year of Father's death?

Mrs Roberts now has her arm outflung, and is pointing to the upper tier of boxes on the other side of the hall. George's flesh is throbbing all over, as if he has been thrown naked into a bank of nettles. He thinks: I am not going to be able to bear this; it is coming my way, and I cannot escape. The gaze, and the arm, are moving slowly round the great amphitheatre, holding the same level, as if watching a spirit form go questingly from box to box. All George's rational conclusions of a moment ago are worthless. His father is about to speak to him. His father, who spent all his life as a priest in the

Church of England, is about to speak to him through this . . . improbable woman. What can he want? What message can be so urgent? Something to do with Maud? A paternal rebuke to his son's failing faith? Is some terrifying judgment about to fall on him? Close to panic, George finds himself wishing Mother were by his side. But Mother has been dead these six years.

As the medium's head slowly continues to turn, as her arm still points to the same level, George feels more scared than the day he sat in his office, knowing that at some point a knock would come and a policeman would arrest him for a crime he had never committed. Now, he is again a suspect, about to be identified in front of ten thousand witnesses. He thinks he must simply rise to his feet and end the suspense by crying, 'That is my father!' Perhaps he will faint and fall over the balcony into the stalls below. Perhaps he will have a seizure.

'His name . . . he is telling me his name . . . It begins with an S . . .'

And still the head turns, turns, seeking that one face in the upper boxes, seeking the glorious moment of acknowledgement. George is quite sure everyone is looking at him – and soon they will know exactly who he is. But now George shrinks from the recognition he wished for earlier. He wants to hide in the deepest dungeon, the most noxious prison cell. He thinks, this cannot be true, this absolutely cannot be true, my father would never behave like this, perhaps I am going to soil myself as I did when a boy on the way home from school, perhaps that is why he is coming, to remind me I am a child, to show me his authority continues even after he is dead, yes, that would not be unlike him.

'I have the name –' George thinks he is going to scream. He is going to faint. He will fall and hit his head on – 'It is Stuart.'

And then a man of about George's age, a few yards to his left, is on his feet and signalling to the stage, acknowledging this seventy-five-year-old who was brought up in India and passed in 1918, seeming almost to claim him as a prize. George feels that the shadow of the angel of death has been cast over him; he is chilled to the bone, sweaty, exhausted, threatened, utterly relieved, and deeply ashamed. And at the same time, part of him is impressed, curious, fearfully wondering . . .

'And now I have a lady, she was about forty-five to fifty years of age. She passed over in 1913. She mentions Morpeth. She never married, but she has a message for a gentleman.' Mrs Roberts starts to looks downwards, into the arena. 'She says something about a horse.'

There is a pause. Mrs Roberts drops her head again, turns it sideways, takes advice. 'I have her name now. It is Emily. Yes, she gives her name as Emily Wilding Davison. She has a message, she had arranged to come here to give a gentleman a message. I think she told you through the planchette or Ouija board she would be present.'

A man in an open-necked shirt, sitting near the platform, rises to his feet, and as if conscious he is addressing the whole hall, says in a carrying voice, 'That is correct. She told me she would communicate tonight. Emily is the suffragette who threw herself before the King's horse and died from her injuries. As a spirit figure she is well known to me.'

The hall seems to take in a vast collective breath. Mrs Roberts starts to relay the message, but George does not bother to listen. His sanity feels suddenly restored; the clear, keen wind of reason is blowing again through his brain. Hocus-pocus, as he always suspected. Emily Davison indeed. Emily Davison, who broke windows, threw stones, set fire to postboxes; who refused to obey prison regulations and was consequently force-fed on numerous occasions. A silly, hysterical woman in George's view, who deliberately sought death in order to advance her cause; though some said she was merely trying to plant a flag on the horse, and misjudged the speed of the animal. In which case, incompetent as well as hysterical. You cannot break the law to advance the law, that was a nonsense. You do it by petition, by argument, by demonstration if necessary, but by reason. Those who broke the law as an argument for obtaining the vote thereby demonstrated their unfitness to receive it.

Still, the point is not whether Emily Davison was a silly, hysterical woman, or whether her action resulted in Maud getting the vote of which George fully approves. No, the point is that Sir Arthur was such a well-known opponent of Women's Suffrage that the notion of such a spirit attending his memorial service is absurd. Unless the spirits of the departed are as illogical as they are unruly. Perhaps Emily Davison thought of disrupting this gathering just as she once disrupted the Derby. But in that case, her message ought to be for Sir Arthur, or his widow, rather than for some sympathetic friend.

Stop, George says to himself. Stop thinking rationally about such matters. Or rather, stop granting these people the benefit of the doubt. You were given an unpleasant shock by a clever false alarm, but that is no ground for losing your reason as well as your nerve. He also thinks: yet if *I* was so scared, if *I* panicked, if *I* believed I might be going to die, then consider the potential effect on weaker minds and lesser intelligences. George wonders if the Witchcraft Act – with which he is admittedly unfamiliar – should not remain on the Statute Book after all.

Mrs Roberts has been giving messages for half an hour or so. George spots people in the arena getting to their feet. But now they are not competing for a lost relative, or rising en masse to greet the spirit forms of loved ones. They are walking out. Perhaps the appearance of Emily Wilding Davison has been the last straw for them too. Perhaps they came as admirers of Sir Arthur's life and work, but are refusing to associate themselves further with this public conjuring trick. There are thirty, forty, fifty people on their feet, heading determinedly for the exits.

'I can't go on with all these people walking out,' Mrs Roberts announces. She sounds offended, but also rather unnerved. She takes a few steps backwards. Someone, somewhere, gives a signal, whereupon a sudden skirling blast comes from the vast pipe organ behind the stage. Is it intended to cover the noise of the departing sceptics, or to indicate that the meeting is being brought to an end? George looks to the woman on his right for guidance. She is frowning, offended at the vulgar way in which the medium has been interrupted. As for Mrs Roberts herself, she has her head cast down and her arms wrapped round herself, shutting out all this interference with the fragile line of communication she has established to the spirit world.

And then, the last thing George expects comes to pass. The organ suddenly cuts off in mid-anthem, Mrs Roberts throws her arms open, lifts her head, walks confidently forward to the microphone, and in a ringing, impassioned voice, cries,

'He is here!' And then again, 'He is here!'

Those on their way out stop; some turn back to their seats. But in any case, they are now forgotten. Everyone gazes intently at the stage, at Mrs Roberts, at the empty chair with the placard across it. The blast on the organ might have been a call to attention, a prelude to this very moment. The entire hall is silent, watching, waiting.

'I saw him first,' she says, 'during the two-minute silence.'

'He was here, first standing behind me, though separate from all the other spirits.'

'Then I saw him walk across the platform to his empty chair.'

'I saw him distinctly. He was wearing evening dress.'

'He looked as he has always looked in recent years.'

'There is no doubt about it. He was quite prepared for his passing.'

As she pauses between each brief, dramatic statement, George studies Sir Arthur's family on the platform. All of them except one are looking across at Mrs Roberts, transfixed by her announcement. Only Lady Conan Doyle has not turned. George cannot see her expression from this distance, but her hands are crossed on her lap, her shoulders are square, her carriage erect; head proudly high, she is gazing above the audience and out into the far distance.

'He is our great champion, here and on the farther side.'

'He is quite capable of demonstrating already. His passing was peaceful, and he was quite prepared for it. There was no pain, and no confusion to his spirit. He is already able to begin his work for us over there.'

'When I first saw him, during the two minutes' silence, it was as in a flash.'

'It was when I was giving my messages that I first saw him clearly and distinctly.'

'He came and stood behind me and encouraged me while I was doing my work.'

'I recognized once more that fine, clear voice of his, which could not be mistaken. He bore himself as a gentleman, as he always did.'

'He is with us all the time, and the barrier between the two worlds is but a temporary one.'

'There is nothing to fear in passing over, and our great champion has proved it by appearing here amongst us tonight.'

The woman on George's left leans across the velvet armrest and whispers, 'He is here.'

Several people are now on their feet, as if to get a better view of the stage. All are staring fixedly at the empty chair, at Mrs Roberts, at the Doyle family. George feels himself being caught up again in some mass feeling that transcends, that overwhelms the silence. He is no longer seized by the fear he had when he thought his father was coming for him, nor the scepticism when Emily Davison was putting in her appearance. He feels, despite himself, a kind of cautious awe. This is, after all, Sir Arthur they are speaking of, the man who willingly used his detective abilities on George's behalf, who risked his own reputation to rescue George's, who helped give him back the life that had been taken from him. Sir Arthur, a man of the highest integrity and intelligence, believed in events of the kind George has just been witnessing; it would be impertinent for George in this moment to deny his saviour.

George does not think he is losing either his mind, or his common sense. He asks himself: what if there was in the proceedings that mixture of truth and lies he earlier identified? What if some parts of what has happened are charlatanry, but others genuine? What if the theatrical Mrs Roberts, despite herself, was truly bringing news from distant lands? What if Sir Arthur, in whatever form or place he now might be, is obliged, in order to make contact with the material world, to use as a conduit those who also deal in fraud some of the time? Would that not be an explanation?

'He is here,' the woman on his left repeats, in a normal, conversational voice.

Then the words are taken up by a man a dozen seats away. 'He is here.'

354

Three words spoken in an everyday tone, intended to carry a mere few feet. But such is the charged air in the hall that they seem magically amplified.

'He is here,' someone up in the gallery repeats.

'He is here,' responds a woman down in the arena.

Then a man at the back of the stalls suddenly bellows, in the tone of a revivalist preacher, 'HE IS HERE!'

Instinctively, George reaches down at his feet and pulls his binoculars from their case. He crams them to his spectacles and tries to focus on the platform. His finger and thumb nervously twirl past the proper focus in each direction, then finally land on the mid-point. He examines the ecstatic medium, the empty chair, and the Doyle family. Lady Conan Doyle has remained, since the first announcement of Sir Arthur's presence, fixed in the same attitude: straight-backed, square-shouldered, head up, gazing out with – as George can now see – something resembling a smile on her face. The golden-haired, flirtatious young woman he had briefly met has grown darker-haired and matronly; he has only ever seen her at Sir Arthur's side, which is where she still claims to be. He moves the glasses back and forth, to the chair, the medium, the widow. He finds his breath coming quickly and harshly.

There is a touch on his right shoulder. He drops the binoculars. The woman shakes her head and says gently, 'You cannot see him that way.'

She is not rebuking him, merely explaining how things are.

'You will only see him with the eyes of faith.'

The eyes of faith. The eyes Sir Arthur brought with him when they met at the Grand Hotel, Charing Cross. He had believed in George; should George now believe in Sir Arthur? His champion's words: I do not think, I do not believe, I *know*. Sir Arthur carried with him an enviable, comforting sense of certainty. He knew things. What does he, George, know? Does he finally know anything? What is the sum of knowledge he has acquired in his fifty-four years? Mostly, he has gone through his life learning and waiting to be told. The authority of others has always been important to him; does he have any authority of his own? At fifty-four, he thinks a lot of things, he believes a few, but what can he really claim to know?

The cries of witness to Sir Arthur's presence have now died down, perhaps because there has been no answering acknowledgement from the stage. What was Lady Conan Doyle's message at the start of the service? That our earthly eyes cannot see beyond the earth's vibration; that only those with the God-given extra sight, called clairvoyance, would be able to see the dear form in our midst. It would have been a miracle indeed if Sir Arthur had managed to endow with clairvoyant powers the various people still on their feet in different parts of the hall.

And now Mrs Roberts speaks again.

'I have a message for you, dear, from Arthur.'

Again, Lady Conan Doyle does not turn her head.

Mrs Roberts, in a slow waft of black satin, moves to her left, towards the Doyle family and the empty seat. When she reaches Lady Conan Doyle, she stands to one side of her and a little behind, facing towards the part of the hall where George sits. Despite the distance, her words carry easily.

'Sir Arthur told me that one of you went to the hut, this morning.' She waits, and when the widow does not answer, prompts her. 'Is that correct?'

'Why yes,' replies Lady Conan Doyle. 'I did.'

Mrs Roberts nods, and goes on, 'The message is: tell Mary –'

At which moment another tremendous blast comes from the pipe organ. Mrs Roberts leans closer and carries on speaking under the protection of the noise. Lady Conan Doyle nods from time to time. Then she looks across to the large, formally clad son on her left, as if enquiring of him. He in turn looks to Mrs Roberts, who now addresses them both. Then the other son gets up and joins the group. The organ peals on relentlessly.

George does not know if this drowning of the message is in consideration of the family's privacy or a piece of stage management. He does not know whether he has seen truth or lies, or a mixture of both. He does not know if the clear, surprising, unEnglish fervour of those around him this evening is proof of charlatanry or belief. And if belief, whether true or false.

Mrs Roberts has finished communicating her message, and turns towards Mr Craze. The organ thunders on, yet with nothing to drown out. The Doyle family look around at one another. Where is the service to go from here? The hymns have all been sung, the tributes paid. The daring experiment has been performed, Sir Arthur has come amongst them, his message has been delivered.

The organ continues. Now it seems to be modulating into the rhythms which play out a congregation after a wedding or funeral: insistent and indefatigable, propelling them back into the daily, grimy, unmagical, sublunary world. The Doyle family leave the platform, followed by the officers of the Marylebone Spiritualist Association, the speakers and Mrs Roberts. People stand up, women reach under their seats for handbags, men in evening dress remember top hats, then there is shuffling and murmuring, the greeting of friends and acquaintances, and a calm, unhurried queue in every aisle. Those around George gather their belongings, rise, nod and grant him their full and certain smiles. George returns them a smile which is no equal of theirs, and does not rise. When most of his section is empty, he reaches down again and presses the binoculars to his spectacles. He focuses once more on the platform, the hydrangeas, the line of empty chairs, and the one specific empty chair with its cardboard placard, the space where Sir Arthur has, just possibly, been. He gazes through his succession of lenses, out into the air and beyond.

What does he see?

What did he see?

What will he see?

Author's note

Arthur continued to appear at seances around the world for the next few years; though his family only authenticated his manifestation at one of Mrs Osborne Leonard's private sittings in 1937, where he warned that 'the most tremendous changes' were about to occur in England. Jean, who became a fervent spiritualist after the death of her brother at the Battle of Mons, kept the faith until her death in 1940. The Mam left Masongill in 1917; the parishioners of Thornton-in-Lonsdale presented her with 'a large watch with a luminous dial in a leather case'. Though she finally came south, she never joined her son's household, and died at her West Grinstead cottage in 1920, while Arthur was preaching spiritualism in Australia. Bryan Waller survived Arthur by two years.

Willie Hornung died at St-Jean-de-Luz in March 1921; four months later, he came through at a Doyle family seance, apologized for his previous doubts about spiritualism and pronounced himself 'no longer handicapped by my horrid old asthma'. Connie died of cancer in 1924. The Rt Hon George Augustus Anson served as Chief Constable of Staffordshire for forty-one years, retiring finally in 1929; he was knighted in the Coronation Honours List of 1937, and died at Bath in 1947. His wife Blanche died as a result of enemy action in 1941. Charlotte Edalji returned to Shropshire after Shapurji's death; she died at Atcham near Shrewsbury in 1924, at the age of eighty-one, and chose to be buried there rather than beside her husband.

George Edalji survived them all. He continued to live and practise at 79 Borough High Street until 1941; then had an office in Argyle Square from 1942 until 1953. He died at 9 Brocket Close, Welwyn Garden City, on 17th June 1953; the cause of death was given as coronary thrombosis. Maud was still living with him, and registered the death. She returned for a last visit to Great Wyrley in 1962, when she gave photographs of her father and brother to the church. Today they hang in the vestry of St Mark's.

Four years after Sir Arthur Conan Doyle's death, Enoch Knowles, a fifty-seven-year-old labourer, pleaded guilty at Staffordshire Crown Court to the writing of menacing and obscene letters over a thirty-year period. Knowles admitted that his career began in 1903, when he joined in the campaign of persecution by sending letters signed 'G.H. Darby, Captain of the Wyrley Gang'. After Knowles's conviction, George Edalji wrote an article for the *Daily Express*. In this last public statement on the case, dated 7th November 1934, George makes no reference to the Sharp brothers, nor to race prejudice as a motive. He concludes:

The great mystery, however, remained unsolved. All kinds of theories were advanced. One is that the outrages were the work of a lunatic seized from time to time with blood lust. Another was that they were done with the idea of bringing the parish and police into disrepute, or possibly the work of some dismissed policeman. One curious theory was suggested to me. A man belonging to Staffordshire told me the outrages were committed, not by a human being, but by one or more boars. He suggested that these animals were sent out at night after being given some kind of dope which made them ferocious. He said he had seen one of these boars. The boar theory seemed to me then – as it does now – too fantastic to be taken seriously.

Mary Conan Doyle, Arthur's first child, died in 1976. She had always kept one secret from her father. Touie, on her deathbed, had not only warned her daughter that Arthur would marry again; she also named his future bride as Miss Jean Leckie.

J.B. January 2005

Apart from Jean's letter to Arthur, all letters quoted, whether signed or anonymous, are authentic; as are quotations from newspapers, government reports, proceedings in Parliament, and the writings of Sir Arthur Conan Doyle. I should like to thank: Sgt. Alan Walker of the Staffordshire Constabulary; the City Archives of Birmingham Central Library; the Staffordshire County Property Service; the Revd Paul Oakley; Daniel Stashower; Douglas Johnson; Geoffrey Robertson; and Sumaya Partner.